Kingdom of Ashes

BOOK I

IN THE NIGHTFALL SERIES

ELENA MAY

This book is a work of fiction. Names, characters, businesses, organizations, places, events and incidents either are the product of the author's imagination or are used fictitiously. Any resemblance to actual persons, living or dead, events, or locales is entirely coincidental.

Cover art by Nadica Boshkovska.

For information visit KingdomOfAshes.net

Contents

Chapter One: In the Shadows 1

Chapter Two: Old World 13

Chapter Three: Survival 25

Chapter Four: Heroes 39

Chapter Five: Innocence 53

Chapter Six: New World 67

Chapter Seven: Temptation 81

Chapter Eight: Captive 91

Chapter Nine: Tests 105

Chapter Ten: Tales and Songs 119

Chapter Eleven: All That Glitters 133

Chapter Twelve: Darkness and Light 145

Chapter Thirteen: Humanity 163

Chapter Fourteen: Justice of the Beast 175

Chapter Fifteen: Golden Cage 191

Chapter Sixteen: The Carrot and the Stick 213

Chapter Seventeen: Heaven 225
Chapter Eighteen: Man and Beast 233
Chapter Nineteen: Wolves and Puppies 243
Chapter Twenty: Night Falls 265
Chapter Twenty-One: The Pen and the Sword 279
Chapter Twenty-Two: Contracts in Ink and Blood 293
Chapter Twenty-Three: Origins 305
Chapter Twenty-Four: The Devil You Know 329
Chapter Twenty-Five: Last Shred of Being Human 349
Chapter Twenty-Six: Prince of Darkness 365
Chapter Twenty-Seven: Predators and Prey 377
Chapter Twenty-Eight: A Wicked Game 395
Chapter Twenty-Nine: Victory 411
Chapter Thirty: Scheherazade 423
Chapter Thirty-One: Metamorphosis 433
Chapter Thirty-Two: Fear 449
Chapter Thirty-Three: The Survivor 461
Chapter Thirty-Four: Madness 479
Chapter Thirty-Five: Obsession 493
Chapter Thirty-Six: Promises 507
Chapter Thirty-Seven: The Right Thing 525
Acknowledgments 535

Chapter One

In the Shadows

Six candles were hardly enough to illuminate the stuffy cellar. Myra raised a hand and rubbed at her eyes. Her head throbbed, but if she stopped writing, she would lose her mind. She considered lighting a seventh candle but pushed the thought aside. The last patrol had returned empty-handed, and she could not afford to waste supplies to satisfy her whims.

The sound of feet tapping against stone startled her, and she put her notebook down at the knock on the door. "Come in," Myra called with as much cheer as she could muster.

The wooden door cracked open, and her cousin peeked in. "The General is looking for you," Thea said. "He requested you come to the Headquarters immediately."

Myra sighed. Calling one of the many underground cells "Headquarters," or Zack "General," did nothing to make their pathetic, ragtag team a real army. "If Zack wishes to talk to me, he can come here himself. You're not his messenger."

"He's busy, and this is important," Thea said with a serious expression on her youthful face. "We captured another one."

Myra snorted. "That's what you call 'important'? Zack should have figured out by now that we can't learn anything useful from that filth." She tucked her notebook underneath a moth-eaten blanket and walked to the candles, extinguishing them one by one. "Let's go, then. Better not keep *the General* waiting."

She followed Thea down the narrow torchlit corridor. Her cousin ran forward, her short golden ponytails bobbing up and down at every step. Myra found it hard to keep up with the pace and enthusiasm, but she tried to remain hopeful for Thea's sake.

About thirty Warriors had gathered inside the Headquarters, waiting for them. Myra spotted Lidia and Thomas, and, of course, *the General*. "Zack, what—"

He cleared his throat. "Captain Andersen, how good of you to join us."

Myra resisted the urge to roll her eyes. "You called for me, General Wong."

"Follow me," Zack said.

Myra looked at her cousin. "You should go now, Thea."

The twelve-year-old pouted. "I'm a part of the Resistance too! In less than four years, I'll be allowed to join the Warriors' Council. I want to see the prisoner!"

"Why would you want that?" Myra asked. "There's nothing glorious about fighting a war or interrogating prisoners. Until you learn that, you can't be one of the Warriors. Go now. Grandma Pia is giving a talk at the school. You should attend as many lessons as you can."

Thea gave her a glare but complied. Once the girl was gone, Myra followed Zack and the rest of the Warriors into a small candlelit cellar. The air was heavier in this place, but she was certain their guest did not mind.

The prisoner was standing with his back towards the stone wall, heavy chains holding up his shackled hands. Another set of thick fetters encircled his ankles. The Resistance had discovered long ago that vampires possessed superior strength, but so far the titanium chains had been effective in detaining the captives.

Myra narrowed her eyes and looked over the prisoner. She had seen only a handful of vampires, all very different in looks, but all had been the same in their vanity and arrogance.

The first thing Myra noticed was his clothes. The bright lilac tuxedo complemented the vampire's dark complexion but made him look no less ridiculous. Vamps always dressed in style—or what they perceived to be style—while Resistance members wore whatever they could get their hands on. She wondered what the vampires would do once all the clothes ever made wore out beyond repair. They had destroyed all of the humans involved in production, and as far as she knew, they had set up no system to replace the goods they used up. These creatures could only consume and destroy and never create anything new.

"So this is the famous Resistance?" the prisoner asked, his sharp white teeth glistening under the candlelight as he gave his hosts a smug grin. "More pathetic than expected."

"You must be quite the fighter yourself to be captured by creatures as pathetic as us," said Thomas, and Zack threw the red-haired Warrior an approving look. "If we are pitiful, what does that make you?"

"We're not here to exchange lame insults," Myra interrupted and glared at the vampire. "We're here to give you a choice. You can die quickly, or your death can last weeks if you refuse to answer our questions."

"So, what are you two supposed to be?" The vamp glanced between Thomas and Myra. "The good and the bad cop?"

"What's he talking about?" Zack asked.

"It's an Old World thing," Myra said impatiently. "I'll explain it to you later." Really, did Zack ever read books? He was almost ten years older than her, but he knew less about the Old World than she did.

Zack turned back at the prisoner. "You heard your options. You can talk now, or you can wait for us to make you cooperate."

The vamp snickered. "You are wasting your time. The WeatherWizard is heavily guarded; you can never reach it and live to tell the tale."

"We know everything about the WeatherWizard," Zack said. "We wanted to ask you a few questions about Prince Vladimir."

The vampire laughed—an ugly, mirthless sound. "You cannot seriously think you can plan anything against him. The Dark Prince will swipe you away with his little finger. You kids have no idea what you are getting yourselves into."

"Perhaps you'll be willing to tell us," Zack said. "Lidia?"

The petite woman stepped forward. "Yes, sir?"

"I'll leave you alone with him. Make him sing. If he refuses, Thomas will take the next shift. One of us will be with him at all times until he agrees to cooperate."

"I can make him talk," Lidia said and threw the prisoner a look. She walked to the wall and took a hammer from the rack. It looked huge in her small hand, but her grip around the handle was strong. "I have an idea or two."

"I know you do," said Zack. "We'll be in the Headquarters in case you need us."

Myra tried to ignore the vampire's snigger at the word "Headquarters," hoping beyond hope that the prisoner would speak before her shift came.

***

Several stone walls separated the Headquarters from the prison cellar, but they did little to muffle the hellish screams. Myra closed her eyes for a moment. "Zack, if you don't need me here, I'll go to the clinic and help Dr. Dubois."

Her leader nodded absentmindedly, and she stood up, barely stopping herself from running towards the door. Once the screams were out of earshot, her pace slowed down. As usual, the corridor leading to the clinic was crammed with people. Patients occupied every bench; many more were standing. Myra sighed, feeling tired just looking at them, and opened the door to the doctor's cellar.

Dr. Dubois stood bent down, feeling a patient's stomach. Gary, her aide, waited next to her with a basket full of vials.

The old woman looked up and smiled at her. "Ah, Myra, it's good to see you. Do you have time to stay and help?"

"Sure. I saw the line on my way here—I think we need to open a second examination room. Do you think any of your apprentices are ready?" *They better be.* Dr. Dubois was the only one among them trained in medicine in the Old World, and she was over eighty years old. She had been training a few aides, but none of them knew as much as she did.

"I've considered this," the doctor said. "They need to start working on their own, but Lidia is the only one close to being ready. Have you seen her? She needs to be here, learning."

"We have a prisoner. Her skills are required for the interrogation."

Dr. Dubois frowned. "I know she likes killing vamps more than she enjoys healing people, but she needs to show some responsibility. Besides me, she's the closest thing to a doctor we have, and she hasn't come to the clinic at all the past three days. You come more often than she does."

"It's not her fault," Myra said. "She's one of our best Warriors. Zack has many tasks for her."

"We have plenty of Warriors. We don't have any doctors. Lidia has a head for medicine—more than anyone else I've seen—but she won't learn unless she comes to assist me."

"I'll talk to her," Myra said. "Do you need help with your patient?"

"I'm fine," the man in the bed said, and Dr. Dubois smiled.

"Yes, he'll be fine. Gary is helping me. If you have time, can you walk through the queue and check everyone's symptoms? If it's something straightforward, give them instructions and send them back to their cellars. If you spot any emergencies, send them ahead of the rest."

"Sure," Myra said and left the room. She hated the responsibility of deciding which cases were important and which were not, but someone had to do it. She had considered becoming Dr. Dubois's apprentice herself, but had discovered that her true passion lay elsewhere.

Myra gazed around the corridor and spotted a pale face at the front of the queue. She frowned and knelt beside the woman. "Nina, what's wrong?" Myra asked.

"It's Erik," Nina said and nodded at her nine-year-old son. "He's thrown up three times in the past couple of hours."

"Do you also have diarrhea?" Myra asked him. The boy nodded, and she turned back to his mother. "Did he drink any unboiled water?"

Nina shook her head. "I always boil his water before I let him drink."

Myra raised her eyebrow at Erik, who was now determinedly avoiding her eyes. "Do you have something to share?" she asked.

The boy looked down. "The water in the underground spring felt so cool and fresh. I hate the taste of boiled water. And it always stays warm, even when you leave it to cool."

Myra smiled and squeezed Erik's hand. "I know," she said. "I also tried fresh springwater once, when I was younger than you. But you have to learn to put up with boiled water. You don't want to be as sick again as you are now, do you?"

He shook his head and looked away.

Myra looked up at Nina. "He'll be fine in a couple of days. Give him plenty of water—*clean* water. He needs to stay hydrated. His sickness will pass on its own."

Nina frowned. "Are you certain? Perhaps he should see Dr. Dubois?"

"I'm quite certain," Myra assured her. "I'll come by the children's cellar and check on him tomorrow."

She stood up and moved on to the next patient. "What is it, Irene?"

"It hurts," the girl said. "Everywhere—my arms, my legs, my back. Even my face."

Great. As common as tummy problems were in their community, this affliction was much more prevalent. "Does it hurt more when you exert yourself? Do your legs hurt when you stand and walk?"

"Yes," Irene said. "And my arms hurt even with the slightest bit of exertion. When I open a door, or even when I brush my hair."

"Have you been taking your vitamin D?"

Irene nodded. "Every three days as instructed."

"We should increase your dosage," Myra said. "I'll talk to Zack; perhaps we can spare some supplies." But even as she spoke, she knew it would not be enough. It would never be enough. Irene needed natural sunlight. They all did.

Someone cleared his throat. Myra looked up, seeing a blob of red hair at the end of the corridor. She raised an eyebrow at Thomas. "Are you here as a patient?"

He snorted. "I'd rather die in my own bed." He took a few steps and approached her. "Zack needs you at the Headquarters. The search party is back."

Myra followed him, her steps quick. Finally, some real news. This last patrol had taken longer than expected, and she was beginning to worry.

Thomas and Myra entered the Headquarters, and Zack greeted them with a smile. "Captain Sanchez," he said as he turned to the tall woman sitting next to him. "Everyone has assembled. Do you have anything to report?"

Alerie Sanchez stood up from her seat. "We met no vampires on the way. All of us returned alive and unhurt."

I should have joined the party, Myra thought. She had almost asked Zack to let her go before her fears had stopped her. She did not feel ready to go Outside, but every day spent in those dark cells made her lose a bit of her mind.

Zack grinned. "It's been a while since a patrol report started like this. Please, go on."

"We found the ruins of a city thirty miles south of here," Alerie continued. "We looked through houses and shops, but the place has been searched. The vamps have taken almost everything, but we still found a few useful items."

She brought a sheet of paper close to the candle. "We found seven cans of peas, three cans of corn, thirteen cans of pork, two bars of chocolate, fourteen large candles, twelve pairs of trousers of various sizes, two pairs of slippers, one pair of flip-flops…"

Myra bit her lower lip as she listened to the list. "Is any of the food still edible?"

Alerie snorted and took a can out of her bag. "It says, *Expiration Date: March 2531*."

Everyone laughed, but there was no joy in the sound. The food had supposedly expired over forty years ago. "With cans you never know," Myra said. "Some of it may still be fine."

"Did you find any grains?" Zack asked. "Wheat? Rice? Corn?"

Alerie shook her head. "No. We searched everything. Someone had been there before us."

"What about medicines?" Myra asked.

"We found a few pharmacies, but they were pillaged. Nothing was left."

"Why would vampires need medicines?" Thomas mused.

"They don't," Zack said. "They knew we would find the place sooner or later. They wanted to cut off our supplies."

Everyone fell quiet. Thomas ran a hand through his red hair, and Zack buried his face in his hands.

"We need the medicines," Myra murmured, wincing as her voice shattered the silence.

"We do," Zack agreed. "But as we don't have them, we need to take necessary measures. For starters, we must reduce everyone's dosage of vitamin D."

Myra looked up. "Zack, we can't! The current dosage is already too low. Most of our people have never seen sunlight, and it shows. You haven't been to the clinic often enough, but I have. Every day we have more cases of bone pain, even amongst children."

"A little pain has never killed anyone," said Zack.

"It's not just pain," Myra protested. "This deficiency could lead to an increased risk of cardiovascular disease or cancer. Now *those* have killed plenty of people."

Zack rubbed at his forehead. "We have no choice. There are four hundred and thirty-seven of us here. Our current dosage with the available supplies gives us enough supplements to last a little over four months."

"And this is not the only thing we lack," said Thomas. "I think we'll run out of food before we have time to start worrying about cancer."

Zack nodded and looked at Alerie. "Captain Sanchez, did your party hunt down any game?"

"Two rabbits," she replied, her words emphasized by a cry from the prison cell.

Myra bit her lip and stared at the stone floor. *Two rabbits for hundreds of people.* She looked up and saw the same worry in her commander's eyes.

"Alerie," Myra said. "Did you come across any living woods?"

Alerie shook her head. "Everything was dead and barren."

"The rabbits must have come from somewhere," Myra said. "There must be patches of habitable ground. We need to find them."

Zack looked about to reply, when the door blew open and Lidia walked in. "The filth refuses to talk," she said as she collapsed into a chair.

"That's because he hasn't talked to me yet," Thomas said and got up.

Myra gave him a smile. "Good luck. And Zack, if you have no more need for me, I'll go check on my cousin."

"Very well," Zack said. "You're all dismissed."

Myra walked out of the Headquarters, and all the Warriors followed one by one.

"Hey, Myra, wait," Alerie called and caught up with her. "You should bring Thea to my room. I have something for her."

Myra remembered Alerie's report and grinned. "Is it what I think it is?"

Her friend smiled. "Don't get excited. There is barely enough for all the children. There will be nothing left for you and me."

"That's fine," Myra said. "Alerie, I wanted to talk to you. I've been thinking about joining the next patrol."

Alerie stopped in her tracks and looked her up and down. "You are eighteen, right?"

"Nineteen."

Alerie nodded. "Nineteen. Yeah, why not? You've been a part of the Warriors' Council for three years now. Most people start raiding later, but plenty of younger Warriors have successfully participated in patrols. How is your training going?"

"I'm passable with the gun and crossbow. Not so much in hand-to-hand combat."

"None of us can hope to defeat a vampire hand-to-hand anyway. I must warn you, though—even if you're perfect at hitting an unmoving target during a training session, shooting at a real vamp is something completely different."

"I'm sure it is," Myra said. "But in general, you don't think it's a bad idea?"

"Depends. I think it makes sense for you to go, as long as you go for the right reasons. If you feel you're ready and want to contribute, then fine. But that's not the main reason you want to go, is it?"

Would Alerie laugh at her if she confessed her true reasons? "Honestly, I want to go Outside. I want to see what it's like." Myra winced. Now that she had said it aloud, the words sounded even more childish than they had in her mind.

Alerie snorted. "Everyone does. But the Outside isn't everything it's hyped up to be: barren ground, rotting and dead trees, and thick clouds covering everything in shadow. Not much to see."

Myra gazed at the dark corridor, barely illuminated by the meager torchlight. "Anything is better than this."

Chapter Two

Old World

Myra entered the small chamber and walked to the long table in the center, lighting all the tall beeswax candles. A gloomy light washed the room, playing across the half-empty shelves against the wall. Were Old World libraries ever so small or so dark?

Myra's eyes moved across the top shelf, stacked with textbooks, encyclopedias, papers, and articles. She reached out to a chemistry textbook and flipped through the pages. The margins were filled with questions she had noted down, things she meant to ask Grandma Pia or Dr. Dubois. Myra frowned. The questions were so many; no one would ever have the time to sit down with her and answer every single one.

Perhaps she had to reread the section and try to figure out some of the answers herself. Myra sighed. Preserving the knowledge of the Old World was important, and she wished to learn everything humans used to know and pass it on to the younger generations. Yet, she had no energy for studying right now. All she wanted was to sit down with a good novel in her hand and lose herself in worlds far away from here.

Myra's eyes moved to the lower shelf, where she had arranged all the fiction titles. She raised the candle and illuminated the thick covers. She had read and reread each of these books so many times that she had stopped counting. It had been years since a patrol had found a new novel during one of the raids. In all likelihood, they would never find anything new again.

Don't be lazy, she told herself. *Stop wasting your time with books you can recite by heart. The shelves won't restock themselves. You have to contribute.*

She knelt on the floor and reached out underneath the lowest shelf, pulling out a box filled with papers and notebooks. A cloud of dust rose in the air, and Myra coughed. She took the top notebook, labeled *Ranger's Quest*, and opened it at the bookmark. Her novel was going very well. She had written over two hundred chapters now, each more exciting than the last. Myra smiled and grabbed a pencil. Perhaps she could steal some time for this before Thea finished her lectures.

Myra grinned as she jotted down words on the paper. She had reached the point where her protagonist, Maryabella, had to fight a band of trolls. Thea always complimented her on her ability to write action scenes, and Myra smiled, anticipating her cousin's reaction once she read the new pages.

Myra paused and absentmindedly chewed on her pencil, staring at the page. She had to describe the scenery—green woods, a running stream, blue skies above. And yet, she had never seen any of those things. She had read about them in many books, but had never experienced anything she was writing about. Did her descriptions make any sense at all?

Would someone who had seen the Old World laugh at her works?

She sighed and ran her hand through her hair. A few wavy brown strands remained in her hand, and she threw them to the floor with a quick, frustrated flick of her fingers. She wanted to write well. She wanted to create vivid worlds that would come to life. But how could she do this when all she had known was fear and darkness?

She could never become a better writer unless she went Outside and saw more of the world. She had to stop being a coward. It was time to ask Zack to send her on a patrol. And yet, there was no protection Outside. Anything could happen Outside.

I have to be more like Maryabella. She's brave, adventurous, and a good fighter. I won't find adventures in books I've read ten times. I'll find them out there.

Yet, she knew how selfish that was. Warriors went Outside, risking their lives, so they could find food and clothes for everyone. She wanted to go so that she could become more sophisticated and find inspiration.

Myra rubbed at her forehead and placed the notebook back into the box. She glanced at the mechanical clock on the shelf. Thea's lesson had to be over by now. She smiled and stood up—it was time to give her cousin a happy surprise.

***

Myra knocked before entering the classroom. Grandma Pia had finished her talk some time ago and was now answering the kids' questions. A group of about forty children surrounded her; the youngest among them had barely turned five, while the oldest were Thea's age.

Myra loved listening to the old woman. Pia was one of the few who had long and extensive memories of the Old World. She had been a little older than Myra during the Nightfall, and she always entertained and educated them with tales of the time before.

"Why did people make the WeatherWizard?" a little boy asked. "Didn't they know vamps could come out if the sun was gone?"

"Scientists created the WeatherWizard for greater control over how many rainy and sunny days each place would get," Grandma Pia explained. "Most days were made sunny so people could enjoy their time outside. But there was also rain to allow crops to grow and to stop the summer days from becoming unbearably hot."

As she spoke, Grandma Pia sketched little pictures using chalk on the blackboard—a circular sun with rays going in all directions, clouds, raindrops, houses, streets, and little human figures carrying inverted basins on sticks; *umbrellas*, Myra's memory supplied. Grandma Pia had told them that people of the Old World used umbrellas to keep the rain away.

"Rain was turned on late at night, to avoid inconveniencing people," the old woman continued. "Sleet and hail were eliminated, as they could damage many plants. You have never experienced rain, children. On a hot day, rain may be refreshing, but it is mostly unpleasant. This wasn't the only reason for the Wizard, of course. It also allowed control over greater problems, like tsunamis and hurricanes."

"Tsunamis sound nasty, but I'll choose them over vamps any day," Myra said.

"No one expected what happened," Pia said. "People in the Old World had no idea vampires existed. There were tales, but they were all attributed to legends and turned into fiction. At the time, vampires were far fewer. They always hid in crypts or caves, going out only at night. They hid their existence well."

"And then people devised the WeatherWizard?" Thea said.

"Yes," said Grandma Pia. "And about a century after the Wizard's creation, this one vampire realized he could use it to take the world away from humans."

"Vladimir," Myra murmured.

Pia nodded. "He was once just another vampire, but ever since the Nightfall he's been styling himself as their Prince."

Myra snorted. "If he wishes to go around giving himself fancy titles, he should have at least changed his name. Honestly? *Prince Vladimir.* He sounds like some Old World Dracula wannabe. It's hard to take him seriously."

"He conquered the world," said Grandma Pia. "It's hard *not* to take him seriously."

"He didn't conquer the world," Myra said. "He destroyed it. He rules over an empty world of ashes and death."

"How did he stage the Nightfall?" a girl asked.

"We never learned all the specifics," Pia replied. "In any case, the preparations must have taken years. He gathered his armies down below, and once all was ready, his accomplices took over the WeatherWizard and covered all landmass where vampires dwelt with permanent clouds.

"And then the Nightfall began. The conquest was short as humans were unprepared. We tried to fight them with full-spectrum lamps, but artificial sunlight never worked against the demons. Vampires killed by the thousands and turned the humans they considered beautiful enough, so their numbers kept growing. Nowadays vampires are many, and we are few. Even if the WeatherWizard is destroyed, the fight will be long and hard. These creatures have a taste for ruling the world. They won't give up easily."

"Is the whole world dead and covered in clouds?" a little boy asked.

"All areas our scouts explored are dead," Grandma Pia said. "Though there must be patches of life here and there. Our scouts have hunted down animals, so there must be living plants."

"There have to be," Myra added, facing the boy. "Vampires need blood. They destroyed us, so now they have to feed on animals. They need to leave parts of the world alive to let animals survive."

"Are there any other humans left besides us?" Thea asked.

"I can't say," Pia admitted. "So far our patrols haven't found any other survivors."

"I hope we meet other humans," Thea said.

Myra had little hope that would ever happen. Ancient spells protected their cellars so that no vampire could find them unless led by a human. Druids had put the wards back in Roman times when people still believed in vampires, and all of their attempts to recover and recreate the spells had failed. She could not believe that there were other places protected by similar wards, or that human communities could survive without protection.

"I hope so too," Pia said, "but to the best of my knowledge, all humans that remained Outside were either killed or turned. I have to say it's strange. Vampires can survive on the blood of any animal, yet they have always preferred humans. Now that they have practically extinguished our kind, human blood is hard to find."

They must be really happy whenever they capture one of us, Myra thought.

"So human blood is their favorite?" a seven-year-old girl, Monica, asked.

"They prefer it to animal blood," Pia explained. "However, there is one single thing they like even better. Vampires enjoy drinking small amounts of each other's blood, not as a means of sustenance, but as part of the games they play."

Myra sighed. This information was not suited for children. "Thank you, Grandma Pia," she interrupted before the old woman could elaborate. "Your tales are exciting as always. I have to leave now. I'll take Thea with me, but I'll come by to talk to you later."

"I'll finish my work in the school in about an hour," the old woman said. "After that you can find me in my cellar."

Thea stood up. "Grandma Pia, I have one last question before I go. You said people in the Old World had legends about vampires. What kind of legends? Were they true?"

Pia smiled. "A few were true, I guess. They did know about stakes, and beheadings, and fire, and sunlight, of course. However, most of their so-called knowledge was silly superstition. Humans believed vampires were repelled by such things as crosses, holy water, even garlic."

"Garlic?" Thea snorted. "Now that would have been handy."

"I suppose they needed some sense of false security," Myra mused.

Monica cleared her throat. "Vamps breathe," she said and blushed as all eyes turned at her. "My mom interrogated one, and she said he was breathing. Can we suffocate them?"

Grandma Pia shook her head. "They breathe so that they can talk and sense smell. They suffer no harm from lack of air."

Myra stood up. "Come, Thea, we have to go."

Thea said goodbye to the children and followed Myra out of the room. "Where are we going?" she asked.

"Alerie returned from a patrol," Myra said. "She found something you might like."

***

Alerie greeted them, and Myra and Thea entered the small cellar.

"I'm so happy you finally found some, after so many years," Myra said with a smile.

"I wish I could give you more, but it's better than nothing." Alerie handed her the small piece. "We found only two bars, and we need to make sure all the children get a bite."

"I'm not a child," Thea protested.

"Problem solved, then," Myra said. "Nothing for you."

Thea glared at her. "What is it, anyway? And why is it only for children?"

"Let's go to the children's cellar, and I'll show you," Myra said.

Once they were in the room and seated on Thea's pallet, Myra held out the precious object for her cousin to see. "It's chocolate," she said. "We haven't found any since before you were born. I've tried some, and now it's your turn. I must warn you, though—it's expired and smells a bit funny, but I think it'll still be good."

Thea stared at the small piece as if she were afraid to take a bite. "Is there enough for everyone?" she asked.

"It's enough for all the children who have never tried it before," said Myra.

Thea looked up. "Do you want to share it?"

Myra smiled. "I've had a few pieces before you were born. Chocolate was easier to come by back then. This one is for you. Enjoy." She paused, wondering if she should continue. "Thea, chocolate was your mom's favorite food. She liked it a lot. I think you'll like it too."

Thea played with the dark piece in her hand. "Then perhaps I should save it for her. In case she comes back."

Myra looked away. "Thea, no one has seen her in over ten years."

"But no one found a body either," her cousin reasoned.

Myra sighed. That much was true. "Do you miss her?" she asked.

Thea shook her head. "To be honest, I can't say that I do. I miss the idea of her, I think, but I don't remember her. You're my family now."

Myra stared at the chocolate in silence. It was so unfair. Aunt Sandra had loved her baby girl more than anything, and now her daughter did not even remember her. "Try it," she said.

"Only if we split it," Thea declared stubbornly.

Myra was about to protest when she spotted something on the low wooden table next to the bed. She frowned and reached out, picking up the red silken ribbon. "Thea, where did you get this?"

Her cousin's face brightened. "Remember the goods Thomas brought from his last patrol? He scavenged what he thought was useful and was going to throw away the rest. He told us to look through the stuff and see if we liked something. I found this!" She reached out to pick the ribbon from Myra's hand.

Myra sighed. "Do you even know what it is?"

"Of course," Thea said, scolding. "I'm not a baby. I've read books and seen pictures." She tied the ribbon around one of her twin ponytails. "See? Don't I look pretty? Now I just need to find a second one."

Myra stared at the ribbon, bright crimson against Thea's dark-golden hair. She had never seen anything like it except in old photographs. Myra frowned and gave her cousin what she hoped was a stern look. "Why should it matter? It's the vamps who want to look pretty. We are above such trivialities."

"Says who? Humans of the Old World wanted to look pretty all the time."

"Yes, they did, and don't you know how it ended? The prettiest of humans became vampires. Is that what you want to happen to you?" Myra untied the ribbon from her cousin's hair. "We are better than that."

"Better?" Thea said. "Why would wanting or not wanting to look good make you a better or a worse person? It is only one of the many facets of your essence and it neither negates nor validates your other qualities."

Myra stared at her baby cousin at a loss of words. "A facet of your essence? It doesn't negate your qualities? *Where* did you learn to use such words?"

"At school," Thea replied with a grin. "So do I get to keep the ribbon?"

Myra handed it back. "Fine, if it makes you happy, but don't lose sight of what really matters."

A soft knock came from the door, and Myra fell quiet and looked up. The door opened and Lidia's dark curly head popped in. "Sorry to be the bearer of bad news," she said. "But the prisoner isn't talking, and Zack says it's your turn."

Myra suppressed a shudder. "Do I have to? You enjoy this. Feel free to take my shift if you like."

Lidia grinned. "I don't hate it, I admit, but I'm practical. I've seen enough to know that I can't make this one talk. Your tactics are different. Perhaps you can do something with him."

Myra had no desire to do anything with the prisoner, but if Zack insisted, she had little choice. "Fine," she murmured. "Let's get this over with."

Chapter Three

Survival

The vampire prisoner stood on unsteady legs, supported only by the chains that kept his arms up. Angry cuts and bruises decorated his face, arms, and bare torso. His fingers hung down, bent at unnatural angles. Still, he looked up and gave Myra a grin. "The next one," he said. "Let's see if you can come up with something more creative."

Myra tore her gaze from him. She would never break him with pain. If Lidia and Thomas had failed, she stood no chance. Her best bet was to be the good cop, as the prisoner had said earlier.

"I'm not here to torture you," she said.

He snorted. "Right. So you fight for love and peace among all beings?"

"Far from it," she said. "I know it will be pointless. My commander insists on me interrogating you, but that would be a waste of both your time and mine. I'm not going to make this even more unpleasant than it already is for either of us."

"Who says it's unpleasant?" the monster said. "I am enjoying myself."

She forced herself to smile and sat down in front of him. "I admire you, really. You are ready to suffer so much in order to protect your Prince. He must be a remarkable vampire to inspire such loyalty."

He laughed. "Is that your way of getting me to talk about His Highness?"

Myra bit her lower lip, but did not allow her smile to falter. Too obvious. "I'm just curious. He united all vampires and brought them together to work for a common cause. I admit I can't imagine how he rules over the entire world. How do you even communicate with the faraway places? You have let all technology, except the WeatherWizard, fall to waste. It must take ages to send a message."

He remained silent, but she pretended not to notice. "I guess your society must have something of a feudal structure. The Prince is the ruler in name, but every small region is under a local vampire lord or lady, who in theory reports to the Prince, but holds all the power."

He stared at her and grinned. Myra sighed. She had done a poor job hiding the fact that she was fishing for information.

She stretched her legs on the floor, faking a yawn. "I should have brought a book along to pass the time. This is such a waste. I keep telling Zack we should just focus on survival and forget this nonsense, but he never listens."

"Yes, you should," the vampire finally said. "You'll get yourselves killed if you go after the Prince."

"Exactly," Myra cried, trying to sound enthusiastic. "Last time we tried to do something major against your kind, it led to the Great Massacre, and over half of our Warriors died. If we target the Prince, it will be even worse. That's what I keep telling everyone."

"And your commander disagrees?"

She snorted. "Have you met Zack? He's obsessed. *Kill the Prince. Kill the Prince.* It's like a mantra to him." She stood up, brushed the dust off her pants, and took a few steps away from him. "Forgive me. I know you don't want to talk to me. I'll let you brood in peace."

He laughed. "No, please. I am bored. Tell me about Zack."

"He's not thinking straight," Myra said. "He wants to attack the Prince full force. Can you imagine?"

The vamp laughed. "Honestly, I cannot. Your pitiful Resistance cannot hope to stand against an army of eight hundred vampires. You are right—this is insane."

Eight hundred vampires. Myra fought hard to suppress a grin. They already knew the Prince ruled over the world, but naturally, it would be impossible to call all vampires from faraway places to his aid if he was under attack. The Warriors' Council had often wondered how many soldiers were in the Prince's immediate vicinity, ready to rise, and finally they knew.

She wished she could mock the monster and inform him that he had fallen into her trap, but she kept her facade. If she wanted to get any additional information out of him, she had to keep this up.

But what if the prisoner was deceiving her? What if he had seen through her game and had said that number to trick her? Perhaps the vamps were fewer and were vulnerable to an attack, but he had said a higher number to discourage any attempts. Or perhaps the number was greater, and the vamp wanted the Resistance to underestimate the Prince and fall into an ambush.

Myra looked at the captive, bound and helpless, tortured and in obvious pain, and yet still cocky. Did he still have the presence of mind to deceive her?

"Yes, I know we'd all die long before coming anywhere near the Prince," she said. "To tell you the truth, I don't know if I'd want to kill him even if I had the chance."

"How so?"

"He conquered the world," Myra said. "I keep thinking about the Nightfall and how he organized everything. It's quite incredible. Honestly, I find him fascinating." She walked closer to the vampire. "Tell me, what's he like?"

The prisoner's dark eyes narrowed. "Why, you sneaky little idiot. You think you can manipulate me into talking about the Prince? Who do you think you are?"

Myra bit her lower lip and looked away. She had pushed too hard and too fast. She would never get anything more from this captive, but perhaps she could do better with the next prisoner.

She looked up and raised a hand towards a trail of bleeding cuts on his arm. "You bleed, and yet your heart doesn't beat. How does that work? I've always wondered."

"I thought you would have figured that out by now," he said. "The dark magic that gives us life circulates our blood."

"And this dark magic is fed by blood?" Myra said. "I see. That explains a lot. I've seen Old World depictions of vampires, and they were all sickly pale, while you're not. I guess that's how people of the past imagined the risen dead to appear. But truth is, the blood that flows through your veins gives you some color. Though I suppose you can never get a suntan."

"Well, neither can you."

She glared at him. "Yes, thanks to your Prince, my people have never seen the sun. You must be letting sunlight reach the ground in some places. Where are they?"

"Look, my dear. You said it yourself—let us not waste each other's time. If you are not going to torture me, I suggest you go back home and do whatever you people do around here."

Myra stood up and walked slowly and deliberately to the far wall. She picked a stake from the rack and held it up so the prisoner could see it.

"I could end it, here and now. Tell me what I want to know, and I'll grant you a quick death."

He smiled. "And what part of 'I'm enjoying it' did you miss?"

"I'm not going to torture you," Myra said walking back to him. "But once my shift is over, one of my friends will come to relieve me, and they won't be so gentle. I want to spare you the pain. Please, I want to help you."

"Do I look like I care what you want?"

She gazed at the chained and hurt prisoner. Soon her friends would come one by one and resume their torture. The vampire claimed he enjoyed the torment, but she had heard his screams. Myra had no pity for this monster. He had killed many humans and would kill more if given the chance. Yet, abusing him did not seem right. At this point, he would reveal no new information. How long before they, the humans, turned into bigger monsters than the vamps?

Myra took a deep breath and plunged the stake deep into the vampire's heart.

***

"He could have talked," Thomas said.

Myra raised her water glass and took a slow sip. The thirty Warriors seated around the Conference Table at the Headquarters were all staring at her, and she was willing to bet that no more than one or two of them approved of her action. "He wasn't going to talk," she said. "He accidentally revealed information about the army size, but he wasn't going to say anything more. We were wasting our time, when we could be doing something more productive."

"I agree with Myra," Lidia said. "This vampire wasn't cooperating. We need to find one who will."

"And what if we never do?" Myra challenged. "Even if a prisoner talks, do we really think any information will help us assassinate the Prince? And if we do assassinate him, will it solve all our problems? Will it help us destroy the Wizard and restore humanity?"

"Killing the Prince will cause disorder among the vamps and give us an opportunity to strike," Thomas said.

"Do we really know that?" Myra said. "Perhaps the Prince will simply be replaced by another tyrant and we won't even notice the change."

"I can't imagine that vamps appoint heirs," said Thomas. "They never plan on dying. If the Prince dies, it will surely lead to some kind of a civil war."

"You're just guessing," said Myra.

"What do you suggest, then?" Thomas asked.

"We could skip all the dubious intermediate steps and jump right into an attack on the Wizard," Lidia suggested.

Thomas snorted. "Our Warriors are too few."

Myra's eyes darted towards Zack, who was sitting at the head of the Conference Table, strangely quiet. "Thomas is right," she said. "We're not ready to attack, but there might be something else we can do."

An elderly Warrior cleared his throat, and everyone fell silent. "Our Warriors are too few, you say," Andre said. "Well, there is a very easy way to get more."

Zack stood up and started pacing back and forth, but said nothing. Andre followed him with his eyes before continuing. "I'm turning seventy next year. I'm one of your best and most experienced Warriors, and I won't be allowed to fight." He stood up from his chair and stared at Zack. "Remove the age restrictions. Allow everyone who can hold a weapon to be a Warrior."

"Yes," a girl, Estella, cried, and all eyes turned at her. "I turned sixteen last week, so this is my first Warriors' meeting. A week ago, I wasn't allowed to fight. Back then I could fight just as well as I can now. Age shouldn't come into it."

Zack stopped in his tracks and swept the room with his gaze. "We could remove the upper boundary and allow the elderly to fight, but only if they volunteer. I will not force anyone over seventy to take up arms." He looked at Estella and added, "But I won't allow children to fight."

"But—" she started to protest, and he interrupted her.

"Enough. I am not allowing anyone under sixteen to be a Warrior. In any case, even with the babies and the oldest among us fighting, our numbers are far from enough to get through the Wizard's defenses."

Myra sighed. That much was true. Removing the upper age boundary would only add a handful of Warriors to their ranks.

After all, few in the Resistance lived beyond the age of forty, and ten years ago the Great Massacre had further diminished the number of older fighters. "We can't launch any attack if we starve to death," she said. "There might be a way to find better food supplies."

"Speak," said Zack.

"The animals we hunt down must be feeding on something. There must be growing plants somewhere, which means the vampires leave the place sunlit. If we find that place, we could find edible plants and more animals to hunt. Moreover, if the place is sunlit, it will be safe during the day. Zack, I know how important the attack is, but we need to have a sustainable food source before we attempt anything."

"Why would the vamps keep a sunlit place?" Thomas challenged.

"They do need something to eat after all," Myra said. "They couldn't let all animals die out."

"If such a place exists, they must have set up some traps for us," Zack said. "I don't think it's safe to go searching for it."

"May I suggest something crazy?" Estella said.

"You're now a member of the Warriors' Council," Zack said. "You have as much right to speak as anyone."

Estella grinned. "Rat farm," she said. "Think about it. Right now we kill and bake the rats that we capture right away. What if we kept them alive and put them together, so they could reproduce and multiply in a controlled environment? They're low maintenance, and if the farm grows, we would have a steady meat supply."

"It does sound crazy," Thomas said.

"Yet it makes sense," said Andre. "I like it."

"They do multiply fast," Zack mused. "And require little food to survive."

He paused as the door opened, and Alerie stepped in. "General Wong. I have some news. We've captured another vamp."

The silence that followed was deafening. Thomas was the first to speak. "Another? We capture two vamps per year if we are lucky, and now we have a second one in just a couple of days?"

"They are coming closer to our hideout and becoming more dangerous," said Lidia. "We can expect more encounters in the future."

"Any casualties on our side?" Zack asked.

"Tory and Daphne are dead," Alerie said softly. "Three more are wounded but will recover."

Everyone bowed their heads. Myra had not known the fallen Warriors very well, but it stung nonetheless. Death was ever present in their lives, and their small community was growing even smaller. The Resistance had numbered over two thousand shortly after the Nightfall, and now there were less than five hundred of them. Tory had two daughters, she suddenly remembered and closed her eyes.

"Is the captive secured?" Zack asked.

"Yes, she is chained in the prison cellar," Alerie replied.

Zack nodded. "Very well. Let the vamp rot there for now. We'll interrogate her later. First, we'll take the time to bury and mourn Daphne and Tory."

***

Myra knocked on the flimsy door and entered once she heard a reply. The cellar was dark, save for a single lit candle. Zack was sitting at the desk poring over some papers, a half-empty mug in his hand.

Myra leaned on the desk next to him. "What's this?"

"I'm reviewing the inventory," her friend and commander said. "I don't need to tell you things don't look good." Zack ran his hands through his hair. "How am I supposed to do this? How am I supposed to feed hundreds on *this*?" He waved the paper listing their supplies.

Myra placed a hand on his shoulder. "Zack, we don't expect magic from you. We are all facing this together. We'll figure it out." She took the paper out of his hand and left it on the desk. "Have you seen the new vamp? Any chance she may talk?"

He shook his head. "I let Lidia start the interrogation. I haven't seen the prisoner yet."

"More and more patrols fail to return unharmed," said Myra. Suddenly the idea of joining the next party seemed less appealing.

"I know," Zack said, looking tired. "But we can't stop sending them. We are consuming the food faster than we are finding new supplies."

"Yes, of course," she said. "Zack, you were quiet at the conference today. What's wrong?"

"Nothing, really. I just hoped Alerie would find more food."

Myra smiled sadly. "We all did. Honestly, I hoped she'd find some glutinous rice. I was looking forward to your New Year's cakes."

Zack gave her a blank look. "What?"

"You do know it's Chinese New Year next week, right?"

"Honestly, no." Zack raised an eyebrow. "And you didn't seriously expect me to make cakes, did you?"

She frowned. "Zack, you haven't celebrated in the past five years. What happened? This holiday used to mean so much to you."

"It meant a lot to my grandmother," he said. "I never cared much. After her death there was no point in pretending anymore."

That's not true, Myra thought. *I've seen you laugh and enjoy the holiday. Need is turning us all into beasts.*

She took the inventory list from the desk and brought it to her face. "So you focused on fighting and surviving for one more day," she said. "Have you ever wondered what your grandmother would think if she were still alive, watching you? We have become animals—eating, fighting, killing, and hiding in our dark holes. When was the last time we celebrated Holi, or Hanukkah, or Christmas, or Ramadan, or anything at all?"

"People of the Old World celebrated the coming of spring," said Zack. "They celebrated the solstices, and the equinoxes. What would these mean to us when we have no spring? When we have no sun?"

"It doesn't mean we should forget our cultures," Myra said. "We're so busy surviving that we have forgotten about all else. Zack, I finished writing another short story yesterday. Let me give a lecture at the school and make the kids read it."

He snorted. "I'm sorry to be blunt, but the school system doesn't exist to satisfy your ego. We have plenty of Old World books for the kids to read and discuss. I'm sure they can learn more from them than from your stories."

"How would you know?" Myra said softly. "You never read any of my works. Besides, if you must know, we have exactly one hundred and seventeen fiction books in the library. This is hardly enough. We need new works, and we need to encourage the children to create art on their own."

"The children need to train to become Warriors," Zack said. "The combat training is our top priority. We can't destroy the Wizard with art or science."

But can we be humans without it? "Alright," she said. "Let's say we train every day and somehow destroy the WeatherWizard. What then? We'll have to rebuild human society from scratch, and we need to be equipped with the right tools. Humans of the Old World had so much knowledge—on math and science, history, philosophy, art. They worked for millennia to accumulate it; we can't let it go to waste. And, most of all, we can't let the human spirit and the desire to create go to waste."

"I agree that knowledge in a variety of subjects is important," Zack said. "But there will be no world to rebuild unless we destroy the Wizard here and now." He paused. "Still, I see your point. Perhaps it won't hurt to organize another spirit-lifting event. We won't be celebrating Chinese New Year or any other specific holiday. We'll simply celebrate life, culture, and the strength of the human spirit."

Myra smiled and placed a hand on his arm. "Thank you. How can I help?"

"You'll stage a play. One of your own or something from the library. Something funny and uplifting. And, Myra, I can't spare any Warriors at the moment. You should use child actors for all parts."

"I can work with that," she said and paused. Someone was knocking.

Lidia entered at Zack's invitation. "General," she said. "I think you need to meet the prisoner."

Zack frowned. "Is the interrogation going well?"

"I'm not interrogating her," Lidia said. "Or torturing her for that matter. She's speaking freely. And she wants to talk to you."

"What do you mean she's speaking freely?" Myra asked. "Is she ready to reveal information about the Prince?"

"I think you had better come," said Lidia. "Both of you."

Chapter Four

Heroes

Myra stared at the prisoner. The vampire was dressed in a red blouse and wore a wide, short skirt over her tight black leggings. Black lace gloves covered her hands, and her dark brown hair, streaked with golden highlights, fell around her shoulders in soft, silky waves.

The Resistance is fighting hard to get food and medicines while vamps have access to hair products. How a dead woman could have such perfect hair, Myra would never know. She ran her hand self-consciously through her own mousy-brown shoulder-length hair, which would turn frizzy at the slightest hint of moisture. She knew the vampires would never pick her as one of them.

As soon as the thought came to her, she realized how ridiculous it was. She would rather die than be turned. And yet, a silly and vain part of her was irritated at the knowledge that she never stood a chance to be a part of the world she hated.

The captive grinned at the many Warriors surrounding her. She held her head high, her dark eyes bright.

"I hear you have information for us?" Zack said. "What is it, and why do you wish to share it?"

"And I hear you wish to assassinate our beloved Prince," the vampire said. "And I can assure you that nothing would make me happier than to see His Highness part with his haughty head."

"Right," Zack said. "And I'm supposed to believe you?"

"You would be a fool to think His Highness is the most fit to rule among us, and no one strives to overthrow him," the captive said. "But before you start throwing questions and accusations at me, let me make the rules clear."

"The rules?" Lidia blurted out. "You're our prisoner, and you want to set the rules?"

Zack raised his hand for silence. "What is your name?" he asked the vampire.

She smirked. "Rim."

"Very well, Rim," Zack said. "Name your terms."

"No torture," Rim started. "I will tell you all there is to know about Prince Vladimir, but if you so much as touch me, I will stop talking."

"If you wish to work with us, why did you kill two of our people?" Thomas said.

She snorted. "What was I supposed to do? I was minding my own business when your people attacked me. I never planned to get captured, but now that I am here, and I learned that we share the same goal, I think we should all try to make the best of it."

"Fair enough," said Zack. "Your terms sound reasonable. No one will torture you."

"I am not finished. I am going to share everything that can help you assassinate His Highness, and nothing more. If you ask any questions I deem irrelevant, I will leave them unanswered. And"—she paused—"you are to release me once I have told you everything."

Zack and Myra exchanged a glance. The vampire had been blindfolded when the Resistance had brought her inside, and she would not be able to find their hideout. Still, the request posed another problem. "What are you planning to do once you're free?" Myra asked. "Are you going back to the Prince?"

"This question falls into the 'irrelevant' category," Rim replied.

"We can't agree to those terms," Zack said. "Your proposition is suspicious as it is. I find it much easier to believe you're sending us into a trap. And now you want us to release you? And I'm supposed to believe you're not running back to the Prince to tell him exactly where you've sent us?"

"Believe what you will," the vampire said. "These are my terms."

"What if we release you after we've killed the Prince?" Myra suggested. "Our party goes and does the job, they return safely, and then we let you go. How does that sound?"

Rim fiddled with her chains, as if testing them. "Thrilling," she said. "Am I supposed to place my trust in your skills? What if you fail? I will end up rotting in this hole forever."

"Trust what you will," Zack echoed. "These are our terms."

The vampire grinned. "Well, well, General, you are starting to grow a spine. Fine. I will talk to you, and you will release me after the Prince is dead. You will, of course, not mistreat me in the meantime. Can you give me any guarantee you will keep your side of the bargain?"

"I can give you my word," he said. "I'm afraid I can't give you anything else."

"The enemy of my enemy is my friend," Rim said. "Very well. I will trust a friend's word."

"You claimed to have information about the Prince," Lidia said. "Where does he live?"

"He is based in the Palace," Rim said. "It is an old castle, up in the Highlands."

Myra nodded. It made sense; most former cities were turning to ruin, slowly falling apart, while medieval stone buildings were easier to maintain.

"How far away is this castle?" Zack asked.

"Less than ten miles from the place where your people captured me, though I am not surprised you have never discovered it. There are many patrols on the way, so I suppose your people met them and turned back. I can draw you a map, or help one of you draw it since I doubt you will untie my hands. I can also show you how to avoid the patrols."

"That would be helpful," Zack said. "Now, about the Prince. Who is he exactly?"

"An arrogant upstart who thinks the world belongs to him." Rim's face twisted into a grimace.

Myra sighed. "Can you try to be more specific and less subjective?"

Rim shrugged, as much as her fetters allowed. "He is the one who destroyed your world and caused the deaths of millions of your people. What more do you need to know?"

"Fine," Zack said. "How much power does he have? How many soldiers does he command?"

"Over eight hundred soldiers are in the Palace alone. Many more are in nearby castles or in the camps around the Wizard and can be called if needed. You cannot attack the Palace full force if that is what you are planning."

Myra stole a look at Zack. *Over eight hundred soldiers.* This matched what the previous prisoner had said. Oddly enough, Rim appeared to be telling the truth.

"And the nearby castles will answer if he calls?" Myra asked.

"A local noble-vampire rules over each castle, but they all report to His Highness. A few may disagree with him, but they will still send troops if he asks. He holds too much power; no one would oppose him openly."

"You said some of your people wished for his death?" Myra asked. "How many? Are they in the Palace too?"

Rim glared at her. "Little girl, I hope you realize that the people you send to assassinate His Highness can be captured and tortured for information. I would not risk any intelligence on my accomplices leaking to the Prince. Let us just say that most people at the Palace are still loyal to the Prince, or are too afraid to oppose him. You will not find allies. You must rely on yourselves."

"You said we can't launch an assault on the Palace," Zack said. "I assume you have other suggestions?"

Rim rolled her eyes. "Must I make your plans for you now, General? Obviously, you need to send a small group of assassins. One or two will be best."

"And how would my people get close enough to the Prince and live to tell the tale?" Zack asked.

"You cannot enter the Palace. It is a proper castle, with a moat and a drawbridge. You cannot get inside, and even if you do, you will not make a single step before someone spots you. You will have to kill the Prince once he is outside."

"Does he regularly leave the castle?" Thomas asked.

"Almost every day," the vampire said. "One option is to catch him while he is hunting, though he is usually not alone and it will be harder. The better alternative would be to attack when he is reading in the Rose Gardens."

"Rose Gardens, you say?" Myra said. "Are real roses growing there? That must be one of the places you keep sunlit. Are there any others?"

Rim laughed. "None of your business."

Zack cleared his throat. "Fine. Then let me ask you another question, and if you refuse to answer this one, our deal is off. You claim your Prince spends time alone in those Rose Gardens. You claim that you, and possibly others, wish for his death. If killing him is so easy, why haven't you done it already?"

"I never said it would be easy."

"Is he well guarded?" Lidia asked.

"He thinks he can guard himself," Rim said. "He is an exceptional fighter, but he is not infallible. I admit we might have had opportunities. The main reason we hold back is caution. Many vampires would oppose a violent overthrow, and we wish to avoid a rebellion. If the Prince is killed by your people, it will unite us and help me and my associates place our preferred ruler on the throne."

"How would the vampires know it was us who killed the Prince?" Zack asked.

"They will know," she said.

"The Rose Gardens," Myra said. "Are they sunlit every single day? All day?"

"At this time of year, yes," Rim replied. "Your people will be safe there during the day."

"And what if the Prince learns my people are coming and switches on the clouds?" Zack asked.

"This is not how the WeatherWizard works," Rim explained. "The control is not instantaneous. You can program all weather changes in advance, by the minute, but if you want to make an unplanned change, it may take a few days to take effect."

Zack nodded and walked out of the room. He returned in a minute, carrying paper and pencils. "Alright, then, let's do this," he said.

They sat for over an hour, Zack jotting down all the details—vampire patrols on the way, numbers, the Prince's nightly comings and goings. Once he was satisfied, he handed Lidia his notebook.

"Lidia, please continue the interrogation. Rim will walk you through the route, and you'll sketch a map. Everyone else, please join me in the Headquarters." Zack turned to Rim. "We have a deal. Help my captain draw the map, and we will kill Prince Vladimir."

***

"Alright, just say it," Myra muttered when she could no longer stand the aura of smugness radiating from her commander.

"You want me to say it?" Zack asked, and a mischievous twinkle appeared in his dark, catlike eyes.

"Most certainly not," Myra admitted. "But *you* want to say it, and I can't stand watching you sit there and bask in your glory."

"Alright, then, I'll say it." The General made a dramatic pause before continuing. "*I told you so!*"

"So what?" Alerie challenged. "You were right, Zack. After capturing and interrogating tens of vamps, one was bound to talk. We have everything we wanted to know about Prince Vladimir. What are we going to do about it?"

"We have to act fast," Zack said. "The Prince has no idea we have this information. Now is the best time to send an assassin."

"Zack, that would be suicide," Myra said. "There's so much about this I don't like. For starters, how do we know Rim isn't sending us into a trap?"

"The vamps would benefit from such a trap only if many of us go, and they destroy us all with one stroke," Zack said. "Rim suggested we send only a couple of Warriors. Why would she do that if this were a trap? The vamps gain nothing by killing one or two of us."

The door opened and Lidia walked into the Headquarters with a few papers in hand. "I have the maps," she said. "The Rose Gardens are well outside the Palace. The vamps want to keep the Palace in shadow at all times, for obvious reasons."

"Good," said Zack. "Did you get any more information?"

Lidia nodded. "We talked a bit about the vamps' means of transportation. Apparently they mainly use horses and carts."

Myra looked up. Horses? Horses would need grass. The vampires would have to take them to living fields, so some sunlit spots had to be close to the Palace. She had seen horses only in pictures, but she hoped to see real ones one day, and to travel in a cart. It sounded magical, but there was no place for magic in her life.

Zack nodded. "I can imagine electrical and hydrogen cars are out of the question. Sun-powered ones even more so."

"They do have some old gas cars left," Lidia said. "The engines run on propane, but the vampires' fuel supply is limited and only very important vamps get to drive them on special occasions."

"And by 'very important vamps' you mean the Prince?" Alerie asked.

Lidia grinned. "Apparently he's the only one driving. Our captive was bitter about it."

"Speaking of our captive," Myra said, "what should we do with her?"

"We'll kill her," Zack said.

She stared at him. "What? Zack, you can't. You gave her your word."

"She killed two of our people," he said. "Will you tell Tory's daughters that we're releasing their father's murderer? You got a chance to stake the vamp who killed your parents. Surely you understand why others need the same justice."

"Staking him brought me no peace," Myra said.

"Letting him go would have brought you even less peace, believe me," Zack said. "What's wrong? You hate vamps more than most of us. Every vampire has to die if we are to restore human civilization. Surely you know that."

"I hate vampires as much as anyone," she said. "But what I hate even more is watching us become monsters like them. Zack, you gave her your word. If you break it, we're no better than them. Yes, she has to die, and she will. But not now. Not like this."

Zack was silent for a moment, but nodded slowly at last. "Very well. Once we've killed the Prince, I will set her free. I hope we won't regret it."

An anguished scream echoed through the hall, and Myra paled and turned to the door. There, behind a high cupboard, peeked a little girl. Her dark eyes were wide and moist, and she was shaking her head. *Shanice*, Myra's mind supplied. *Tory's daughter. Ten years old.*

A whimper escaped Shanice's lips, and she turned around and bolted out the door. Zack sighed and looked at Thomas.

"Tommy, please, take care of this," he said.

Thomas nodded and ran after the girl.

Zack ran his hand over his face. "I'll have to talk to Shanice later," he said and turned to Myra. "Something else is troubling you?"

"The vampire told us all about her Prince," Myra said, "And perhaps she wants us to succeed. Yet, she doesn't seem worried that we might use the ensuing chaos to attack the Wizard. Why? My guess is, she doesn't expect any chaos. They already have a substitute ruler in place and the transition will go smoothly. What if we don't gain anything from the Prince's death?"

"I can't believe that," said Zack. "Rim may have a ruler in mind, but other vampire factions likely have candidates. There's no way to avoid chaos once their leader is gone. Perhaps Rim hasn't guessed that attacking the Wizard is our final goal, so she's not worried. Lidia, do you think you can find these Rose Gardens?"

"Sure, the map is clear."

Zack hesitated. "I wish to send only a couple of good fighters. Lidia, I hate to ask this of you, but you would be my first choice. Alerie, you'd be my second. I'd like to send you both."

Lidia seemed taken aback, but quickly recovered. "It would be my honor, General Wong."

"Mine too," Alerie whispered.

"Zack, you can't send Lidia," Myra protested. "She is too valuable. We can't afford to lose her."

"I know," Zack said. "She is one of my best Warriors, but we are all valuable."

"This is not about fighting," Myra insisted. "Lidia is the only one among us with adequate knowledge of medicine. Dr. Dubois is over eighty. If something happens to her, we're left without a doctor."

"I know it's important to have a doctor in our community," Zack said. "But if we don't do this here and now, we won't live long enough to worry about disease."

"If Lidia fails, we'll lose all chances of survival," Myra said. "Even if we destroy the WeatherWizard and overthrow the vamps, we'll have no doctor. The medicine books in our library don't cover all topics, and there is only so much you can learn from a book."

"If Lidia fails in the mission, and we don't assassinate the Prince, we'll all die anyway, sooner or later," Zack said. "It's an all-or-nothing gambit. I will send a few Warriors, and if they succeed, we all live. If they fail, we all die. I have to send the ones best suited for the task."

"Fine, but must you send Lidia?" Myra said. "Thomas is also a good fighter."

"Thomas is needed here," Zack said sternly. "I will ask you not to question my decisions. I have reasons for them."

Andre stood up in his chair. "I'll go. I'm a good Warrior, and I am more disposable. I've lived longer than any of you. Death doesn't scare me."

Zack massaged his temples. "How many times do I need to say it? This is *not* supposed to be a suicide mission. I'm not sending whoever is most disposable. I'm sending whoever can do the task best. Andre, you're a great Warrior, but you are past your prime. No offense."

Myra fell silent, thinking on Zack's words. He had a point, and yet sending their only potential doctor on such a dangerous mission seemed insane. What if Lidia and Alerie did succeed, but were killed on the way back? Then the Resistance had a real chance of survival, but they wouldn't last for long with no knowledge of medicine. Myra closed her eyes. Her heartbeat accelerated until her ears started ringing. "If you must send someone," she said softly, "send me."

"Myra, don't be ridiculous," Lidia snapped.

Zack shook his head. "I made it clear that we want to send a good fighter. You're average. Your strength is strategy. You have no experience in fieldwork."

"And how am I supposed to gain any experience if you never send me out? Zack, I want to learn."

He sighed. "Captain Andersen, do you realize that Prince Vladimir's assassination will be the single most crucial mission the Resistance has ever undertaken? I can't take the risk that this task will fail, and I will not use it as your training exercise."

"My strength is strategy, you say," Myra argued, "and I believe we will need more than brute force to assassinate the Prince. In fact, I think brute force will have nothing to do with this. You're sending Alerie, and she is an excellent fighter. You need her partner to be someone with a different skill set."

Alerie stood up. "Myra, this is a serious mission that could change our future. We don't have time for this. If you want to play the hero, do it in one of your theater plays."

Myra felt like she had been slapped. Play the hero? Was that what she was trying to do? She had to admit it had felt good to volunteer. Her heart had pumped with excitement when she had said the words. She was offering to sacrifice herself to save their community. She was like the characters in the books she loved to read, fighting the oppressors and doing what was right. She knew she had not thought this through, but it mattered little. After all, Zack would never accept her offer anyway.

Zack leaned back in his chair. "Myra has a point," he admitted. "Vamps are better fighters than any of us. We cannot expect to defeat them in combat. We must rely on stealth and careful planning as well. Myra, do you think you can do this?"

"I can do this better than anyone else in this room," Myra stated with confidence she did not feel. The moment she spoke the words, she wondered if she could take them back. What was she doing? This mission was suicide, she had said so herself. She had always dreamed of going out there, of seeing more of the world, but not like this.

With a pang of guilt, Myra realized why she had made the offer. She had been certain that Zack would refuse. If she had thought there was any chance the General would pick her, she would have never volunteered. She was a coward. That was the safe way to play the hero, so she could later lie to herself that she had done the right thing.

"Very well," Zack said. "Captain Andersen, the task to assassinate Prince Vladimir is assigned to you."

Chapter Five

Innocence

Torch flames danced in the gloomy corridor, like snakes fighting to devour one another. Myra reached to the stone wall to steady herself. Light and shadow played around her, creating images on the wall—battles, blood, death. She took in a deep breath. Her head was spinning, but she had to keep walking. She had to reach the children's cellar and tell Thea what she had done. But what could she possibly say?

If you want to play the hero, do it in one of your theater plays.

Was it all a dream? Or had the play become reality? She finally saw it all clearly—the moment she had volunteered, she had not believed any of this was real. But it was. She was really going *Outside*, really sneaking into a vampire's lair.

The task to assassinate Prince Vladimir is appointed to you.

The Resistance had been trying to assassinate the Prince since long before her birth. How could she hope to succeed where so many experienced Warriors had failed? What had she been thinking?

"You look gloomy today."

Myra jumped, staring at her cousin who was standing in the middle of the passage barring her way. "Thea, sorry, I was distracted."

"Clearly," Thea said. "What's up?"

Myra opened her mouth to speak, but no words came out. *I should have planned this in advance.* "Can you join me in the library?" she said after she finally found her voice. "I have something to show you."

Thea nodded and fell in step next to her. "What is it? Did Alerie find any other super-food?"

"Do you always think about sweets?" Myra asked, forcing a smile. "You'll learn soon enough. A little patience won't hurt you."

Thea stayed silent until they reached the library. They entered and Myra raised her candle, casting light over the shelves. She loved the sight of books, the feel of paper in her hands, the characteristic smell. She often told herself that she wanted to go outside and experience adventures just like her favorite characters, but in all honesty, she would have been happy to spend her life in the library, reading one novel after another.

Reading. That was what she was always doing. Reading other people's adventures, and reading her own. Up until today her fate had been written down, every single day predefined. Get up, train, study, cook, clean, wash and sew clothes, hunt rats, discuss plans at the Headquarters, interrogate prisoners, eat, sleep. She had been a reader of her own life, and the story had been dark and dull. Now the time had come to become the writer of her own fate and to decide what happened next.

"Can you believe that in the Old World, authors often romanticized vampires?" Myra wondered as she took in the titles.

"Grandma Pia said people had no idea vamps existed," Thea said. "For them it was only a fantasy."

"A strange fantasy," Myra said. "I wonder if any of those authors would exchange their place with mine and come and live it for real." She trailed her hand over the row of books, brushing off the dust. "Ah, sorry, Thea. I brought you here to show you something."

She knelt down to reach the bottom shelf and took out a box filled with her notebooks. "Last week I finished writing another play for the kids. It's about two little pandas, exploring the world. I thought you and Anastasia could play the main roles."

"Sounds great," Thea said. "When are we performing?"

Myra hesitated. "Thea, I'm going Outside on a mission, and I don't know how long I'll be away. I'm showing you the play because I want you to organize the performance in case I am delayed. You've seen me directing before; I know you'll do fine."

Thea had blanched. "What kind of a mission is this? And why do you sound like you don't expect to come back?"

"What are you talking about? Of course I'll come back," Myra said, trying to hide the tremors in her voice. "Where else would I go?"

Thea's lower lip trembled, and her eyes were filling up with treacherous moisture. "You better come back. If you don't, I'll sabotage your play and make a tiger eat the baby pandas."

Myra laughed at that. And then, she cried. And as she held her distraught cousin, she whispered promises she did not know how to keep.

***

Zack took his high chair at the end of the Conference Table and leaned back. "What is your plan?"

Myra unfolded the map and placed it on the table. "We need about three hours to reach the Rose Gardens. We should leave three hours before dawn, so that we arrive there in the early morning. If the place is sunlit, there will be no vampires before sunset, and we'll have plenty of time to investigate the terrain before the Prince arrives."

"That's assuming Rim didn't lie about the vamps keeping the sunshine on," Alerie said.

"For now let's assume Rim was telling the truth," Zack said. "Otherwise we have no starting point."

"Alright, then," Alerie said. "We leave, we follow the route Rim outlined, and provided she told the truth, we reach the Rose Gardens by sunrise. Then what?"

"We'll have the whole day to look around the Gardens and find a good hiding spot," said Myra.

"And we'll sit and hide, waiting for him to appear?" Alerie laughed. "Now I see why we picked you for this mission. A brilliant strategy indeed."

Zack frowned. "Captain Sanchez, now is not the time for sarcasm. If you have something to say, say it."

"Myra has no field experience," Alerie said. "She's endangering herself, and she's endangering me. Even worse, she puts the mission at risk."

"How am I putting the mission at risk?" Myra asked. "Alerie, I understand your concerns, but I can assure you I won't do anything to give away our position. I'll follow your orders. You'll be in command; I'll just advise."

Alerie stood up, walked behind her chair, and squeezed the backrest until her knuckles turned white. "Advise? How exactly will you advise when you have no idea what we are doing? You suggest we simply hide in the garden and wait? Do you even know how keen a sense of smell vampires have? Has it occurred to you that the Prince might catch our scent no matter how well we hide?"

"Yes, you need to conceal your scent," Zack said. "Captain Sanchez, I assume you have a suggestion?"

"Of course. There are some very old fish cans in the storage. We could check if anything is smelly enough and rub it on our skin."

"Wouldn't the Prince wonder why there's dead fish in his garden?" Myra said. "If the gardens are anything like what Rim described, there should be fresh grass and flowers there. We could rub those on our skin instead."

Alerie reached out to pick the map and stared at it. "If you say so. Any thoughts on the actual killing?"

"You're the expert here," Myra said.

"You are *the strategist*," Alerie shot back.

Zack sighed. "Captain Sanchez, I cannot tolerate this hostility. You are one of my best Warriors, and I'd like to have you on this mission. Myra claims she can contribute, and I trust her. I need both of you, and I need you to work together."

Alerie frowned and stared back. "As you command, General." She looked at Myra. "So? Any ideas?"

What answer did Alerie expect? All the vamps Myra had staked had been chained and incapacitated. Her only experience came from talking to the Warriors who had been out on patrols.

"Vampires are quicker and stronger than us," Myra said. "I've heard that the best way to kill them is to weaken them first. It's best to start with the guns. Once they're wounded and slower, we can take crossbows and go for the kill."

"Yes, you've heard this," Alerie said. "While I have actually done it, several times. Myra, I know you have good intentions. And I promise to guide you and help you achieve all you are capable of on this mission. But you must understand that saying something and doing it are two different things. We start with guns, then we take crossbows; it sounds so easy when you say it. Yet, I can tell you it won't be easy at all."

"I know that," Myra said. "Prince Vladimir has destroyed human civilization. He rules over the world and has armies at his command. Killing him can't be so simple."

Saying it aloud made their mission sound even more hopeless. Really, what were they thinking? This was the vamps' leader they were talking about. He would never put himself in any position that would endanger his life. Myra stared at the map showing the road they had to walk. What had she gotten herself into?

***

Myra held her empty backpack and gazed at the supplies on the pallet. Guns and bullets, crossbows and arrows, stakes, water flasks, biscuits, smoked meat, blankets, a notebook and pencils. "Do you think that's enough?"

"You're the strategist," Alerie said. "You tell me."

Myra ran a hand through her hair. "Why do you have such a problem with me? You said it yourself that it's a good time for me to start going Outside."

"I meant you could start joining raids in search for food," Alerie said, "not that you should join the Resistance's most important mission ever. Look, Myra, I have nothing against you. You're a good, caring person, and you've contributed to our community. In fact, I like you, and that's one of the reasons I don't want to see you killed. Which is exactly what will happen if you come with me."

"Can you try to have a little faith in me? I know what I'm doing."

"Do you? Well, then—are the supplies enough?"

Myra sighed. No matter what answer she gave, she would never convince Alerie that she was ready for this. "The food here is enough for a week. If all goes well, we should accomplish the mission and return in less than two days."

Alerie sat on the pallet and started putting the supplies in her backpack. "Still, we may need to camp out at the Gardens for longer if necessary. We don't know for certain that the Prince will come on the first day. Or he may come with company, and then we would need to hide and wait until he returns alone."

"Rim said he goes there almost every day."

"Almost," Alerie said. "How many days in a row would he typically miss? How often would he bring others with him?"

"I guess we should talk to the prisoner again and ask her the specifics."

Alerie took a crossbow from the pallet and started checking the string. "And the notebook and pencils are necessary because…?"

Myra looked at the floor. Alerie would not be happy to hear she was hoping to find inspiration out in the open and do some writing. "We might need to record information on the way."

"We should record as little as possible. Anything we write down could fall into enemies' hands."

"I know how to use our secret code," Myra said.

Alerie snorted. "Ah, the code. That's one of Zack's worst ideas. The vamps have lived for centuries and witnessed the rise and fall of all kinds of sophisticated encryption systems. Do you think they can't crack a simple Vigenère code?"

Myra had never considered this. The code had seemed so intricate and complicated when Zack had first taught her how to use it, and she had honestly believed it to be unbreakable. Alerie was right—the vamps were beasts, but they were likely more knowledgeable than any of the Resistance.

Alerie raised an eyebrow. "Do you still think you're up to this? It's not too late to turn back."

Myra looked away. "I don't know. This mission is unpredictable, and I can't say if I'm better suited than anyone else. What I do know is that I'll never forgive myself if I let Lidia go instead of me and leave our people without a doctor. And honestly, even if we succeed, we still have many battles ahead. Our army isn't big enough to assault the Wizard, whether the Prince lives or not."

"It's much smaller than it should be," Alerie said. "Zack is wrong, keeping the minors from fighting."

"You can't mean that."

Alerie put the crossbow in her backpack. "Why not? Adulthood is a fluid notion. At some points in human history, twelve was a respectable age to fight in a war, to make your own living, or to get married. And a few of the minors are very good fighters. Better than some of our Warriors."

"Better than me, you mean? This isn't about ability or maturity. They're children. They haven't lived long enough. We can't place them in danger like that. And, to be honest, I can't imagine Thea holding a weapon."

"She's like a baby to you," Alerie said. "She's twelve, you know."

"I know. But I've held her when she was this big." Myra put her hands two feet apart. "It's hard to think she's grown up and even harder to imagine her fighting. I hope to end this war before she has to." She reached out to take a stake from the supplies and twirled it before placing it in her pack. "I'm going to talk to the prisoner. Will you join me?"

Alerie stared at her scattered supplies. "I suppose packing can wait."

***

The heavy door came into view and Myra gasped and stopped in her tracks. The prison cellar was one of the few places in the Resistance with metal doors—the patrols had found only a handful of these in abandoned towns, and Zack had decided to install them in the dungeon, where security was the most important. Yet, Resistance members could never be sure that the titanium chains and the metal doors would be enough to contain vamps, so it was customary to have a guard or two in the passage in front of the door whenever they had a prisoner.

The corridor was empty.

Myra's throat grew tight. "Where are the guards?"

"Sean was on guard duty today." Alerie grabbed Myra's arm. "The vamp has escaped. I don't know what she's done to him, but it can't be good."

Myra shuddered and took a step towards the closed door, but Alerie pulled her back. "Wait. The vamp couldn't have gotten out unnoticed. We have too many patrols on the way. She's probably still in there, biding her time."

"Should we call for reinforcements?" Myra asked.

Alerie put a finger against her lips and walked away from the door, gesturing at Myra to follow. Once they had taken a turn into another section of the corridor, Alerie stopped. "If she's in there, she was probably listening to us and planning her next move. She might want to take us hostages and use us in her escape."

"Rim doesn't even know the way out," Myra said. "She was blindfolded when they brought her in."

"She could have memorized the steps and the turns," Alerie said. "But I agree—I don't think she'll manage to get out. Still, if she's running free inside the Resistance, she can do a lot of damage before we kill or recapture her. Sean is probably dead already, and she could kill others. We need to get reinforcements, but we can't abandon this post. If she's still in the cell, we need to watch her moves."

"Should we split up?"

Alerie nodded. "I'll stay here. You go and tell Zack."

"Are you sure? If Rim is free of her chains, she'll be stronger than you."

"I know," Alerie said. "But I don't see any other options. Go."

Myra had barely taken a few steps when she stopped, listening. Someone was running down the corridor, approaching them. Thankfully, the steps were heavier than what she would expect from their delicate vampire prisoner.

She gasped as a tall man appeared in front of her. He wore a shirt of faded red, his head was shaven, and a dark woolen patch over his left eye socket concealed the damage done in an old battle.

"Sean!" Alerie cried. "What happened? Is the vamp out?"

Someone else was approaching, running almost as fast as Sean had. *Oh no, this can't be good.* Myra's heart stopped when Zack appeared.

"Shanice was here," Sean said breathlessly. "She said Zack was looking for me. She claimed he ordered me to leave my post and come immediately."

"As you can imagine, I've done no such thing," Zack said. "Come, and let's hope it's not too late."

Myra's heart raced as she followed them back to the cell. "She couldn't have gotten in, right?" she said, her voice breaking. "The door is locked at all times."

"All Warriors have keys, Tory included," said Alerie. "Shanice could have taken his keys, or someone else's."

Myra opened the door to the prison cellar, her hand shaking. It was unlocked. She breathed in sharply as she walked in and pressed a hand against her mouth. Alerie pushed her aside and cursed.

Alerie and Zack were saying something, but Myra could only gape at the scene in front of her. Shanice stood there, her face, arms and gown spattered with blood. A bloodied stake was in her hand, and her empty eyes stared into nothingness.

The prisoner's body hung from the chains, a stake in her heart. A few more wounds surrounded the stake—the killer had not hit the heart the first time. A bloodied hammer lay on the ground, perhaps used to drive the stake in.

Myra's eyes moved back to the ten-year-old girl. "What have you done?" she breathed.

Shanice turned angry dark eyes at her. "You planned to let her go. She killed my dad. And you planned to let her go."

Sean looked away, shaking his head. "It's my fault. I should have known."

Zack frowned. "We'll discuss this later. This isn't about you."

Alerie knelt in front of Shanice and tried to take the stake from her hand. "Shanice, there were bigger things going on. The situation was more complex than—"

"Complex?" the girl cried and pulled back. "She killed my dad. What's complex, exactly?"

Alerie took a step back to give the girl more space. "In the end, we want to defeat all vamps," she started, but Shanice glared at her.

"I don't care what you want! It doesn't matter anymore!"

Myra stared at the girl's clothes, stained with blood. It would wash away, but she doubted anything could erase the blood from Shanice's memories.

"What is done is done," Zack said. "Come, now, Shanice. Let's go to your mom."

"You go," Myra said. "I'll take care of the body."

"Shanice, come." Alerie pulled the girl out, practically dragging her. The bloodied stake was still in Shanice's hand. Zack and Sean silently followed.

The door closed with a bang. Once the sound of fading footsteps died away, the prison cell was silent as a tomb. Myra forced herself to look at the vampire. No, not a vampire. A body. A *human* body. Rim had been a human woman once, before some vampire had killed her and turned her into a monster. Myra sighed and started with her grim task.

Rim is Shanice's first kill, Myra thought as she unlocked the shackles around the vampire's wrists. How many children had to turn into soldiers before all was said and done? Myra pressed her lips together and stared at the body. If she had any say in the matter, Shanice would be the last.

Chapter Six

New World

Myra stumbled and waved her arms before she regained her footing. The sparse torches did a poor job illuminating the steep passage, and she strained her eyes to see better. Soon the corridor became so narrow that two people could not walk side by side, and Myra fell behind. If one was to lead, it had to be Alerie. She had walked this path countless times, while Myra had never gone past this point.

The corridor led them on a long descent, going even deeper underground before returning closer to the surface. Myra's heart pounded so fast it made her ears ring. She was going *Outside*, into the world that had once belonged to her ancestors; in the world where people had lived, and laughed, and created. She had dreamed about this moment so many times, and yet all she wanted now was to turn back and run.

Myra had spent so much time in the library, reading about heroes and their fights. She had written tales of her own about brave adventurers fighting oppression. And Myra had wanted to be like the characters in her books and go on her own adventure. Now she was on a quest, the fate of the world in her hands. Why was she not happy?

Myra reached for the stake hanging at her belt, clutching at it as if it were a lifeline. Saving the world was a hero's job. She was a dreamer, not a hero. The only adventures fit for her were the ones she had in her mind, from the safety of her own bed. What had she done? And was it too late to turn back?

They passed by a pair of guards, and Myra greeted them even though her throat was so dry she could barely make a sound. Sweat broke across her palms and her heart threatened to burst out of her chest. When were they going to reach the entrance? With every turn, she expected to see the end of this dark underworld, yet it never came.

Finally, the air felt fresher and much cooler. Myra pulled her worn-out denim jacket tighter around herself. She smelled something in the air, something strangely familiar, and yet she could not say what it was.

They passed by the last pair of guards, and there it was at last: a large hole in the stony wall, hidden from the outside world by a curtain of dead branches and protected by ancient magic. Once they left, there would be no protection. No safety.

Alerie pushed the branches away and left the cave without a moment's hesitation. Myra froze, taking a deep breath to steady her heartbeat. It did not help. She exhaled slowly and stepped Outside.

All was dark at first, until Alerie lit a torch, and their surroundings came to life. They were in the middle of a dead forest, leafless branches cracking in the wind and fallen, rotting trees littering the stony ground. Night had fallen and the vampires had allowed the clouds to disperse, revealing twinkling stars and a crescent moon.

The wind caressed Myra's face, and she smiled. She had read so much about the moon and stars, and now here they were, not in a picture, but right above her head, vivid and real. It was worth it. All her fears, all her worries, all the risk, it was worth all that. If Myra were to die right now, she would die happy.

She took a deep breath, savoring the smell of moist earth. Yet, there was another scent, one much more pervasive, and finally Myra realized what it was.

It smelled like *nothing*.

For the first time in her life, Myra was not surrounded by the scent of many people stuffed in a small place, baking food, rats, burning fire, rotting wood. Many smells mixed with each other deep in the Resistance's hideout, creating a unique blend. It felt strange to lose it. Strange, and good.

Myra reached out and placed a palm against a tree's bark. She felt connected, a part of the world. This world had belonged to her grandparents once. One day, it would belong to her and her friends.

"Come," Alerie said, and Myra followed.

After they walked for about half an hour, the trees started to disperse. Myra could see no more than a few paces ahead, as far as the torchlight reached.

"We're coming close," Alerie said.

"Close to what?" Myra asked.

"To this." Alerie stepped aside, letting Myra peek behind the tree.

The forest suddenly ended. They had reached what had probably once been a field, but was now a desert. No plants, no animals, only stony emptiness, as far as the light could reach.

"That's good," Alerie said. "We're going in the right direction."

"Aren't we too exposed here? The vamps can see us from far away, and we can't see in the dark."

"Our prisoner said there were no regular patrols on this route," Alerie said and walked forward. After a few steps, she seemed to realize Myra was not following. She turned back. "What's wrong?"

Myra hesitated. "Nothing. It's just that I never thought I would be going so far away from home."

"The dank caverns are not your home," Alerie said and gestured around her. "*This* is. It's time we reclaim it. Come." Alerie stretched her hand.

Myra took it and stepped forward. "Are we still above the caves?"

Alerie laughed. "Your sense of direction needs improvement, doesn't it? The underground tunnel is running the opposite way. I know it's hard to tell left from right when you're underground, but you need to start learning. Here's the map. Which way should we go?"

Myra took the paper and studied it under the torchlight. Alerie was testing her. It was her chance to show that she was not clueless, but she was not sure how. She had seen many maps in old atlases, but had never used one to find her way. All she could see was that the dot saying "Rose Gardens" was to the upper right of the point marked as "Woods." "Northeast?"

"Obviously. I was asking which way that is."

The map remained silent, giving her no answer. Myra looked up. "Do you know?"

"Of course I do."

"How?"

Alerie grinned. "Think."

"You know this terrain by heart?"

"That too. What else?"

"The stars? You can use them to figure out the direction."

Alerie snorted. "Stop stating the obvious. Which way should we go? I'm still waiting for an answer." She smiled. "Come, now, Myra, we both know you're a nerd. I've caught you many times, studying maps of the stars. Surely you remember something."

Myra bit her lip. Her maps had looked very different. For one thing, they had not been twinkling. The stars had been just stylized dots, with lines connecting them to show the constellations. She could not relate her maps to what she was seeing, but she would never admit this to Alerie.

She fell silent and gazed at the stars. The more she looked, the more her eyes adjusted to the dark, and more twinkling little dots appeared. She tried to find the bigger ones and to recognize familiar patterns. She gasped. "Ursa Major."

Alerie grinned. "Very good. See, it's not hard. Now, keep looking."

"The others are harder to recognize," Myra complained, but to her surprise, now that she had spotted one constellation, the others started coming. "That one's Cassiopeia," she whispered, "and there is Pegasus."

"Are you looking for something specific?" Alerie prompted.

"Ursa Minor. At the end of its tail is Polaris—the North Star. It will show our way north. And there it is!" Myra was grinning now, her heart pumping wildly. She had read so much about travelers using stars to navigate, and now she was one of them. She was an adventurer.

"Lead on," Alerie said.

Myra looked up. "Well, northeast should be a bit to the right of Polaris, I guess."

Alerie rolled her eyes. "That's not very specific, is it? Luckily, I know exactly which way we're going."

"Of course you do," Myra said. "You just wanted to torture me." She gazed at the map in her hands. Even though the route was clearly marked, she still had no idea how to reach those Rose Gardens. Being so dependent made her uncomfortable. If she lost sight of Alerie, she would have no idea how to find her way.

As they walked on, encountering no signs of vampires, Myra started to breathe more easily. She grinned, savoring the wind on her face, the fresh air in her lungs, and the twinkling stars high above. Words and sentences twirled in her mind as she thought about her book. A story started to take shape—a new chapter of Maryabella's tales. Myra's fingers curled into fists and her heart beat faster. Her hands itched to grab a pencil and write it all down. If only she had the time and safety to put it all on paper!

Her character's adventures mirrored her own—Maryabella was tracking her missing friends through a stony desert, with the wind in her face and the moon and stars to light her way. In her head, Myra described every step, every stone, every gust of wind. Her smile grew. The words were coming to her so easily. It was working. Seeing the world would help her become a better writer, just as she had hoped.

The stony desert stretched endless before them; it was a miracle Alerie still knew the way. The wind blew in their faces, with no trees to stop it, and Myra's fist clutched her jacket at the front. After a while, the wind's caress turned from refreshing and exciting to mostly annoying.

They walked for almost an hour when Alerie stopped and brought the torch forward. Myra frowned. Dead branches covered the ground ahead, laid down like a carpet for as far as the light could reach.

"That can't be natural," Myra said.

"Why would the vamps make this?" Alerie murmured. She bent down to take one of the branches and used it to push the others aside. Underneath was nothing but stony ground, and they continued on their way.

The progress was slow since Alerie insisted on testing the way and removing all branches before they stepped anywhere. Myra was not sure why that was necessary, but her opinion changed when Alerie pushed aside a few more branches, revealing a gaping hole beneath.

"A trap," Myra whispered.

"No animals live here," Alerie said. "It's placed for the Resistance. For us." She looked up, her dark brown eyes meeting Myra's. "Rim said nothing about this."

A shiver ran down Myra's spine. "You think she lied to us?"

"I don't know. But we failed to keep our end of the bargain. It's only fair she failed to keep hers."

"In any case, there must be more traps underneath the branches."

Alerie nodded. "If the vamps set this up, they must be returning to check on the traps. This place isn't safe. Let's backtrack and go around the covered area."

They returned to the point where the branches had first appeared and started circling around. To their surprise, the covered area stretched on and on. The wind grew stronger, blowing in their faces and pushing them back. Myra put a hand in front of her face to stop the dust from flying into her eyes. She could barely see anything. The torchlight flickered in the wind, the flames dancing in all directions, thinning and almost disappearing.

After half an hour, the covered area gave no sign of ending. Why had the vamps built such a large trap area? That must have taken a lot of effort, and they were not known for hard work.

The road took them far away from the original path, and Myra had no idea where they were or how to find the Rose Gardens. Hopefully Alerie knew what she was doing; otherwise they were lost. The wind was blowing from all directions, whipping at their faces. Myra could no longer see what she was stepping on.

Prince Vladimir controlled the WeatherWizard. He must have decided he wanted strong wind, at this time and place. Why? Was it another line of defense around the Palace?

Alerie stopped in her tracks and raised a hand.

"What is it?" Myra asked.

"There's something ahead of us." Alerie walked forward slowly, raising the torch.

A thick wall of dead trees rose ahead of them.

"Another forest?" Myra whispered.

"We should continue our way through the woods," Alerie said. "We'll be less exposed, and we won't steer far from our original path."

"Rim claimed there were no patrols on our original route," Myra said. "We know nothing about this place."

"I think we should take everything Rim said with a grain of salt. We're on our own now. We should trust our instincts."

The woods grew thicker as they ventured deeper, but all the trees were still dead—rotting trunks, some fallen on the ground and some still standing. Myra had expected they would provide protection against the wind, but the tempest was as strong as ever.

She looked up, trying to get a sense of their direction from the stars. Only, the stars were gone. Over an hour was left until sunrise. Why would the vamps need clouds?

Something hit her face. A drop of water, cold and wet, and then another, until the wind was blowing the rain full force into her eyes. Myra unbuttoned her jacket and put it over her head, trying to stop the torrent of water and air.

The torch flame sizzled and hissed, and then it was dead. Darkness engulfed them, pressing around them on all sides. Not a single light could be seen, neither on the sky, nor around them. All was black.

Myra shivered from the cold, her clothes soaked. Alerie grabbed her hand so they would not be separated in the darkness, and they walked on, not sure where they were going.

"We need to find shelter," Alerie said. "We have to wait for the rain to stop."

Myra nodded, then realized her friend could not see her. "What if it never stops? The vamps control the rain. What if they've made it rain until sunrise and then all day?"

"We have no choice. We can't go on like this. We have enough food and water for a week. If we find shelter, we can wait for a few hours, even days."

Finding shelter was easier said than done. They walked through the darkness, blindly feeling their way. Myra saw nothing but black.

Vampires could see in the dark. They were quiet and stealthy. What if there were vamps around them, watching them? What if they were just a few steps behind? Myra shuddered. At any moment, a vamp could grab her, sinking sharp teeth into her neck and drinking her alive.

A sharp, painfully bright light tore through the skies, illuminating the dead forest for a second. Myra gasped. "What was that?"

"A bolt of lightning," Alerie replied, her voice drowned in the thunderous boom that followed. "Come, we should keep moving."

Keep moving, but where? Were they even going in the right direction? Myra strained her eyes, trying to see something, anything, but all was blackness.

Another flash of lightning tore through the sky, and Myra squeezed her eyes shut and pressed her hands against her ears. When the thunder was over, Alerie grabbed her arm. "Did you see that?" she asked.

"See what?" Myra had been too afraid to look, but now she realized her mistake. The bolts of lightning were their only chance to examine their surroundings.

"I saw a large wooden house. Four stories high. We can hide there until the storm passes."

"What if vamps live there?"

"A house like that needs maintenance," Alerie said. "It looked to be in bad shape. Vamps wouldn't pick a place such as this. Come. I remember where I saw it." She pulled her arm, and Myra followed.

Another bolt of lightning illuminated their path, and this time Myra saw it too: a large building, right in front of them. "We are almost there," Alerie said. Myra's feet sank into thick mud as she followed. The water had soaked through her shoes, and her socks and feet were completely wet. She no longer cared about vampires and danger—as long as the house was dry and warm, it would be all she needed.

Alerie pushed on the door. "Come on, it's unlocked," she said and pulled Myra inside.

Even though Myra's clothes were soaked and she was still freezing, it felt so good to be away from the wind and rain. She leaned against a wooden wall and slowly exhaled. "Do you think the torches in our backpacks are dry enough?"

"Time to find out," Alerie said. "I'll light one for now, but we have to be careful—light is easy to spot in the darkness."

Myra heard some shuffling and in a minute a bright flame was dancing merrily before her eyes. She could not help a mad grin. Finally she could see something other than endless blackness.

Now that there was light, Myra saw that they were standing at the end of a long corridor. They followed it to the rotting wooden door at the far end, into a spacious living room. The chamber was empty, apart from a table, eight chairs, a cupboard, and a cast-iron wood burning stove. Alerie opened the cupboard. "No food, no kitchenware," she murmured.

Myra examined the stove. "No one has used this in a while. And everything's dusty."

"The inhabitants were probably killed during the Nightfall, or shortly after," Alerie said. "We can use the stove to dry our clothes. But come; let's first check the other rooms. We need to make sure the place is safe."

Myra opened the next door, and her breath caught in her throat. She stopped in her tracks, pressing a hand against her mouth. Pieces of a shattered mirror were scattered all over the floor. Among them lay the remains of two people, the skin and flesh so decomposed that only the bones remained, pale under the torchlight.

Alerie pushed her aside so she could step in. She knelt by the skeletons and reached out to examine them. "The vamps must have drunk them and left them here," Alerie said softly and stood up.

"They lived so close to us," Myra choked. "Do you think this happened after the Nightfall? We could have met them. We could have helped them."

"The Palace is too close to this place. They couldn't have survived long here," Alerie said. "Even if they died after the Nightfall, it must have been long before we were born. Come, now, let's search the other rooms. We may find something useful."

They found nothing; no medicines, clothes or durable food, only the rotten remains of a third person. "This makes no sense," Myra said when they stopped to take a break on the fourth floor, after examining the last room. "This could have been a comfortable home for twenty people."

"And an uncomfortable home for a hundred," said Alerie. "Yet, we found only three. What happened to the rest?"

"Perhaps the vamps couldn't eat everyone and took the remaining humans to finish them later," Myra whispered, her stomach turning. "And what happened to all the supplies? I can't imagine the vamps needed them. Did they really destroy everything just to prevent us from finding it?"

"I don't know," Alerie said and approached the wall, pressing her ear against it. "The rain is still strong. Let's make camp for a few hours."

"Should we light the stove and dry our clothes?" Myra asked.

Alerie frowned. "I'd love to, but I'm worried about the light. There could be vampires in the woods." She walked to the window. "The shutters are closed, but there is a crack between them. The light would be visible."

"If we do nothing, we'll freeze to death," Myra said.

Alerie nodded. "Very well. Let's use the stove, but we'll put it out as soon as the clothes are dry."

Myra walked downstairs to light the stove and hang her jacket on a chair in front of it. She picked up their backpacks and carried them back to the room on the fourth floor. She shuddered. They were staying in this house full of death. She wished she could do something for the dead people, but she could not bury them in this rain. She had never before seen a human skeleton, she realized, startled. She had seen so many dead bodies, but never one so decayed that no trace of the person remained.

"We should take some rest while we wait for the rain to stop," Alerie said once Myra entered the room. "After we leave this place, we'll likely make no stops before the Rose Gardens. One of us should keep watch."

Myra was certain she could not sleep anytime soon. "I'll take the first watch," she said.

Alerie nodded and stretched out her sleeping bag on one of the beds. Myra sat by her side, watching the flames. The rain kept tapping against the roof and the wooden walls. A bright light shone through the shutters, and a loud thunder shook the house.

A shudder ran down Myra's spine, and she stood up, smiling, facing the shut window. Out there, behind these flimsy wooden shutters, the storm was raging. Out there was the world, wide and dark and dangerous and terrible. Out there was her true home, scary and insecure and unknown. And now that she had seen it, she could never go back to the life she had lived before.

Chapter Seven

Temptation

Myra put down the pencil and stretched her fingers. Her eyes ran over the last paragraph she had written. Her heroes were now facing a thunderstorm and fighting to find their way through the woods. Myra grinned. Writing came so easily out here—she had already written over twenty pages while Alerie slept.

She tilted her head to the side, listening. The rain had stopped. She walked to the wall and peeked through the crack between the shutters. The sun had started to rise, but the clouds were so thick that it was impossible to see much apart from the dark shapes of rotting trees.

Myra walked downstairs, put out the stove, and picked up her jacket. It was already dry and felt warm around her shoulders. She returned to the bedroom and stretched. She had to wake up Alerie—now that the rain had stopped, they could resume their journey. They had lost some time already, but still had a very good chance of reaching the Rose Gardens well before sunset. Myra reached out to shake Alerie, but her hand stopped midair and her eyes turned to her notebook.

She was almost done with the current chapter. She would not get another chance to sit down and write before they accomplished their mission, and there was still so much she wanted to say. The words were fresh in her head, burning to be written down. What if she forgot it all before she had the chance to put her thoughts on paper?

Myra took her pencil once again and went on writing. The journey could wait. They would have many hours in the Rose Gardens before darkness fell, and a few minutes would make no difference.

She kept writing on and on, the words flowing through her mind faster than she could write them down. *Just one more paragraph*, she thought. And then, *just one more.*

Alerie stirred, and Myra quickly pushed the notebook back into her backpack. "Alerie," she called. "The rain stopped."

Alerie blinked and stood up, instantly alert. "What time is it? We should get going."

"About half an hour after sunrise," Myra said and took her jacket from the chair. "Our clothes are dry already, so we can leave right away. We are good on time."

"We are already behind schedule," Alerie said. "We were supposed to be in the Gardens already." Her eyes widened. "Give me your jacket," she whispered.

"Why?" Myra whispered back. She complied, startled by her friend's urgency. To her shock, Alerie wrapped it around her burning torch. Darkness fell over the room. "What are you doing?"

"I had to put out the light, and all around us is wood," Alerie said. "Look." She tapped on the crack between the window's closed shutters.

Myra squinted and saw a few lights not far away. "Vamps?" she breathed. "Do you think they saw our light through the crack?"

"I saw theirs," Alerie said, "Ours must have been easier to spot, and they have better eyesight. Stay here and watch them. I'll go and bar the doors."

Myra laid down her backpack and took out a gun and a crossbow. She squeezed the gun's handle, her palm starting to sweat. She swallowed hard. This was not good. Even if they fortified the house, they could not defend it for long. They were only two against…how many? She squinted through the crack, until her eyes focused on the figures; there were about ten. Not good at all.

The window had no glass, only two sets of shutters, one that opened on the inside and one on the outside. The crack between them was too small to shoot through, but it gave her a good vantage point. And, despite Myra's fear, she could not help but stare in awe.

She had met only a few vampires in the Resistance's prison. She had never seen many of them at once, and never out in the open. And now she was observing them in their natural habitat as they interacted with each other. Curiosity won over terror, and she looked more closely.

Vampires preferred long hair, she noted, men and women alike. Whether this was some current fashion trend or they were imitating their Prince, she did not know. Not only was their hair long, it was also well maintained, even if not always tastefully. One of the male vampires, for instance, clearly hailed from what had once been northeastern Asia, and Myra expected his hair to be jet-black and perfectly straight—just like Zack's. Instead, it was curled and bleached to a strange orangey color.

Their clothes followed a similar trend. Each of them had apparently put great care into picking their outfit, with varying degrees of success. The garments combined a hodgepodge of styles from the different places and periods the vampires had lived through, mixed with more contemporary and practical clothing. Kimonos and high-heeled boots, leather jackets and saris. Heavy woolen ponchos, fez hats, khaki pants, Victorian shirts and vests, jeans, red and purple turbans, sometimes put together in seemingly impossible combinations.

"So these are our enemies," she whispered as Alerie returned and crouched next to her.

"Yeah, a motley band of peacocks," Alerie said. "Unfortunately, they fight better than they dress."

A face popped right in front of the crack, and Myra stifled a scream.

Alerie rushed to the table, broke off a leg and handed it to her. Without thinking, Myra shoved it through the handles of the inner shutters, effectively barring the window.

"The other windows," Alerie called as she reignited the torch and secured it to the wall. "I've already blocked the front door, and all other doors leading here."

Three more windows remained in the room, and Myra frantically grabbed a chair and broke off a leg. They were on the fourth floor. Had the vamp climbed up the wall? Were there any others?

Her question was answered when someone tried to break the window shutters Alerie had just barred. There were vamps at two of the windows at least, trying to get in. She had not even seen them approach. They were not a part of the main group she had observed; she was sure of that.

Out of the corner of her eye, Myra saw Alerie look at the map for a long moment before she held it over the flame until it turned to dust. Wild banging sounded from all four windows, and she and Alerie exchanged a panicked glance. "Get ready," Alerie said, raising her gun. "We shoot at the first vamp who comes in."

A loud thud from behind made Myra turn around. Someone was at the door. Alerie had barred all doors on the way, but the windows at the adjacent room remained vulnerable. The vamps must have gone through and come to the door. She shivered. There were vamps inside the house.

"I saw at least ten around the torches," Myra said. "Who knows how many more might have come here unseen?"

"I've escaped direr situations," Alerie said, pointing the gun at one of the windows.

"Have you?" Myra doubted that, but now was not the time to panic. The window burst open and she and Alerie fired at the same time.

One bullet hit the vamp in the throat, and the other in the chest. He hissed and pressed a hand against his chest wound, but remained standing. Myra raised her crossbow. He was weakened now, and slower. She had to act before he had time to recover.

She fired a wooden arrow, but missed his heart. The projectile hit the vampire in the shoulder and propelled him a step back. He pulled the arrow out of his flesh, broke off the metal tip and hurled it forward while Myra reloaded, but failed to hit her.

Alerie released her arrow before Myra could fire. It struck true this time, hitting the vamp straight in the heart. He fell to the floor with a thud, limp and lifeless, and his skin grew pale and taut in seconds.

Myra was taking quick, ragged breaths as she lowered the crossbow and raised her gun once again. They had done it. They had killed a vampire. This had been the first time she had engaged the enemy in combat, out it the open. And they had done it. She had no doubts now. Alerie and she could kill the Prince once they met him.

"One down," Alerie said. "Dozens to go."

A second vampire crawled out of the open window, and another after her. Just then, two of the three barred windows and the door burst open at the same time. Myra gasped and took a step back as more vampires swarmed into the room, pointing swords, daggers, arrows, and guns at them.

She recognized the bleached-orange-haired vampire she had seen earlier—so the vampires she had observed had joined the fray after all. He raised his bow and fired two arrows in rapid succession, and Myra yelped as her gun was knocked out of her hand. A quick look showed her he had disarmed Alerie with the other shot.

An idea came to her then. It was a desperate gambit, but she knew nothing could make their situation any worse. After all, their vampire prisoner had claimed some of their people opposed the Prince.

"Rim sends us," she called. "We're here to help you get rid of the Prince."

The orange-haired vampire laughed. "I am sure His Highness would love to hear that. Too bad we are not taking you to him."

Alerie raised her crossbow, but another vampire shot it out of her hand. "You'll kill us, then?" she said, glaring at their attackers. "I can assure you, we'll take many with us."

The orange-haired vampire grinned, exposing his sharp teeth. "I wonder how you plan to do that. You mistake our intentions—we will not kill you. Surrender now, and we will let you live."

"They want us to surrender so they can torture us for information," Alerie whispered, and he rolled his eyes.

"No point in whispering, we can hear you perfectly well." He frowned. "You are wounded. Did this fool throw some blade at you?" He glanced at the dead vampire on the floor. "I thought my orders were clear."

Only now did Myra notice the crimson spot on her friend's shirt. The vamp had not missed after all. "Alerie…"

"I'm fine," Alerie said.

Myra paled. It appeared to be a stomach wound, but the bloodstain was large, and it was hard to say where exactly the arrow tip had struck. This was bad, very bad. Her friend needed immediate help.

Alerie was right. If they surrendered, the vampires would most likely interrogate them. A quick death was preferable, and who knew what these monsters had in store? Besides, Myra was not sure she trusted herself to keep quiet under torture. She had never tested her endurance, and had no desire to. Yes, fighting to the death made the most sense.

There was only one problem with that option: Myra had no intention of dying. She clenched her fists, trying to stop her shaking. If they did not surrender, the vampires were going to kill them. There was no way around that. The vamps would bite them and suck them dry. There would be pain, and blood, and fear.

Myra bit her lip, taking deep breaths and trying to calm down. The vamps would bite her, their sharp fangs piercing her skin and flesh, and they would devour her like she was some animal shot down for food.

"If we surrender," she said, "will you take care of my friend's wound?"

"Of course," the orange-haired vampire said.

"Myra, that's a bad idea," Alerie cried.

Myra looked at her, trying to meet her eyes and give her some signal. It was not cowardice, she told herself. If they refused, the vampires would either kill them, or injure them badly and capture them anyway. It would mean the end of their mission. Surrender bought them time. Perhaps an escape opportunity would present itself later, and the risk was worth it.

She held her friend's gaze for a moment until Alerie nodded. Myra smiled and nodded back. "We surrender."

She tried to fight her panic as the vampires took away the stake at her belt and bound her hands. She had been helpless before, but now was worse. She had no means to defend herself. They could do anything they wanted to her, and she could do nothing to stop them.

Myra struggled instinctively against the vampire tying the rope around her, but it made no difference. She took a deep breath, trying to fight her panic.

"Yong, should we interrogate them now?" a female vampire asked.

The orange-haired vamp shook his head. "No. Resistance members are tough. We will get nothing out of them here. We will take them to the Dark Cell."

"The Dark Cell is occupied," another vampire said.

"No matter," Yong said. "We can keep them in the dungeons until it is empty."

Resistance members are tough. Myra was not at all sure she was tough. And what was that supposed to mean, anyway? Had they tortured other Resistance members?

Don't panic. This was to be expected. The vamps were planning to torture them; she had known that when she had surrendered. It mattered not. She would find a way to escape.

"You said you'd help my friend," she said.

"I did," said Yong. "I need both of you alive and healthy for long enough to speak. Natalia, take a look at the wound."

The vampire called Natalia knelt down, and Myra's heart sank as she looked at Alerie. Her friend had appeared well only moments ago, but was now deathly pale, her face bathed in sweat and her breathing labored. Myra felt bile rise in her throat. The vamps would patch Alerie up, only to kill her slowly later.

Myra gasped when Natalia tore Alerie's shirt and wiped the blood from her stomach, revealing a large blue-black bruise. "What are you waiting for?" Myra snapped. "Stop the bleeding."

The vampire looked up and shook her head. "The arrow tip has hit her liver. The internal bleeding is strong. She will not survive the road to the Palace without surgery."

"Well, then," Yong said. "Let us not waste the fresh blood."

It took Myra a moment to realize what the vamps meant to do. "No!" she screamed. "Wait, no, please, we surrendered. You said you wouldn't kill us if we surrendered!"

Yong shrugged. "I did, but she is dead anyway."

"Please, there must be something you can do to help her. You didn't even try. Please, just try, I'll do anything!"

"Anything?" the vampire raised an eyebrow. "Would you tell us how to find the Resistance's hideout, then?"

Myra froze, her blood draining from her face.

He grinned. "I did not think so."

Yong made a gesture with his hand, and two vampires bit Alerie's neck, while Natalia bent down to drink the blood from the open wound. The vampires' skin grew pale, almost transparent, and Myra could see dark veins running underneath; veins, carrying Alerie's blood. Alerie gasped, too weak to cry, but the scream that tore from Myra's lips was loud enough for them both.

Chapter Eight

Captive

So many times, Myra had dreamed of traveling in a cart, of seeing real horses. She would be like one of the princesses in the books she had read a dozen times, going on an exciting adventure. Tears rolled down her cheeks. She was in a cart now, and two stunning black horses pulled her towards her destination. And she wished for nothing more than to be back in her cellar with a book in hand.

The wooden wheels creaked over the asphalt road. The cart rocked and jumped up and down as the wheels passed over potholes along the way. The vamps had done nothing to maintain the road, but the unsteady journey provided a welcome distraction.

Alerie is dead.

Myra could not comprehend the notion. Just hours ago, her friend had been smiling, teaching her about navigating, and making plans for the future. And now she was left to rot in the abandoned house, to join the other skeletons.

Her tears had not yet dried, but new ones were already spilling. This was so unfair. Alerie had deserved to live, to be happy. She had fought so hard for so long. She had dreamed of a world where humans ruled, where the sun was shining and no one had to hide in fear. If this world ever came, Alerie would not be there to see it.

Most likely, it would never come. Killing the Prince had seemed possible while Alerie was still alive, but now it was an empty fantasy. Myra was an average fighter, captured and with no escape plan. And she was a coward.

Yes, there was no point denying it. She was terrified. All she wanted was for this nightmare to be over, so she could go back home.

The sun had risen somewhere behind the thick clouds, casting a gloomy light over the world around her. Two vampires sat on the front bench—Yong, his long orange hair falling over his black shirt, and a tall dark-haired female vampire, dressed in jeans and a black leather waist cincher over her white medieval shirt. Myra was at the back, tightly bound and weaponless. She could not move and could barely see what was happening around her. A wave of panic rose in her chest at her utter helplessness, threatening to suffocate her. They would eat her. Their sharp teeth would pierce her skin, and they would drink her blood drop by drop. Myra blinked against her tears.

"What are you going to do to me?" she sobbed.

"What we do to all Resistance members," Yong said.

"I have no idea what you're talking about," she said, unable to hide the tremors in her voice.

Her other captor snickered. "Do not worry, girl. We have ways to refresh your memory."

She fell silent. Talking to these monsters would do her no good. She struggled against her bonds, but it was fruitless.

Even if she somehow got free, she had nowhere to run and could never hope to overpower her two captors. Finally, she gave up and tried to concentrate on the monotonous song of the wheels. Perhaps an escape opportunity would present itself later, and the best she could do for now was preserve her energy.

Alerie is dead.

It was all her fault. If only she had awoken Alerie earlier the attack might have been avoided. They might have left the building before the vamps' arrival. It had been the logical thing to do, and yet Myra had stayed, desperate to finish her writing. She had allowed her mind to stray in the clouds while the real world around her collapsed.

Alerie had claimed Myra would compromise the mission. She had been right. If Lidia had come in her place, Alerie would still be alive.

She could not afford to think of that now. Her duty to the Resistance, to herself, to Thea, and to Alerie's memory, was to stay alive, escape, and complete her mission. Only then could she redeem herself.

The cart passed by rolling hills that had perhaps once been green, but were now barren. No grass grew without the sun, and Myra wondered if seeds for all plant species lay dormant or were stored somewhere, so they could one day be restored once the WeatherWizard was gone.

Soon, a stone castle came into view, rising on top of the highest of the surrounding hills. It matched the description Rim had given them, and yet the numerous flags waving proudly atop the high towers confused her. Every banner was the same—a golden sun in the middle of a clear blue sky. Sun was deadly to vampires—it was their greatest enemy—and a blue sky was what they had destroyed with the WeatherWizard. None of it made sense. What kind of vampire would take the clear blue sky as his sigil?

The cart went up the hill, and the huge gates opened. The drawbridge was lowered over the water-filled moat, and Myra winced at the sound of cracking wood as the cart rolled over it. She hoped it would not break and wondered if she had only imagined the scaly brown-green creatures in the dark waters.

The inner bailey was paved with stones, and she breathed a sigh of relief once they were on solid ground. A few vampires rushed over to take care of the horses, and her guards pulled her down and dragged her to the front gate.

Two male red-haired vampires in light blue livery stood on both sides of the large metal door. Engravings covered the door top to bottom—men on horses with raised swords, tables laden with fruit and game, a stag in the woods. Two lion heads served as door handles, round metal loops hanging from their mouths.

The door opened and Myra's captors pushed her inside and then down the narrow winding stairs. Torches lit the stony passageway that led deeper and deeper into the gloomy underworld. She stumbled and the vampires dragged her forward, until they reached an empty cell. Her captors pushed her inside and locked the door behind her.

Myra fell to the cold ground and stood up immediately, brushing the dirt off her knees. She turned back to the door, but the vampires were already gone. The torches were sparse in the corridor and there were none inside the cell, so she could barely see her surroundings. The cell was empty, the stone floor covered in dirt. Her stomach made a noise, and she sat down, placing a hand over her belly. The vamps had taken her supplies, including her food. Myra's eyes scanned the floor and discovered a few pieces of old, filthy bread. Had someone been here before? A human? A Resistance member?

She shuddered and tore her eyes away. The bread looked as if it has been there forever, and she knew that eating it would do her more harm than good.

Voices sounded from far away, and Myra's eyes widened. She ran to the barred wall facing the corridor, straining to hear. She could not make out the words, but there was agitated speaking, and then a scream. She froze. Did vampires have some conflicts in their ranks, or was that a human? But how would a human get here? Had the Resistance sent someone after Alerie and her?

She tried to hear more, but the voices died out and complete silence descended over the cell. Myra stared into the dimly lit corridor, trying to make out any shapes, any sounds, but there was nothing to see. The nearest torch went out, leaving her in nearly complete darkness.

Myra started pacing back and forth. She had to find a way to escape or the mission would be a complete failure. But even if she got out, could she go back to the Resistance? Could she face her friends?

No, she could not return unless she accomplished her mission and assassinated the Prince. But what could she do? Even getting out of the cell seemed impossible. She could not pick locks and had no tools. The next time the vamps came, they would likely take her to that torture chamber they had hinted at, and that would be the end. If they drank her like they had drunk Alerie, it would be a mercy.

She shivered and wrapped her arms around herself, unable to ward off the cold. Her hunger was growing, but it was a welcome distraction. They would kill her. They would cause her pain and harm until she talked about the Resistance, or until she died. And there was nothing she could do about it.

With a sob, Myra collapsed to her knees and let her tears fall.

***

Myra awoke shivering. She rubbed her hands and arms, but the cold had seeped deep inside, reaching her very bones. Her legs felt stiff and started hurting once she stood up.

All around her was silence. No voices, not even from far away, and no movement in the corridor. How much time had passed? Minutes? Hours? Was it day or night?

She paced in a circle around the cell. The iron bars were hard and unyielding—there was no way to break them. She saw nothing she could use to dig a hole through the floor or the wall, and the stone was unlikely to give in anyway. She could do nothing until someone came for her. Nothing at all.

Was this a part of the vampires' game? Leave her alone until she slowly lost her sanity? If so, she had to fight it. She had to stay focused.

Myra went on pacing in a circle, then in a square, then in a triangle, trying to bring some variety to her routine. Perhaps if she walked fast enough, she could get warm. Her feet made a soft, hollow sound every time they hit the stone floor, and she tried to focus on the rhythm. *Use this time to come up with a plan. The vamps will return sooner or later.*

What would she do once Yong came back for her? She had to get away before they took her to that torture room, but even if she miraculously escaped her captors, where would she go? Her only hope was to find the vamps who supported Rim, but would she ever get a chance to meet any of them?

When her feet started to hurt from walking, Myra ran her hands through her hair and lay back down on the cold stone floor. She stared at the ceiling, dark like everything else.

The next time she awoke, she found a bowl of water next to her. She sniffed at it and took a long sip once she was satisfied there was no strange scent. Someone had come to bring the water, which meant someone could likely come again, this time while she was awake. She could try to talk to them and determine their allegiance.

Right. In all likelihood, the next time anyone came to her cell, it would be to take her to the torture place.

She paced, and slept once she could no longer walk, and paced, and slept once again. Had the day passed? Had anyone at the Resistance started to worry?

She walked to the wall and made a small scratch on the dirt with her nail. *Day One.* But had one day passed? Or perhaps two? Or five? Or just two hours, that had felt like a lifetime?

Judging by her growing hunger, it had to be more than a few hours, more than even a day. But how long? And when would anyone come to talk to her?

***

Myra awoke to a strange sound, her hands and feet cold as ice. She looked up around the gloomy cell, trying to determine if the sound meant harm, but could not identify the source.

She then heard it again and sighed, burying her face in her hands. It was her own stomach.

She stared miserably at the dirty bread on the floor. Suddenly, the idea did not seem so bad. After all, she would likely be dead before she had the chance to worry about disease. Myra reached out to take one of the pieces.

The bread was hard as stone and tasted like death. She nearly broke her teeth at first, and then slowly and cautiously she scraped off little crumbs and swallowed them, ignoring the stench of mold and rot. When all the bread was gone, she wanted more.

Voices sounded in the distance, and Myra ran to the bars, her heart hammering. She saw approaching torchlight and froze when she recognized Yong. The vampire was frowning, his eyes dark and gloomy. When he was close enough, he threw her a glare and she instinctively stepped back.

Three more guards joined him and stopped in front of her door. Myra walked to the far wall, shuddering. They had come for her.

"This way," Yong said and raised the torch, and only then did Myra realize that they were waiting for someone.

Her curiosity got the better of her, and she approached the bars once again, staring as the newcomer came into the light.

The man—nay, *vampire*—must have been turned in his early to midtwenties. His clothes looked very fine, all in varying shades of blue. He wore a knee-length tunic of light azure brocade shot with silver, its sleeves open and lined with blue silk. His leggings were of suede dyed a deep midnight blue, and a silver belt of intricately linked spiderwebs circled his slim middle. His gleaming platinum-blond hair was flowing down, reaching almost to his waist.

He stepped forward and came close enough for Myra to see his face. All vampires were extraordinarily beautiful, she had noticed, not because of some magic that happened after turning, but because vamps carefully selected whom to turn, and only the most exceptional-looking humans ever stood a chance. And yet, this one would turn a few heads even among vampires, with his high cheekbones and silver-grey eyes. The only thing that marred his fairness was the fact that his face seemed frozen into a state of a permanent frown.

The vampire walked purposefully towards the cells and stared at Yong. "Where is she?" he asked.

The guard gestured at Myra, and the blond vampire walked to the bars and knelt to her level. He reached through the bars, and Myra's heart hammered as he touched her hair and turned her head around.

"No one is to touch her," he said. "She is for the Prince."

"But, Tristan, she must be a member of the Resistance. We can question her."

Tristan stood up and grabbed Yong by the collar. "I said, *she is for the Prince*. His Highness has not had a single drop of wild blood in months. I will kill anyone who tries to deny him that." He turned around and stormed back out.

"She is for the Prince," Yong repeated in a whiny voice that was probably supposed to be an imitation of Tristan's. He glared in the direction Tristan had gone, and the other guards chuckled.

Myra stepped forward and reached for the iron bars to steady herself. She was for the Prince? What did he need her for? Would he drink her?

His Highness hasn't had a single drop of wild blood in months, Tristan had said. Wild blood. What was that supposed to mean? She supposed the vamps rarely had the chance to drink human blood nowadays, but why 'wild'?

Yong and his mooks left after a while, leaving her alone. Myra stared into the darkness and rubbed her hands together, trying to warm them. It looked like she had escaped torture. The Prince had picked her for himself instead, to enjoy her blood, but she was not sure if this was an improvement.

Don't be a coward. Of course it's an improvement. I need to kill the Prince. Perhaps when I meet him, I'll get a chance.

She frowned and started pacing again in an attempt to keep warm. Yong had wanted to torture her for information, but Tristan had denied him that, picking her as a delicacy for his master instead. Yong had looked unhappy. Was there some tension between the vampires? Some conflict? Rim had claimed many opposed the Prince and his policies, but when Myra had mentioned killing the Prince to Yong, he had given no indication this was his goal.

Were there more factions among vampires than she had thought? And was there any way to use them before she turned into a meal?

***

Myra dreamed of Alerie. Her body decomposing, a feast for worms, and rats, and crows. Her eyes empty sockets, her skin leathery and wrinkled, the shape of the skeleton visible underneath. *Alerie is dead and I am alive. Do I deserve it? Why was I the one to survive?*

The sound that woke her up this time was painfully familiar. Myra allowed herself a small smile as she listened to the persistent scratching. She had heard it so many times in the Resistance that in a strange, twisted way, it made her feel at home.

She pushed herself up on her elbows, trying to figure out where the rat was. She had nothing to bake it with, but she was certain she would be able to chew on a raw rat if she managed to capture it. The corners of her vision were growing dim with hunger, and she was not certain if she would be able to move at all unless she ate something soon.

Ah, there it was. A dark shape next to the wall at the far end of the room. Myra lunged at it, but it ran along the wall, fast as a shadow, and disappeared inside an invisible crack. She collapsed on the ground, rubbing at her knees. Myra scanned the ground for more bread, but she had eaten it all.

Voices sounded from the corridor and she looked up, but had no energy to move and go to the bars. Yong stepped forward with a torch, and two shapes appeared behind him.

Myra recognized Tristan, grinning and looking ready to start jumping up and down, which did nothing to diminish his perma-frown. "Come, my lady," he called. "It is here."

A few steps behind him walked a stunning female vampire, wearing a bright red evening dress, which matched her lipstick and nail polish. Her emerald-green eyes shone brightly on her pale face, and her silky burgundy hair was flowing around her bare shoulders and past her waist in soft waves.

She smiled at Tristan. "Will you show me this gift, my sweet, or do you want me to guess?"

"It is her." Tristan pointed at Myra, his eyes bright.

She laughed. "Tristan, dearest, as much as I adore you, if you are spending your time going through the cells and picking out girls for my beloved, we may have a few disagreements."

The vampire lady approached the cell, and Myra frowned. She was not some curiosity for her to look at. She crossed her arms in front of her chest and gave the vampire what she hoped was a defiant glare.

The vampire stared at her for a brief moment, her green eyes wide, before her lips curled into a smile. "Tristan, His Highness always values your gifts, but you have outdone yourself this time. A wild one? He will love it."

Tristan beamed, somehow managing to smile brightly and keep frowning at the same time. "Should I bring her to him now or later, my lady?"

"Have her brought to his study at dinnertime. This is a special event. He would want to make it more than a quick snack."

Tristan nodded and disappeared into the darkness.

The red-haired woman lingered behind, giving Yong a sweet smile. "I am sure Tristan did not capture the girl himself. I bet all he did was stick his pretty nose everywhere and listen for news, and then come here and snatch her from you before you have found a better use for her. Will you let him take all the credit? You deserve the Prince's gratitude no less than he does, perhaps more."

The guard pouted. "You know how His Highness is, Armida. Try telling him something against his puppy dog, and you may as well sign your own death sentence."

"Don't worry, my friend. I will make sure His Highness is made aware of your contribution and appreciates it properly," she promised.

"Thank you," Yong said.

Armida smiled. "And I suppose you would like me to skip the part where you never planned to give the girl to him, or even let him know you had her? He would not be happy to learn you planned to torture her in the Dark Cell."

He looked away and cleared his throat. "I would be most obliged, my lady."

She nodded at him as he took his leave. Armida turned to the cell, and Myra was surprised to see compassion in her warm green eyes. "I am sorry you got caught up in this, sweet girl," the vampire said. "Let me give you a piece of advice. One way or another, the Prince will kill you. However, the better you entertain him, the longer you will stay alive. It is your decision if you prefer a quick end, or would like to live for a while longer."

She turned around and left before Myra could wonder if she was supposed to be grateful for the tip.

Chapter Nine

Tests

W*hy do they need four guards to escort me?* Myra wondered as the vamps dragged her out of the dungeon and up the stairs. *Do they think we have superpowers in the Resistance?*

After uncountable floors of winding stairs, they entered a long stone passageway. A thick red carpet covered the floor and numerous glowing torches lit their way. At the end of the corridor, they reached a high oaken door, covered in floral-shaped carvings. The only solid gold Myra had seen before now was Andre's old locket, but she was quite certain that was what the handle was made of.

One of the guards pushed down the handle and dragged Myra inside. She stifled a gasp. A huge glass window covered most of the western wall. The heavy drapes were pulled back, and it must have been sunset, for the barest hints of orange and pink could be seen from behind the eternal, impenetrable clouds.

A large ebony piano was in the corner, and five round tables of blue marble were arranged in a cross, surrounded by cushioned armchairs. The largest table in the middle was covered with cups, plates and teapots of the finest china, and a wave of nausea washed over her as she hoped the set was not used for drinking blood. Playing cards lay scattered on the smaller tables, as well as various games—wooden, ivory, jade, and marble chessboards and intricate pieces, backgammon, go, checkers, Nine Men's Morris. Myra had played some of those games in the Resistance, but most she had only seen in books.

A huge tapestry, showing high peaks and a deep blue cloudless sky, covered the southern wall. The other two walls were barely visible behind the numerous shelves, filled with hundreds of books. And as much as Myra desired to burn this place to the ground, she could not help staring.

The makeshift library was superbly organized, by genre, period, and author's origins, spanning all kinds of literary movements, from the heroic epics of the ancient world, through literature from the Middle Ages, Renaissance, Enlightenment, Realism, all up to the neo-Romanticism of the twenty-fifth century.

Novels, short stories, poems, plays, from literary fiction to a wide variety of genres—mystery, fantasy, science fiction, romance, historical fiction, some written in languages she did not recognize, the titles in alphabets she could not place.

Myra desired to reach out and touch the books, pick one and read it. Her eyes filled with tears. She would never again read a book. She would never write a story, or stage and watch a play. She would never see her friends again. She would never again talk to Zack and Lidia, or hug Thea. She would never again listen to one of Grandma Pia's lectures.

She bit her lower lip and took a slow, deep breath. It was not fair. She was only nineteen, and she had seen and done so little. She had never seen the sun. She had never climbed a tree, or ridden a bike, or played in the snow.

The vamps bound her to a chair facing the window, and Myra closed her eyes. She had hoped to distract herself by looking at the books, but the monsters had denied her even that small mercy.

"You will have the honor to be His Highness's dinner," one of her captors said, sounding annoyed. "Of course, you would have been more useful in the Dark Cell, but this is not for me to decide."

Myra did not deign a reply and waited in silence as her four guards exited the room and closed the door behind them. She opened her eyes and gazed at the darkening world outside, trying to push all thoughts of her impending fate out of her mind. As the orange hues died away, the clouds started to dissipate, revealing bright stars.

Myra remembered the first time she had seen stars—just a few nights ago, and yet it seemed ages away. Alerie had shown her how to recognize constellations and how to use them to find her way. Would she ever be able to look at the stars without thinking of Alerie?

"Andromeda and Pegasus are my favorite," a deep voice behind her said, and Myra was glad her bonds prevented her from jumping. "After centuries of looking at the stars, I still cannot get enough."

She would not talk to him. She would not give him the pleasure. And yet, his comment sparked her curiosity. Had he seen the night sky change? Had he seen stars die and new ones be born?

No, she would not talk to him. She stared forward, at what she guessed to be the North Star, and waited for him to come into her line of sight.

He was tall and raven-haired, dressed in black and burgundy. A thin golden circlet with a red ruby adorned his high brow. A sheathed sword hung from his leather belt, the handle and scabbard encrusted with gold and gleaming jewels. He appeared around ten years older than Tristan though Myra knew their age difference could well be centuries or even millennia. And while the Old World image of the deathly pale vampire could fit Tristan, whose porcelain skin contained next to no natural pigmentation, the Prince's honey-bronze complexion did not betray that he had not seen the sun in centuries.

Myra shuddered. So this was *him*? This was the monster who had covered the world in darkness and killed millions. He was the one truly responsible for the deaths of Tory and Daphne, her parents, Aunt Sandra, Alerie, and so many more whose names she would never learn. He was the beast they had been trying to kill for so long. He was the one she was now supposed to kill to redeem herself and give the Resistance a chance.

Prince Vladimir walked in front of her, his thin lips curled into a barely perceptible smile. "It has been a while since we last captured a human. You are a member of the Resistance, I assume?"

Myra glared at him. "If you think you can get any information from me, you are wrong," she said and winced as her voice cracked. No matter what, she did not want to die. And she was certain she could not withstand any form of torture for more than a few minutes.

The Prince chuckled. "Information? Why would I want information, darling girl? You do not think I plan to bring down the Resistance, do you? Why, it is the one thing that brings some semblance of excitement to my life nowadays."

Myra stared at him in disbelief. "You must be insane."

The Prince laughed and in one fluid motion jumped onto the windowsill and opened the window, letting a gust of wind into the room. He turned towards her, his dark cape and hair waving behind him, his figure framed by the starry sky. "Insane? What makes you say that?"

"Every now and then we manage to capture and kill one of your people."

"So what?" he asked.

"So what? As long as we persist, you are in danger. Are you telling me that if you had the chance to end it all, you wouldn't take it?"

The vampire sat on the windowsill, letting his left leg hang on the outside, high above the ground. "If all our enemies were gone, we would be immortal," he stated calmly. "*Truly* immortal. Even though our bodies are free from the restraints of natural decay, there is still some danger. Still, every single day, each one of us can be captured and killed. Chances are slim, yes, and do not delude yourself—your pitiful Resistance is far from the worthy opponent I would have asked for, but it is better than nothing. Without you, even this minimal danger would be gone. Now, where would the fun in that be?"

"You *are* insane," Myra stated. She did not care if her words would anger him. If he was going to eat her anyway, she might as well speak her mind. "You need a war to fight to keep you happy, and you can't bear the peace. You are unfit to rule. You enjoyed conquering us, but ruling over obedient masses is not to your taste."

"And this is where you are wrong," the Prince said, the smile never leaving his lips. "I do enjoy ruling. Oh yes, I enjoy it very much."

As he spoke, he jumped back into the room and took a few steps towards her, his hand going to his belt. He raised it then, his long fingers curled around the ivory handle of a gleaming knife.

Myra tensed and instinctively tried to pull back as much as her ropes allowed. Why would the vampire need a blade? She had assumed he was planning to kill her the traditional way—by sinking his razor-sharp fangs into her neck and drinking her blood.

"No need to fear me. I will not hurt you," he said as he cut her bounds. "Come with me."

Myra stared at him. "What? Where?"

He arched an eyebrow. "Are you always so eloquent? We are going to my private dining chambers. You look like you could use some dinner."

She stood up on shaky legs and followed him as he led her into an adjacent room. Why would he feed her? Did he want to fatten her up, like a pig, before he slaughtered her?

Myra pushed away her dark thoughts and stepped into the room. The floor was of white marble, and paintings of laden tables and people dining covered the walls. A small round table was in the middle, covered by a silken white cloth. A most intoxicating scent of baked sweetness filled her nostrils, making her dizzy.

Myra's mouth watered as she took in the scene before her. A platter of golden bread rolls sat in the middle of the table. In front of each of the two chairs was a small plate, with a slice of a strange purple vegetable. Some green paste covered the slice, with pieces of something red and a few green leaves on top. Whatever this was, it was the most appetizing thing she had ever seen.

She blushed as her stomach made a very loud sound, and her eyes wandered to the bigger plates, placed behind the smaller ones. On each of them was a piece of grilled meat, larger than anything Myra had seen. This most definitely did not come from any rat or a rabbit. Next to the meat were baked yellowish things—were those potatoes? Myra had seen pictures, but the Resistance had never gotten hold of anything like this.

"Please, take a seat," the Prince said.

Myra wanted to resist, she really did, but her stomach hurt so badly, and the edges of her vision were growing black. She collapsed onto the chair, grabbed the meat with her right hand and stuffed it into her mouth.

Her left hand reached out for the bread. A crunchy golden crust on the outside, and white and soft on the inside. How did vampires bake such good bread? Had they found well-preserved flour supplies from the Old World, or were they growing their own wheat? And, most importantly, why?

The Prince cleared his throat, and Myra looked up to meet his eyes. He had seated himself on the opposite chair, holding a knife and a fork, staring at her with a raised eyebrow. Only now did Myra notice that there were two pairs of golden knives and forks in front of her, one bigger than the other. On her left was a folded white cloth. The Prince took the cloth in front of him and laid it across his knees. Myra blushed and followed suit, reluctantly putting the half-eaten steak and the bread back on the table.

"Bon appétit," he said, cutting off a tiny piece of the purple vegetable thing.

What was the right answer to that supposed to be? "You too," she said, and took the smaller set of utensils, following his example. "You eat human food?"

"Not truly. This food can provide me no sustenance. No matter how much I eat, it will neither harm me, nor make me stronger. Only blood can feed the magic that gives me life. Still, I can appreciate the taste, and I do not mind eating to keep you company."

Myra frowned. "The taste? So it doesn't taste like ashes or something?"

The Prince laughed. "Only ashes taste like ashes. But it is true that when you become a vampire, your senses change. I can see colors I never knew existed when I was a human. I can distinguish between hundreds of shades of red, blue, and green. I can hear a blade of grass bend in the wind, or an ant crawling on tree bark." He placed his palm on the table and ran his fingers along the white cloth. "When I touch the tablecloth, I sense more than smooth silk. I sense the woman who wove it and the family of five who ate from it." He cut off a small piece of his steak. "When I taste this meat, I can taste the grass the deer grazed on, the cool water it drank, and the distant stars it looked at in the night."

"How about smell?"

He smiled. "You truly want to know? I can smell the blood flowing in your veins. I can smell your fear, your confusion, your grief."

Myra shuddered and pulled back. "Why are you feeding me?" she asked.

"Why do you think?"

"So that I taste better and have more blood when you eat me," she said, glaring at him.

"Wrong." He reached out to a cupboard behind him and produced two golden goblets, studded with red gems. He placed one in front of her and took out a bottle of blood-red liquid from underneath the table. "Do you like wine, dear girl?"

Myra froze. She had tried wine once, at the Resistance, when Zack had decided to open one of their four surviving bottles. She had drunk less than a sip, and had no idea what her limits were. After her starvation, the first sip would likely go straight to her head. She could not do this. Something strange was going on here, and she needed to be in a full possession of her mental faculties.

"I don't like the taste," she lied.

He uncorked the bottle and poured himself a small sip. His long fingers curled around the goblet's stem and he raised it, his gaze fixed on Myra. The Prince drank and nodded appreciatively before filling Myra's goblet, and then his own. "Perhaps this is because you have never found the right kind of wine. I will not force you to drink if you have no desire, but if you wish to try, be my guest. Smell it. What do you sense?"

Was this a test? Myra took her goblet and lifted it to her nose. There was a very faint smell like—something—but she had no idea what.

"It smells of wine," she said. "Alcohol. Grapes."

"Do not be in such a hurry. Twirl your glass. Let the oxygen in. Let it release the flavors. Now, what do you sense?"

Myra did as instructed, but the smell did not really change. "Smells of the Old World," she said. "The world you destroyed."

He twirled his own glass, bringing it up to his face. "I smell cherries, sun-dried fruits, and coffee." He took a slow sip and closed his eyes. "Full-bodied and generous in the mouth. Acidity is low, leaving it smooth and silky on the palate, with a bright, wild berry finish. It will go well with our venison steaks."

What? It was just wine, how could it be all of that? Myra lifted her goblet, momentarily tempted to taste it and experience what he had described, but placed it back down.

He smiled. "You are cautious. You fear me. You believe I will drink you."

"Won't you?" she said and cut off a piece of the vegetable. She put the bite into her mouth, and her eyes widened at the explosion of tastes that bombarded all her senses. What *was* that?

He shrugged. "Perhaps. Or perhaps not. I might find a better use for you."

She held her breath. Was he playing with her? Or did he really consider sparing her life and using her for something other than food? "What use?"

He leaned back into his chair, his amber eyes never leaving hers. "That remains to be seen."

Myra swallowed hard and looked back to her food. What was that supposed to mean? Armida had advised her to entertain him. Was she expected to amuse him? But how?

She was too starved to think. Myra finished her vegetable in mere moments and moved to what was left of her steak and potatoes. She reached out to the soft warm bread, spread butter on it and sprinkled it with salt and herbs. *I could spend my life doing this*, she realized with a start. *Eating*. Never before had she considered eating to be a pleasure. The things that made her happy were writing, reading, talking to Thea, and perhaps listening to lectures at the school. Eating was a chore—stuffing a stinking baked rat or a moldy biscuit into her mouth, so that she would not faint from hunger. And now, for the first time, she was enjoying it.

Alerie is dead. She paid with her life for my carelessness, and now I'm glutting myself on food bought with blood. The only way Myra could redeem herself, the only way Alerie's sacrifice would make any sense at all, was to kill this beast. But how?

The silence stretched between them as Myra cleared her plate. This was not good, she realized once she was sated enough to think clearly. He expected her to entertain him. He would kill her if he decided she was unfit. Perhaps he was being quiet on purpose, waiting for her to start a conversation. But how?

Possible questions she could ask flew through her mind, each one more meaningless than the other. *What meat is this?* Right. He had already said it was venison; she would look stupid and inattentive if she asked it. *Do you often eat human food?* No, she had already raised this topic. *Did your servants prepare this?* Useless. This was a yes-or-no question that would not push the conversation any further.

Myra pointed at her fork. "Is this solid gold?" she said and immediately wanted to slap her forehead. How was that *not* a yes-or-no question?

He leaned back in the chair and took his fork in his hand, twirling it. "What makes you think it is gold?"

Great. Back to the test. Perhaps a monosyllabic answer would have been better.

"It's yellow and shiny," she said.

"So are bronze, brass, copper, and various alloys. Not all that glitters is gold. Tell me, dear girl, what else characterizes gold besides being shiny and yellow?"

It is a test, she thought and looked down, her eyes fixed on her empty plate, as she tried to focus. Thinking was not easy when her life was on the line. She looked up. "It is precious," she said. "From what I have seen of vampires so far, you like to flaunt your possessions in people's faces. You would be the sort to use golden cutlery."

"Interesting," he said. "The answer I was looking for was, gold is soft." He tried to bend the fork, but its shape changed only barely in his hands. "Gilded silver. Sturdy enough to be useful, yet the gold on the surface preserves the taste. Your cutlery can affect the taste of your food. This is why tea from a porcelain cup would taste better than from plastic or paper, and why people used to eat caviar with a pearl spoon. A zinc fork would make a baked fish horrendous, but will work well with sweet-sour fruits, such as mango. Tin is perfect for pistachio curry, and gold"—he raised the fork for her to see—"gold is good with anything."

Myra frowned. Did anyone in their right mind actually spend time considering what type of cutlery to use with each type of food? Did it really matter? To her, food had always been about surviving another day. "Is that a vampire thing?" she asked.

"Vampires rarely partake of human food," he said. "When we do, pleasure always matters, but it is the humans of the Old World who put so much thought into how to take tastes to new levels. It saddens me that your kind has lost this art, along with many others."

Yes, we lost this art and many more when you wiped out our civilization. The silence stretched between them once again, but she had no desire to strike up another conversation.

"What is your name, sweet girl?" he asked at last.

"Myra," she said.

"Myra," he repeated. "I knew a girl named Myra once."

"Did you eat her?"

He leaned back in his chair, smiling. "You truly think I am going to eat you?"

She steeled herself and looked up, meeting his eyes. "Aren't you? Don't play with me. Let's put an end to this theater and get to the point."

He stood up from his chair and started pacing back and forth. "Indeed. This is precisely what we must do. Tell me, Myra, can you draw?"

"What?"

He swept his hand in the air. "Paintings. Sketches. People. Animals. Nature. Abstractions. Anything."

She shook her head. "I've never tried."

"Never? You never felt the desire to give it a try?"

"We don't have drawing utensils in our place."

He paused and stared at her. "Did the cavemen need utensils to create the drawings on the walls? Humans have always felt the desire to draw, to create, improvising tools out of the most unlikely objects and substances to satisfy the urge. Has humanity truly lost this drive?"

"There was nothing in our place to improvise with."

"I cannot believe that," he said. "Draw me something."

Myra froze. Was this it, then? Would he spare her life if she could draw? Or was he expecting her to draw something specific? What was the right answer?

"Will you give me paper and pencils?"

"You have all you need."

Myra frowned. All she needed? She had nothing to draw with, and nothing to draw on.

Or perhaps not. He eyes wandered towards her empty plate, and then to the unfinished gravy in his. Here they were—her canvas and paint. She hesitated for a moment and then, with newfound confidence, stood up in her chair.

Before she could reach out to dip her finger in the gravy, he turned away from her with a sigh.

"I believe I have seen enough," he said, and without a look back, he walked out of the room.

Myra paled, her throat constricted. If that had been a test, she had failed. Her eyes darted towards the table for one last time and she felt no shame when she grabbed his barely touched steak and stuffed it inside her pocket before the guards came in.

Chapter Ten

Tales and Songs

Myra sat on the cell floor, her knees drawn to her chest. She did not know how much time had passed after the guards had brought her back, but it must have been hours because she was growing hungry again. She took the cold steak out of her pocket and nibbled on it. Perhaps it made sense to ration her food—she had no idea when the next meal would come.

In all likelihood, *she* would be the next meal. Was the Prince still planning to eat her, or would he let his people torture her for information? She was not certain which one was worse.

Someone approached, and she put the steak down. A hooded figure walked in front of the cell. A pale, slender hand pushed back the blue hood, letting wavy red hair spill out. Myra was on her feet in an instant. "Lady Armida? What do you want from me?"

The vampire smiled. "I want nothing from you, dear girl. I merely came to bring you this." She handed her a bright red apple. "I thought you might be hungry. You looked on the verge of fainting yesterday."

Myra took a step back. "Where do all these living plants come from? Why have you left sunlit places?"

"Why do you think?"

Myra sighed. She was tired of tests. "I suppose the animals whose blood you feed on need something to eat."

Armida grinned. "The animals whose blood we drink need something to eat? You could put it like that, though I bet you would have phrased it differently if you knew what was going on."

"Then what *is* going on? Why did the Prince offer me dinner?"

"He wanted to know if you have what he seeks," the vampire said and handed Myra the apple in between the bars. "Come, now. Take it."

"What does he seek?" Myra asked, making no move to take the fruit.

"The one thing he does not possess. Humanity."

Myra frowned. What was that supposed to mean?

"Do not be proud, girl," Armida said. "Take the apple."

Myra knew it was probably foolish to refuse food, but it was not much smarter to accept gifts without knowing the giver's intentions. "I don't need your help."

"Very well." Armida left the apple on the floor of the cell and turned to go.

"Wait," Myra said. "I don't need your help, but perhaps you need mine."

The vampire turned and raised an eyebrow. "I doubt this. What can you offer me?"

Myra knew this was desperate, but if she wanted to get out of here, she needed an ally. Perhaps it was not so far-fetched to think Armida would help her if she could give something in return. "Information."

The vampire nodded. "Speak."

"Do you love the Prince?"

Armida grinned. "I thought you were the one giving me information, not the other way around."

"My people have captured vampires in the past," Myra said. "And we have learned things from them. I know for a fact that some of your subjects want your beloved dead."

The vampire stared at her, her face expressionless. "If you want to trade information with me," she said, "then tell me something I do not already know."

Armida pulled her hood up and disappeared into the darkness.

***

Myra paced around the cell, playing with the apple in her hand and musing over Armida's words. The Prince had no humanity. And he was looking for someone who did? What did that mean? How was humanity manifested? And what would the Prince do with the person who possessed it?

It made no sense at all. She clearly possessed humanity by virtue of being a human. But then why were the tests necessary? What was he looking for exactly, and why?

The sounds of a scuffle took her out of her thoughts, and she rushed to the bars to see what was happening. She heard hurried talking and then a scream. Approaching footsteps sounded and Myra froze when she caught sight of long dark hair and recognized Natalia—the vampire who had drunk Alerie. She was dragging a chained male vampire behind her and Myra's eyes widened as she examined the unlikely pair.

This vampire was a prisoner. What had he done? Was he one of those who opposed the Prince? Did he live in the Palace, or had he sneaked in from another place? He looked different from most vampires she had seen—less flamboyant, with short brown hair, dressed in jeans and a sweater. He tried to struggle, but he must have been wounded as Natalia had no trouble overpowering him.

Myra smiled. Whoever he was, it could mean only one thing. The fight was not simply humans versus vampires. There were vampire-versus-vampire conflicts as well, and some vamps opposed the existing order. If she could get in touch with any of them, perhaps they could strike an alliance.

Natalia pulled at the chains and the prisoner cried out.

Myra froze, stunned, the apple dropping from her limp fingers and falling to the floor.

When the prisoner had cried out, his mouth had fallen wide open, and Myra had caught a glimpse of his teeth. His short, blunt, perfectly *human* teeth. She fell to her knees, staring as Natalia dragged her prisoner forward, disappearing along the corridor.

He is human.

He was human, and Myra had never seen him before. He was not from the Resistance. The man looked no older than thirty—he must have been born after the Nightfall. This meant that his parents had survived and lived long enough to have a child. Were they still alive? Did they have any other children? Had others survived as well? Were they all captured or killed, or were some of them still free?

Myra grabbed the metal bars and stared along the corridor, where the man had disappeared. Where was Natalia taking him? Did the Prince want to test him too? Was she competing against this human, or was the Prince willing to keep them both alive if both passed the test?

She let go of the bars and stepped back as Yong appeared, followed by three guards. He unlocked her door and grabbed her, pulling her out of the cell. Myra tried to wriggle free, but his grip was strong. "Where are you taking me?" she asked, her heart hammering. Had he come to torture her, or to bring her to the Prince? The vampire remained silent.

When they left the dungeon and Myra recognized the way to the Prince's study, she was not sure if she was supposed to be relieved. They entered the room and Yong deposited her into one of the armchairs, turned on his heels and left, followed by the rest of the vamps.

Myra squeezed the armrests, her knuckles turning white. She was not restrained but doubted it was possible to escape. What did the Prince want from her this time? More games? Or had he given that up and decided to eat her?

A chessboard was laid out on the table in front of her, and Myra glanced at it nervously. Did the Prince wish to play chess with her? She knew the rules, but that was as far as her skills went. Armida had said the Prince was looking for humanity. Did expertise in chess relate to humanity?

The door opened and she looked up to glare at Prince Vladimir. "What do you want with me?" she asked even before he had taken a step.

"You are frustrated," he said. "You do not understand the reasons for my actions."

"You don't say."

He smiled. "Perhaps I have been unfair to you. It is time to tell you why you are going through all of this." He took the chair opposite hers and moved one of the white pawns. "You see, I have been looking for someone to do a job for me. I was wondering if you might be qualified."

Myra frowned. A job? Something no one else was able to do? Was this the thing that required humanity? "What kind of a job?"

"You will learn in time."

Myra sighed. These riddles had to end. "Fine. Just tell me—is this job open to many, or is it a single position? Do I have competition?"

He leaned forward and moved a black pawn and then a white one. She raised an eyebrow. Was he playing against himself? "What do you think?" he asked.

"Well, one possibility is that you need many for your project, and some of your people are already working on it. For some reason, you think I can also contribute and you are testing me to see if that's the case."

"And what is the second option?" he prompted.

"That this is a single-person project," she said. "If you haven't found anyone until now, that makes me think it's something a vampire can't do." She leaned forward in her chair, briefly considering moving one of the black figures, but then gave it up, afraid she would do something stupid.

"So in neither case do you have competition," he said.

"On the contrary," she said. "If it's a single opening, and you are looking for a human, I do. I saw a human in the dungeons. Are you testing him too?"

He frowned. "You saw a human?"

"Yes, Natalia was pulling him somewhere."

His eyes cleared. "Ah, I see. Well, I can assure you, this man is no competition to you." He reached out to move a black pawn and a white bishop.

Myra sighed in relief. Her move would have been different, and she was glad she had not made it. "Why? Did he fail your tests?"

"I did not need to bother testing him," he said. "You should not concern yourself with him. Think about yourself now." He picked a deck of playing cards from the table, fanning them out in his hand so they faced Myra. "Have you seen cards before? Pick one."

Myra was not happy to let the subject go, but her main concern was to stay alive. She stared at the beautiful images before pulling out a card.

"Which one did you choose?" he asked.

She frowned. "I thought you were going to guess."

He raised an eyebrow. "Do you think me a trickster? Which card did you choose?"

Confused, she laid it out for him to see and gazed at the exquisite painting of a dark-haired man with a crown on his head and a scepter in his hand.

He smiled. "Ah, this one. Who is he?"

"The King of Spades," she said, relieved to finally know something.

"I know that already. What I am asking is, what kind of a man is he?"

Myra stared at the image. What was he asking? "He's a playing card."

"Must I walk you through everything?" the Prince said. "Who is he? What happened in his past? What awaits him in the future? Who are his loved ones? His enemies?"

"How am I supposed to know?"

He stood up. "Myra, I believe I have seen enough. You are not the person I am looking for."

She froze, her eyes growing wide. She could not do this job for him, which meant he did not need her. Shaking, she looked around, looking for an escape route, but she knew it would be pointless. She would never make it to the door, and even if she did, the Palace was swarming with vamps.

Perhaps she could at least finish her mission even if it would mean her death. But how could she kill him? She saw nothing she could use as a stake, and sunlight was out of the question. He still wore a sword at his belt, but she could not imagine overpowering him to take it. Her eyes moved to the dancing flames in the fireplace. Perhaps that was it. Perhaps she could set the room on fire, but if she did, she would burn as well.

Myra bit her lip, her throat dry, her eyes burning. Whether she set fire to the room or not, she would die. Whether she killed the Prince or not, she would still die. She would never again go home. She would die here, alone, far away from anyone who had ever cared about her.

"Are you going to eat me now?" she said, barely managing to speak around the lump in her throat.

He raised an eyebrow. "Why are you so fixated on getting eaten? Eating you was never on the menu, darling girl. Now go."

Myra stared at him dumbstruck. "What?"

"You heard me," the Prince said. "The door is over there."

She grabbed her armrests, her face pale. "What are you talking about?"

"I have no more use for you. Let us not waste each other's time. Go back to your people."

She did not need to be told twice. Ignoring the growing warning in her mind, Myra stood up and strode to the door. After a few steps, she stopped and peeked back.

"Go on," he said with an encouraging smile. "I have made sure there are no guards on your way out. All you need to do is follow the corridor to the end, go down the staircase, and then turn left. You will see a large metal door that will take you outside. The drawbridge is down, and you can leave the castle."

This could not be happening. Myra's knees went weak at the overwhelming surge of relief. Just a moment ago she had been saying her goodbye to the world, and now he was letting her go. "But why?" she asked. "Why would you set me free?"

"Why do you think?" the Prince challenged.

She shook her head. "I honestly have no idea."

He sighed. "Disappointing. And I had such high hopes. Go on."

Myra was shaking. She did not understand one bit of what was happening, but she would have plenty of time to question his motivations once she was out of here. Slowly, she took another step. And another.

Her fingers curled around the cool golden doorknob. The door opened and she stepped outside. The Prince had spoken the truth—there was no one in the corridor. Myra hesitated. Was it a trap? Did he want her to lead him to the Resistance? If that was his plan, he would be disappointed—she did not know the way back. Myra walked on. She would worry about where to go once she was out of the castle.

She had barely taken a few steps when a strong hand grabbed her and pushed her back inside the room. "This will not do," Prince Vladimir said. "You need to be faster if you wish to escape a vampire. Try again."

She blinked. "What are you doing?"

"Try again, I said. And this time run."

She did, but before she had reached the door, Vladimir was standing in front of her, blocking her way. He grabbed her shoulders, his amber eyes boring into hers. "Come on girl, fight me. Is this the best the Resistance can send me?"

He let her go and Myra nearly collapsed. What had she been thinking? He was only playing with her, handing her a candy only to snatch it back. She had known vampires were cruel, but this took her by surprise. Myra glared at him. "Hasn't your mother told you not to play with your food?"

Something flickered in his eyes, but his smile never went away. "Stop talking and fight me, if you want to live."

Myra wriggled free from his grasp and ran to the right, standing behind one of the tables. One of the Prince's sleeves fell back in the scuffle, revealing a simple tattoo before he pulled it back down. He stared at her, a predatory fire in his eyes.

Myra threw chess pieces and boards at him and pushed over a table, trying to block his way. But it was all in vain, and all she could do was struggle weakly as his hands closed around her arms and held her in place.

Perhaps it would have been better if a true fighter had come instead of her. Perhaps they would have stood a chance and perhaps, with a little luck, they might have seen an opportunity to kill this monster. Perhaps she had been wrong to volunteer. And then, a little voice inside her head laughed mockingly—of course she had been wrong to volunteer. She had been the only one who had failed to see it.

"Pathetic, really," the Prince said. "Come on, another try."

He released her and she whirled around, eyes flashing. "No." Myra said resolutely. "I will not play cat and mouse with you. You want to stalk me like prey, you want to hunt me and capture me before you kill me, but I will not serve for your entertainment. If you are to kill me, kill me now."

She had expected to see annoyance and disappointment in his eyes, but instead there was a sparkle of amusement.

"Indeed? What you lack in muscle and technique, you make up for in spirit. But you are making a bold claim now. Are you saying that I can bite you and drink you dry, and you will not even attempt to fight back?"

"I know it will be useless," Myra stated with a calm that surprised her. "I won't give you the pleasure."

"Let us try that," the Prince said, sounding disturbingly enthusiastic. "I am curious how long you can hold out before you start fighting."

He grabbed her and turned her around. Myra's survival instincts screamed at her to fight him, and she used all her willpower to suppress them. No, she would die with dignity and would not let him win.

His unyielding arms were around her, pinning her in place. It was too late now. There was nowhere to run. Sweat broke on her forehead and her throat tightened. This could not be. She could not die, not here, not like that. Death terrified her, but what made things worse was the knowledge her end would be violent. The pain. The fear. The realization that her life was draining away.

Myra shivered. If she were to die, she would have preferred poison, or anything else that brought painless death. And, most of all, she did not wish to die at all.

Instead, she would be murdered. Butchered like an animal and fed to this monster to sate his hunger. Her only hope was that Thea and Zack would never learn what had become of her.

The Prince was close now, so close that she could feel his icy breath on her neck. His sharp teeth grazed her skin, ready to pierce it.

She closed her eyes, trying to pretend she was somewhere else, anywhere else. Perhaps back at the cellars, singing Thea a goodnight song. And then, Myra sang.

"Little bird, little bird, where are you flying?
Did you see my hometown, where I was born?
Did you see my brothers and my mother crying
For a son forgotten, far away from home?"

Tears came to her eyes. She would never get the chance to sing this song to Thea again. Myra swallowed hard. She could not afford to think of that now; all she could do was die with dignity. She forced herself to keep on singing, barely getting the words past her tight throat.

"Little bird, I wonder where this road takes you
If you'll see the gardens where I played as a boy,
If you'll see the mountains that can tell you stories
Of my greatest sorrow and my greatest joy.
Little bird, I beg you, if you see my mother,

Tell her I am living, tell her I am well—"

Lost in the pleasant images and memories she had called to her mind, Myra did not notice that the Prince's teeth were no longer at her neck. And when she finally wondered why she was still alive and opened her eyes, the vampire was in front of her, an unreadable expression on his face.

"Where did you learn that song?" he asked, his voice intense.

She would not talk to him. No, let him ask—she would not say a word.

"I know neither the lyrics, nor the melody," he said. "What song is that?"

She returned his stare with a silent challenge in her eyes.

"What song is it? How do you know it? Answer me." He shook her forcefully, his eyes glowing orange under the candlelight.

"I—I made it up," she stammered, cursing her own weakness. It surely did not take a lot to make her talk; it was only fortunate the vampire was not questioning her about the Resistance.

He looked at her long and hard, his searching stare seeming to penetrate all her defenses. She felt exposed under his gaze and tried to pull away, but his grip was strong. "Have you written any other songs?" he asked.

"Yes," she said, forgetting her resolve not to talk to him.

"Have you written anything else? Poems, stories, novels?"

"I have," Myra replied, the strength returning to her voice. "All of those. And some plays too."

He did not speak for a long while and simply stared at the tapestry as if it was the only thing he saw. He released her and turned to the wall, stretching his hand and touching the picture in reverence. His fingers slid down the image of the sky, so blue and clear, the likes of which the Earth had not seen in the past five decades.

When he turned back, there was a strange longing in his eyes. "Come with me."

Myra blinked, startled. "Where?"

"Come," he said and led her out into the corridor. "You can try to run if you like, but you know how this is going to end."

She followed him silently even though there were many questions on her mind. He led her to a spacious room. Under the light coming from the torches in the corridor, she saw a large bed, two chairs, and a writing table in the corner.

"You will spend the night here," the Prince said. "The servants will bring you food, tea, bathing water, candles, and clean clothes. I will send for you tomorrow."

Without waiting for a reply, he walked out and closed the door behind him, leaving her alone.

Chapter Eleven

All That Glitters

Myra sat on the bed, staring at the dancing candle flame, her arms wrapped around her legs. She knew she had to get some sleep—the Prince apparently had plans for her and she needed to be sharp—but her mind was racing.

What had happened? The Prince had been about to kill her, but had spared her life. Why? Had she proven she could do the job he required? Or had he never planned to kill her so soon in the first place? Was he still playing his cat-and-mouse game, leading her to believe she was safe for now?

Myra gazed at the table and swallowed hard. Aromatic buns, pears, jams and grilled meat awaited her, but she could not enjoy the food if she had no idea how long this would last. She expected the Prince or one of his henchmen to come at any point and take her back to the cell, or perhaps this time to the torture chamber. Perhaps this was what the game was all about—playing with her mind to drive her insane and prepare her for the interrogation.

She could not trust anything the vamps said or did. What did they want? What was their motivation for treating her like this? If they were rational, their goal would be destroying the Resistance. If they were not, she could never hope to figure it out.

She gazed through the large bay window. Rosy light was trying to find its way through the thick black clouds. Dawn was approaching, and she had to prepare herself for whatever the vamps had in store for her. Myra stood up from the bed and walked to the basin to wash her face.

Once she was done, she looked at the pile of clothes the servants had brought for her. The selection of garments covered the entire spectrum of possible colors and shapes, but Myra had no idea what most of them were, or even how she was supposed to wear them. One was a smooth, shiny orange cloth, many feet long. Was she supposed to wrap this around herself? How? And was that red thing over there supposed to be a skirt or a blouse? Or a dress, perhaps?

In the end, she settled for simple black jeans and a long-sleeved white blouse. So much else was new in her life; there was no need to experiment with clothing. Still, the clothes she had picked out were much better quality than anything she had ever worn.

Someone knocked on the door, and Myra took a deep breath to steady her heart. "Come in."

Tristan opened the door. He was dressed in a stylish black tuxedo and a bow tie, an outfit that might have looked ridiculous on anyone else, but he somehow made it work. The vampire wore his long platinum hair in a ponytail, falling behind his back. Silver bat-shaped cufflinks kept his sleeves in place. "My lady," he said and bowed deeply. "His Highness would like you to accompany him to the opera."

My—what? Myra blinked. Was he talking to her? Was this a joke? Last time she had seen him, he had treated her as a tasty steak, and now he was my-ladying her?

"What opera?" she asked, taking an instinctive step back.

He smiled brightly, still keeping his perma-frown on. "We often stage operas at the theater hall. Today we perform Tosca."

"So vampires watch theater and opera?"

"All the time," he said and walked to the desk, picking up a pear. "You have not eaten much. My lord will be displeased."

She snorted. *Right. Pleasing your lord is the dream of my life.* "And you have vampire performers?"

"Of course. When the Nightfall started, my lord's orders were clear. Turn the ones worthy to join our ranks. Kill the rest. However, he made sure all his favorite singers and actors would be turned, not killed, regardless of other qualities."

Myra's eyes widened. "He turned his favorite singers?"

The horror must have been clear in her voice, and Tristan shrugged. "The alternative was to kill them or worse. He did them a favor, really."

Some people would prefer to die rather than be turned into monsters. "Or worse?" she asked. "What's worse than dying or becoming a vampire?"

"Do not concern yourself with this," he said and offered her his hand. "Let us go. He is waiting for us."

She raised an eyebrow at his outstretched hand, but made no move to take it. Myra turned her back at him and walked out of the room.

***

"Why does the Prince want to take me to an opera?" Myra asked as they walked down the corridor.

"He believes it will help you with the tasks he has for you." He looked at her, his brow furrowed. "Have you ever seen an opera before?"

She shook her head, and his face brightened.

"Ah. It is your first time, then? Brilliant. I cannot wait to see your reaction. Do you understand Italian?"

Was he mocking her? She had spent her life underground, hiding and isolated from any human culture other than her own, thanks to his Prince. "Not a word."

"A pity," he said. "That needs to be remediated. Are you familiar with the story?"

"I'm afraid not." What game was he playing?

"You do not need to understand the lyrics to appreciate it," Tristan said. "But just to give you a little background—Tosca is a singer. She is in love with the painter Cavaradossi. The chief of police, Baron Scarpia, is persecuting an escaped political prisoner, Angelotti, who is also a good friend of Cavaradossi. The painter helps his friend escape and hide. Scarpia is convinced Tosca knows of Angelotti's whereabouts and plans to get the information from her. I do not want to spoil the rest for you, but I will try to keep you updated as the story progresses."

Myra observed Tristan with a raised eyebrow. The vampire's eyes were bright, and he was speaking so fast that she could barely follow. *He is excited*, she realized, surprised. "Have you seen this opera before?"

"Oh yes," he replied with a smile. "Many times in the Old World, at various locations and with different singers. But tonight is the first time we are staging it after the Nightfall. I admit I am looking forward to it."

Yes, I can see that. Myra frowned. It was strange to her, seeing someone so excited about a performance. She had always needed to force the grown-up Resistance members to attend any of her plays. Normally, she herself would have been excited to see the opera, but it was hard to feel anything but terror. Why did the Prince want her there? Was he toying with her once again?

They reached the hall, and Tristan pulled back the heavy red curtains concealing the private loge. Armida, wearing a deep purple evening dress, was sitting at the far right. The Prince, dressed in his usual black and red, sat on her left. Tristan seated himself next the Prince, and Myra took the seat next to him.

"Thank you for coming, Myra," Vladimir said. "I hope you will enjoy the performance."

I rather hope to find out why I'm here, she thought but there was no time to say anything. The curtains opened, and Myra relaxed in her seat. If she had to attend this performance, she could at least try to enjoy it.

And then, the orchestra started playing.

Myra froze, her heart slowly rising up in her chest until it reached her throat. She fought to draw breath, but air barely squeezed around the tight lump. Goose bumps rose on her arms and back, and sweat beaded on her face, mingling with her tears.

Was that what real music was supposed to sound like? They had tried singing at the Resistance; they had tried playing their crude scavenged or self-made instruments. Myra had believed they had succeeded in producing music. Until now.

Myra shuddered and took a deep breath, exhaling slowly. As magical as the music was, the plot was impossible to follow. Tristan had given her the basics, but she had already forgotten all the names. She remembered some characters—a painter, a prisoner, a police chief, but she had no idea how to match them to the actors on the stage.

One of the actors started to sing. But was this supposed to be singing? She had heard nothing like this before. This was not a song one would casually sing to pass the time, while washing dishes or cleaning the floor. It was pure, raw, powerful emotion. It was as if the singer had cut his heart wide open and let all his feelings pour out, unchecked.

"This is Cavaradossi," Tristan explained in a hushed voice. "He is comparing the beauty of the blond Mary Magdalene in his painting to his lover, the dark-haired Tosca."

Myra nodded, although she realized this did not matter. Tristan was right—one did not need to understand the lyrics. She could already feel what the singer was feeling, think what he was thinking.

"And this is Scarpia," Tristan whispered. "He is trying to turn Tosca against Cavaradossi."

Myra wanted to tell him that he did not need to explain every plot point, but one look at him made her keep her silence. He was enjoying this. He was sharing his passion with her, and he liked it.

"Scarpia invites Tosca for dinner," Tristan said, raising his voice a little to make himself heard over the singing. "He cannot find Angelotti, so he imprisons and tortures Cavaradossi instead. He wants to make Tosca tell him where Angelotti is hiding."

"This is so unfair," Myra whispered. "I hope she doesn't tell him."

"She resists at first," he said. "But then she hears her lover's screams and yields."

"Ah. But Angelotti escapes, right?"

"You are new to operas, aren't you?" Tristan said with a grin. "Angelotti kills himself, and Cavaradossi is mad at Tosca for betraying him."

"Why? It wasn't her fault," Myra grumbled and leaned back, letting herself sink into the music.

It was all so professional, so magnificent, so *big*. The imposing stage and the detailed sets, the heavy curtains, the costumes. She had never produced anything close to that at the Resistance. And the orchestra! What she was seeing and hearing now shook her to the core. She had had no idea something like this had ever existed, anywhere.

"What is happening now?" she asked after a while.

"Scarpia is going to execute Cavaradossi," Tristan explained. "He tells Tosca that he will spare her lover only if she gives herself to him."

"What?" Myra cried. "Seriously, I hate this scumbag."

"I hate him too," the Prince chimed in. "Almost as much as I hate people talking during a performance."

"Sorry, my lord," Tristan said and flashed the Prince a bright grin before turning to Myra. "He is right. We must be quiet now. This is my favorite aria. Tosca is singing about how she lived for art and love and cannot understand why God had abandoned her."

Myra fell quiet. The song began, soft and gentle at first, lulling her in. Then it shook and swelled, with rising tension and emotion, shrill, and dark, and powerful, rising to the skies and falling deep into the underworld. The actress stood there, in her red dress, dramatic crimson lipstick, and jet-black hair, pouring her heart out. Pleading. Begging. Questioning. So much pain. So much despair.

Myra grabbed the armrests and squeezed. Her palms were sweating and her heart rose up in her throat. She could not understand a single word, but she knew what Tosca was singing. She had lived for art, for love. Why was God punishing her so? It was so unfair. But life was unfair, was it not? Myra herself had lived to write, to create, and what had she received in return? Life had thrown her into the clutches of the same monsters who had slaughtered her family. She wanted to raise her voice and sing together with Tosca, lamenting the injustice of it all.

But did she have any right to lament her fate? Here she was, pampered, well fed and well dressed, not required to do any physical work, and watching what she was certain to be the most magnificent and heart-wrenching performance ever staged. Experiencing this opera was a dream come true, a dream she had not even known she was having because she could not even imagine that something like this could exist. And here she was, enjoying it all, while her friends at the Resistance starved and struggled for their lives. While Alerie's body lay rotting in a forgotten house. While her parents, her uncle, and in all likelihood her aunt, were all dead.

The vampires had created a beautiful world over the blood of her people. Their castles were built over the bones of everyone who had died during the Nightfall and the following years. It was stunning and shiny, but it was all just a facade, on top of all the death and rot underneath. *You were right, Your Highness. Not all that glitters is gold.*

Shaking, she turned to look at Tristan and could not stifle a gasp. He was staring at the stage, as if in a trance, his grey eyes shining. Was he crying? The bloodsucking fiend who had likely killed many without batting an eyelid was *crying at an opera.* This was so ridiculous that Myra wanted to laugh.

The moment was over. The actor playing Scarpia was back on stage, demanding an answer.

"She won't give in," Myra muttered. "Please, tell me she won't give in."

"Sorry to disappoint, but she just agreed to his demands," Armida said.

The Prince sighed. "Fine. Obviously we cannot enjoy the opera quietly like civilized people, so let us at least do this the proper way. Tosca agreed to submit but demanded a paper that gives her and Cavaradossi safe passage out of Rome."

"Oh, this is fun," Tristan cried. "We can all do a live translation for our human guest."

"Only if you sing the songs," Vladimir countered and Tristan scolded.

"But she can't submit to him," Myra protested. "This is not"—she paused, spotting the prop knife on the stage. "Please tell me she's going after the knife." She moved to the edge of her seat. "Take the knife. Stab him! Yes!" She turned towards Tristan, bright-eyed. "She killed him. And she has the safe passage. This is brilliant!"

"Keep watching," said Tristan with a grin. "There is one more act."

Myra listened with bated breath to Cavaradossi's heart-breaking song, followed by the reunion with his beloved.

"She is explaining to him that the execution will be staged," Tristan said. "The guards will shoot with blanks, and he is to play dead."

The guards did shoot, and the actor fell. And when he failed to rise, Myra wanted to scream. "What? How? But the execution was staged, right?"

"That's what Tosca thought," Tristan said. "Scarpia lied to her."

"This is so unfair," Myra protested. "They had the safe passage. They were so close." She watched in stunned silence as Tosca ran away from the guards and jumped to her death. "You have to be joking," she said. "This can't be the end. What kind of a story ends like this?"

Armida laughed. "Welcome to the world of opera. If you plan on seeing any more, you should get used to it."

Tristan stood up. "Do you wish me to bring the girl back to her room, my lord?"

Prince Vladimir shook his head. "No, thank you, my boy. I would like to talk to her first, and then I will escort her myself. You may go."

Tristan bowed and left. Armida caught Myra's eye and winked at her before turning to the Prince and giving him a quick kiss. "May you find what you seek, my love," she said and followed Tristan.

"Why did you ask me to join you?" Myra asked when she was alone with the Prince.

He raised an eyebrow. "I was expecting gratitude. Unless you disliked it?"

"Don't misunderstand me. I enjoyed this, but I need to know what is happening and what you expect of me."

"You mentioned you had written plays," he said. "Were you the one to stage and direct them?"

"Always," she said. *No one else would.*

"Wonderful. Perhaps you will be interested in helping with the next opera?"

She froze. "There will be another one?"

He smiled at her. "I am planning a few more operas, musicals, and plays in the near future. Tell me, Myra, did you find this inspiring? Does it make you want to write?"

Myra nodded. "Honestly? There is nothing I want more right now than to go back to my room and start writing."

He smiled. "I am happy to hear that. I will make sure you have unlimited supplies of pens, paper and candles. What would you like to write about?"

She hesitated. "I've started working on a novel. I'd like to continue my work. Unfortunately, the chapters I have so far are back home, and my newest writings got lost when your people captured me. I would need to write them again from scratch and then continue with the rest."

He nodded. "What kind of a novel is it?"

"Fantasy," she said. "With a bit of adventure."

"Splendid," he said. "Here is what we will do. You will write your novel's outline—short summaries of all the chapters you have so far. You will also make a list of all your main characters along with short descriptions, personality traits and backgrounds. How much time do you think you will need? Is tomorrow morning feasible?"

Myra stared at him. "I could. But… why?"

He smiled. "Because, darling girl, you wish to stay alive. And if you do this little thing for me, I could perhaps grant this desire."

She shuddered. "Of course. What I meant was, why do you need this?"

"I told you already. I am trying to determine if you are the right person for a job I need done."

She frowned. So the test was not over? She had believed she had somehow passed it, but it looked like her life was still on the line. "I will have the outline for you by tomorrow morning," she said, her voice steady even as her heart clenched.

Chapter Twelve

Darkness and Light

Myra stared through her window, watching vampires on foot and horseback coming and going in the courtyard below. The chocolate on the table was tempting, but her stomach was tied in a knot, and she doubted she could enjoy any food. The Prince had asked her to write an outline of her book, and a few hours ago she had given it to Tristan. The Prince had made it clear this was a part of the test. Would the contents of her book decide if she lived or died?

She tore her eyes from the moving figures down below and sat on the bed, her head spinning. She had somehow ended up in the Prince's inner circle even though her position was still precarious, and at any point he could decide he did not need her anymore. And yet, she was certain that in the past couple of days she had spent more time with him than an average servant would. It was a blessing. Her mission was to kill him, but now that she was so close to him, perhaps she could also use the opportunity to find out more about the WeatherWizard.

Myra ran her hands through her hair so forcefully that a few strands remained in between her fingers. Was the Prince reading her outline right now? Would he think it was good? Back at the Resistance her works had received either praise or lack of interest, but this was different. Judging from his library, he must have read so many books. Would her own be better, different, memorable? Or would he find it average and forgettable?

Someone knocked, and Myra held her breath. The door opened and Prince Vladimir stepped in, a notebook in his hand. She gulped and scanned his face, looking for hints that he had read her outline and enjoyed it.

"May I come in?" he said.

She blinked. "Yes—yes, of course. It's your castle after all."

He sat in a cushioned armchair and stretched out his long legs. "These are your chambers, so you are the lady here."

Until you decide to eat me. "Did you look at my outline?"

He was silent for a moment, and Myra's heart clenched. Had he seen it and hated it? Did he think she was a terrible writer?

"I did," he said.

Myra's throat constricted as he failed to elaborate. "And—"

"We have a lot of work ahead of us," he said and smiled at her as she paled. "Do not look so worried. You are certainly very imaginative."

This did little to alleviate Myra's worries. He sounded as if he was trying to come up with a compliment when there was nothing to compliment her about. "But you disliked it?"

"I did not say that. You are inexperienced, but experience is something people gain. Your plot, if I can call it that, is a mess, and your book is ridiculously long—two hundred and four chapters in which nothing significant happens. As for your characters—well, we need to talk about them."

Myra's knees grew weak and she was glad she was sitting down. Her plot was a mess? She had been so proud of her story. Her friends had either told her they liked her stories, or that they did not have time to read them, but no one had ever claimed her tales were poorly written. And why did he wish to talk about her book? What did he hope to accomplish?

"Let us start with your protagonist," he said and opened his notebook. "Maryabella. Honestly? *Maryabella*?"

Myra paled and looked up at him. "I thought it was a beautiful name."

He sighed. "I have traveled every patch of land on this earth, and I have never encountered anyone named Maryabella. An unusual name would work if you had created a complex culture within a well-established universe, with its own language and naming conventions. However, your other characters' names do not fit the pattern, so this is not the case here. Besides, the name seems derived from your own, which leads me to believe she is a self-insert. You probably enjoy fantasizing about your alter ego being amazing, but this does not mean others will want to read about it. You need to *make* people want to read your story, and you must recognize that their reasons for enjoying it might be different from yours."

She clenched her fists, treacherously close to tears. She liked Maryabella a lot, and now he was tearing the character apart, without knowing much about her. "Why are you doing this?"

"Obviously, I want to help you improve," he said. "Look, Myra, there are many ways to make your character special. Giving her an unusual name or appearance is not one of them.

It will make your readers roll their eyes rather than take her seriously. You want them to like your character because she accomplishes extraordinary deeds and grows as a person, not because she is a very special snowflake."

Myra placed her hands over her knees, shaking. She liked Maryabella's name. Thea, and everyone else who had agreed to read the story, had liked it too. She wanted to lash out at him, to defend her choices, but then she realized that he was not attacking her. He was *teaching* her. But why would he do that?

"Now," he said, "let us look at your actual story. I will be blunt—the plot has no structure at all. Here she is, fighting trolls, then a faery kidnaps her friends, she goes on a quest to save them and slays a dragon on the way, then everyone is saved, then there are some griffons, minotaurs, cyclopes, and a few orcs, because why not? Your mythology is a hodgepodge of random creatures whose existence is never justified, and your story lacks progress."

"How can it lack progress?" she protested. "So much is happening."

"Action does not mean progress. How is your character better off or worse off in the tenth chapter than she is in the second? She is going on random adventures that do not move the story forward and have no direction. What is the point of the whole thing?"

"She is doing good," Myra said. "Saving her friends. Fighting the enemy."

"Your story needs to start with some kind of a setup," he said. "Introduce us to your world and your characters. Then something happens, some trigger that changes the status quo. Your character goes on a quest and accomplishes something.

Possibly, she changes and grows in the process. At this stage you can have various problems for your character to overcome, growing in severity. It all builds up to a climax, followed by a resolution and an establishment of a new status quo."

Myra's eyes widened, and ideas started popping up in her head as she listened. "We could start at Maryabella's home," she said. "I'll describe her life and her everyday interactions with her friends. It's all stable, but then the peace is shattered when something terrible happens, and she needs to go on a quest to fix things."

He massaged his forehead. "Can we change the name? Maryabella is distracting me."

Myra was about to argue that she liked the name, but realized that he had a point. "Alerie," she said. "Her name is Alerie."

"Now, this is a proper name," he said. "A beautiful Filipino name. Ordinary enough, and yet unusual enough, so that you will not have tens of thousands of book characters named the same. Go on."

"I am thinking her home is attacked by some creatures of darkness. It's destroyed and she can't go back."

"Let us work on your creature of darkness for a bit," he said. "Right now we have a wood where trolls, dragons and griffons live as good neighbors. The next wood is the same, and so is the next one. Traveling farther from home does not become more dangerous. Your world is too homogeneous in terms of strange creatures."

"What do you mean?"

The Prince opened his notebook and drew a vertical line. "The ancient Greeks divided the world vertically and horizontally." He made a little dot in the middle of the line. "The center is where humans lived. High above were the gods, and below was the underworld." He flipped to a new page. "The horizontal division is even more relevant in your case," he said, drawing a circle with a dot in the middle. "You have a center and a periphery. Your hometown is your center. It is known and familiar. The farther away you go, the more dangers and wonders you encounter, and the stranger the creatures and the landscapes become."

"So you are suggesting I structure my world like this?" Myra asked.

"This is only one of many options, but your world does need a clearer structure. Your biggest problem, however, are your creatures of darkness. Even though you have so many different kinds, all of them appear to be pure evil."

"Why is that a problem?"

"A story like this could make for a good children's book, but nothing more. The real world is never black-and-white."

"It is," Myra said. Perhaps it was a bad idea to make him angry, but she was tired of playing games. "The real world is exactly black-and-white. We have vampires and humans."

He laughed. "We are the complete monsters, are we? And your kind are only saints? Myra, some of my people have disappeared throughout the years. Tell me, what did the Resistance do to them? Invite them for a pint of hot blood and integrate them as useful members of society?"

We tortured and killed them. She looked him in the eyes. "You can't put that on us. You are our oppressor. You destroyed our civilization and killed many, including our families. We are only fighting to stay alive."

"You are not fighting to stay alive," he said. "You do not need to kill vampires to stay alive. You want more than that. You want to overthrow me and destroy the world I created."

"You created this world over my people's graves," she said. "Humans and vampires coexisted for millennia. You are the ones who broke the peace first."

He stood up and walked to the window, staring at the darkening sky. "Coexisted? Peace? Is this what you call it? Your ancestors have hunted our kind since the dawn of time. Once humans developed better weapons, we were forced into hiding and lived in dank holes, keeping our numbers low, until your people believed us to be a myth. We wanted to partake of your world, to visit your theater plays, your museums and libraries, but we had to do it in secret and at a great risk."

"So now you force us into hiding instead?" Myra said. "This is ridiculous. Humans of the past hunted your kind because you were killing people. What did you expect them to do?"

"Nothing else," he said. "Your people fought, and we fought back. We won. This does not make us evil. It makes us stronger and smarter. It makes us better." He left his notebook on the desk and turned to the door. "I have to leave you now. Tomorrow I expect the first chapter of your story. No outline this time—I want to see your actual writing."

"Why?" Myra said.

"I told you already. I need to know if you are suitable for the task."

"And what do I get in return? And don't tell me you'll keep me alive—that doesn't count. You asked something of me. I'll ask for something back."

He raised an eyebrow. "You are forgetting your place. I would hate to give you a reminder."

Myra froze, her heart beating wildly, and with an effort she held his gaze. "My place? And where is that exactly? What am I? Your prisoner? Your dinner? You plaything? Your servant?"

"You are my potential means to an end," he said. "But you said you wanted something. What would you like? Clothes? Food? Books? Games?"

A stake, Myra thought. *Freedom and safety for all humans. Information on the WeatherWizard. Your head on a spike.* "I saw a human in the dungeons," she said instead. "I want to know the truth. Who is he? Where did you capture him? What did you do to him? Are there any others where he came from?"

"These are far too many questions in exchange for a simple chapter," he said. "Thankfully, they all have the same answer. You do not want to know."

"I do," Myra said. "I was unaware there were other surviving humans. I need to know who he is."

"You neither *need* nor *want* to know that," said the Prince. "Though I am inclined to grant your request, if only to teach you to be careful what you wish for. Very well. Next time we meet, I will show you something. And once you see it, you will learn all you wished to know about that man, and a lot you never did."

***

Myra sat on the bed, staring at the notebook in her hands. It was opened to the page where he had drawn the center-and-periphery circle, and she had made a few more marks and notes around the diagram.

Maryabella's house could be here. And here could be the woods where she encounters trolls for the first time. She would have never seen such creatures before and would have no idea how to fight them.

Alerie, Myra corrected herself. *Maryabella is called Alerie now.* Why had she picked that name? Now working on her book would always bring pain.

Myra reached out for the pen. She could start by describing her character's domestic life before it turned upside down. As she scribbled the words down the page, a small smile appeared on her lips and slowly grew into a full grin. It felt so good to write.

Once she had written two pages, Myra paused and read them, making a few corrections. The story was shaping up better than ever. *Thea would love it. I can't wait to show it to her.*

She pressed her lips together and put the notebook down. In all likelihood, she would never see Thea again, and her cousin would never get the chance to read her story.

Someone knocked on the door, and Myra stood up, expecting the Prince. She frowned when Armida stepped in. "Lady Armida," Myra said. "To what do I owe the honor?"

The vampire swished her long blue skirts and sat on the bed. "No need to be so formal, sweetling. I merely wished to know how you are faring, and to reassure you if you are afraid. The Prince sees potential in you. If he believes you can give him what he seeks, he will keep you alive for a very long time."

Myra took a step back. Armida had been kind to her from the very beginning, but that was more frightening than open threats. "You said the Prince seeks humanity," Myra said. "But what about *you*? What do you want?"

Armida smiled. "I just want my beloved to be happy. If you can give him what he desires, it will make me happy too."

Did Armida love the Prince after all? "Can vampires love one another?" Myra asked.

"Of course. Does that surprise you?"

Myra nodded. "It's just something so human. I thought you lost your humanity once you were turned."

"We do lose a lot," Armida said. "But not this. A vampire can love as strongly as a human, perhaps even more so."

"How would you even know that?"

"I was a human once, you know."

Myra sat on the bed and clasped her hands together. Of course. It made sense Armida had been a human once. Vampires did not simply spring from holes in the ground. Each one of them must have been a human at some point, even if Myra sometimes forgot it. The Prince himself must have been human once. She shuddered at the thought.

Armida smiled. "You seem confused. I was indeed a human girl, long ago. And I can tell you that I had never loved anyone more than I love the Prince—neither my parents, nor my baby brother—no one."

Myra considered this. After all, vampires were sentient creatures—it stood to reason that they would have loved ones. And yet, the Resistance captured and tortured them, and then butchered them like animals. Did Rim have someone waiting for her in the Palace, someone who would mourn her death? And what about the prisoner she had killed herself, the one whose name she had never bothered to learn?

She pushed the thought aside. This was ridiculous. The vampires had destroyed her people. They had killed her family.

She had watched them eat Alerie as if she was nothing more than a steak. "Why did you come here, Lady Armida?" she said. "I'm sick of riddles."

Armida smiled sadly and stood up from the bed. To Myra's shock, the vampire knelt down in front of her and held her hands in her own. "Oh, sweet girl. You think I am here to play games with you?"

Armida's large jade eyes shone brightly on her pale face, and her dark red hair fell around her bare shoulders in soft waves. She looked so angelic, so good and kind and compassionate, and Myra wanted to trust her, to have an ally, a friend in this place so far away from everyone she cared about. But she knew she could not. She still remembered her own scream as the vamps drank Alerie like a butchered pig. She still remembered the Prince's cold breath against her neck, his teeth grazing her skin as he prepared to drink her. The vamps were all tricksters and manipulators, set out to mess with her mind for whatever end.

"Why are you here?" Myra said, keeping her voice cold and level.

The vampire rose from her kneeling position and offered Myra her hand. "I want to show you something. Come."

Myra knew that resistance was useless, and besides, whatever Armida wanted to show her could hopefully answer some questions. With a resigned sigh she stood up and followed.

Once they left her room, the guards stationed at the front turned around and followed them. Myra tried to ignore them. She wished to talk to Armida, to ask her more questions, but all the other vamps were within earshot, and they made her uncomfortable.

"What do you want me to see?" she asked.

"My love told me of your conversation today. You seem to think vampires are pure evil, while humans are pure good. I wished to give you some food for thought."

Myra had had plenty of food for thought ever since her arrival. "I never said humans were pure good," she said. "And why do my opinions matter anyway? I'm a prisoner. The Prince gives me orders and I obey. Who cares what I think of you?"

"Whatever you think of us, your black-and-white perspective is very limiting," Armida said. "If you expand your horizons, you will be better suited to give my love what he seeks."

Myra threw a glance back at the guards following a few steps behind. "Why am I the one who can give him what he seeks? Why can't you do it?"

Armida froze in her tracks, suddenly paler than usual. Her red lips pressed tightly together and her eyes focused on something far away. She turned around, raising a palm at the guards. They stopped instantly, and Armida walked on.

Myra followed, trying to steal a look at the vampire's face. "Did I say something wrong?"

The vampire was silent, focused on the path ahead. Once the guards were far behind, she turned to face Myra, her warm green eyes shining.

"I never could," Armida said. "Not even when I was human. I have never been what he needed, what he was looking for. He is always surrounding himself with objects of art and people who appreciate it. Even Tristan used to be a poet before the Prince turned him."

Myra frowned, confused. "Used to be? He doesn't write anymore?"

Armida quirked an eyebrow. "You can be very slow sometimes." She sighed. "My love told me he was first drawn to me because of my name. It was from a poem he liked, he said. To tell you the truth, my parents could not have named me after the character. I doubt they had ever heard of the poem. You see, they were illiterate. I myself only learned to read and write when I was fifteen."

Fifteen? So how had Armida spent the first fifteen years of her life? What had she done? Myra had been able to read and write for as long as she could remember. It was the one thing that gave meaning to her gloomy life. She did not wish to imagine a lifetime without it.

"Why are you telling me this?"

Armida stopped in front of a door and opened it. "To help you understand that we were also human once. And that we also have weaknesses. I know next to nothing about writing, but even I think that creating beings of pure darkness will not make your story very strong."

Why was everyone so intent on helping her create a better story? Myra took in a deep breath and stepped inside.

The candle in Armida's hand illuminated the small room. Large cupboards stood against the wall, and dusty sculptures and framed paintings were stacked on the floor. Myra looked at the vampire. "What is this place?"

"Here we keep all precious objects that are not currently on display in the halls or the library. Hold this," Armida said and handed her the candle. The vampire walked to a stack of paintings and started lifting them and looking at them one by one.

"I think what I am looking for must be larger," she murmured. "Ah. That must be it."

Armida walked to the far end of the room, where a large rectangular object stood against the wall, covered in linen. The vampire pulled the cloth away, revealing a dark painting beneath. "Come closer," she said. "Take a look."

Myra stepped closer and raised her candle to illuminate the painting. She gasped and took a step backwards.

A magnificent white horse with a shining silvery mane and tail had bolted in fear. A large tiger bit at the rider's neck, trying to drag him off the horse, its front legs clawing at the man's head and neck and its hind legs searching for a foothold on the horse's back. Two men in black armor had raised their swords, charging at the tiger from behind. Below them a tigress was struggling desperately, with a cub in her mouth, and two more baby tigers were jumping pitifully at her feet. A leopard lay on the ground, slain, spears sticking from its bloodied hide. In the lower left corner two men were wrestling a lion, prying its jaws open with their bare hands.

"What is this?" Myra asked.

"*The Tiger Hunt* by Paul Rubens."

They had a few books on art history in the Resistance's library, and Myra had read each of them at least ten times. She gasped, her eyes widened, and her heart beat faster. "You have an original Rubens? And you're keeping it hidden?" This could not be happening. Rubens had painted this himself. He had held this canvas and painted these shapes with his own brush. Myra had never hoped to be so close to a piece of history. A sudden desire to jump up and down overwhelmed her, and a mad grin spread across her lips.

The vampire smiled. "We are not keeping it hidden. We have so many impressive paintings that we cannot have them all on display at the same time, so we rotate them. Step closer, Myra. Look at the painting. Feel it. Who is the enemy here? Who is the hero? What is the mood?"

"We have Man versus Nature," Myra said. "This tiger is biting one of the riders, and it is horrific, but then these two hunters are charging from behind and will kill it. Humans are stronger than nature and will defeat it. The mood is triumphant. There is loss, but there is also victory."

"And how do the poor tigers feel, with the humans coming with their swords and spears, slaughtering them and their young ones?" Armida asked. "Come here. I want to show you something else."

The vampire opened a cupboard and Myra stepped forward to look inside. She gasped and reached out to touch the statue. The figure was almost half of life size, made of painted wood. A man with a black hat and a red coat lay prostrate on the ground, a large tiger pinning him down, biting at his throat. Armida pressed on a handle at the back, and to Myra's horror, the man's mouth opened, emitting a pitiful, wailing sound. The vampire pressed on something else, and the man's arm started flapping back and forth, the wailing rising in pitch.

"We see a tiger killing a man," Armida said. "What is the mood of this work?"

"Triumphant," Myra said, surprised. "Victorious. It celebrates the man's death."

The vampire nodded. "We saw one work of art, in which a tiger bites a man and it looks horrific. The action needs to be avenged, and it is, by the men attacking the tiger from behind.

The picture clearly shows the hunters will triumph, and we are supposed to celebrate that. Here, we see the opposite. The human is violently killed and humiliated, and we are expected to cheer it on."

A shiver ran down Myra's spine. "Who would produce something like that?"

"This is Tipu's Tiger," Armida said. "It was created in the late eighteenth century for the Tipu Sultan, ruler of the Kingdom of Mysore. The tiger was his personal sigil, and he commissioned this work because of his hatred towards the British of the East India Company."

The vampire pressed the switch again and the horrific wailing stopped. "You see, Myra, when the British arrived in Asia, they saw themselves as heroes. Explorers and conquerors, discovering new lands and claiming them as their own. Stealing the treasures and bringing them back home. Acting as if they were the masters and the lands belonged to them. Needless to say, the local rulers saw things differently."

Was Armida trying to tell her the same applied to the Nightfall? That there were always two sides to each story, and she had heard only one? That was ridiculous. Vampires were not humans with a different point of view. They were unnatural, bloodsucking beasts. "Why are you showing me this?"

"I only ask that you keep what I showed you in mind when you think about us, and when you create your characters. Without considering different perspectives, you can never be a good author. And you need to be a good author to give the Prince what he seeks."

"What *does* he seek?" Myra said. "How can I give him anything if I don't know what he expects of me?"

Armida closed the cupboard, hiding the tiger figure behind the wooden doors. She turned to Myra to give her a small, tired smile. The candle flame danced, throwing a play of light and shadow on the vampire's sad and beautiful face. "He seeks one of the many things his enemies denied him when they tore his world apart," she said. "Closure."

Chapter Thirteen

Humanity

Myra paced around her room, occasionally stealing glances at the door, waiting for it to open. Yet, it remained closed and silent, and she continued in her lonely march. *If no one comes here soon, I might make a hole in the floor.* She smiled. Now that would be an unusual way to escape.

Did anything the Prince and Armida had said make any sense? It seemed true enough that vampires valued culture, beauty, and high tastes. They loved collecting books and paintings, and staging plays and operas. Perhaps before the Nightfall the vamps had been forced to hide in their dark caves and sewers, unable to experience the world as they wished. Perhaps they had simply wished to create a beautiful world for themselves, and they had certainly succeeded.

And yet, all this beauty could only exist because so many had died in horror and pain. And while she was here, enjoying what her captors had to offer, her friends back at the Resistance were struggling to survive with no food and medicines. Myra shuddered. The only reason she had watched an opera, the only reason she had seen an original Rubens, was that her people were on the verge of extinction.

She stole a glance at the table, laden with more bread, meat, fruits and vegetables than she could eat in a day. A few unopened wine bottles awaited her, and a selection of chocolates, marzipan and caramels stood there, tempting. What was Thea eating right now? Had her friends captured enough rats, or did they have to survive on stale biscuits and canned foods? Had they found any flour to bake real bread?

Myra remembered the piece of chocolate she had given Thea. So small, and yet Thea had insisted they share it. And now she had so much chocolate, more than she would ever want to eat, and all of it was paid for with the blood of Alerie and many others.

Next to the table lay her notebook, and Myra frowned when she saw it. Now, that was the most confusing of all. The Prince was teaching her to write, and she had noticed improvement even after a single brief lesson. Myra sighed. She had always wanted to become a better writer, but not like this.

The door opened, and Myra jumped and twirled around.

Prince Vladimir stepped in, giving her a small bow. "Forgive me. I knocked but heard no reply."

"I—I'm sorry. I was lost in thought."

"I see. How is your story coming along?"

"Very well. I should have the first chapter soon."

He walked to the table, uncorked a bottle and poured himself a goblet. "I am glad to hear it. I am looking forward to reading it."

And she was looking forward to him reading it and telling her what he thought, but she would never admit it to him. "Why have you come? Did you decide to answer my questions?"

He twirled his goblet before taking a slow sip. Myra's eyes darted to his dark hair. He was not wearing his golden circlet. It was the first time she had seen him without it and she wondered what it meant. The rest of his appearance was the usual—a wine-red silken shirt with a sleeveless black vest on top. Black leather trousers and a black cape, trailing behind him as he walked. Myra raised an eyebrow at the cape. *Seriously, did he dream of becoming a vampire when he was a little human boy?*

The Prince placed the goblet down. "I promised I would. I will tell you the truth about the human you saw."

Myra's breath caught in her throat. So it was true—other humans had survived. How large was their society? How had it developed? Did they value art, or were they focused on survival? "Is he still alive?"

"I am not sure which exact human you saw, but quite possibly he could still be alive."

Myra's head was spinning. *Which exact human?* There were more than one? "Will you take me to him?"

"I am uncertain if that is a good idea," he said. "Tristan advised me to wait, but Armida believed you were ready to know the truth. I think she is right—if you cannot handle it, you are clearly not the person I am looking for. If that is the case, it is best for me to know it and resume my search."

And what if she was not the person he was looking for? Would he kill her? Myra pressed her lips together. Whatever she saw, she had to convince him that she could handle it. "Show me."

He led her down the corridor, her guards trailing at a distance. They reached the western tower and Myra's stomach tightened when she recognized the spiral staircase leading to the dungeons. She did not wish to go back there. The darkness, the stench and the hunger were still with her every time she closed her eyes.

Myra took in a deep breath. "I am ready."

"Very good," he said. "I will wait here. I only go down there on special occasions, and this is not one of them. Your guards will take you there. Once you are ready, you will come back up, and we can talk about what you saw."

Yong and three of his people approached them, and the Prince nodded at them. "Show Myra what she desires to see."

Myra followed her guards down the stairs, her heart sinking deeper and deeper with every step. She had too many memories of this place, none of them good. She choked—the air was stuffier down here. Myra frowned, realizing with a start that it was still much fresher than the air at the Resistance. When had she grown so spoiled?

They passed by her cell, and she shuddered, momentarily afraid they would throw her back in. She did not release her breath until it was many steps behind.

After a while, they reached a large door and stepped on the other side. The air was fresher in this place, and the floor was cleaner. The corridor was still surrounded by cells with barred walls, so it was obviously still a prison. Myra walked forward until she froze, her legs heavy as lead.

She tried to take another step, but failed miserably. Yong grabbed her elbow and dragged her forward, and she watched all that was happening around her, shivering. Humans. Hundreds of them, inside the spacious cells, some as old as Dr. Dubois, others mere babes in their mothers' arms. So many humans lived still! So many had survived the Nightfall. And if so many of them were captives in the Palace, how many were still Outside, still free?

Some paid no attention to her, while others stared at her with vacant expressions. None of them appeared gaunt or sickly, or mistreated in any way. In fact, the cells were more luxurious than anything at the Resistance. Thick soft carpet covered the floor, and many tables were laden with food. The humans were well dressed, in clean and well-preserved clothes.

"Who are you?" Myra called at them. "Where do you come from? How long have you been captives?"

Yong pressed a hand against her mouth. "His Highness gave you no leave to speak to them," he hissed in her ear and then looked up to glare at the humans. "And neither did he give you leave to talk back to her." He dragged her back the way they had come. "If you have any questions, you can talk to His Highness."

Myra's mind reeled. Where had so many humans come from? Were they all a part of the same community? Had the Prince captured all of them, or were their friends and relatives still hiding out there? And if the Prince was looking for humanity, and he had so many humans, why had he taken such an interest in her? How was she different?

The guards led her back up to the Prince's study. He was sitting in one of the armchairs, waiting, and Myra required all her willpower to stop herself from blurting out all the questions on her mind. She waited until he had dismissed the guards, and she turned wide eyes at him.

He twirled his goblet and smiled knowingly. "You saw what you wished to see. Did it make you happy?"

"Where did all those humans come from?" she asked.

He gestured at her to take a seat, but she stood there, standing and staring at him. He took a sip from his goblet. "They live here."

"I saw that. But where did you capture them? How long ago?"

He raised a dark eyebrow at her. "Myra, I refuse to believe you can be so daft. You know exactly when I captured them even if you refuse to accept it. I captured them during the Nightfall."

"The Nightfall was fifty years ago. Many of those humans were clearly born much later."

"I fail to see how that contradicts what I said."

Myra's eyes widened. "They were born and raised in captivity!" She started pacing across the room. "You captured young humans and encouraged them to reproduce. They were always prisoners and never had a real life. You are breeding them like livestock!"

"Precisely," he said. "We provide them with food, clothes and medicines. They live well."

Myra felt tears prick at her eyes and blinked them away, her body shaking. "How can you do something like that? These are human beings, not some animals for you to raise and feed on."

He shrugged. "The domesticated humans are little more than animals."

She stared at him. "The *domesticated* humans? This is what you call them?"

"This is what they are."

Myra stepped away from him, shaking. "And so you raise them and kill them?"

"Unfortunately, we cannot afford to kill a human every time we feed," he said. "They do not reproduce and grow fast enough to sustain that. We aim not to kill, and we drink only as much as the human can handle. We provide them with plenty of iron supplements, B vitamins, red meats and green leafy vegetables to help them recover from the blood loss and prepare them for the next meal. We cannot always hold back, especially if the human tastes too good, so incidents do happen, but in general most domesticated humans survive the first bite and a few even live to an old age."

Myra stood frozen. How could he talk about these people so casually, so callously? She glared at him, her eyes burning. "Why would you do something like that? You can survive on animal blood. Why do you need to destroy people's lives?"

"And humans could survive on vegetables, and yet the majority chose not to. They chose to raise animals in farms for meat." He paused and took a long sip. "Yes, we find human blood tastier than animal, but there is more to it. Human blood gives us strength that nothing else could. What is your excuse? Meat was not necessarily healthier for you. In some cases it was the opposite."

"You can't honestly compare humans with animals. Humans are sentient. We have thoughts, and feelings, and aspirations."

"And animals do not? Do you know it for sure? Did you ever bother finding out? You never cared. You did not eat animals because they were not sentient. You ate them because you liked it and because you wanted to. I am not judging—the world belonged to you, and you had the right to do anything you pleased. All I ask is not to be judged in return."

Myra's fists clenched. How could this monster speak of humans as if they were mindless beasts? If she could, she would have staked him right on the spot, but she saw nothing that could serve as a weapon. She had to bide her time and strike when she was ready. But first, she needed to get out of here before she did anything stupid.

"I would like to go back to my room," she gritted through clenched teeth.

He smiled and waved his hand, dismissing her, and she wished nothing more than to wipe that smile off his face forever.

***

Myra paced back and forth at an almost jogging speed, but it did little to diminish her rage. The vamps were holding people captive from birth, raising them like animals, only to feast on their blood. This was even more monstrous than she had thought, and she had no intention of letting it go on for any longer than necessary. She had something the Prince desired, and once she figured out what it was, she would finally gain some leverage over him.

Myra sat on the bed, leaning her head against the wall. She opened her notebook and stared at it as if the blank page could give the answer to her questions.

Why? she wrote down and stared at the word. Why did the Prince want her works? And why did he need her to improve her writing skills? Obviously, he enjoyed reading, but he had so many books already.

And yet, he was immortal. He had millennia ahead of him—enough time to read every single book ever written. The *domesticated humans*, as the Prince had called them, were unlikely to produce any books. If the vampires wanted any new literature, they would have to create it themselves.

Unless… they could not. Myra gasped. She had often wondered what happened to a human's personality upon turning. She had questioned the Resistance's prisoners, but it had given her little insight. Her impression was that vampires were similar to the humans they were before, only vainer and more entitled, and with a distorted sense of justice and conscience. Vampires lost a part of their souls. They were no longer human.

And without humanity one cannot create art, Myra wrote down. A smile spread across her face. The Prince was desperate for new literature, desperate enough to let her live. If she refused to give it to him, he would need to find another way to get new books. And the only way was to restore human civilization.

It all made sense now—this explained why Armida had told her the Prince was looking for humanity, and why only she, a "wild human," could give him what he was looking for. And she was not planning to give him anything, unless she got something in return.

Myra flipped through her notebook, her eyes scanning the words. This was her best chapter so far, and she was so proud of it. She ran her hand over the paper, almost lovingly, caressing the beautiful words. Myra smiled sadly and flung the notebook into the fire.

The paper hissed and sizzled and Myra watched, transfixed, as her work disappeared into the nothingness. *You can't have it. I won't give you anything.*

A knock sounded, and the door flew open. Myra turned her back to the fire as Tristan stormed in. The vampire was wearing a light green tunic and white trousers, and his long silver-blond hair was perfectly coiffured and shining under the soft candlelight. His perma-frown, Myra noted in amusement, was as deep as ever.

"My lady," he said with a bow. "I am here to collect your latest work." He approached her desk and started rummaging through the various notebooks and piles of paper. After a while, he turned at her, waving a few sheets.

"What is this?"

She raised an eyebrow. "Perhaps paper was not invented back in the century when you were born? Then let me enlighten you. Paper is made of wood or substitutes and is used for writing, drawing—"

"I know what paper is," Tristan interrupted her, his steely eyes cold as ice. "Why is it empty? My lord was expecting a chapter."

"Yes, he was," Myra replied calmly. "I burned it."

The wide-eyed look on his face was worth whatever punishment Myra would suffer for her insolence. "You did what?"

"The Prince wanted me to write," she said. "And I figured out why."

"Good for you. I fail to see how this excuses you from following orders."

"You didn't simply conquer the human world," she continued unperturbed. "You *destroyed* it. You are not only unable to create anything new; you could not even maintain what already existed. You destroyed the entire infrastructure of this planet, and now you have no electricity, no running water, no efficient means of long-distance transport. You are lucky that the WeatherWizard can work without maintenance."

She stood up from the bed, walked to him, and pulled the papers from his hands, her eyes never leaving his. "Your so-called Prince is ruling now, but he is ruling over the ashes of the world that once was. Of course, inconvenient as this is, you can live with it. After all, you require fewer comforts than we do. But there is one thing you didn't take into account."

"That we have failed to eliminate all humans, and now we are doomed to listen to their stupidity?" Tristan guessed.

"That there is one single resource that you can't produce and you cannot live without," Myra said. "Art. You still appreciate literature and music, but you can neither write a new book nor compose a new melody. I am sure many of you can survive without reading. And yet, I know that for some of you, your immortal existence will lose all meaning if there are no new books to read."

Tristan's grey eyes were so cold they could freeze the fires of Hell. "You know nothing, human."

"I know enough, *vampire*. I have seen enough to know that your Prince is one of those who can't survive without reading. I won't play his game. If he wants new literature, there is a simple way to get it—destroy the WeatherWizard, release the humans he is keeping prisoners, and give this world back to humanity. You can go back to Vlad and tell him that."

In a heartbeat Tristan's eyes had turned from frozen ice into raging fire. He took a step forward, grabbed the front of her shirt, and lifted her up in the air. "He is 'His Highness' to you," he hissed in her face.

Myra's heart was in her throat, but with an effort she managed to suppress her terror and maintain her composure. "Styling yourself as a Prince doesn't make you one. Fifty years ago he was just another vampire."

Tristan released her and walked to the door. He took a step outside, but before leaving, he turned back, his intense eyes boring into hers. When he spoke, his voice was barely above a whisper, and yet she could clearly hear every single word. "I have known my lord since long before the Nightfall. I have spent centuries by his side. And I can tell you one thing—he was *never* 'just another vampire.'"

Myra sighed when he left. That had been stupid. Obviously, the Prince was not going to destroy the WeatherWizard, and taunting his puppy dog had not been her best idea. She sat back on the bed and took one of the crumpled empty sheets of paper from the desk.

Final goal: Destroy the Wizard and kill the Prince, she thought, but did not dare write it down. But how? Myra started mindlessly drawing sketches, trying to focus her thoughts, but her mind came up blank. She put the paper down.

Preliminary goal: Survive long enough to come up with a plan. Now, this sounded more manageable. Indeed, Myra had an idea how to achieve this. There was a trick she knew—a trick as old as time. However, the story of Maryabella-Alerie's adventures would not do the job—the Prince had already shown his lack of interest. If she wished to succeed, she needed something new, something better. Myra smiled, picked up the discarded sheet of paper, and began jotting down story ideas.

Chapter Fourteen

Justice of the Beast

Myra was almost ready with her story plan when the door opened and four vampires appeared. She suppressed a sigh—when would the Prince learn that sending four guards to fetch her was a waste of resources?

"We are here to take you to His Highness," one of the vamps declared, and Myra followed.

They stepped into a spacious hall and Myra gasped. The place was monumental, the floor covered in white and blue marble tiles, with the Prince's sun-and-sky banners hanging from the high ceiling. A narrow red carpet led from the door, up to the dais and to the imposing throne made of black stone. But what made Myra stop in her tracks was the altar rising next to the high throne.

On top was the body of an indistinguishable animal, which could have been a dog or a cat. The Prince stood there, a bloodied dagger in his hand, staring transfixed at the animal's blood that flowed in small rivulets through the specially made little chutes carved into the stone and onto the floor.

"Welcome to the Great Hall," the Prince said, not taking his eyes off the blood. "I have good news for you. Even after your little scene, my god says that keeping you alive will give me what I seek."

That took her aback. "Vampires worship no gods," she said.

He looked at her, smiling sadly. "Well, I do." He left his dagger on the altar and approached her, motioning to the guards to step aside. "Tristan tells me you want me to destroy the WeatherWizard and give the world back to humans."

He did not sound angry, but Myra was unsure if that was a good sign. She knew it was probably pointless, but she could not help taking a chance. "If you want to keep literature and art alive, this is the only way," she said, forcing herself to meet his eyes. "You have to return the world to us, take your vamps with you, and crawl back to the crypts and sewers from whence you came."

"From whence we came," the vampire echoed, as if testing how the words rolled off his tongue. "Interesting vocabulary you have. What kinds of books have you been reading? To be honest, I am surprised the Resistance has access to any books at all."

"We have assembled a very good library," Myra said proudly, and the vampire laughed.

"Library? You have no idea what a real library is, darling girl, and if you are cooperative, I may decide to show you one." His eyes hardened. "But from what I hear, you refuse to cooperate. Burning your writing, really? Do you know, historically, what kind of people burned books? I must advise you to tread carefully. If you dislike carrots, I have plenty of sticks."

"I fear you have been misinformed, Vlad," she said calmly. "I will do as you ask. I will tell you a story. A story you've never heard before, for I only thought of it today."

The Prince raised a dark eyebrow. "Vlad? Ah yes, Tristan told me about *that* too. We need to teach you how to properly address your betters, but I suppose that can wait. Let us hear the story."

He walked up the dais, swung his black cape to the side, and sat on the throne, nodding at her to go on. Myra took a deep breath, suddenly self-conscious. With a last glance at the sacrificed animal that had apparently served to give a prophecy in her favor, she started.

"Lily rode her horse along the path. She was on her way to visit—"

"Wait, stop right here," the Prince said. "You are barely on the second sentence, and you are already on the verge of losing my attention."

"Excuse me?" Myra said, feeling strangely hurt. Her writing was good—everyone who had read her stories had said so. And the Prince had not even heard the story; what right did he have to judge?

"I appreciate that you are trying to throw me straight into the action, without a lengthy exposition," Vlad said. "In general, this is not a bad technique. However, I know nothing about this Lily, and I could not care less if she is riding her horse, or swimming in the lake, or brushing her teeth. You need to give me more information. So far, I only know her name and that she has a horse. The name does not tell us where she is from, and the horse does not tell us the setting—could be in the distant past when horses were commonplace, or after the

Nightfall when cars were rare, or in the recent past and she is riding for sport."

"Actually, it's set in a fantasy universe," Myra said, "not that it matters much."

"I see," said Vlad. "First of all, it matters. It always matters. Second, why is it so that every time a human comes up with a fantasy universe, they populate it with horses? Fantasy universe means something that is not our earth, or an alternative history of our world, or practically anything you can come up with. Fantasy does not need to mean horses and castles. Lily may as well be riding a bike."

"Horses look nicer," Myra argued, realizing her reasoning was not especially convincing.

He smiled. "A horse it is. Describe it. What kind is it?"

"Do you think I'm familiar with different horse breeds?" said Myra, annoyed. "I have spent my entire life hiding away from the world."

"Give me as much information as you can," he said patiently.

"A black mare," she said.

He nodded. "How about this? 'Lily urged her steed forward, along the steep mountain path. The black mare whinnied and shook her head. It was as if the horse knew as well as she did how bad this idea was. The Shadowy Mountains were perilous to cross at this time of year.' See? This creates a better visual, and we learn that she is in a hurry to reach her destination since she is urging the horse. Also, as there has never been a place called the Shadowy Mountains anywhere in the world, we also learn that this is set in an alternate reality. And we also get foreshadowing that something horrible is going to happen."

"I thought you couldn't write," Myra commented with a frown.

"I cannot create anything new," he admitted. "I can build on what already exists, but first I need something to work with."

"Why did you decide that something horrible is going to happen?" she asked.

The Prince smirked. "My dear girl. All humans are the same—they can rarely create a compelling story without something bad happening, and so they always pick disasters to build their tales on. I assumed you would do the same. Was I wrong?"

"No," she admitted. "Alright, then, should I continue?"

"Please," he said.

"Lily was on her way to meet Eduardo, her beloved."

"Are you reading the news report?" the Prince asked. "You sound like a machine."

Myra's heart skipped a beat. "What do you mean?" This was a disaster. Vlad had not liked a single word so far. If her story failed to hook him, her plan would fall to pieces.

"We are seeing the story from Lily's perspective," said the Prince. "She does not go around thinking 'I am going to see Eduardo, my beloved.' It should be more like 'She rode on as fast as she dared. Only three more days and she would see Eduardo. She had missed him these past three months—she had missed his smile, his strong, yet gentle hands, his warm and caring voice. One more day away from him would be too long.' Of course, you can replace the three months by years, decades, centuries, or whatever suits your story."

"Centuries?" she said.

"You never said she was human. You are working with a fantasy universe. She could be any kind of creature."

"Yes, she can be, and I decide she's human," Myra said impatiently. "Do you wish me to continue?"

The Prince smiled. "Forgive me. You are right, of course, this is your story, not mine. Please, go on."

This time the vampire behaved and allowed her to describe the journey without interruptions. Unfortunately, this only lasted until Myra reached the point when Lily was attacked by bandits.

"Bandits, really?" Vlad asked. "You story is set in a made-up world. You are not confined in your choice of baddies. They could be anything—goblins, werewolves, flying killer monkeys—"

"Vampires," Myra said. "Lily was attacked by a pack of vampires."

The Prince chuckled. "Alright, then. I will overlook the fact that vampires do not hunt in 'packs,' and that a single one could have overpowered any human in seconds. Let us say that in your world vampires work differently."

Myra suppressed her annoyance and continued the story. She told him how Lily tried to fight off her attackers but was outmatched and badly hurt. But then she was saved. A brave man had come from the mountains, armed with a sword and a torch. It was Eduardo. He took her to a shelter to take care of her wounds, and she was surprised that he was there, in the middle of nowhere, instead of back in his mother's palace. He explained that he had been keeping watch, over the path and over her.

Vlad interrupted her only a few times when Myra revealed the other source of Lily's surprise—Eduardo was wearing a scarf, and she had never seen him wear one before. Later in the night, Lily tugged at the cloth to reveal a deep scar across her beloved's neck, but he refused to talk about how he had received the wound. But Lily's confusion turned to worry when Eduardo announced that once she recovered, she had to continue her journey to his mother's palace alone, while he would stay here to watch the path.

"This made no sense, Lily thought as she lay in the makeshift bed, trying to fall asleep," Myra continued in a soft voice. "Eduardo had seemed happy to see her, and yet a strange sadness lingered around him like a cloud she could not see through. And what was this nonsense about staying here? Was there more trouble with the mountain vampires than what he was willing to tell her? It made no difference. She would not leave him here alone. Once she got better, she would drag him back to the palace if that was what it took. With that encouraging thought, Lily went to sleep."

"And then?" the Prince prompted when her pause lasted longer than usual.

"This is it for now," Myra said. "I'm tired. I will continue with this story tomorrow."

The Prince narrowed his eyes. "I want to hear the end now."

She met his gaze unflinchingly. "And I said I will finish tomorrow."

There was nothing friendly in the smile he gave her. "What are you doing, girl? Do you think you can pull a Scheherazade on me? You must know by now that I am too genre savvy to fall for that. Besides, your story is far from being the most fascinating piece I have heard."

"It may not be that good, but it's the only new literature you'll ever be able to get." Myra held his gaze. "And yes, you caught me. You know what my plan is. And what of it? You can't kill me, or you'll never hear the end of the story."

"Oh, I *can* kill you, never doubt that," the Prince said. "But it is true that I would prefer not to. Make no mistake—I can make you tell me the rest of the story, right now. And I will not do it by promising libraries, or food, or any other kind of gifts. I am done with the carrots. If you choose to disobey me, I will use a stick."

"We have already established you're not going to kill me," Myra said. "I'm curious to see that fabled stick of yours."

The vampire's gaze darkened. "This was the wrong thing to say, little girl," he said and motioned to one of the guards to come closer. The Prince whispered something in the other vampire's ear, and the guard swiftly left.

Myra followed him with her eyes. "Where did he go?"

"You will know soon enough," Vlad said with finality in his voice that deterred her from questioning him any further.

And indeed, no more than fifteen minutes had passed when the vampire returned, leading a scared-looking boy, no older than ten. The guard pushed the boy forward and handed him to his Prince.

Vlad stood up from his throne and placed his hands on the child's small shoulders. "Tell me the rest of the story," he said. "Or I will kill him."

Myra's heart stopped beating. "You wouldn't."

The Prince smiled, but there was no humor in his eyes. "Would you like to test that claim? We have plenty of children in the Farm. If you do not believe me before I have killed this one, maybe you will change your mind after the second, or the third."

Myra froze, a heavy lump forming in her throat. She had no doubt that the vampire had no trouble killing the boy, and he seemed intent on killing until she obeyed. And she would be damned if she let this child die to satisfy her pride.

"Fine," she said. "I'll tell you the rest of the story."

"I am listening," the Prince said and raised an eyebrow when she hesitated. "You have no idea what happens next, do you?"

"I know the ending, but not the details of how to get there," she admitted. "I was planning to come up with the second part tonight. I often make up stories on the spot, sometimes not knowing where they are going."

"Well, then, I would advise you to come up with what happens next right now and share it with us."

Myra ran a hand through her hair and continued, sometimes making pauses to give herself time to design the next sentence. She told him how Lily woke up the following morning, only to realize that Eduardo was not there. She looked for him everywhere, but there was no trace of anyone coming or going. She waited for him for another day, before she reluctantly decided to head for the palace.

"Oh no," the Prince groaned. "Please do not tell me she is going to reach the palace and learn from Eduardo's mother that he has been dead for some time? He was probably beheaded, which would explain the scar."

Myra's eyes widened. "How did you know?"

He sighed. "This trope is so overused. You humans are always predictable."

"How can it be overused?" Myra asked, disappointed. She had genuinely believed that the story was original and the

Prince would like it. "I've never read this scenario in another story."

"You did not have to. You humans think alike. You come up with the same ideas over and over again even if you have never seen them before. And it makes sense—there are a finite number of stories that can be told and at some point, they start to repeat. It can be expected, but is still disappointing." He smiled. "Don't be sad, Myra. Your prose needs refinement, but your style improved after my tips, so you are learning fast. And you have the necessary imagination. Your story was entertaining enough," the Prince said before he sank his teeth into the boy's neck.

"No, wait! What are you doing, are you mad?" Myra screamed, taking a step forward before the guards restrained her. "Stop it! You're killing him, stop it! I told you the story, what more do you want? Vlad, stop this! Your Highness, my lord, please, please stop! I will tell you another story, I will write down stories and poems for you to read. Stop this, please!"

He ignored her and continued drinking calmly until the boy's cries of pain and fear had died down, and his face had gone pale as a sheet. Vladimir's own face grew pale and translucent, and Myra could see light blue veins running underneath his skin, pulsing with life. The vampire's eyes were closed as he drank, and when he opened them, they were bright yellow and glowing like burning coals.

Hot tears rolled down Myra's cheeks as she watched the small body slide listlessly to the floor, his eyes unseeing. And then it was not the boy's pale and drained face anymore. It was Alerie staring back at her, her brown eyes wide and glazed over.

Alerie had died because of her. This boy, whose name she would never learn, had died because of her. How many more would die as she kept failing?

"Why did you do that?" she sobbed, turning furious eyes at the Prince. "Monster. You are all monsters."

The Prince looked up, casually licking a few drops of left-over blood from the corner of his mouth. "Monsters, are we? And what makes us monsters? Yes, we have a human farm and breed humans for food, just like you used to have pig farms. And yes, we chase down and kill the few of you who are still running free, just like you humans hunt prey. We are no monsters. We are just a superior species, and that puts us at the top of the food chain."

"You are not a superior species," Myra said, glaring at him. "You are not even a different species. You are unnatural. You are human yourself, only… dead."

"I believe 'undead' is the word you are looking for. And this changes nothing. We need to feed, we are strong, and we take what we want, just like you used to do. It was fun for you, humans, when you ruled the world, but this time is past. It is our turn now."

Myra fisted her hands, her body trembling in barely suppressed rage. "A vampire killed my parents. Are you telling me they were only prey to him?"

The Prince smiled, but his eyes were sad. "And now you hate us all? A man killed my own parents. And my wife. And my children. And my aunts and uncles, and cousins, and their wives and husbands, and their parents, and their children. I barely escaped and was turned shortly after. Now tell me, little girl, should I hate all men just like you hate all of us?"

"Your argument falls apart on so many levels that I am not sure where to begin," Myra said. "One vampire killed my parents, and yes, I hated him, until I drove a stake through his heart. But this isn't why I hate you all. You are all killers. Each one of you has killed men, women and children, and will kill many more. And yes, there are evil men. And yes, men have performed unspeakable atrocities. But your wife and children were human, weren't they? There are humans who do nothing but good, who live and love and create beauty and happiness. It's unfair to hate us all for the deeds of a few."

"And what a fine world you humans have created," the Prince said.

Myra threw him a confused look. "I thought you enjoyed our world. The art, the music, the literature…"

"The art was good, yes," he said. "In fact most of your world was good, and I admit that I miss it." He paused and gazed through the high window, at the cloud-covered sky. "Do you know what happened to the man who killed my family?" he asked, so softly that she could barely hear him.

She assumed it was a rhetorical question and waited for him to continue. "No," she said at last, when it became clear that the Prince would not go on until she had spoken.

"Take a guess," he prompted.

Normally Myra would have expected the killer to receive retribution, be it dungeons, execution, or whatever the practice had been at the time and place where the Prince had spent his human life. Yet, looking at the fire in the vampire's eyes, she knew this was not the case. "He got away with it?" she guessed.

He laughed then, and it was the bitterest sound she had ever heard. "Got away with it? That is a mild way to put it. Why don't you try, 'Historians call him one of the greatest persons in history'? Why don't you try, 'He was canonized as a saint'? Then you might get closer to the truth."

Myra stared wide-eyed at him. She had read whatever history books they had at the Resistance, but she had no idea what he was talking about. "How—"

"This was the justice of the Old World," the Prince continued. "But it is gone now. Now I rule the world, and I decide who deserves what."

"And this boy deserved to die?" she asked incredulously.

It all happened so fast her eyes could not follow. In a heartbeat the vampire was standing right in front of her, his hand grabbing her throat and pulling her closer. "Now listen to me, and listen well," he said calmly. "I do not hate humans. I *feed* on them. Do you hate the chickens you butcher for meat? The boy died to teach you a lesson. You have forgotten your place. You are not my friend, and you are not my enemy. To me, you are food. You belong on my plate. You think these tales you can spin give you power? I can crush you at any time, and I can crush all you hold dear. From now on, you will show respect. You will call me 'Your Highness' and you will do as you are told. Now the guards will take you back to your room. Tomorrow you will have a new story for me, with a beginning and an end, and no smart comments. Understood?"

Myra desperately tried to get some air into her lungs through her smashed airways. Her heart hammered wildly, threatening to break out. Pride and sense battled in her mind, as she struggled to reply.

She would not bow to this monster and do his bidding. She had some dignity after all, and if she were to die, she would do it with rebellion in her eyes and defiance in her words.

And yet, the rational part of her kept telling her that this would achieve nothing. What was her final goal? To return to Thea and her friends, to bring down the Prince, to destroy the WeatherWizard, to give this world back to humanity. Would dying help her achieve any of this? What was her pride compared to her final goal?

No. If she was meek and obedient and able to gain his trust, she would live, and perhaps one day she would get the chance to escape. And then maybe, just maybe, she would get the opportunity to complete her mission and drive a stake right into the Prince's unbeating heart.

"Forgive me, Your Highness," she wheezed, and Vladimir relaxed his hold. "You are right. I have forgotten my place. I am your prisoner, and it is your right to kill me. Instead, you have shown me nothing but kindness, and I have repaid you with disrespect. I give you my word that I shall not disappoint you again."

The Prince put her back on the ground and raised an eyebrow. "No need to overdo it, it breaks my suspension of disbelief. Niko, Edric, take her to her room, please. And you." He stared at Myra. "I will come to you tomorrow to hear your new story, and I will wait for the day when you speak those same words, and they are sincere."

Never! Myra wanted to scream, but swallowed her angry words. She had read many books and articles about the Old World, on history, society, and psychology. She was aware of cases when hostages learned to care for their captors and sympathize with their causes. If Vlad believed she would develop something of the sort and grow to enjoy her time here, he was dead wrong. He had said he was too genre savvy to fall for her tricks. Well, so was she. He wanted her to play his game. Why was he so certain she would not play *him* instead?

"I'll be looking forward to your visit, Your Highness," she said, trying to suppress the challenge in her eyes.

"Oh, I am sure you will." The Prince grinned at her, and for some reason she found that smile more unsettling than any possible threat.

Chapter Fifteen

Golden Cage

Myra closed the leather-bound notebook. Finally, the new story was ready. Now all she could do was wait and hope it would be enough to convince the Prince to keep her alive.

Writing could perhaps buy her time, but time for what? She could not idly wait for an opportunity to come her way. She had to start looking for ways to destroy the Prince and get out of this place.

First, she needed weapons. Her eyes wandered across the room, lingering on her wooden writing desk. There was no way she could break off a piece of that without anyone noticing. Her gaze moved to the fireplace. The Prince sent servants to maintain the fire and bring the larger logs. He had given her only paper and small twigs to keep it going, and none of them were sturdy enough to work as a stake. Perhaps she could take one of the logs out of the fire and see if the wood in the middle was intact. Perhaps there was a way to break off a part. But could she do that without anyone noticing? Vampires kept coming and going through her room without warning. What if someone walked in on her?

She knelt down to examine the bed's legs. They were wooden and long enough, but how could she break one off without anyone noticing? She lowered herself on her hands and knees and stuck her head underneath the bed. There. The leg at the far corner was invisible unless you looked under the bed. Perhaps she could find something to replace it and break it off. She stood up and brushed off the dust from her hands and knees. Vlad had given her many notebooks. She could stack a few on top of each other and place them underneath the bed to support it, allowing her to remove the leg. But how could she break the wood? She needed something sharp and sturdy to use as a saw, but she had nothing of the sort.

Myra sat back on the chair and opened a blank notebook. She stared at the page, her brow furrowed. There was no way to pull this off without allies. She had to find some discord among the vamps and use it to her advantage. Myra started writing down names around the sheet's edges—Vlad, Armida, Tristan, Yong, Natalia. What did she know about each of them and their relationships? Were there any conflicts she could exploit?

Natalia served under Yong, and seemed to obey him without question. How much of that was just for show, Myra had no way of knowing. She had not seen her interact with any of the other vamps. Myra crossed out the name.

Yong. Now, here was something. He seemed to get along with Armida, but despised Tristan. Also, he disagreed with the Prince's policy of keeping wild humans alive and had been planning to disobey him and torture Myra and Alerie in secret. Myra drew a straight line between Yong and Armida and jagged lines towards Vlad and Tristan.

Vlad and Armida. Armida claimed to love him, but did he love her in return? Armida had expressed some insecurity, lamenting her inability to give him what he needed. Myra drew a straight arrow from Armida to Vlad, and a dotted arrow with a question mark from him to her. Perhaps there was something useful here.

Vlad and Tristan. Yong had implied that Vlad would punish anyone speaking against Tristan. But even if the Prince cared about Tristan, did it work both ways? The guards called Tristan 'the Prince's puppy dog,' and he had sounded outraged when Myra had spoken disrespectfully of his master. Still, Armida had said that Tristan had been a poet, and Vlad had turned him, taking this ability away from him. Tristan had to be angry. Myra's ability to write was one of the things she valued the most, and she would have killed anyone dreaming to take that away from her. She drew a straight arrow from Vlad to Tristan, and a dotted one the other way. But even if there was any discord here, would it be enough to make Tristan stand against the Prince?

Armida and Tristan. Now, this one was tricky. Myra had seen them together only in the prison and at the opera, and they had been amiable enough. Armida had spoken dismissively of him with the guards, but that could have been to earn Yong's sympathy. Myra drew one big question mark. She had not yet seen enough to decide if there was anything to be exploited here.

The door opened without a knock and Myra turned around in her chair, stuffing the paper into her pocket. She forced herself to smile when Tristan and a female vampire walked in. Myra had never seen the female vampire before. She was tall, with a yellow ribbon around her dark auburn spiral curls and a golden kimono fitting her slender form.

"His Highness has a present for you," Tristan said. "It should be your size. He thought it would help you feel like you belong here."

Myra's fists clenched, but she kept her smile on. "The Prince is very kind. Send him my thanks."

The female vampire walked to the bed and laid down the dress she was carrying, so that Myra could take a better look. The long wine-red ballgown was stunning, puffy in the back and with a ring around the lower rim.

"It's beautiful," Myra said. "Though I'm not sure it will help me fit in."

"How so?" Tristan asked.

"From what I've seen of vampires so far, this seems too plain for your tastes," she said. "Maybe I should add, say, a leather jacket and a cap—"

To her surprise, he burst into laughter. "I see you have met Yong and his merry fools. You must not judge us all based on them. Many vampires have impeccable taste, and I more than anyone."

Myra resisted the urge to roll her eyes. "Of course. Forgive me, I meant no offense."

"None taken," he said and nodded at the other vampire. "Lucy here will help you put on the dress. Once you are ready, my lord would like to show you the Rose Gardens."

He walked out, and Myra grabbed the chair's backrest, her knees weak. The Rose Gardens. She had wanted so much to reach this place, to see it, but not like this. She had expected to be with Alerie by her side, and free.

"Sit down," Lucy said. "We need to get you ready."

Myra sat on the chair and watched as Lucy opened her bag and produced an evil-looking device. She blanched when she realized what it was. "Can we do this without a corset?"

"No," the vampire said.

"I really don't think it's necessary."

"It is," Lucy insisted. "It will make the dress fit much better."

The vampire put the corset around her and pulled the strings. Myra gasped as all air was forced out of her lungs. The corset felt like heavy chains around her, keeping her captive, suffocating her. But that was what the Prince had wanted, was it not? To take away her free will and make her a prisoner.

She stood up, letting Lucy put the dress on her and tighten all strings. The gown was lovely, and yet it felt like a tight cage built around her.

Myra turned around. The dress was too long for her, and she had to hold it up as she walked. She was certain it was no coincidence the Prince had chosen a gown like this one. It came from a time when noble ladies were supposed to be no more than ornaments—flowers for people to admire. Everything about that dress screamed, "Look at me! I'm not doing any work. I physically can't."

It was limiting, incapacitating. She felt disabled somehow, like a bird with clipped wings. There was no way she could run with this thing on, let alone fight. She could barely walk.

Vlad got what he wanted, she thought, her fists clenched. She took her notebook from the desk and reached out to put it into her pocket. Her hand froze midair.

"I have no pockets," she said, examining the dress in wonder.

Lucy snorted. "Of course you have no pockets. It is a gown."

"Will I then get a purse or a backpack to put my things in?"

"You need nothing," the vampire said.

Myra frowned. Honestly, she had never worn anything without pockets, and it added to her discomfort. She could carry her notebook in her hand; that was not the problem. The issue was that she had no place to hide a weapon or anything else useful. She had no belt, and the dress's sleeves were short, leaving her arms exposed. She was not supposed to do anything physical; she was just meant to stand there for the vampires to look at her. She wished she could at least put something around her shoulders and hide herself from the world.

"Will I get a scarf?" she asked. "I'm freezing."

"You will get used to it," Lucy said. "Come."

They walked out the door, where four guards joined them and accompanied them to the inner yard. A four-wheeled carriage was there, its wooden frame carved and gilded. Red velvet drapes covered its windows. Myra's eyes ran over it. She could not see any piece of the carriage that she could easily break off without anyone noticing, and even if she somehow managed to produce a stake, she had nowhere to hide it.

Yong sat at the front bench, holding the reins. Four magnificent horses were tied at the front, their snow-white coats gleaming under the torchlight.

The Prince stood by the horse at the front-left side, grooming him with a large brush and speaking softly. He smiled and took a few apple slices out of his pocket and handed them to the animal. Tristan approached him and said something, but Myra was too far away to hear the words.

The two vampires were talking now, and Myra's heart clenched as she tried to hear the words. Were they discussing her? Was Tristan reporting on their earlier conversation? Would Vladimir find anything unacceptable in the way she had acted and punish her?

Myra looked away. She was probably being paranoid. Something touched her elbow and she jumped, barely suppressing a yelp.

She turned around, and Armida smiled at her. The vampire was wearing a flowing light green dress that looked much more comfortable than Myra's. "It is so good to see you again, Myra," she said. "Will you join me in the carriage?"

Myra followed, concentrating on not tripping as she lifted her long gown to climb into the carriage. Armida sat next to her on the cushioned bench and lit a few candles. She reached out and trailed her slender fingers over Myra's dress. "A beautiful gown," she said. "Though I suspect the Prince cannot win you over with gifts; not after what he did to you. I suspect it is not even a step in the right direction."

Myra frowned. Was the vampire genuinely understanding, or was she testing her? Would she report every word to the Prince? Would Vlad kill another child if he was unhappy with her response?

"The dress is lovely, my lady," Myra said. "His Highness is very generous."

Armida smiled. "I see. Look, I know he scares you. But he will not kill you if you please him. Try not to provoke him. Do what is expected of you, and you will live to an old age."

"He won't kill me, you say. Will he kill others?"

"He will always kill others, no matter what you do. This is out of your control. You should not worry about it."

Out of my control? Myra pressed her lips together. Nothing would be out of her control if she managed to stake this monster.

"We need to do something about your hair," Armida said, apparently unaware of Myra's dark thoughts. She took a red flower-shaped hairpin out of her purse. "May I?"

Myra stiffened. For the first time after her arrival at the Palace, someone had bothered asking for permission before making a change to her appearance. Yet she knew her choice was an illusion—refusing Armida was not an option. "Of course," she said.

Armida combed through Myra's hair with her fingers and twisted it in a bun, securing it with the pin. "There. Much better."

Myra forced herself to smile. She could not care less what her hair looked like, but what mattered was making the vampire happy. Something occurred to her then, and her smile turned genuine.

"Thank you, my lady. My hair is hard to tame and I'm conscious of it all the time. Do you have any ribbons? I wish I could tie it myself whenever I want."

"Of course," Armida said and opened her purse. "Red, violet, green, blue. Which one would you like?"

"The red is lovely, thank you," Myra said and tied the offered ribbon like a bracelet around her wrist. She suppressed a smile. If Vlad insisted on her walking around in ballgowns, she could use this ribbon to tie something around her leg underneath the skirt and smuggle various objects in and out of her chambers.

The carriage's door opened and the Prince stepped in, followed by Tristan. Vlad took a seat and smiled at Myra.

"I am glad you were able to join us, Myra. I hope you will enjoy this trip."

She stared at him. Why did he bother pretending to be nice after he had shown his true colors? These fake courtesies were exhausting. She wished she could go back to telling him how much she hated him to his face, but she knew he would likely punish her by killing another child.

"Thank you for your gift, Your Highness," she said instead. "The dress is beautiful. You are very kind."

He grinned. "I know. My kindness knows no bounds. It is unbelievable how certain humans fail to appreciate it."

Myra clutched the armrest, resisting the strong desire to smack him. "Unbelievable indeed," she said through clenched teeth.

"Yong, we are ready to go," the Prince called. A cry sounded from outside, and the carriage started moving.

Myra pulled back the curtain and gazed outside. Night had fallen and the darkness stretched endless as far as eyes could see. The clouds had moved away, and bright stars were twinkling far above.

"Your Highness," she said, "I finished writing a story today. It's one of my old ones, but I embellished it a bit as I wrote. I hope you like it."

He took the notebook she handed him and tossed it in the overhead luggage compartment. "Good," he said. "I will have a look when I have time."

Myra's heart sank. She had expected him to dive into it straight away, but apparently he was not as impatient to read her works as she needed him to be. And it made sense—one day the Prince would reach the stage when he had read all existing books, but it was not today. Vlad still had plenty of works to read, most of them probably better than hers.

They traveled for about an hour when the carriage slowed down and stopped. Vlad stepped out first and turned back, offering Myra his hand. She took it and followed.

At first, Myra saw nothing. All around them was darkness, and yet she knew right away that this place was unlike any other. A strange scent engulfed her, strong, sweet, intoxicating, *alive*. It smelled of life, of freshness, of joy and rebirth.

Her foot touched the ground, sinking into the unfamiliar softness. She gasped and fell to her knees, running her fingers through the grass. It was cool and soft under her fingers, and slightly wet, and so much alive. The grass had collected the sun's life force throughout the day, and Myra now felt this energy touching her, flowing through her.

Myra bit her lip to stop herself from laughing aloud. She would not show the monster how happy she was. She was determined to find out his weaknesses and turn them against him. Letting him see her own weakness was not a part of the plan.

Yong hurried forward and started lighting the two rows of torches, placed around a narrow path. Myra stood up and gasped. She had seen roses in photos, but the pictures did them little justice. Blooming blossoms, blood red, bright orange, yellow, pure white, and of mixed colors covered the bushes around the path. The soft torchlight played over the buds, dancing, revealing and then hiding their shapes.

Myra ran to a bush of white roses, her long dress sweeping the ground. She would probably destroy the fabric, but she could not bring herself to care. She grabbed the blossom and brought it close to her face, breathing in the scent. The thorns cut through her skin, but she barely noticed.

Yong returned to the horses, and the Prince instructed him to untie them and let them graze. Vlad walked towards the path, and the others followed.

Myra tried to subdue her excitement. She was not here to enjoy herself. She was here to kill the Prince. She had to use any opportunity to plan and observe. Still, the garden offered her little to work with. The bushes and grass were plenty, but they offered nothing she could use to make a stake. But as Myra's gaze moved around, searching for useful items, she noticed something else.

The bushes are thick, yet I could get behind them if I crawled. Alerie and I could have hidden behind that one. Or perhaps over there.

Tears came to her eyes, and she blinked them away. Such thoughts would not help her, but it was hard to push them aside. She was supposed to be here with Alerie, planning the Prince's assassination. She was not supposed to be a prisoner. And Alerie was not supposed to be dead.

Her dark thoughts evaporated and she smiled as they stepped into a small clearing. A large oak grew in the middle, surrounded by rose bushes on all sides. Now, this could produce a good stake. If only she could reach one of those branches.

Underneath the oak was a wooden bench, with torches on both sides. Myra guessed it to be the place the Prince came to read, and she expected him to take a seat. Instead, the three vampires stretched on the grass, lying on their backs and gazing at the sky.

Myra hesitated, unsure what the Prince expected of her. She knelt down slowly and then stretched on the grass next to the vampires, carefully adjusting her dress. Thousands of stars watched her from above and she smiled at them, trying to forget where she was and with whom.

"Myra, can you recognize your constellation?" Vladimir asked. "You are Pisces, correct?"

"What?" she blurted out.

"Your zodiac sign. It must be Pisces, unless I am mistaken."

She blanched. "How do you know?"

"I have known you for a couple of days now. It is enough for me to figure you out."

Her fists clenched. He thought he had figured her out? And yet, the fact remained—he had no way of knowing her date of birth, and still he somehow knew her star sign. Was he telling the truth? Had he really guessed it just by observing her? She was supposed to figure *him* out, not the other way around. "What is your sign, my lord?" she asked, trying to make her voice steady.

"I will let you find out yourself," he said.

Right. She knew next to nothing about star signs, but if there was a sign associated with an arrogant, heartless monster, that had to be it.

"So, do you know which constellation is Pisces?" he asked.

She bit her lip. He thought he was so clever. She wanted to show him that Resistance members were also smart and educated, and knew as much about the world as he did. But the truth was, although she had studied maps and knew many constellations, she had no idea about that one. "No," she admitted. "I suppose it must look like fish."

He laughed. "If you use a lot of imagination, perhaps it does. Over there, see those stars forming a hexagon? Then there is this line of stars going down and to the left, and then up. These are two fish, tied on a string."

Myra watched out of the corner of her eye as Tristan stood up, walked to the large oak, and sat on the grass, leaning his back against the tree. She turned her attention back to the Prince. "So a fisherman caught them?" she asked.

Vlad raised himself on his elbow, so he could look at her. "Not at all. The ancient Greeks believed these to be Aphrodite and Eros, who leapt into the sea and turned themselves into fish to escape Typhon. They tied themselves together with a string, so the waves would not separate them. You know who these are, right?"

And again, he assumed she was some ignorant idiot. "Aphrodite is the goddess of love, and Eros is her son," she said. "I've no idea who Typhon is."

"Indeed? It surprises me you have not heard of him. He was the most fearsome monster in Greek mythology." He turned to face her fully. The wind blew his long hair back, and his amber eyes shone under the torchlight as he spoke.

"His upper half was humanlike and reached as high as the stars," the Prince continued, his voice hushed. "As he outstretched his arms, one would touch East, and the other—West. But he had no human head. Instead, hundreds of dragon heads erupted from his neck and shoulders. Gigantic viper coils made up his lower half, and black wings covered his entire body. Fire flashed from his eyes, striking fear in anyone who met him."

A shudder ran down Myra's spine. "Who killed him?"

"No one did. Zeus defeated him in the end and trapped him underneath Mount Etna, but according to legend, he lives still. And before his capture, he sired legions of monsters, including Cerberus—the three-headed guardian of the Underworld—and the Sphinx, who slays everyone who fails to answer her riddles."

"Did he sire vampires too?" Myra could not help asking.

He laughed. "My dear girl. We are no monsters."

Right. They would never agree on that point. And once again, Vlad was proving himself to be an arrogant jerk. He was surprised she had not heard of some obscure mythological creature? Myra had read every single book on mythology and history available at the Resistance's library multiple times. If their collection was limited, it was hardly her fault.

A sudden, grating sound made her draw in a sharp breath. She looked up, trying to identify the source, and her eyes found the large oak. Tristan sat there, filing his long pale nails, one eyebrow arched and his perma-frown as deep as ever, a look of pure concentration on his face. He looked strangely detached, as if lost inside his own world.

Vlad followed her gaze with a grin. She sighed and looked back at him. "Have you lived in ancient Greece, my lord?" she asked, realizing she had no idea how old he was.

"I never witnessed it firsthand," he said. "I was born later, during the Byzantine period. Still, I know a few vampires who hailed from there."

Myra silently stored the new information. Byzantine. This could mean anything between the fourth and the fifteenth century. It narrowed down the possibilities, but the pool of options was still large. She looked back at the stars.

"It looks nothing like fish to me," she said.

He smiled. "Many will agree with you. The Greeks saw fish. The Chinese saw a marsh and a pig farm, and a fence to keep the farmer and the pigs from falling into the marsh. What do *you* see?"

Myra fell silent, staring at the constellation. Was he expecting something profound and imaginative? She wished to impress him, to show him that humans were smart, but no matter how much she stared at it, it looked like nothing more than a circle, with a line coming out of it. "It looks like a yo-yo," she said.

He laughed. "Do you have any yo-yos at the Resistance?"

Myra winced. Every time Tristan moved the nail file, the sound pierced her brain like a knife. "No. But I've seen pictures and they looked fun. I've always wanted to have one."

"Good," the Prince said. "I can help with that. We do have some at the Palace."

Myra frowned. Did he think he could buy her with dresses and yo-yos?

Armida laughed. "My love, I do not think you can impress Myra with toys."

He smiled. "Perhaps you are right. What should I impress her with?"

"Culture," Armida said and winked at Myra. She stood up and stretched. "Tristan, dearie, did you bring your flute? Play me a song. I feel like dancing."

Myra felt movement to her right and turned around to see Tristan put away the nail file and take a silver flute out of his bag.

"How can he play that?" Myra asked. "I thought vampires couldn't create art."

"Same way as the players and orchestra could perform at the opera," the Prince said. "Once a song is written, we can reproduce it by singing or playing an instrument, but we cannot compose a new melody."

Tristan pressed the flute to his lips, and Myra gasped.

Never before had she heard a melody so clear, so lively, so melancholic and yet uplifting at the same time. Her eyes were glued to Armida as the vampire started to dance.

Armida's hands drew circles in the air, her shoulders, hips and legs moving in time with the music, faster than any human ever could. She arched backwards so that her hands touched the ground and then straightened up faster than an eye could blink. She jumped around and twisted her body, drawing figures with her feet over the grassy floor.

As she danced, she undid her braids and ran her fingers through her long wavy hair, setting it free. She kicked her shoes away, so that she stood barefooted on the grass. Armida's green dress and red hair waved around her, and to Myra she looked like a forest sprite.

Myra stared, transfixed. She wished she could dance like that, but knew that this was something no human could do. She had thought vampires used their superior speed and strength only to sow death and destruction. She had never imagined a vampire would use her abilities to create something beautiful.

Armida stopped in front of the Prince and curtsied, smiling. "Your Highness. Will you do me the honor?"

He grinned back and took her outstretched hand. The two vampires danced under the stars, twisting and turning, so fast Myra's eyes could barely follow. Vlad lifted Armida high up and tossed her, and she turned up in the air, landing gracefully in his arms.

Vlad jumped up, grabbed an oaken branch and pulled himself up into the tree. Armida followed, each move they made perfectly synchronized with the music. They jumped from one branch to another, chased each other high across the treetop, peeked from behind the trunk and teased each other with smiles and gestures. They kissed and broke apart, climbed high up and slid down, every move a part of their elaborate dance.

Myra knew she was witnessing something otherworldly. She dared not breathe as the two figures danced across the branches, telling a story of beauty and passion. Then the two vampires jumped down, landing gracefully just as Tristan played the last note and put the flute down.

Vlad reached out to a bush with red roses, picked one and handed it to Armida. Sharp thorns pierced his skin and blood tickled down, but he did not seem to notice. Armida took the rose with a smile and brought his wounded hand to her lips. At first, Myra thought she was kissing it, but as the vampires' faces grew paler and strangely luminous, she knew she was witnessing a kind of magic no kisses could induce. Myra shuddered as she realized what Armida was doing.

She was drinking his blood.

And then, all magic was gone. All beauty Myra had seen in the performance evaporated and she placed a hand on her stomach to suppress her queasiness.

Armida kept drinking, her lustrous jade eyes never leaving Vlad's as she raised the rose with her free hand and smelled it. She then ran it across her neck, the thorns making shallow scratches, drawing crimson blood. Vlad kissed her, his lips moving down her pale neck until they found the cut.

Both vampires were drinking each other's blood now, and Myra looked away, trying to concentrate on a yellow rose and forget what was happening around her. The oak was tall, she thought. There was no way she could reach the branches to break one off and make a stake, and she had seen no fallen branches on the ground. She had to find another way to devise her weapon.

"Tristan, dearest, will you join us?" Armida's voice sounded from her right, but Myra still refused to look, afraid of what she would see.

Tristan stretched out his long legs before him and placed the flute in his bag. "Perhaps later, my lady."

Myra was not sure how much longer the blood-drinking lasted, and she stubbornly refused to look. After a while, Vlad and Armida approached them, and the Prince looked at Tristan, his amber eyes still shining with iridescent fire from the blood exchange.

"What is wrong, my boy?" he asked. "Something is bothering you."

"Nothing important, my lord."

The Prince raised an eyebrow and grabbed Tristan's left hand. "Did you break a nail?"

The blond vampire scolded and pulled his hand away, muttering something under his breath. His nails left small scratches across Vladimir's palm, and Tristan stared at the blood, transfixed, before looking away.

Vlad sighed and turned his back to the blond vampire. He never saw Tristan bring his bloodied fingernail to his lips and briefly close his eyes.

Do you wish to taste his blood? Myra wondered. *Do you wish to make him suffer for what he has done to you?*

The Prince turned back and said something in a language Myra could not understand. Tristan seemed to hesitate for a moment before nodding. Vladimir looked at Armida. "My love, will you entertain our guest for a while? I need to speak to Tristan alone."

"Of course," Armida said, and Myra did not miss her brief frown.

Myra watched as Vlad and Tristan walked away, disappearing behind the bushes. "What was that about?" she asked. "Is it something I did? Are they talking about me?"

"What?" Armida raised her eyebrows. "Why would you think they are talking about you?"

Myra hesitated. She was uncertain if she could share her doubts with Armida, but this vampire was the closest thing to a confidant she had. "I know some vampires are against the Prince keeping me alive. I know they want to torture me for information in the Dark Cell."

"And you think Tristan might be one of them?" Armida said. "You think he is lobbying for your death?" She started to laugh. "Myra, I know it is hard to believe, but not everything is about you. Tristan has other troubles on his mind, unrelated to you. And yes, some vampires want you tortured, but I can promise you—Tristan is not one of them."

"Why?" Myra asked. "What does he gain from keeping me alive?"

"This is his own business. And I told you, you should stop worrying. As long as you keep the Prince happy, he will not let any harm come to you. Do what he asks of you, and you will live." Armida tilted her head to the side, and her eyes narrowed. "But your death is not what you fear, is it?" she asked. "You know he will keep you alive. You fear he may kill others to keep you under control."

Myra pressed her lips together. Again, she was not sure if Armida was testing her and if she would report any of their conversation. "His Highness may do as he pleases. He is the Prince; it is his right."

Armida laughed. "You do not need to play this game with me. What is the point of lying when no one believes you? You think he is a monster."

"And you don't?" Myra asked. "He has killed so many, and you still love him."

"Yes, I love him," Armida replied calmly. "More than anything."

Myra frowned. Of course, Armida was a vampire. She had a different value system, and in all likelihood, she did not see anything wrong with killing humans by the thousands. Armida was so friendly when she talked to her, and Myra realized she had almost forgotten what she was. But the truth was simple—Armida was a monster, just like the Prince.

Myra turned to the left, watching as Vlad and Tristan returned. Tristan seemed in a better mood, laughing at something the Prince had said. Myra allowed herself a small smile.

If the vampires truly loved one another, then perhaps there was a way to use that against them. And if they did not—then perhaps there was a way to use that as well.

Chapter Sixteen

The Carrot and the Stick

Myra closed her eyes, shaking. For the past few days, the Prince had allowed her to dine alone in her room, but tonight he had decided it was time for her to start joining the evening feast. Food, however, was the last thing on her mind. All her thoughts were focused on keeping herself from being sick as she took in the scene around her.

Three vampires stood in the corner, playing violins. By all rights, she should have been happy—so many times, she had dreamed of hearing skilled musicians play beautiful music on high-quality instruments. And yet, her current predicament was more like a nightmare than a dream come true.

The rest of the guests sat at a long rectangular table, covered in a silken red cloth. The Prince sat on a high chair at the end, with Tristan on his right and Armida on his left. Next to them were humans, and the sight of the two young men, chained and eating obediently, made her stomach turn.

They were not the only ones. Next to each vampire sat a human, and it was easy to guess why. Did the humans know what was awaiting them? Had they been through this before?

And why were they eating silently, like obedient lambs? If the vampires got carried away, this could turn into the prisoners' last supper.

In front of each vampire and human stood a golden chalice, engraved with pictures and encrusted with precious stones. Each one was unique, and the one in front of the Prince was a work of art. It was made of a nautilus shell mounted in silver, engraved with dragons among clouds. An inscribed silver band ran around the lip, supported at the sides by mermaid figurines. The back of the shell was shaped like a sea monster with an open mouth. A long stem, shaped like a festoon of fruits and flowers, supported the shell, ending with a base in the form of a bird's claw.

Two male vampires walked around the table, carrying a large Greek vase, inscribed with figures of heroes killing monsters, orange on a black background. Next to them walked a golden-haired female vampire, dressed in a white toga. She used a golden dipper, shaped like a palm leaf, to scoop dark red wine from the vase and pour it into the goblets.

Vampire servants dressed in red togas, their faces hidden behind golden masks, walked around the table, placing silver plates in front of each human. Boar and hare meat, cooked with potatoes and various herbs, and small, wild apples for dessert. Myra forced herself to take tiny bites, but she did not trust her stomach to hold anything more than that.

Some of the vampires would also try a bite or two. However, the true food would come after, and Myra had to swallow the bile rising in her throat.

The feast was coming to an end, and Myra looked down, unwilling to witness what was to follow. Still, she heard the screams and the pleas as each vampire reached out to the human next to them. She heard the desperate struggles, the gurgling, the wheezes. The stench of blood made her stomach turn.

She hated them; she hated them so much. She wanted to scream, to fight, to tell the vamps exactly what she thought of them, but most of all, she wanted to kill them all. Yet, she knew she could do nothing—she had no chance of harming any vampire, and even if she tried, the Prince would likely punish her by demonstratively killing another child.

Her eyes filled with tears at her helplessness. She was their prisoner in more ways than one. Myra closed her eyes and traced her finger over the diamond bracelet around her wrist—it felt like an iron shackle, keeping her chained.

When she opened her eyes once again, her gaze wandered to the knife next to her plate. A somewhat blunt blade, meant for cutting food. Even if it was sharper, she could have done nothing. And yet, vivid fantasies of what exactly she wanted to do ran wildly through her mind. She imagined the knife cutting, slashing, and blood, *vampire* blood, pouring on the ground. She would stake them and free the humans from their chains. She wished to be the hero, to fight, to defeat evil with the heart-wrenching music of the violins playing in the background. But she was no hero.

Myra swallowed hard and raised her face. No one seemed to be watching her and she slowly and casually brought the knife under the table. No one reacted, and now the knife was out of the vamps' line of sight. Carefully, Myra lifted her skirt and found the ribbon tied around her leg. She secured the knife, hoping it would not accidentally cut either her or the dress as she stood up and walked, or worse—fall off and give away her ruse. Once she was done, she turned her attention back to the vamps.

The Prince was the only one not feeding. He was observing everyone with a soft smile on his face, lazily twirling his wine goblet. He caught her gaze and nodded at her, raising his chalice as if in toast. "Myra, my dear, is the feast to your liking?"

Her hands were sweating as all gazes turned to her. How many of these vamps wanted her dead? "I… the food is good, Your Highness. Thank you for inviting me."

"And yet, you have barely eaten," Vladimir observed.

"Leave the girl alone, my love," Armida said with a smile. "Surely you understand our ways must be foreign and frightening to a human."

"We have very little food at the Resistance, my lady," Myra said. "I'm unused to eating so much, is all."

Tristan raised his head from the human he was drinking to give her a curious look. As he did so, he licked his bloody lips, and Myra looked down again, her stomach queasy. If not for the thick blood trickling down his chin and the half-dead man in his arms, Tristan would be a vision. Graceful and refined, he was like a classic marble statue, a Renaissance portrait come to life. In the books she loved to read a character like him would be a hero—kind and brave. The pale blond hair shining like a halo around his face made him look like an angel. And yet, he was as different from an angel as anyone could be.

For a moment, Myra closed her eyes, wishing she would be trapped in an old-fashioned fairy tale or a high fantasy world, where the beautiful were good, the evil were misshapen and hideous, and everything was straightforward.

"Your Highness," a female vampire spoke, and Myra breathed a sigh of relief as the attention turned away from her. Myra frowned when she recognized Natalia. "I ask for permission to turn my human," the vampire continued.

The Prince looked at her sternly. "Natalia, you can see that there are many of us, and the humans are not reproducing and growing any faster. We have barely enough human blood for ourselves. We cannot afford to turn anyone, unless they are exceptional."

"I like her blood," Natalia said stubbornly. "Who is to say she will not make an exceptional vampire?"

The dark-haired young woman in the vampire's arms was barely conscious, and Myra doubted she could follow any of the conversation that was to decide her fate. What would she choose if she could? Would she prefer to live as a slave, or as a slaver?

"You have not even talked to her," Tristan grumbled. "Have you heard nothing of what His Highness said? We cannot go around turning every single human who looks and tastes nice."

"And yet, we should not close the door to everyone," Armida countered. "There may be gems hidden amidst the filth. We should not discard them."

"You expect to find gems among the domesticated humans?" Tristan said incredulously, and Myra wanted to punch him. "They have no education system, no books, no musical instruments. How could any of them grow up to be passable, let alone exceptional?"

Armida smiled. "Tristan, sweetheart, I was not aware you ever went to school."

The fair-haired vampire started to protest, but the Prince silenced him with a raise of his hand. "Do you have a proposition to make, my heart?" Vladimir asked.

Armida nodded. "Revive the girl and bring her to my chambers. I will talk to her and decide if she is worthy to be one of us."

"As you wish. Natalia, feed and bandage the human and bring her to Lady Armida once she feels better," he said as he stood up. "Myra, please come with me."

As soon as the Prince's back was turned, Tristan glared at Armida, and she shot him a victorious grin. Myra noted the exchange before she followed Vlad on his way out of the Great Hall.

"I thought only looks mattered when you decided whom to turn," she admitted once they were alone. "I didn't know you considered anything else."

"We do," he said. "Or at least we used to. In the past, we were very picky when choosing who could become one of us. Many vampires never turned a single human, and most turned just one or two special ones. When we had chosen a human, we would spend time observing them, until we were certain they were suitable. We used to be an elite society, a society of beautiful, intelligent and educated individuals."

"But the Nightfall changed this?" Myra guessed.

"Unfortunately, yes. I needed armies, so numbers were of the essence. We turned humans by the dozens, and anyone who satisfied a set of some loose criteria could become one of us. To be honest, nowadays I have half a mind to put most of them under the stake." He laughed when he noticed her shocked expression. "Do not worry, my dear. I was only jesting. These are my people now, and they live in the world I have created. It is my responsibility to give them safe and happy lives."

"And you have done an excellent job in this regard, Your Highness," Myra said, forcing herself to smile. It pained her to be so servile to this monster, but if this was the price to stop him from hurting anyone else, she would gladly pay it. He threw her a grin that seemed to say, "I don't buy a single word you say, but keep trying," and she fought to keep up her facade. Vladimir knew she was pretending, and yet this was what he expected of her. Did he take pleasure in humiliating her? Or did he hope she would somehow become the mask?

"You have given your people a world where sunlight is no threat, and they can wander the earth at any time of day," Myra continued. "A world where they have no need to hide and fear persecution, a world with an endless food supply. They have every reason to be grateful."

"And they are," the Prince said. "The problem is, it is also my responsibility to teach my people what it means to be a vampire, and the younger among us lack those skills. They have never experienced living as undead in the Old World, and to them our old lives seem mythical and terrifying. They have never known what it means to fear the sun or to have to hunt for food and fight for survival on the brink of starvation."

I have an easy solution, Myra thought. *Destroy the WeatherWizard, and they'll get a taste of fearing sunlight and not being rulers of the world soon enough*. Unfortunately, the time when she would have spoken her thoughts freely was past.

"You are worrying needlessly, Your Highness," she said instead. "Many humans in the Old World also experienced hardships that taught them useful skills, but they fought to prevent their children from facing the same trials. Whole generations struggled with starvation, wars, diseases, but they did everything possible to give their children safe and comfortable lives. Was that a mistake? Is hardship an integral part of being a human? Of being a vampire? Removing unnecessary struggles gives us time to focus on what really matters."

"What you say makes sense for humans," he agreed. "We, on the other hand, have all the time in the world. We should fill our immortal lives with as many different experiences as possible, and I feel some of my people are missing that. Do not get me wrong—I am not complaining. And to be fair, some of those we turned during the Nightfall have become decent vampires." They reached the doors to his study and walked in. "You seem interested in our world today. You are trying to get to know your enemy, I suppose."

"Your world and culture are fascinating," she said as she took the seat he offered.

"Yes, you looked positively fascinated at the dinner table." He removed the golden circlet that marked him as royalty and placed it on the table, before sitting in one of the armchairs. A thoughtful grin spread across his face, and she did not like it one bit. "I caught you stealing glances at Tristan. I cannot blame you, of course."

Myra frowned at the suggestion. If she had stared, it was for a very different reason from whatever Vlad assumed. However, she had no desire to explain to him her thoughts on beauty and evil. "His looks are unusual, is all," she said nonchalantly.

"I mean, the only blond person at the Resistance is my cousin, and her shade is much darker. I've never seen hair like his. It's natural, I suppose?"

He chuckled, probably thinking she was trying to deflect his suspicions. "Completely natural. Remarkable, is it not? To be fair, that shade was not unusual in his village. He, however, was extraordinary among his fellow men." The Prince leaned back in his armchair. "I admit I am glad you found one thing to fascinate you tonight," he said. "Asking you to join was thoughtless of me. From now on, you will not be required to attend any feasts of this kind."

The admission surprised and relieved her, but she tried not to show it. "Thank you, my lord. This is very considerate of you."

He smiled. "Yes, I know it is. Now, I am sure you cannot wait to get away from me. There are guards outside who will take you back to your chamber if you wish to leave."

She did wish to leave. Truth be told, Myra could hardly wait to return to her room, ask a servant to prepare a bath, and wash away all the memories of that evening. And yet, there was one thing she desired even more. She tried to suppress the fearful eagerness in her voice as she spoke her next words. "My lord, there is one more thing before I go. Please, tell me, did you have a chance to look at my new chapter?"

The Prince seemed pleased by the question. "Indeed, I did." He opened a drawer and handed her a notebook.

Myra opened it and cautiously peeked inside. Her throat constricted. What was the meaning of this? She thought she had been improving. The Prince had given her tips, and she had applied them all. Now she was a much better writer than she had ever been. And yet, there was so much red ink all over her writing—words were crossed over and replaced by others, the order was changed and more words were added, whole sentences were restructured, and the wide margins were filled with comments, written in a small, neat script. "Did you use to be a teacher, Your Highness?"

Vladimir smiled. "I do tend to be overly critical, but it must not dishearten you. The only reason I spend so much time carefully reading and editing your stories is that I believe you have potential. I cannot yet tell you why, but it is important to me that you learn to write well."

The comment sparked Myra's curiosity, but she knew that tone of voice and was certain any questions she asked would remain unanswered. Instead, she looked through the pages, carefully reading the notes the vampire had inserted.

"I disagree with your comment that the speaker's identity should be revealed earlier," she said. "That way the reader goes through a few pages not knowing from whose point of view this is written and it comes as a surprising twist."

"Surprise or boredom," the vampire argued. "Your readers spend pages having no idea what you are talking about. When you reveal Gregory's identity, they need to go back and reread the chapter, and most will not even bother. But forgive me, Myra, I have other plans for tonight, and we must postpone our discussion until tomorrow."

Myra knew she had to be happy—she could return to her room early, and if the Prince had something else to do, he would not visit her. She could spend time by herself and forget that she was a prisoner, required to speak and smile on demand. And yet, she had been looking forward to hearing his feedback. Her disappointment surprised her. "Of course, my lord. Thank you for your time."

He smiled. "Do not look so sad. I will not deprive you of my pleasant company. The plans I speak of involve you too, dear girl. Since you have been so good and exemplary, I have decided to give you another carrot."

Rage flared in her heart, but she did her best to hide it. Did Vlad think he could train her like a dog, giving her rewards and punishments in varying order? She was not happy about how pleased he was with her obedience, but tried to remind herself that her time would come, if only she stayed low.

"Another carrot? Besides the paintings, and the tabletop games, and the wonderful food and beautiful clothes? You are spoiling me, Your Highness. I am not certain I deserve this."

He grinned. "My dear girl, you are misunderstanding how this game works. It is not about you saying pretty words. It is about making me believe you. First of all, you sound too humble and eager. Tone it down a little; it is unrealistic. And your eyes betray you. You should try practicing in front of the mirror. Now, try again."

"Are you teaching me how to better lie to you?"

"Of course I am," the Prince said calmly. "If you get better at this, it will be more fun for me to try to figure out when you are telling the truth. Right now, it is no real challenge."

He *was* insane, Myra decided. He wanted a worthy opponent, and since she was not good enough in his eyes, he was willing to train her until she became the cunning enemy he desired. Honestly, she did not mind. If Vlad wanted to hand her the weapons she needed to defeat him, she would not complain. She would learn, and she would lie to him until he believed her, and then she would strike. "I was only curious what else you wish to offer me," she said. "I admit I liked the paintings and the other presents, so I'll probably like this one too."

"Good. This was more convincing. And yes, I believe you will like what I have to offer." He leaned back in his chair, interlacing his fingers in his lap and looking smug. "I have noticed you are interested in tales and knowledge of the Old World. Myra, how would you like to see a real library?"

For a moment, she could not breathe. If the book collection in the Prince's study was anything to go by, this library had to be something spectacular. Her pulse was racing so fast that she had to struggle to find her voice. "I would like that," she admitted.

He grinned. "And I believe this is the first truthful thing I have heard from you since you agreed to behave. Follow me."

A lump formed in her throat. What was she doing? He was giving her a treat to reward her obedience, and she was *happy*? Yet, when they stepped into the library hall, all thoughts of guilt melted away and she nearly fell on her knees. Ever since leaving the Resistance, she had been lost. And now, for the first time, she knew exactly where she was.

She was in Heaven.

Chapter Seventeen

Heaven

The chamber was larger than anything she had seen. Shelves laden with books covered each wall completely and went on for as far as the eye could see. Some volumes looked centuries old, while others were probably printed shortly before the Nightfall. Myra took a deep breath, savoring the smell of paper and ink. *That must be the most beautiful place in the universe.* She pressed her eyes shut. The Prince was playing with her mind. She had to be strong.

Myra opened her eyes, taking in the wonders around her. Along the shelves stood marble statues of gods and heroes. A woman in a toga, with a shield in her hand and a large helm on her head. A nude bearded god with a trident fighting a sea monster. A lion, eating a horse.

In between the statues were tall pedestals, covered with various treasures—jade dragons and demon masks, ivory figures of Indian gods, painted glass snuff boxes, sea snail shells engraved with pictures of people and animals, and so many stones. Minerals and gemstones, some crude, some polished, and others carved into figurines, red, pink, purple, bright rich green, the colors interlacing and forming circles and spirals on the surface. On one pedestal lay silky fine fibers, thin as human hair. Myra reached out to touch them and frowned in surprise when they were hard underneath her fingers.

"Is that a stone?" she asked.

The Prince laughed. "It certainly is. This is called bushmanite, as it comes from the Bushman river in South Africa, but many other minerals can have this shape or be even more wondrous. Look at this." He pointed at a bright red cube, nested in what looked like a black-and-white coral.

"This can't be natural," Myra said.

"It is," he said with a smile. "Nature has created more treasures than humans ever could. I myself admire art and beauty created by both humans and nature, and I aim to honor and preserve it."

"This is admirable," Myra said. "But how did you find all these stones? Did you go up the mountains and down the rivers, digging and looking for hidden gems?"

He laughed. "I have done that in fact, but I never found anything as fine as what you see in this gallery. I had to get these in other ways. After the Nightfall, no humans were left to go to museums, and I thought it would be a shame to leave all those treasures just lying there forgotten."

Myra paled, suddenly nauseous. Vlad had looted museums? And he had most probably looted libraries, and castles, and the homes of the people he had murdered. Her eyes clouded and she reached out to a pedestal to steady herself.

"What is it, my dear?" he asked. "You look unwell."

"I'm fine," Myra said. "I'm simply overwhelmed by all this beauty."

He raised an eyebrow. "You have said nothing of my book collection."

"It's big," she said.

"Are you surprised? This is *my library*, not some small village bookstore. This part is mostly encyclopedias. Fiction is in the West Wing."

"The West—are you telling me there is more?"

"Of course," he said. "I will let you browse it later. It should be easy to navigate—I have organized the sections by language and genre and sorted the books alphabetically by author's first name."

"*You* have sorted them?" she asked. "You have done all this yourself?"

"Naturally," Vladimir said. "I like to know where each book is. I have spent centuries acquiring all these treasures. I remember when and where I have picked up each book. Let me show you around. This part is biology. In different sections you will find taxonomy, genetics—"

"All the medicine books look well used," Myra observed.

"And for a good reason," the vampire said. "I have used them extensively for my research."

"Your research, my lord?"

A sad, wistful smile appeared on his face. "It was fruitless in the end. And yet, I believe in knowledge for the sake of knowledge, so I suppose it was not a complete waste."

"May I ask what you were researching?"

Vlad grinned. "You may, of course. It does not mean I will answer."

Myra suppressed a sigh. "This is all nice, but I guess a lot of the information here must be outdated. Take this book on extinct and endangered species, for example. I can imagine the list must have grown tremendously after the Nightfall."

He raised his eyebrows. "What makes you say that?"

"Plants can't grow without sunshine," she said. "And lack of plants breaks the food chain on all levels up."

"Who said there is no sunshine anywhere?" Vladimir asked. "We cover the sky in the places where we live, or where we would like to go. But I keep many spots sunlit for large parts of the day especially for plants to grow. The domesticated humans need food after all, and besides, I am committed to preserving the planet's biodiversity. The endangered species' natural habitats are sunlit and undisturbed, and I am happy to tell you that many animal populations have grown after the Nightfall."

He had to be joking. He had no trouble breeding humans for food and killing children to make a point, but he was *committed to preserving the planet's biodiversity*? She hoped he was not deluding himself that this somehow made him a good guy. "How do you know this, my lord? Surely you haven't traveled to the distant corners of the world using post-Nightfall technology and transportation means, just to check on animal populations?"

His grin widened. "Does that surprise you? I am a scholar, and this is of great interest to me. Tell me, what books would you like to see? I noticed your interest in the stars. Astronomy, perhaps?"

"That would be lovely," she said. "But first I would like to see your history encyclopedias."

"Ah, I see. You want to learn more about the Old World. You know, there is only so much one can glimpse in books. You can read about the Old World all you want, but I have lived in it for around seventeen centuries. I have traveled many places and known various cultures."

The flames of the torches rose and fell, casting shadows across his face and giving him an otherworldly appearance. His amber eyes shone like charcoals and his voice was hushed as he spoke.

"I saw the Vikings sow fear throughout Europe and joined their nightly raids. I fought with Saladin against the Crusaders, and I joined Tamerlane's forces as he invaded the lands around the Caspian Sea. I traveled west with the Spanish Conquistadors and saw the Inca civilization before it crumbled to dust. I fought with Sundiata when he defeated Ghana and founded the Mali Empire. I witnessed the rise and fall of the Mughal Empire and the collapse of the Ming dynasty."

One of the torches went out, and he smiled, looking his usual self once again. "If you are interested, I can tell you more about the world as it once was. I can tell you things you will not find in any book."

Myra smiled back, strangely excited despite herself. "I would be grateful if you do, my lord. Do you have time now?"

"I am going hunting with Armida and Tristan tonight," he said, "but if you have a quick question, perhaps I could take it."

"I would very much like to know where you are from."

He casually reached out to take a thick book and flip through the pages. "I like to think of myself as a citizen of the world," he said without looking up at her.

Myra had to admit the answer was expected, even if disappointing. If the Prince did not wish to discuss his past, it was understandable. His family had been massacred after all, and she could imagine he would not wish to relive the memories just to satisfy her curiosity.

Yet his vague answer had only piqued her interest. Where had he lived? What lands had he traveled? Who was the man who had killed his family? How long had he known Armida and Tristan? Did he have any other close associates? Was Armida his first lover, and if not, who had come before? Myra had to admit the answers to those questions were unlikely to help her defeat him, but she was curious.

She hoped she would eventually put together the pieces of the Prince's life story from the hints he had dropped. For now, he had said he was seventeen centuries old, which meant he must have been born around the ninth century. That was a start. "There is no doubt about that," she said. "You are not only a citizen, but a ruler of the world. Forgive me. I did not mean to be intrusive."

Vladimir closed the book and stared at it for a moment, as if wondering what to do with it. Finally, he placed it back on the shelf. "Apology accepted. Now, if you have no other questions, I will ask the guards to escort you to your room. I bid you goodnight."

Myra took a step towards him. She had been planning something for a few days, and now was as good a time as any. "Please, my lord, stay for a minute. I have something else to discuss with you."

He eyed her carefully, seemingly surprised by her boldness. "Can it not wait?"

"I'll be quick," she promised, and he nodded at her to speak. "You want me to become a better writer, and I want the same. Unfortunately, I don't have everything I need."

"I gave you plenty of pens and paper. You need nothing else to write."

"I need nothing else to put words on paper," she said. "But I need more to be a writer."

He signed and leaned against one of the pedestals. "What do you require?"

"Experience. I need to get to know this world, to feel it, to understand it. I need to draw inspiration from the people around me and their life stories. Unfortunately, I've seen so little of the world. I only know my society at the Resistance, and now I am meeting you and your people, but I need more. I need to open my eyes."

"You certainly do," he said. "But we are short on cultures around here. If you wish, I could take you for a visit to another castle and let you get to know the local society."

Great. More vamps. "I'm sure that would help, but I had something else in mind. I was hoping to get to meet other humans—humans not from the Resistance—and see how their society has developed after the Nightfall. I thought it would give me insights into human nature."

"I see," the Prince said. "You have a point, but I wonder how you propose to accomplish this? Are you about to tell me the Resistance are not the only surviving humans?"

Myra suppressed her frustration. "I mean the humans in your dungeons."

"The domesticated humans? What could you possibly learn from them?"

"I beg you, don't call them that," she said. "And I'm sure there is plenty to learn from each of them. They are humans. They think, and dream, and create. I want to hear about their values and aspirations."

He snorted. "The aspirations of domesticated humans. Sounds fascinating. Very well. I will send Tristan to pick out a human for you. In return, I will ask you to join me in my study for a lesson."

She frowned. "What kind of a lesson?"

"You will see. Are you happy with the arrangement?"

Not at all, Myra thought, but she needed to meet these humans. They were imprisoned and powerless, but they were many. Perhaps she could find a way to free them, so they could join the Resistance's ranks. Myra took a deep breath and smiled at him. "This is more than what I expected, Your Highness. Your generosity knows no bounds."

He sighed. "Myra, my dear girl, what did I tell you about making me suspend disbelief? I will leave you to enjoy the books if you wish. The guards outside can bring you back to your chambers once you are ready."

She glared at the door through which the Prince had exited and briefly wondered how her eyes were not burning holes into the wood. If this presumptuous, arrogant, pathetic excuse for a monster thought he could train her like an animal to jump and smile at his command, he was gravely mistaken.

Chapter Eighteen

Man and Beast

Myra carefully lifted her dress and knelt down. The servants had removed her ordinary clothes and left her with nothing but ballgowns to wear. Even walking across the room was a challenge. Vlad was doing it on purpose, no doubt.

With an effort, she managed to lie facedown on the floor and peek underneath the bed. She reached out to the pile of notebooks she had thrown down next to her, and started stacking them one over the other until they produced a makeshift column. The bed was stable now. It would hold even if it was missing one leg.

Myra held the knife she had smuggled from the dinner and made a cut into the wooden leg. It was small and shallow, but it was there. Smiling, she made another. In a few days she would have a stake.

She froze at the sound of approaching footsteps and quickly crawled out from underneath the bed, adjusting her skirts. The door opened, and Tristan stepped in, dragging a man behind him. *A human.* Myra's heart leapt.

The man appeared to be in his midtwenties, dressed in a green T-shirt and blue jeans, lazy golden brown curls falling over his chubby face. He looked around the room, his blue eyes wide, until Tristan pushed him in.

"I found you a human," the vampire said and left, closing the door behind him.

Myra grinned at the man. "Welcome. I can't tell you how happy I am to meet another living human."

"Who are you?" the man asked, frowning.

How much had the vamps told the Farm humans about the Resistance? Probably nothing at all. "My name is Myra. I'm a member of the Resistance—a group of people who live in freedom and fight to bring this world back to humankind."

"You live outside the Palace?"

She nodded.

The man walked to the desk and stared at a loaf of bread. Myra raised an eyebrow. "Would you like some?"

He grabbed the loaf and took a large bite. "How do you survive?" he asked. "Who feeds you?"

"We feed ourselves. We scavenge and hunt, and we cook if we manage to find any supplies."

Her guest plopped on the chair and propped his legs up on the bed, taking another bite. "Hm. So what do you eat?"

Honestly? I just told him there is a group of humans fighting his oppressors, and this is his question? "Many things. Canned goods, biscuits, sometimes birds, rabbits, or rats if we have a successful hunt. Whenever we find flour, we bake bread."

"Ew, rats?" He put the bread down. "You can't survive like that. Why don't you come live with us? There's plenty of room in the Farm."

Myra stared at him wide-eyed. "What? Are you serious? The vamps raise you like animals and feed off you!"

"The masters are good to us," he said. "They give us great food and take care of us when we are sick. They even take us out for walks."

"They take you out for walks?" Myra echoed, not sure if she was dreaming. "You're not dogs."

"Sounds like your life is crappier. I'm serious. Come live with us. The masters have enough food for everyone."

Myra took a deep breath. "Look—what is your name?"

"Samson."

"Look, Samson, you can't tell me you and your people like this life. I saw a man struggling in the dungeons as a vampire led him out. I attended one of the dinners and heard the screams."

He stretched and reached out to one of the wine bottles. "Is all of that for you? Nice. The masters give us wine only occasionally." He poured himself a full goblet and took a long sip. "Yes, I guess the biting is a bit painful, but it passes quickly, and the masters let you be for a few months before they bite you again."

Myra slowly massaged her temples as her plans crumbled to dust. She had hoped to make allies out of the Farm humans and to offer them a chance to join the Resistance. Instead, one of them was trying to convince her to join them and live like an animal. "Samson, can you read and write?"

He snorted, making wine splatter from his mouth. In her mind's eye, Myra saw Prince Vladimir, his long graceful fingers curled around the goblet's stem, twirling it softly, bringing it to his lips, smelling, analyzing, savoring every sip. Every sip was an unspoken pleasure, an experience, a celebration of taste and sense and life itself. And then, here was Samson, pouring the liquid down his throat, anxious to get the alcohol to his head as fast as possible. "Of course, I can read," he said. "I'm not stupid."

"So someone is teaching you?"

"A few of us like to teach. Franka most of all."

Myra took a step towards him. "Who is Franka?"

"She's old," he said. "Very old. She's been around since before the Nightfall."

Of course. Myra smiled for the first time after meeting Samson. The humans born before the Nightfall were likely to have more spirit. If only she could make Vlad let her meet one of them.

***

Myra's eyes wandered across the vast shelves in the library. Even the multitude of books all around her failed to take her mind off the human she had met. Tristan had returned shortly to take Samson back to the Farm, and Myra did not consider it a great loss. She had planned to give the man a message to the other Farm humans, but had changed her mind. Could she look for allies among these people? Could she trust them enough to tell them her mission was to assassinate the Prince? In all likelihood, they would get mad at her for trying to harm their *master.*

How was it possible? *The domesticated humans are little more than animals.* Vlad's words came back to her, but she refused to believe it. No one could truly domesticate a human, no matter what the Prince claimed.

Her eyes brightened as she spotted a book on art history. Myra rose up on her toes and pulled it from the shelf. She sat on one of the stuffed armchairs placed against the wall, opening the heavy book in her lap. Myra smiled and ran her hand over the glossy paper. The print was of astonishing quality, so bright and smooth and detailed—it was like seeing the real paintings in front of her.

If Zack could see me now, he would tell me to stop wasting my time and do something useful. I should be looking for books that could help me kill vampires, or destroy the WeatherWizard.

Myra bit her lip and stood up, returning the book to its place. Imaginary Zack was right—there had to be books on the WeatherWizard in this library. Her mission was to kill the Prince, but Vlad's death would do no good unless the Resistance was ready to strike at the Wizard while the disorder created by the power vacuum still lasted. If another vamp rose to power and the WeatherWizard was still standing, it would be a wasted opportunity.

She passed by the history section and threw the long rows of books a longing look before moving on. Perhaps in one of those tomes she could find the secrets of the Prince's past. She already knew enough to give her a starting point. She had seen him perform an animal sacrifice, so his people had likely been pagan. And the man who had killed his family was canonized as a saint. This had to be connected to a conversion to Christianity.

Myra stopped in her tracks, turning back. Perhaps one quick look would not hurt. The books on the WeatherWizard were not going anywhere.

And how exactly will knowing more about the Prince help you accomplish your mission? Imaginary Zack said inside her head. *Stop giving in to flights of fancy and get to work.*

But I need to know my enemy if I'm to fight him, she argued.

She could see Zack's face in front of her, his eyes stern and his mouth set in a straight line. *You don't need to know his hopes and dreams to drive a stake through his heart. While you are here, looking at pretty books, we are starving. Disease is spreading, and we have no medicines. Our vitamin D supplies are running low. We struggle to get through every single day, and you frolic around in fancy dresses.*

Myra sighed and with an effort tore her gaze off the shelves. She walked on until she found the section on meteorology.

Her face immediately brightened, her eyes focusing on a dark blue spine sandwiched between a book on deadly hurricanes and another on types of clouds, with the title written in bold white letters—*The Day the Rain Stopped.* That had to be it.

Myra stole a glance in each direction and rose up on tiptoes, reaching for the book. She brought it down and stared at the front page.

A two-story-high structure stood on top of a stony hill. The hill was in the middle of a deep valley, surrounded by steep cliffs on all sides. Suspension bridges connected the surrounding cliffs with points around the middle of the central peak. Myra gasped and opened the book, flipping through the pages. Most of it was text, but there were also charts—maps of the surrounding area and blueprints of internal structures.

Myra's heart was beating wildly. This was perfect. She could tear off a few pages and look for a way to send them back to the Resistance. If Zack could see this, their odds in the fight would improve tremendously.

She nearly jumped and clutched the book tightly as she heard someone approaching. Shaking, Myra returned the book—she had nowhere to hide it, and would have to come back later and pick the pages she needed.

Tristan's pale blond head appeared from behind a shelf, and the vampire grinned at her. "Losing ourselves among the books, are we?" He looked around, scanning the surrounding titles. "Are you looking for something in particular?"

Myra tried not to blush, tearing her eyes off the Weather-Wizard book. "I'm writing a story," she said, "and the characters are out in the sun. I've never seen the sun. I was thinking perhaps I could find a book about it to better understand what it feels like."

"Then you are in the wrong section," he said. "Besides, the sun is overrated. I never had much affection for it anyway."

She gulped. Did he suspect her true reasons for being in this section? And what was he doing here anyway? Her eyes wandered to the book in his hand, and she stared at the wood-carved cover, decorated with butterflies, plants, and symbols she could not read. "You came here for a book? What language is that?"

Tristan raised the book to let her take a better look. "Japanese. It is one of my favorite poetry collections. I must have read it over fifteen times."

Myra frowned. "You must miss it? Writing poetry?"

He arched an eyebrow. "How do you know about that?"

She grinned. "I know things."

"I see. If you must know, I do miss it. It used to be a large part of who I was. And writing poetry was the thing that ultimately saved me from mediocrity."

"You must be angry at the Prince for taking that from you."

He stared at her, wide-eyed. "What? Why on earth would I be angry at my lord?"

You better be, Myra thought. She was still looking for some discord among the vamps she could exploit, and any resentment on Tristan's part would work nicely. "You used to write, to create art and beauty," she said. "He destroyed that. He killed you and turned you into a monster with a broken soul. You read the words others write, but can't write your own. It must hurt. He did that to you. I'm certain you must be angry, and no one would blame you."

"You have no idea what you are talking about," Tristan said. "He took nothing away. And he gave me so much."

"How so?" Myra asked. "I know that my ability to write is one of the things I value the most. It is who I am, and if I lost it, I would lose myself. I would hate anyone who tried to take it away from me. What could the Prince give you that is more valuable?"

Tristan smiled sadly. "Everything."

"Would you care to elaborate?"

He leaned over the shelf and ran his finger along the spines. "Perhaps I should tell you how I was turned. It could help you understand us better."

Myra held her breath. She had wanted to learn more about the Prince, but hearing about Tristan's past sounded almost as exciting. And it could give her glimpses into Vlad's story as well. "I would love that."

He grinned. "I am sure you would. Myra, dear, nothing comes for free. You want to hear my story? You need to give me something in return. So, what can you offer me?"

She hesitated. "What would you like? I could write you a story."

Tristan threw his head back, laughing. "Sweet girl, you will write me a story whether I demand it or not. It is in your blood. Come, now, you have to come up with something better than that. Until you do, I fear my past will remain dark and mysterious."

Myra rolled her eyes. What could she give him? Besides art, vampires could do anything better than she could. And even if she did come up with a skill she could trade in for a favor, was it not better if she asked for something that would help her learn more about the WeatherWizard or defeat Vlad instead of Tristan's tale? She was hopeless. She had to concentrate on the mission at hand, but her curiosity was about to push her five steps back.

Tristan smiled at her. "Come, now, let me show you those books about the sun you have been looking for."

Myra followed him, resisting the urge to cast a look back at the shelf, where she had left the WeatherWizard book. She had to come back for it. Finding out more about the WeatherWizard—this had to be her only goal now. This, and nothing else.

Chapter Nineteen

Wolves and Puppies

Myra opened the door to the Prince's study and stepped inside as her guards waited in the corridor. "You called for me, Your Highness? Yong said it was time for the lesson you talked about."

The vampire stood up from the piano chair and gave her a small bow. "Indeed it is. Please, come in, my dear, and take a seat." He sat back down and started playing.

Myra had heard the orchestra at the opera, Tristan's flute, and the violins at the dinner table, but this was the first time she was hearing someone play the piano. The melody was hauntingly beautiful and tugged at her heartstrings in ways she had not expected. She wanted to hum along, but restrained herself and sat down, waiting for the Prince to speak.

"Have you heard this music before?" he asked.

She shook her head. "I'm afraid not, my lord. Sadly, we have no pianos at the Resistance's Headquarters. The only musical instruments in our hideout are crude woodwind instruments we have made ourselves and an old balalaika salvaged from somewhere during the Nightfall, but no one knows how to play it. None of us have any real training. Most of the music we hear is simple unaccompanied singing—songs from the Old World the eldest among us have taught us, or songs we have made up ourselves."

"This is how music first started, after all, by creating your own instruments, making up songs, and experimenting. Humans are born to create, to compose, and if your small community survives long enough, I am certain they will produce some remarkable pieces," the Prince said. He continued to play as he spoke, never pausing. "What you are listening to now is my own piano arrangement of Shostakovich's Second Waltz. It sounds better when performed by a proper orchestra, and you will have the chance to hear it at the concert I am having in the Great Hall in two weeks. For now, this will have to do for your lessons."

"What lessons do you have in mind, my lord?"

"I am planning to teach you how to waltz, if you would like it, of course. If you are able to dance, you will enjoy yourself much more at the upcoming ball."

Myra could not believe him. A ball? And he would probably gift her with a lovely flowing gown and lead her on a dance? What was the vampire thinking? That just like that she would start seeing the castle as a place of beauty, music, dances, literature, and blooming culture, instead of as a disgusting butcher house?

"Your offer is generous, my lord," she said.

"I know it is," the arrogant jerk said. "And yet, you are not grateful. Why?"

"I'm grateful, Your Highness, please don't misunderstand me. I'd love to learn." That much at least was true—she did want to learn how to dance. She still remembered Armida in the Rose Gardens, dancing gracefully under the torchlight. Myra wanted to learn how to do that. She only wished for it to happen under different circumstances. *Any* other circumstances.

The Prince looked about to say something, but a knock on the door interrupted him and Tristan entered without waiting for an invitation. "The wine and chocolates you requested, my lord."

Vlad sighed. "Tristan, you should send servants for such requests. It is not your duty to wait on me."

The silver-haired vampire placed the tray on the central table and plopped on an armchair, leaning back casually and flinging one leg over the armrest. "If you rely on these idiots, you will have to wait until the next millennium to get any service," he said and reached out for the chocolates.

Myra gazed thoughtfully at the wine and the severely expired chocolates. She wondered for how long these supplies would last until the vamps realized that they had to actually work and produce something if they wished to maintain their current lifestyle.

"I can see you have invited yourself to the party," Vlad said dryly, eyeing the three golden goblets. "Well, then, you can perhaps do something useful. I am planning to teach Myra how to waltz."

Tristan choked on his chocolate and stared at the black-haired vampire with wide, unbelieving eyes.

The Prince raised a dark eyebrow. "Is there something amusing you would like to share?"

The other vampire had managed to regain control over himself and smiled innocently. "Forgive me, my lord, but *you* are planning to teach her?"

"And what is that supposed to mean?" Vladimir asked icily.

"It is just that everyone knows I am better at the waltz than you. Much better."

The Prince had raised both eyebrows now. "Is that so?"

Tristan nodded. "It only makes sense, does it not? The waltz was not even invented when you were born, old man."

A dark smile appeared on Vladimir's lips. "I learned to waltz easily once it was invented. I am a nobleman after all, and the cultured dances are in my blood. But I can imagine ballroom dances must have felt unnatural to a peasant boy, such as yourself."

"A *nobleman*? You?" Thankfully, Tristan had given up on the chocolate or he would probably have choked once again. "Your grandfathers were savages, drinking fermented horse milk. The only reason you call yourself noble is that you conquered the locals and ruled over them. You were the ones with stronger bows and sharper arrows, not higher culture and nobler blood."

The Prince's eyes burned dangerously as he crossed his arms. "First," he said with chilling calmness, "I would have you know that my people were highly cultured and had well-established aristocracy system even during their nomadic years. Second, the drink you describe is delicious and has numerous benefits. Third, we did not conquer the locals—we *liberated* them. And last, even if there was the slightest amount of substance to your arguments, which is not the case, they all fall apart as I was born well after we had settled down. My own upbringing was very different from that of my grandfathers."

"Are you saying you have not been raised in the way of the horse lords?" Tristan challenged.

The Prince casually leaned back against the piano. "I do not deny that I was taught how to ride before I could walk, and tutored in horseback archery since I could hold a bow. Yet I fail to see in what way this makes me any less civilized. In fact, similar activities were a standard part of a young nobleman's education in many courts. Besides, the rest of my learning did not suffer in any way, and I continued improving long after I was turned. You are aware that I am versed in literature and history, art and music, mathematics and the natural sciences, and that I am fluent in forty-two languages, even if some are now extinct or have evolved beyond recognition. How many 'savages' can say that?"

Tristan flung both of his legs across the armrest and ran a hand through his long hair. "Fine, fine. Arguing with you gives me a headache."

"This is what you get for picking the wrong side in the argument," Vlad said with a smile. "You were right about one thing, though. You *are* the better dancer. Now, will you teach the girl?"

The two vampires turned at Myra, and she looked away, trying to hide her shock. What was wrong with Tristan today? He was always so servile around the Prince, but now he was inexplicably cheeky and cheerful. It was like watching a completely different person.

"What is it?" the fair-haired vampire asked, apparently noting her confusion.

Myra shook her head, trying to collect her bearings. "Forgive me, Lord Tristan," she said and chastised herself as he raised his eyebrows at the title. No one called him that. "I noticed you were different today, and it surprised me. I meant no disrespect."

"Different?" The Prince looked at her quizzically. "I noticed no such thing. How is he different?"

"Well, you know…" Myra glanced at Tristan helplessly. "You must have heard what everyone says about you." He *had* heard, right? She had noticed that many of the vampires were talking freely in front of her as if she was not even there. It was annoying, and yet convenient as it gave her the chance to hear most of the gossip around the Palace.

The silver-haired vampire crossed his arms and stared at her. "Enlighten me."

Myra hesitated. She did not wish to anger him, and yet she saw an opportunity. If he was indeed unaware of what everyone was saying behind his back, she could prove herself useful. Perhaps she could be a spy for them—hearing things no one would speak in front of Tristan and the Prince. If she could convince Vladimir that he would benefit from her cooperation, perhaps she would at last gain some leverage over him. Perhaps she could also use it to make Tristan tell her his story. Myra bit her lower lip and looked up, meeting Tristan's eyes.

"You know. Many say you are so puppylike around His Highness, and—"

"*Puppylike*?" Tristan cried indignantly, while the Prince collapsed into the piano chair with laughter. "What do you mean puppylike?"

"These are not my words," Myra said, hoping she had not crossed a line. "Everybody says so—the guards, the servants, the noble-vamps."

"Today is nothing unusual," Vlad explained with a grin. "Tristan is always like this, but he tends to be a bit reserved in front of other vampires. You do not think I would enjoy his company if he was 'puppylike' all the time, do you?"

"My company is always extremely pleasant, whether I am *puppylike* or not," Tristan scolded.

Myra tried to come to terms with this new side of Tristan—and of the Prince—that she had witnessed. "But you always look so unhappy with the other vampires around," she said.

Tristan wrinkled his nose in distaste. "This is because I *am* unhappy with them around. I have an extreme dislike for other vampires. I know that the feeling is mutual, and I could not care less."

Vlad sighed overdramatically and gave Myra a tired smile. "See what I have to deal with? I have to protect my people and ensure their happiness and well-being, and my closest friend could not be happier than to see them all burn to dust. What happened to you, Tristan? You used to like vampires, even before you were turned."

"That was because you and Lady Callisto were the only vampires I knew at the time," Tristan said as he uncorked the wine bottle and poured three goblets. "You never warned me what the others were like."

Myra took her chalice and sniffed at the wine. An idea had come to her mind. She knew that no matter how well she learned to lie, the Prince would never trust her. He would always assume that she was playing a role, that she was lying, before she even started to speak. She needed to change the game, to mix the truth and the lies, and make him believe that she was always sincere. And the only way to do that was to make him permit her to speak freely. Myra raised her goblet, meaning to take a small sip for courage, but then put it back down. If she was to do this, she had to be completely sober.

"There is something I can't understand, Your Highness," she said. "You claim that you enjoy Tristan's company because he isn't puppylike all the time—"

"Oh, enough already," Tristan cried, but Myra ignored him.

"Then why is it that you require the opposite of me?" she asked. "Why do you ask me to grovel at your feet, instead of to speak my mind? Why do you want *me* to be puppylike, Vlad?"

This was the first time she had called him that out loud since the boy's murder, and she fervently hoped she had not overstepped her boundaries. She expected a violent reaction if not from the Prince, then at least from Tristan, but both vampires regarded her silently.

"You do have a point," Prince Vladimir said after a while. "Perhaps I will indeed enjoy you better untamed."

"*Untamed*? You must have tamed many horses in your lifetime, but you can't put a leash on a human being. Even if you keep me a prisoner here, you cannot take away my free will."

"Oh, I can do that and much more, never doubt that. Though I admit I am intrigued by the idea of a wild human talking to me freely. I suppose I do not need another puppy. After all, I have Tristan already."

"Hey!" the vampire in question scolded and aimed a chess knight in his lord's direction, which the Prince caught easily.

"You know, 'Vlad' is not even the proper way to shorten my name. But it matters not, I like it well enough," the Prince said and reached out for his goblet. "You may continue calling me that if it is to your liking. But come, now, I promised you a dancing lesson." He sat on the piano chair and started playing.

Tristan showed Myra the basic steps and led her on a dance. The steps themselves were easy enough, but doing them without thinking and coordinating her legs and moves with the music was more challenging. Still, Tristan was a patient teacher, and Myra soon realized that the vampire was doing most of the work in the dance and all she had to do was follow.

"My lord tells me you were interested in my hair," Tristan said with a smile.

Myra glared at Vlad. Did he blabber about their private talks to everyone? "Your hair is quite interesting."

"*Everything* about me is interesting, human," Tristan said smugly. "You will do well to remember that. And if you would like, I would be more than happy to give you a few hair care tips."

"What, give me a vampire makeover?" she asked incredulously. "Many thanks, but I'll decline your generous offer."

The dance was slow, but tiring for Myra's untrained feet, and after a while, she and her partner collapsed into the stuffed armchairs. "When shall we see your admirable dancing skills, my lord?" Tristan asked, taking a sip from his chalice.

"Not today, I fear. Myra has done nothing to deserve that. She has been such a good girl," the Prince said, and the younger vampire grinned, probably thinking his lord was admitting defeat. He should have known better, Myra thought and smiled when Vlad continued. "If I am to dance, you need to play the piano."

Tristan glared at his Prince. "Are you insulting my pianist skills, my lord?" he asked, his voice low and dangerous.

"Not at all, my boy," the Prince said cheerfully. "How could I insult something that does not exist?"

Before Tristan could retort, the door opened without warning and Armida walked in. The vampire was wearing a glittering black dress, and her long burgundy hair was falling around her bare shoulders in intricate braids.

"You are late, my love," Vlad said and turned around, giving her a long kiss.

"And I have missed much from the looks of it," she said, smiling, and sat on the arm of Tristan's chair. She ran her fingers through the vampire's silver hair, smoothing it down, and started to braid it.

"You did indeed. I will tell you all about it tonight," Vlad promised and took a sip from his wine.

Armida's eyes moved across the filled goblets. "Interesting. Only three. Tristan, dearest, am I to assume you did not want me at this party?"

"Any party without you is not worth attending, my lady," Tristan said. "I simply assumed you would be sharing my lord's chalice."

"I could," Armida mused. "But, to be honest, I never liked goblets. Tell me, dearie, how much wine is flowing through your veins?"

"Not much, I am afraid," Tristan said. "I only had a glass."

"Well, then," she said thoughtfully and brushed the vampire's half-braided silver hair away from his neck. "I suppose I would need to drink more."

Myra could not stifle a gasp when the vampire sank her sharp teeth into Tristan's neck. Tristan threw his head back and closed his eyes, inhaling sharply. Myra looked at Vlad in confusion, expecting him to do, or at least say, something, but to her utter shock, she found the Prince gazing at the two other vampires with an affectionate smile, as if the scene playing before him was the most natural thing in the world.

Armida twisted her long red-lacquered fingers into Tristan's silver hair, pulling his head back and exposing his pale throat to her hunger. She drank deep, and Tristan gasped, whether in pleasure or pain, Myra could not say. She tried to look away, but found her eyes strangely glued to the scene. She shuddered as both vampires' faces grew pale and translucent, and their eyes shone with otherworldly light—Tristan's soft blue-grey, and Armida's bright emerald.

"Myra, I wish to discuss something with you," Vladimir said.

She stared at him in disbelief. "Here? Now?"

He frowned. "Forgive me. I am losing my touch with human customs and lifestyle. Is it your bedtime already?"

"It's not my bedtime," Myra said incredulously. "Vlad, you mean we are to have this discussion here and now? While they are"—she gestured at the other vampires, trying to find the right words—"*doing stuff?*"

The Prince arched an eyebrow. "They are not 'doing stuff.' Armida is drinking a blood-and-wine cocktail. The combination has an exquisite taste, but if it bothers you, we can move to your room. See, my love, you scared the human."

Armida lifted her head, her eyes large and round like bottomless jade pits, her small mouth curved and wicked. She licked her bloody lips. "Forgive me, love, this was never my intention. Tristan, muffin, you know I like my cocktails stronger."

Tristan opened bleary silver eyes. "As my lady commands," he mumbled and reached for his goblet. His slender hand shook with the weight, and Armida reached out to steady it and guide the wine to his lips.

Myra sighed. "I would really like to leave *now*," she whispered.

The Prince picked up their two goblets and a backgammon set. "My love, when you two are done, could you have another bottle sent to Myra's room? Thank you. And don't drain him too much."

"I'll leave enough for you, love," Armida said, and Myra breathed a sigh of relief as she followed the Prince out of the room.

"Our ways may disgust you now, darling girl, but one day you will learn to tolerate and even desire them," Vladimir said once the door closed behind them.

He has to be mad, Myra thought. "Can he die of this?"

"Tristan, you mean?" the Prince said. "Of course not. You cannot kill a vampire by drinking their blood, but it can weaken them, and they would need to feed to regain their strength. If a small amount is drunk, it will leave the vampire in a pleasant, drugged-like state, which will not last too long."

"So this is what Armida is doing right now?" Myra said. "But what happens if you drink a lot?"

"A greater blood loss is not so much fun," he said. "If a vampire loses too much blood, it could weaken them a lot, so much that they might be unable to hunt and feed, or even walk or move. Then someone has to feed them if they are to recover. If enough blood is lost, the vampire may lose consciousness and remain in this state for centuries until someone feeds them enough blood to wake up."

"Like a coma?" she asked.

"Not exactly. Vampires suffering from severe blood loss are not brain-dead. They are trapped in a sea of dark nightmares until someone brings them back to life. Still, this will not kill them; even if the last drop of blood is drained from their bodies, they will still live. And yet, they will be completely dependent on someone to save them. There must be dozens of vampires around the world, trapped in such a state, waiting for someone to revive them."

"Why does no one save them?"

"In some cases they are simply forgotten, buried, or lost somewhere and no one is looking for them. In others, someone keeps them like that on purpose as a form of punishment for past wrongs. And more often than not, nobody cares enough."

"This is terrible," Myra said.

The Prince looked at her sharply. "I thought you desired death for all vampires?"

"I do," she said. "And I would gladly give them all a clean death with a stake to the heart, but to be trapped in eternal torment is something no one deserves."

"I agree," the Prince admitted. "It is a fate I would not wish upon my worst enemies."

"So only blood can revive a vampire?"

"No other food can sustain us," Vlad said. "Blood feeds the magic that keeps us alive. Any other food or drink, we take only for taste and enjoyment, and alcohol affects us to an extent, but it has no nutritional value for us. Indeed, a vampire who has not drunk blood in a long time can lapse into the same weakened state. Same applies for wounds—almost nothing short of a stake right through the heart, a decapitation, fire or sunlight could kill us, but any other severe wound can weaken us considerably, especially if a blood loss is involved. Why are you so interested in this, anyway? Looking for ways to kill me?"

"Of course not, my lord," Myra protested, a bit too quickly. "I only find it strange that you would drink each other's blood if it has such negative effects upon your kind. I'm simply trying to understand you better, is all."

The Prince grinned and raised an eyebrow at her. "There is nothing strange about it. As I said, a small amount gives more pleasure than pain. You must understand that sharing blood plays a great role in our culture and society. For one thing, it is a way to share intimacy, a way to express both a bodily connection and an emotional and spiritual closeness."

Her disgust must have shown on her face, and his grin broadened. "Why are you so disturbed by this? It should not be foreign to you. The concept of blood brothers has existed in a variety of human cultures since the beginnings of time. Sometimes the men would cut their thumbs, press their wounds together and mix their blood, other times they would squeeze their mixed blood into a cup and drink it. After the ritual, they believed themselves to be blood brothers, ready to do anything for each other, simply because the same blood flowed through their veins. It is the same with us. I drink a vampire's blood, and he drinks mine. My blood flows through his veins now, and his through mine. We are brothers, in spirit and blood."

"So you only drink the blood of vampires you are close to?" Myra asked.

"Not necessarily. This is only one of the uses. You can drink a vampire's blood as a form of domination. Say, for example, one of my people disobeys me. Then I could overpower them and drink their blood, until I have brought them to their knees, begging me for mercy."

"Is that how you came to lord over all vampires?" she asked, trying to keep her voice neutral.

He laughed. "I did have to resort to such means occasionally, but there is no need for that anymore. My people obey me now."

"They certainly do. Are there any other uses of blood-drinking that will not make me sick?" Myra asked, unsure if she wanted to know.

"All I told you about are trivialities," the Prince said. "Most of all, blood is food, blood is life. It is a way to save lives. Imagine, for example, that you are trapped in the wilderness, together with another vampire, who is weakened by blood loss or starvation. There is no living being around, and so there is only one way to help your companion—let them drink your blood. Let them feed off you, like a babe feeds off its mother's milk."

Myra sighed. "I thought I specifically asked for ways that would not make me sick." She regarded the Prince carefully. "Have you ever been saved in such a manner?"

"I have not," he said. "And your attempts to figure out my past are becoming pathetic."

As they spoke, they passed by the guards stationed in front of her chambers and entered. "Please, take a seat," Myra said, remembering that he considered her a host in her chambers and was expecting an invitation.

Vlad sat on the chair behind the desk and reached out to take one of her notebooks. He flickered through the pages without looking inside, all the while staring at the desk's edge.

"You wanted to discuss something with me?" Myra prompted.

"Yes… yes, I do," he said.

When he made no move to continue, she raised an eyebrow. "Well? Are we going to discuss it tonight, or do you prefer to come back tomorrow? Perhaps you have other duties to attend to?"

"No, to be honest, I have been meaning to talk to you about this for some time."

Myra nodded, waiting for him to continue.

"One thing I noticed about you was your approach to writing longer stories," he said. "You seldom have a plan how the story is going to reach the end; you simply start somewhere and keep writing, on and on, relying on ideas to keep coming to you. And they always do."

She ran her hand through her hair impatiently. Were they going to discuss this again? "Yes, I know, we have talked about this already. It's a bad practice, and I shouldn't rely on it. I should learn to be more organized and to plan my plots in advance."

She was surprised when he shook his head. "No, not at all. In fact, I was happy when I learned this was your manner of writing."

Myra frowned, trying to detect some irony in his words and finding none. "How so?"

The Prince hesitated. "Because it gave me hope that you may be able to help me."

Now this was the last thing she had expected. The Prince admitting that he needed her help? And the nerve of him! After all he had done to her and to so many humans, he thought he could ask her for a favor?

"What do you want from me?" she asked icily.

Just then, someone knocked on the door and a guard entered, carrying a bottle of wine. Vlad poured two goblets after dismissing him and handed one to Myra. "Would you like to play backgammon while we discuss it?" he offered.

She narrowed her eyes at him. "Would you like to stop procrastinating and tell me what this is all about?"

He smiled and took a sip from his wine. "I was just like you once," he said. "I used to make up stories, never knowing the end, coming up with ideas as I went along. I had even started writing one of them down. You see, at the time and place I grew up, writing fiction was not at all common. Hardly anyone could read or write, and the two most common languages of the realm I lived in had no writing systems of their own. The concept of a novel did not exist at the time, and writing itself was rare and mostly intended for correspondence between rulers or defining laws.

"It mattered not to me. I wrote my tale for myself and to entertain my wife and my daughters. I wrote the chapters and read them to my family, one after another, never planning more than two chapters in advance. And then, my loved ones were taken from me because I refused to let my people's legacy be forgotten."

He took another long sip and fell silent. Myra patiently waited for him to continue.

"I was turned shortly after, and for many years my book was the last thing on my mind. After a few centuries, the burning agony gradually turned into a dull ache, and I finally found the courage to reread my story. I liked it a lot, even if I say so myself, and I wanted to know what happened in the end. But I did not. I had never come up with the ending, and had relied on ideas coming to me. And they would have come if only I had remained human for a while longer. You know the rest of the story—I am a vampire now. I am devoid of my imagination and cannot weave any new tales. My book will always remain unfinished, and I will never learn what happens in the end."

"You want me to finish your book?" Myra guessed. "You want me to think of an ending and write the remaining chapters?"

"Yes, I would like that. I saw that you have imagination, but your writing talent was unrefined. However, in the past weeks you have improved greatly, and I trust you enough for this."

Myra's heart beat wildly in her chest. She wanted to tell him she owed him no favors and that she would not finish his book unless he released all humans and let her go home. She wanted to tell him that if he had spent lifetimes wondering what happened in his book, it was the smallest of punishments he deserved for his cruelty. And yet, she was so curious to read the Prince's book. Perhaps it would finally give her some insight into his past and his mind before he was turned.

But most of all, she was overwhelmed. The Prince trusted *her* to finish his work. This book must have meant so much to him, and now he had enough faith in her skills to let her do this.

"I can give it a try," she said.

He seemed to breathe a sigh of relief. "Thank you. I suppose you will first need to read what I have so far. I am going hunting tonight, but I will try to translate one or two chapters before I leave."

"That would be a good start," she said. "But I will need something from you to help with the writing."

He raised an eyebrow. "Something besides everything I have already given you? What else could you possibly want?"

"I told you I wanted to talk to humans from other societies to expand my horizons. I met with that Farm human you sent me, and you were right—there wasn't much to discuss with him."

"I told you so," he said. "They are no more than animals."

Her fists clenched. *And you made them that.* "Of course, my lord. But he said that one human, Franka, who was born in the Old World, was trying to teach them and keep their spirit alive. I would like to meet her."

"You believe she will be different?"

"I have to try. I feel my perspective is limited, and I won't be able to give you the quality writing you need."

"Very well," he said. "I will find this Franka and send her to you."

Myra smiled. "Thank you. And one more thing—"

He frowned. "You agreed to help with my book. I owe you one favor. Not two."

"It's not a favor really, just something to help me write. I've been having some problems recently."

The Prince nodded. "What kind of problems?"

"I've been having trouble sleeping after I attended that dinner. I keep hearing the screams in my nightmares and wake up. I sleep badly, I have headaches throughout the day, and it's difficult to concentrate."

"You should have told me sooner. I will send someone to pick valerian from the woods and make you tea."

"Thank you, Vlad, but I'm not sure if this would help. I think I'll need something stronger."

"You need sleeping pills?" He leaned back in the armchair, taking a long sip. "You are not planning to kill yourself, I hope?"

She forced herself to laugh. "If I wanted to kill myself, I would have jumped from the window."

"Good point. Remind me to bar your windows."

She smiled. "I promise you, I have no desire to kill myself. I simply want to sleep better."

"We do have sleeping pills in the pharmacy," he said. "I will prescribe you the dosage and you will let me know if you have any side effects."

"Sounds good," she said and raised her own goblet. He raised his in a toast. "Always wine," Myra said. "Why do you drink it? Does it make you forget?"

"Forget? Why would I want to forget?"

"Your family died horribly. I assume you don't like to think about that."

"I would never try to forget," Vlad said. "It would be a dishonor to their memory. No, Myra, the reason I like wine is much simpler. When I drink, my intelligence quotient drops temporarily. Less intelligent people are happier, don't you agree?"

Myra watched him silently as he took another sip. Alcohol affected vampires, so it was likely drugs affected them too. And if she could grind these sleeping pills into powder, perhaps they would dissolve in wine. And once they took effect, Myra would find out if the stake she had devised from the bed's leg was sharp enough.

But not yet. First she needed him to translate his chapters, so she could read his book.

And how exactly does reading his book advance my mission?

Myra massaged her temples. She wanted to kill him, to hurt him, to take revenge for all the monstrosities he had committed. Yet at that moment, she wished nothing more than to read his book.

Zack would not have hesitated. Lidia would not have hesitated. Alerie had died so Myra could be here, with a chance to strike.

Less intelligent people are happier, don't you agree?

"Yes," she said softly. "Yes, I believe they are."

Chapter Twenty

Night Falls

Myra stared silently at the human in front of her. Short and skinny, her head barely reached Tristan's chest. Wispy snow-white hair framed her pale, wrinkled face, and her large blue eyes were lively and clear.

"Is she the one you requested?" Tristan asked.

Myra met the old woman's gaze. "Your name is Franka?"

She nodded.

Myra turned to Tristan. "You will not bring her back to the Farm. She will stay here with me, or you will find her separate chambers."

The vampire raised a silver eyebrow. "Indeed? Is that a part of your agreement with His Highness?"

She held his gaze. "His Highness wants me to improve my writing. I can't do this without talking to actual humans."

"Right. I will check with my lord and see if he approves of these arrangements. Anything else you require, *Your Majesty*?"

She rolled her eyes. "Thanks, Tristan, really."

He grinned and left the room, closing the door behind him. Myra turned to the old woman, who was now staring at her wide-eyed.

"And who the hell are you?" Franka said.

"My name is Myra Andersen. I'm a member of the Resistance—a group that fights to destroy the Prince and bring back the sun."

The old woman snorted. "I've heard the vampires mention this Resistance thing years ago, but I thought it was a myth. You're telling me there's a bunch of humans fighting against His Evilness? Wow. What a marvelous job you've done."

Myra frowned. "You can't blame us. It's hard to survive out there, let alone fight."

Franka flung herself on the bed and reached out for the chocolates on the table. "Well, then, you might want to rethink your mission statement." She bit on a chocolate. "You claim to fight the vampires, and yet here you are, living in their Palace and eating their food. And I don't see any bite marks on you."

Myra shuddered and placed a hand protectively over her neck. "My commander sent me here to assassinate the Prince, but I was captured."

Franka laughed. "And again—marvelous job. So now he keeps you as his pet and pampers you, is that it?"

"It's a bit more complicated."

"But in a nutshell—yes," Franka said in between bites. "Does he give you any cigarettes?"

"What? No. I mean, I never asked."

Franka scolded and stood up from the bed. "Next time ask. I haven't had a smoke in decades."

"I'm sure that's a big problem for you," Myra said, "but right now we have other priorities."

Franka walked to the window and pulled the curtains, letting the moonlight in. "Priorities? You and your Resistance people have been living your jolly lives out in freedom, while the vampires bred us like cows, and you did nothing to help us. Don't talk to me about priorities."

"I'm sorry you have been treated badly," Myra said, "but we couldn't have done anything. We had no idea you existed. Besides, I thought your people were happy at the Farm."

"What? That's ridiculous."

"I thought so too," Myra said. "But I talked to one man, Samson—"

Franka burst into laughter. "Samson? Honestly? I bet the vampires let you meet Samson of all people on purpose, to prove whatever point they were trying to make. I can assure you, not all of us agree with him."

Myra smiled. "You're telling me your people want freedom? Will they be ready to join us if we make a stand?"

"Of course," Franka said. "You shouldn't have asked Pretty Boy to give me my own quarters. I could move back and forth between the Farm and your place and carry your messages to my people. If you have any messages to give, that is."

Did she have any messages? Myra frowned. She had no immediate escape plan. She had not even found the time to return to the library and get information on the Wizard.

"So why did His Evilness decide to keep you alive?" Franka asked.

Myra sat on the bed and invited the old woman to take a chair. Slowly, she started her tale—how Vlad had discovered she could write, how he had killed a boy to control her, and how he wanted her to continue his book.

"He is toying with you," Franka said. "You must be cautious. The Prince is no fool, and he knows what he's doing in keeping you here. You must be careful not to fall for his tricks."

"I won't, I promise," Myra said. "Do you know anything about him? Have you seen him much during your years of imprisonment?"

"I've seen him a few times," Franka said, "though he seldom comes to the dungeons, and I was imprisoned at another place before. It's a bit of a coincidence I ended up here."

"You are not from around here, then?" Myra asked.

"Not really," the old woman said. "I was born in a small town in the Netherlands, and moved to Amsterdam for my job after I finished my studies. It seems like hundreds of lifetimes ago. Those were simpler times—worrying about finding a flat or putting bread on the table."

Myra sat on the bed, wrapping her arms around her knees. "I wish I could worry about all that, and not about getting eaten. It sounds so surreal—having a flat, and a job, and going to work every day. What did you do?"

"I was a consultant. Nothing terribly exciting, I'm afraid," Franka said. "Mostly staying long hours at the office and lots and lots of travel. Often I had to get up at three to fly somewhere for a project, and fly back on the same evening."

Myra stared at the older woman. Nothing terribly exciting? Yes, she supposed Franka's life had been ordinary—the old woman had finished university and become a working professional, like so many other people. And yet, Franka's life sounded so strange, so varied, thrilling even. Myra wondered how she would describe her own past. *I was born in darkness. I lived in darkness. I never went Outside.* Yes, her criteria for 'exciting' were somewhat lax. "So you didn't mind the long hours?" Myra asked.

Franka shook her head. "I was young and single, so it was fine for me. The only thing I minded was that I couldn't always plan my holidays—if I was on a project, it was impossible to take a single day off. This was why I was so happy when my manager allowed me a two-week Christmas holiday."

Christmas… this was something Myra had read a lot about, but had never truly experienced despite her efforts to preserve Old World traditions. "I can imagine you wanted to celebrate with your family," she said.

"I did," said Franka. "I often had to work on the weekends and seldom had the chance to travel to my hometown and see my mom and dad. I had only seen them for a few days or so during the past year, and you can't imagine how much I looked forward to getting back home. And then, about a week before my holiday, my manager told me I had to fly to London for three days."

"You weren't happy I imagine?"

"Honestly, I didn't mind—I was going to be back in time for Christmas, and if I got any spare time, I could go shopping for presents. It was perfect. The evening before my flight I called my mom and told her I would see her soon." Franka smiled. "I remember she told me that my grandma was asking what meals I would like when I got back home."

Myra tried to return the smile, but could not. She already had an idea where this story was going and did not like it one bit.

"On the first day in London, the weather was dreadful," Franka continued. "Clouds covered the sky and not a single sunray reached the ground. It surprised me. I had heard nothing good about London weather in the past, but after the WeatherWizard's creation, it was often sunny in most big cities around the world. I asked some of the people working for our client company, and they said that indeed weekends were kept sunny, but clouds were not unusual for a workday. And so I never suspected anything. I didn't know something was wrong until it was too late."

The old woman fell silent and Myra wondered if the tale was too painful and her companion would stop here. She was just about to break the silence, when Franka spoke again.

"I was at the office, absorbed in my work, when a fire alarm went off. My colleague Simone said they were simply testing it, so we could ignore it and stay in the building. Then a strangled scream came from somewhere on the floor, outside of the little conference room our clients had given us. Simone and I exchanged a glance and she rushed to bar the door with a chair. Through the matted glass wall, we saw people running.

"I asked if we shouldn't get out—it could indeed be a fire after all, but Simone disagreed. We heard more screaming and fighting, and she was convinced it was a terrorist attack—our client was a big corporation and could be a target. We decided to stay inside, but that choice was taken from us when the glass door shattered.

"A stunningly beautiful blonde woman stepped into the room. With her strange clothes and jewelry, she seemed to have come straight from a Renaissance Fair. Blood was smeared across her lips, and in her hand she still held the chair she had used to break the glass, raised high as if it weighed nothing.

"It was so surreal; I thought I was trapped inside a dream. Everything was happening so fast. I had no time to wonder who she was and how she had gotten here before she grabbed Simone and bit her neck. Simone screamed and tried to struggle, and I wanted to help her, I truly did. Yet when I tried to fight the blonde, she pushed me away with such ease that I knew it was hopeless."

"And you ran?" Myra said. "I couldn't blame you. I can't imagine what horror it must have been."

"And I can't properly describe it," Franka admitted. "I couldn't comprehend what I was seeing. All around me there were people running, and other people in unusual clothes chasing after them, biting and drinking them. Bodies littered the floor and there was blood—so much blood everywhere. I ran down the stairs and didn't look back to check if anyone followed.

"I reached the ground floor to find the security gate broken and the robot guard shattered on the ground. The concierge lay facedown, blood pouring from the wound in her neck. I ran outside and never looked back.

"The streets were eerily empty. I ran on and on until I fell down. I barely registered that I had slipped in a pool of blood before I was running once again. I had to get away from there, as far away as possible. I wanted to stop a car, but there were none on the street. You see, an empty street in London, in the middle of a workday, was something unheard of. There was nothing natural about this.

"When I reached the larger road, I nearly collapsed. There were cars on the street. Some had crashed against stores and buildings or against each other, but most were simply parked in strange positions in the middle of the road, their windows broken. I saw bodies, arms and legs hanging from the shattered windows. Only the self-driven black taxis kept moving among the carnage, some empty, others with dead bodies at the back seats.

"I had to be strong. I had to get far away from here and find help. I turned around and descended into the nearest tube station.

"I saw nothing wrong at first, apart from the strange emptiness. There were no robot security guards, but my card worked and the gate opened, which gave me a sense of normalcy. The timetable was also working and I saw that the next train was coming in one minute.

"The doors opened, and I stepped inside. The carriage was full of people. Dead people. Some on the ground, others still in their seats. I collapsed on my knees and threw up."

Myra thought she would throw up herself. "There were no survivors?" she asked softly.

"I saw none at first," said Franka. "But then something moved. It was just a girl, a black girl no older than fifteen. She wore a blood-smeared white shirt and torn jeans. She was bleeding from a cut on her arm, but I saw no bites on her neck. A desire to protect her surged in my heart. She and I were the only survivors in this city of monsters and dead men.

"I told her to be brave. I told her I would help her. She smiled at me then, and I saw her teeth."

Myra gasped and pressed a hand against her month, breathing in deeply. The need to throw up was growing stronger.

Franka continued, "She told me I shouldn't fear her. She said she would not kill me—she had orders to capture a few humans of breeding age for the Farms. When she grabbed me and twisted me around with strength I could never match, I had no will left to fight back. I tried to talk to her, to ask her who she was—*what* she was. Why she was doing this. The only thing she told me was that the Prince commanded and she obeyed.

"We got off the tube at the third station and she dragged me to the Tower of London. The monsters had taken a large group of people in the yard inside the walls, all chained. Our captors were laughing at us, teasing us. Then all went silent and they stepped aside, making way for a woman.

"Her impossibly long golden hair was held up in an intricate style—that thing must have weighed at least ten kilos. Her elaborate snow-white ballgown was so long it was brushing the floor and trailing behind her as she walked. One step behind her was a man, wearing nothing but black leather pants. A thick dog collar encircled his neck, and crisscrossing straps wrapped his bare upper body. He had a ring piercing on his right nipple, attached to a delicate silver chain. The chain's other end was in the woman's hand.

"'See, my pet,' the blonde woman said, running her fingers through his hair, 'I have so many humans for you. Men and women, all young and juicy. You can have any one you want.'

"'Thank you, mistress,' the man with the collar said, and I wanted to scream."

"I want to scream myself," Myra admitted, "I cannot imagine how much worse it would be to witness that, and to have no idea what's going on. I hope he didn't pick someone to drink?"

Franka snorted. "Keep hoping. He drank a young woman, while the blond monster woman was drinking him at the same time. I really don't want to go into detail. Those freaks wanted to pick another human, but thankfully they were interrupted when he arrived.

"He was tall and broad-shouldered, his long cloak and dark hair waving in the wind. As he approached us, a flock of ravens rose from the field around us and disappeared into the cloudy sky. He smiled at the blonde woman and bowed. 'Duchess,' he said.

"She curtsied. 'Prince Vladimir. I trust you are satisfied with our progress?'

"'Very much so,' he said. 'Everything is going according to plan.'

"'You will stay here, then?' the Duchess said.

"He laughed. 'Oh no, not at all! A big city is not for me, and I cannot imagine what will happen to all those buildings once people stop taking care of them. I have picked a good old Scottish castle for myself. It is close to the WeatherWizard, so it would be easier for me to organize and monitor the defenses. It has a large dungeon; perfect for a Farm,' he added, throwing a glance at us. 'It is somewhat plain for my taste, but I have arranged for the best furniture, carpets, clothes and silverware to be delivered there. You prefer to stay here I imagine?'

"She smiled. 'It must be a relief to you. I hear your silver boy is scared of me, though I cannot imagine why. Have no fear. I have always wanted to rule over the Tower, ever since I was tortured here as a human. And if it is all the same to you, I would like to keep the Crown Jewels. I suppose you would want a share of these humans to be delivered to your castle?'

"'Naturally,' he said. 'As I would expect you to recognize my authority. You rule over the Tower, but you still report to me.' He looked away, and, to my horror, stared straight at me. Prince Vladimir took a few steps towards me and reached out. Only then did I realize he had seen my phone sticking out of my pocket.

"'You will not need this anymore, sweet girl,' he said. 'It probably will not even work in a few days.'

"I was crying. 'Please, sir,' I begged. 'I need it. I need to call my mom.'

"He looked almost sympathetic. 'Darling girl,' he said gently, 'your mother is dead.'

"I knew it could not be true, and yet a shudder ran down my spine at the words. 'She's not,' I told him. 'You might have killed everyone in this city, but my mom is far away from here. She is back in our hometown in the Netherlands.'

"'Sweet, silly girl,' he said. 'Do you think your puny town is untouched? What you see around you is happening everywhere, in every single place in the world. After tomorrow, the only humans alive will be captives in our Farms. This world no longer belongs to humankind. It belongs to me.'"

Franka fell silent and Myra raised a hand to brush her own tears away. It was fruitless, she realized, they kept on flowing. "I am sorry," said Myra. "I am so sorry. I wish there was something I could do."

There was no sadness in Franka's blue eyes, only grim determination. "There is," the old woman said. "Kill him."

Myra nodded. "I will."

Franka snorted and stood up from her chair. "Right. There's no time for fake bravado and badass boasts. You'll kill him, you say? Very well. How? What's your plan?"

Myra stared at her. "Can I trust you?"

The old woman laughed. "That's perhaps the smartest thing you've said since I walked into your room. You think His Evilness put me up to telling you a sappy story, gaining your trust and making you reveal your secrets?"

"I wouldn't put it past him," Myra said.

"And neither would I," said Franka. "But I can assure you, my story is true, and so is my hatred for him."

Myra gathered her skirts and knelt down. She stuck her hand underneath the bed and felt around until she found what she was looking for. She stood up and raised the stake and a transparent box filled with white pills.

The old woman reached out to touch the stake. "It's crude and not very sharp. Did you make it yourself?"

Myra nodded. "I'm planning to sharpen it as much as I can. I have a knife, though it's for cutting food, not wood."

Franka's eyes brightened. "Good enough. I'll help you. And the pills?"

"Sleeping drugs. I won't be able to stake him while he is awake."

For the first time, Franka smiled. "Brilliant. Do they dissolve in water?"

"One way to find out," Myra said.

The old woman looked around the room and walked to the shelves to pick a small marble statue of some god in a toga. "This will do," she said.

Myra and Franka set out to work. It took them almost an hour to turn the pills into fine, even powder, but in the end it was done. Myra sniffed at the final product. "I can't smell anything," she said, "but vamps have a better sense of smell."

"It appears odorless to me," Franka said and poured a goblet of wine.

Myra spilled a small amount of the powder into the goblet and twirled a spoon inside. The powder disappeared and the color never changed. Myra slowly poured the wine into a bowl and examined the goblet's bottom. There was no residue.

"It dissolved completely," she said. "Still, we don't know how much we can add to a cup of wine before the solution becomes saturated, or what dosage we need to do the trick."

"The more the better," Franka said. "Should we give it a try next time you talk to him?"

"Not next time," Myra said. "First, I need an escape plan. There is information on the WeatherWizard in the Prince's library. I need to get it and take it back to the Resistance. We'll gain nothing if we kill the Prince and then die. My friends at the Resistance won't even know he's dead until another vamp has solidified power."

"I don't think you can kill the Prince and escape," Franka said. "It has to be one or the other. You said you'd kill him."

"And I will," Myra said. "Just not this time."

Franka rolled her eyes. "Whatever. Just try not to fail me like your people had failed mine."

Myra sighed. Franka was right—the Prince had to die if the Resistance was to have any chance against the Wizard. And yet, there was still so much she could learn from him. Every new story she wrote was better and better. Did he know how much her writing had improved? Did he notice her progress? Was he proud?

Myra frowned at the thought. No one had ever been proud of her. Her parents had died years ago. Zack had given her tasks and had been satisfied enough with her accomplishments, but had never expressed any pride. She had been proud of herself every time she had written a new tale, but she now realized there had been nothing to be proud of. All her old works were a naive child's scribblings.

But her new works—now, that was something else. She had improved tremendously, and a big part of that was thanks to the Prince's tutelage.

I will make him say he is proud of me, Myra thought. *And then, only then can I start thinking about killing him.*

Chapter Twenty-One

The Pen and the Sword

"So," Franka said, "what's your progress?"

Myra looked up from the picture she was sketching. Vlad had given her color pencils and art textbooks, and though her works were still hideous, each one was better than the previous. Still, she doubted Franka was asking about the progress of her artistic skills. "On what?"

The old woman threw her hands in the air and turned around. "On killing the Prince, of course. Yesterday you said you had a plan, and yet he's still alive and drinking human blood."

"You should speak more softly," Myra said.

"Why?" Franka took a pull from her cigarette. Myra wished she had never asked Vlad about that. "Surveillance bugs can't work without electricity."

"There are other ways to listen," Myra said. "Spies were no less common when this castle was built, and the rulers often designed their homes so they could keep an eye on their subjects—hollow walls, hidden rooms. Besides, vamps' hearing is better than ours."

"Whatever," Franka said, lowering her voice. "I see you've made no progress with your sleeping powder thing. Have you thought about fire? There are torches everywhere."

"If we light a fire, we'll be the first to die," Myra said. "And it would be hard to target a specific vampire. I told you, my plan is good. I just need an escape plan first, and I need that book from the library."

"Don't put all your eggs in the same basket," said Franka. "You must have plans B and C. And D. His Evilness has weaknesses, you know. Weaknesses we could exploit."

"Like what?"

Franka was thoughtful for a moment. "For one, he's unreasonable."

Myra looked up from her notebook. "How so?"

"After I was transferred here, I would sometimes see him. He came to the dungeons more often back then," Franka said. "I remember one time, it was just a few days after I arrived, when Armida came down to join him. She reported she had been following a group of surviving humans, whom she had lost, and needed reinforcement. 'Let them be,' the Prince said. Armida protested, saying that they had agreed to kill, turn, or enslave everyone and let no one live in freedom, but he insisted that the humans shouldn't be prosecuted."

"He doesn't want to destroy the Old World completely, and makes irrational decisions because of it," Myra said. "I've noticed it too. He should have tortured me to learn more about the Resistance. Or he should have killed me—it must be clear to him my mission is to assassinate him. He takes a risk by keeping me here, and he even gives me tips how to lie to him and how to kill a vampire. He likes to play with fire."

"He does," Franka agreed. "But how do we use it against him?"

Myra felt strange. Vlad's attachment to the Old World was perhaps his single redeeming quality. It seemed dishonorable to use the lessons he had taught her to kill him. Yet, if he was stupid enough to underestimate her, then all that followed was his own fault. She was about to reply, but fell quiet as the door opened and Yong appeared.

"You are required in the throne room," he said, glaring at Myra before he turned to Franka. "You stay here. I will send someone to escort you to your new chamber."

Myra followed obediently, briefly wondering if the vampire had come to collect her by himself for a change. She suppressed a grin as they exited the room. Nope—predictably enough, four more vamps were waiting to accompany her. She followed them, eager to get to their destination as fast as possible and be rid of their company.

The high doors opened and she stepped inside. A long red carpet ran from the entrance up along the dais and to the foot of the black stone throne. Tristan sat on the throne sideways, his legs flung over the armrest. In his lap were an open leather-bound journal and a bowl of cherries. The vampire was lazily eating the cherries, spitting the pits onto the stony floor.

"Ah, our honored guest," he cried, not moving from his position. "Leave us."

Yong looked doubtful, and Tristan glared at him. "I think I can overpower a single human if she decides to try anything. Now, wait outside."

The vamps hesitated but finally complied, throwing Tristan dark glares. The silver-haired vampire followed their way out with a smile, pretending not to notice the murderous glances shot in his direction.

"Approach," he called to Myra. "I do not feel like standing up." He raised the journal for her to see. "My lord has translated the first two chapters of his tale. He read it to me centuries ago, with live translation, but this is the first time I see it written on paper. It is heart-wrenchingly good, but I will leave you to make up your own opinion."

"What language was it translated from?" she asked.

Tristan shrugged. "I suppose Old Church Slavonic written with Greek letters, or some other ridiculous combination no vampire in his right mind should be able to read." He grinned when he noticed her surprise. "I guess it is unusual, but apparently the Cyrillic alphabet was only in the process of being invented at the time, and my lord never had any particular love for it anyway."

"How can one dislike an alphabet?" Myra wondered.

The vampire's smile disappeared. "Trust me, he has a valid reason. I beg you not to ask him about this—it is not a pleasant story."

Myra stepped forward and took the book in her hand, resisting the urge to look through it right away. "Where is His Highness?" she asked.

"My lord went out hunting with Armida," Tristan said. "He should be back anytime now. Why, you miss him?"

"I was just wondering. What is he hunting exactly?" she asked with a clenched heart.

Tristan smiled at her, seemingly reading her thoughts. "No worries, he is not hunting humans. Deer, rabbits, foxes, wolves, the usual."

Myra breathed a sigh of relief. "I suppose you keep a sunlit forest nearby."

He nodded. "We go there hunting at night, or we cover it in clouds if my lord feels like hunting during the day. You may perhaps know about it? Where does the Resistance send its hunters?"

She glowered at him. "You can't expect me to answer that."

He grinned. "You still think my lord wants to destroy the Resistance?"

"I know *he* doesn't," she said. "I'm not sure about you."

"I want what my lord wants," Tristan said, grinning even more. "After all, I am—how did you put it again? *Puppylike*, right?"

Just then the doors flew open and Vlad and Armida entered, purposefully striding forward. Both were clad in tunics, breeches and riding boots made of tanned leather and were covered in dust, blood, and leaves from head to toe. The Prince held a bow in his left hand, and a half-empty quiver was strapped to his back. Myra had never seen either of the two vampires disheveled like that, but she could have accepted it easily enough. What was a bit harder to accept was the small wolf wrapped around the Prince's shoulders. The *alive* wolf, still struggling weakly but determinedly.

"Welcome home, my lord, my lady," Tristan called. "How was the hunt?"

"Very productive," Armida said. "We drank our fill and enough unspoiled meat is left to feed the humans. But right now I cannot say no to a hot bath."

"I could not agree more with you, love," Vlad said. "Please go ahead and order the bath prepared for us."

She frowned, looking between the three of them, but left the throne room without a word. The Prince walked forward.

"Behold, the refined nobleman!" Tristan called cheerfully. "You look positively civilized, my lord." He eyed the wolf. "And you certainly know how to accessorize."

Vlad reached the throne and placed his bow on a low table to its right. "And how exactly did *you* spend your night?" He grabbed Tristan's hand and brought it to his face. "Doing your nails by the looks of it?"

Tristan pulled his hand back, scolding. "It would not hurt *you* to get your nails properly cleaned and shaped once in a while. But then again I suppose clippers, let alone nail files, were not invented back when you were born." He eyed the Prince carefully. "Quite a bit of blood you have on you, my lord. Is any of it yours?"

"Why, you want a lick?" The Prince raised an eyebrow at the cherry pits on the floor. "You will clean this mess."

"Make me," Tristan challenged and spit another pit at the other vampire's feet.

The Prince grabbed the fair-haired vampire by the front of his shirt, lifted him up in the air, and dropped him down. Tristan fell on his back unceremoniously and lifted himself on his elbows, glaring up at his lord.

"You almost make me regret that I brought you a present from the hunt," Vlad said and dropped the wriggling wolf into Tristan's lap. "Can you eat it like this, or would you require a plate and silverware?"

Tristan's face brightened. "Thank you, my lord, this is very thoughtful," he said and bit the animal's neck.

Myra rolled her eyes and raised an eyebrow when she felt Vlad's eyes on her. "Wolf blood is his favorite," the Prince said as a manner of explanation.

"Favorite after human I suppose?" Myra said acidly.

"Nothing compares to human, true," Vlad said, "but we need some variety on our plates. If your favorite meal is, say, stuffed peppers, you still would not eat it every day, would you?"

Myra snorted. "You do realize you just compared people to stuffed peppers?"

"I did. Now tell me, did you get a chance to look at my book?"

"Not yet," Myra said, wondering if she had only imagined the flicker of uncertainty that passed across his features at the question. "Tristan gave it to me just now. He has been reading it apparently." The younger vampire threw her a warning glare and shook his head, and she grinned inwardly. "He said it was heart-wrenchingly good." Tristan looked positively murderous and Myra winked at him.

The Prince smiled smugly. "Did he now? *Heart-wrenchingly good*? I will not forget that."

"Oh, please, my lord, surely you know the human is exaggerating," Tristan protested. "I believe my exact words were along the lines of 'not too bad.'"

"I am sorry, my boy, but I believe Myra this time." He frowned. "Myra, my dear, forgive me, I did not bring you a present from the hunt. I have another gift for you, though. How would you like to attend a real ball tonight?"

Myra raised an eyebrow. "I love it how you make it sound as if I have a choice."

He smiled. "It is settled, then. I will take my leave of you now; Armida is waiting for me. I advise you to try to get some sleep before the dance."

"Easy for you to say, I just got up," Myra complained as the guards escorted her back to her room.

As she walked, thoughts of the sunlit woods never left her mind. She needed to know where it was. The vamps kept it sunlit most of the time, so it would be safe to visit under daylight. The Resistance could send hunters there and get plenty of food at almost no risk.

She needed to find out where these woods were. Only then could she make a shot at escape.

***

Myra did not even have the willpower to try to sleep before the ball, for there was something way more exciting to do. The first thing she did upon returning to her room was plop down on the bed and open the leather-bound journal.

The words flowed before her eyes and she read on with bated breath. She did not realize when she had moved to the edge of the bed, her heart beating wildly, her muscles tense with excitement. And when the last word came, there was one single, all-defining thought in her mind. *I need more.*

Someone knocked on the door, but she closed her eyes, ignoring the sound. She was not ready to return to reality, to leave behind the wondrous world that she had briefly stepped into. But then the knock came again, and with a resigned sigh, she called an invitation to enter.

The moment the door opened, all images and fantasies the book had instilled flew away, and her head was clear once more. "Lady Armida?" she said, surprised and somewhat worried. "To what do I owe the honor?"

Armida smiled. "Do not worry, dear. I simply wished to learn the answer to a question that has been bothering me lately."

Myra forced a smile. "What do you wish to know?"

Armida walked to her, grabbed her chin and forced their eyes to meet. "These days he spends more time with you than he does with me," she said. "What can you give him that I cannot?"

Panic gripped Myra's heart. If this was what Armida was thinking, she was done for. "My lady, I never meant—"

"Oh, be quiet," the vampire said softly. "None of this is your fault. I have always known I was not what he was looking for."

Myra tried to think, but the blood was rushing to her head. Armida was insecure. She had admitted the Prince surrounded himself with artistic people, and she was none of that. And suddenly Myra had a vague idea how to use this insecurity. But to use it, she first needed to feed it.

"You shouldn't blame yourself," she said. "No vampire can create what I can. The Prince understands this and doesn't hold it against you."

"He has given me everything I need," Armida said softly. "Yet, I cannot give him what he needs."

"You feel that you love him more than he loves you?"

Armida looked up sharply. "Of course I do. Is it not obvious? And here you are, spinning your tales and reminding him of everything I can never offer."

"This was never my intention," Myra said. "And it's ridiculous to think such thoughts, my lady. The Prince adores you."

"Does he?" Armida said. "Strange that he seems to spend more time with everyone else."

Myra remembered something. A throwaway comment Tristan had made when Vlad challenged him on liking vampires once and disliking them now. *You and Lady Callisto were the only vampires I knew*, Tristan had said. And, perhaps, a shot in the dark was worth it.

"I understand your fears," she said. "After all, many vampires in the Prince's circle used to write when they were still human—Tristan, Callisto. But this mustn't bother you. They all lost this ability, so it makes no difference now."

For a moment Armida froze, but then she turned to look at Myra, perfectly composed. "He talks to you about Callisto?"

Myra nodded. "He does."

"What does he say?"

Myra gulped. This was a slippery slope. She had no idea what she was talking about and how much Armida knew on the subject. Was this Callisto even still alive? Had Armida met her?

"Not much. He grows melancholic when he talks about her, but he says she used to write when she was a human." She observed Armida's face. Nothing the vampire did indicated she had caught the lie, and Myra decided to take another shot. "He also says his wife was a writer before she was killed."

Armida stared at her, wide-eyed. "He talked to you about his wife?"

Myra frowned. He must have never talked to Armida about his wife, she realized. "My lady, you've been kind to me," she said. "I want to help you."

"How could you possibly help me?"

"I could help you convince the Prince you used to be a writer before you were turned."

Armida face was still as stone. "This is impossible."

"Why impossible? I could write a story for you. You can give it to the Prince and tell him you wrote it when you were human."

Armida burst into laughter, but the joy never reached her eyes. "Myra, this is the daftest plan I have ever heard. You expect him to believe that? He would not find it strange that I am only telling him about this now and never mentioned it before?"

"He has no reason to doubt you," Myra said. "You could tell him you wanted him to love you for who you are now, and not for who you were as a human. And now is a good time to bring it up—he's working on translating his own book. It makes sense for you to mention that you've also written one."

"This is ridiculous. My beloved is a smart man. He cannot believe that I suddenly became a writer."

"You didn't suddenly become a writer," Myra said. "You have to make him think you wrote a story as a young girl, then you stopped writing for a few years, and, of course, once he turned you, you couldn't write anymore. It goes like this—you can say, 'My love, how is your book translation going?' He will reply something, and then you say, 'Can you read to me?' He'll read you a few pages, and you'll say 'You write so beautifully. You know, I also wrote a story once, long ago, though it was never as good.' He'll be surprised you've never mentioned it before, and you'll say, 'This happened years before we met. I haven't thought of it in a long time.'"

Armida was grinning madly, and this time her bright green eyes danced with laughter. "Myra, dearest, this was hilarious. Do you realize my love and I sound *nothing* like that when we talk to each other in private?"

Myra sighed. "Alright, then. *What* do you talk like?"

"You would like to know that, wouldn't you?" Armida asked with a wink. "None of your concern."

"Fine," Myra said. "Armida, think on it, please. Is it really impossible that you could convince him? Think of the benefits. He would believe you used to be a writer. Isn't that what you always wanted?"

Armida was silent for a moment, her brow furrowed. "Very well," she said. "Suppose that he somehow believes that. Can you write the story so that the style matches the time and place where I lived and avoid anachronisms?"

"I've never done it before," Myra admitted. "I believe I can, but you'll have to tell me more about yourself."

"I lived in eighteen-century Italy, a small village near Naples," Armida said. "Can you work with that?"

Myra nodded. "I would have to do some research, of course, and—"

Armida snorted. "Research? How, by reading books? Myra, my beloved actually lived through this time. He saw it and experienced it. He will not be easily deceived."

"That's why I'll need your help. We will discuss the plot and you'll tell me if anything doesn't make sense."

Armida massaged her forehead and started walking back and forth. "You make it sound so easy. You can't even write in Italian, let alone my local dialect."

"You could tell him you translated the story for him."

Armida rolled her eyes. "My love can read eighteen-century Italian. I would have no reason to do that."

"Then I could write the story, and you'll translate it into your language and tell him it's the original. Can you do that?"

"I could," Armida said and smiled. "You know, that might actually work."

Myra grinned. "Do you want me to do it?"

Armida nodded. "Yes. Let us give it a try. How much time do you need?"

"I suppose you don't want a full novel? If you're fine with a short story, I could have something for you in a week or so."

"Yes, a short story would be perfect." Armida smiled brightly. "Thank you. Thank you so much."

Myra's gaze hardened. "I said I *could* do it. Not that I *would*."

Armida laughed. "I see you are learning. A favor for a favor. Fair enough. What would you like?"

The WeatherWizard destroyed. A stake through the Prince's heart. No way she could be honest. She had to be reasonable with her request, and now the thing she needed the most was her freedom. Once she had taken the pages she needed from the WeatherWizard book in the library, she had to return to the Resistance and share the information.

But could she really ask Armida for something as big? And, even if the vampire agreed to help her, could Myra trust her?

"Let me think on it. Let's talk after the ball."

"Very well," Armida said. "Think on it, and think well. I will come for you after the dances."

Myra stared at the floor once the vampire left the room. What was she doing? Armida was the only vampire who had shown her some measure of kindness after her arrival here. And how was she repaying her? By manipulating her, feeding her insecurities, and using her to achieve her goals?

I'm not using her—I'm helping her, Myra tried to convince herself. *If the Prince believes Armida was a writer, it's actually good for her.*

But was it really? Armida was lying to present herself as someone she was not, so that she would better fit the idea of the Prince's perfect companion. In what way could that turn out well?

Myra sighed. She could not spend time and energy worrying about doing right by vampires. When had they ever done right by humans?

But if she stopped caring, was she not becoming as bad as a vampire? Was she forgetting what it meant to be human?

She pressed her lips together and reached out to her notebook and pen. So be it. If a good-hearted human could not win this war, she would become whatever was required.

Chapter Twenty-Two

Contracts in Ink and Blood

Myra gazed at her reflection as Lucy helped her get into the large yellow gown and secured all the numerous strings. The vampire tied her hair with a silken golden ribbon and stepped back.

"You no longer complain about corsets," Lucy said. "Did you change your mind, or are you simply resigned?"

I discovered other ways to feel in control, besides wearing comfortable clothes. "It does make the dress look better," she said.

A soft knock interrupted them, and Lucy called out an invitation.

Tristan stepped in. "Forgive me the intrusion, my ladies," he said. "If Myra is ready, my lord and I would like to escort her to the Great Hall."

Lucy nodded and left, and the Prince stepped in.

"Myra," Vlad said once the door closed behind them. "Did you have a chance to look at my book?" He looked down instead of meeting her eyes.

She frowned. She had never seen him like that. He seemed worried and strangely self-conscious, as though if she said the book was poorly written, his world would collapse.

"I did," she said, and he paled. "It's good. I liked it. It's much better that anything I could have written."

The Prince breathed an audible sigh of relief and a small smile appeared on his face.

"You used to have a beautiful soul," Myra added, and her eyes hardened. "Too bad it's gone now."

Vlad stiffened but maintained his composure. "Thank you for the feedback. I shall translate the rest, and then, hopefully, you will continue reading. Now, will you please join me in the Great Hall?"

Myra took his offered hand and followed him outside the room. Tristan threw her a sharp look but said nothing.

"Are you looking forward to the ball?" the Prince asked her as the three of them walked on.

"It should be interesting," Myra said. "But I admit I'm worried. To be honest, I don't feel comfortable dancing with other vampires. I know many still want to torture me for information."

"Unfortunately, I cannot give you my undivided attention as I am expected to dance with each of my guests tonight," Vlad said. "But you are lucky. Tristan also has no desire to dance with other vampires. You can spend the night dancing with him."

"What?" Tristan cried. "Did it occur to you to ask me if I was happy with this arrangement?"

"I know you are," Vlad said and looked at Myra. "I hope you are happy too, my dear."

"It doesn't sound like I have a choice," she said. "I admit I was looking forward to spending some time with you. It's disappointing I won't get the chance."

He laughed. "Of course. You must be terribly disappointed. Did you wish to discuss something?"

"Several things, actually." He nodded, and she continued. "I loved the hunting scene in your book."

He smiled. "I enjoyed writing it."

"I can see that," she said. "It's obvious that you knew exactly what you were talking about, and what each of your characters would be thinking and feeling during the hunt. When I write about something I don't know, I base it on books I've read. And you have actually drawn inspiration from something you've done yourself numerous times. I bet you didn't need to do any research to write this scene."

"You are correct," he said.

"And that's my problem," she said. "I have experienced practically nothing. All I know about the world is from books and from talking to you. I was thinking, perhaps I would need to write a similar hunt scene later in the book, but I would have no idea how to do it."

He raised an eyebrow. "You want me to take you hunting?"

"I can't say that I actually want it," she said. "But I think it will help me write better."

The Prince and Tristan exchanged a long glance. "I see no harm in that," Vlad finally said. "And I agree that diverse experiences will help you be a better writer. I will take you on a hunt."

Myra suppressed a mad grin. This was too good. If she went to the sunlit woods and remembered the way, she could lead the Resistance back there and get supplies. "Thank you. When are we going?"

He laughed. "So eager? I cannot take you at night as your eyesight is not good enough, and the skies above the woods are clear during the day. I will program the WeatherWizard to send thick clouds, but the area will only be safe in three days. If we go before that, the weather would be unstable and we risk the clouds dispersing without warning."

"Yes, we wouldn't want you to burn to dust," Myra said.

He grinned. "I am sure that would make you very sad. Can you ride a horse?"

"I had never seen a real horse until your people captured me."

"We will have to teach you, then. Have no worries, it is not hard at all."

Tristan snorted. "Not hard? Myra, let me tell you this, as someone who has not been a master rider since the age of four—it takes ages to learn. One lesson will be far from enough, and your whole body will hurt for days afterwards."

Vlad smiled. "Do not listen to him. He is exceptionally untalented. It took him forever to master some basic skills."

"*Basic skills?*" the younger vampire cried. "Including, but not limited to, standing upright on a galloping horse, hanging upside down off the side, jumping up and down atop a galloping horse, standing on top of *two* horses at the same time, one foot on each—"

"Yes, basic skills, as I said," Vlad said calmly. "And you surely took your time learning. I am certain Myra will not be that pathetic."

Myra was not so sure about that. "Why would you need all that for a simple hunt?" she asked, and Tristan started nodding vigorously.

"My point exactly," he cried.

"Everything you are able to do on the ground, you should be able to do on horseback," said Vlad. "Myra, dear, you said you had several things to discuss?"

"The other is mostly out of curiosity," she said.

He grinned. "Of course. All the questions you ask are always out of a pure academic interest, and have nothing to do with my imminent destruction."

She sighed. "Vlad, I'm not planning your destruction."

"You almost convinced me," he said. "Now, what would you like to know?"

"We had this talk about blood and what it means in your culture," she said. "I've been thinking a lot about it."

"I am glad you find the subject fascinating."

"I was mostly thinking about vampires sharing blood as a way to become closer to each other, and how this relates to human culture and the concept of blood brothers," Myra said. "I admit I see the similarities, but there is also a huge difference. Blood never had the same meaning for us as it does for you. People would sometimes swear a blood oath, by mingling their blood, and then break it with no consequences."

"This is not the case with vampires," the Prince said. "For us a blood oath is sacred, and we will keep it no matter what."

"What would happen if you break it?"

"The magic that keeps us alive would be tainted forever. The consequences would be dire, but I cannot tell you more unless you tell me why you need to know all this."

"Academic interest, as you said," she said. "I was just wondering, could a vampire strike a blood oath with a human, if they mix each other's blood? Would it still be sacred to the vampire?"

"Of course," he said. "Why, you want to strike a blood oath with me?"

She blushed. "Perhaps. I need to think about it."

They stopped in front of the door leading to the Great Hall. "Very well," he said. "I need to entertain my guests now, but if you wish to tell me more, you know where to find me."

Myra stepped inside and gasped. The music was already playing and vampires were dancing, some in couples or triplets, and others by themselves. Bright silken gowns were flying around, covered in glitter. The vamps were dancing skillfully, so fast and perfectly synchronized, bending their bodies, jumping, and throwing each other up in the air in a way no human ever could.

Armida was wearing a magnificent long gown of blue-and-black lace, sleeveless and with a low neckline, exposing her snow-white skin. On top she wore sheer lace sleeves of the same color, coming together at her neck in the shape of bat wings, held together by a red ruby. She locked eyes with the Prince, and he walked to her across the hall. Vlad placed one hand on her waist and the other in her hand and led her in a dance.

Myra stole a glance at Tristan, who stood still next to her. "That's not a waltz," she said. "I don't know how to dance it."

"That works out nicely, then," he said. "I have no desire to dance."

Myra went back to watching the dancers, but soon the piece was over and the dances stopped. Then the music started once again, and she recognized the rhythm.

"Now that's a waltz," she said. "Shall we?"

He sighed and took her hand.

Myra frowned and looked up to him as they started dancing. "Tristan, what's wrong?"

"I have no idea what you are talking about," he said, his voice icy.

She rolled her eyes. "Come, now. You act as if you are angry with me."

"Perhaps it is because my soul is gone now," he said. "You cannot expect a soulless monster to act any different."

"*What* are you talking about?"

He frowned and twirled her around. "You know what I am talking about. Telling my lord that he used to have a beautiful soul, but it is gone now and he can no longer write. That was mean."

"*Mean?*" Myra said. "He keeps me a prisoner and brutally murders children as a means to control me, and *I* am mean for reminding him he is no longer human? I hope you realize how absurd this is."

"You have no idea how it feels," Tristan said softly. "Wanting to write, *needing* to write. Having the words burn inside your chest, striving to get out. And then holding the pen and paper in your hand, with nothing coming out. With all these thoughts and emotions locked inside you, fighting, burning, suffocating you from the inside." Tristan fell silent and swallowed hard. "This book means a lot to him."

"So what?" Myra said. "He has never cared about sparing my feelings, or my people's feelings. Why should I care about sparing his?"

Tristan gave her a hard stare. "You will refrain from any similar comments in front of my lord again," he said. "If you think it—fine. If you have the need to say it, say it to me. But do not say it to him."

"And why would I do that?" she said. "Tristan, we are not friends. I don't do favors for free."

Tristan's grey eyes turned cold as ice. "You want something in return?"

Myra smiled. "You said you would tell me the story of your past and how you were turned if I could offer you something in return. Tell me the story, and I will watch my tongue with the Prince."

Right. She could have asked him for something more practical, something that would have helped her escape or get more information on the WeatherWizard. Tristan appeared seriously affected by this, and she should have exploited it. But it was too late now. Thankfully, she had another escape plan, and she was not planning to mess it up this time.

He snorted. "Oh. I see you are learning how this is done. Very well, your request is fair. After the ball, we will go to my study and I will tell you everything."

Myra grinned. "We have a deal."

The music stopped and a flurry of blue and black approached them. Armida smiled at them.

"Tristan, sweetest, would you mind if I steal your lady for a moment?"

Tristan stepped in front of Myra. "My lady specifically requested that she dances with no one but me tonight."

Myra rolled her eyes. "Tristan, it's alright. Thanks."

Armida took her hand and led her to a small niche in the far wall, away from the dancers. "Are you enjoying yourself, dear?"

Myra nodded. "The dances are beautiful, my lady." She stole a look around, making sure no one was close enough to hear them over the loud music. "I thought about what we discussed."

"Wonderful. What is your price?"

"My freedom," Myra said. "You must help me escape."

The vampire grinned at her. "You do have guts. I like that. But you know this is a high price, and hard to accomplish."

"I think you'll be happy to be rid of me," Myra said. "After all, you were complaining the Prince was spending too much time with me."

"You have a point," Armida admitted. "To be fair, I had other plans for you, but now that you mention it, I could use another human in your place, and it might work even better."

Myra frowned. "What plans?"

"This is none of your concern," Armida said. "Not anymore. But do you realize that if you run away, my people will not take it well? They will demand human blood."

Myra's eyes widened. "Franka. Do you think they would believe she had something to do with my escape?"

"Certainly, and they will kill her for it," Armida said.

"Then help her escape together with me," Myra said. "Can you do that?"

The vampire grinned. "Your requests are getting bigger and bigger. Thankfully, helping the old woman escape would be easier than helping you. Alright, then. If you write the story, I will help you both."

Myra felt dizzy, unable to believe her luck. "Do you have an idea how I could escape? You said it yourself that it would be difficult."

"Yes, I said it would be very hard to arrange your escape," Armida said with a confident smile. "I never said it would be hard for *me*. Come, now, you should go back to Tristan. If we are to plan this escape, people should not see us together too often."

Tristan raised an eyebrow at Myra when she returned to his side. "What did she want?"

"Some people might just want the pleasure of my company," Myra said. "Is it so hard to believe?"

"Right," he said. "Well, then, can I have the next dance?"

***

By the time the ball was over, Myra could barely stand on her feet. She took a step and grabbed Tristan's arm, leaning against him.

He grinned. "Should I escort you back to your rooms, my lady?"

She shook her head. "No. I want to hear the story."

"I thought you might. Come."

They climbed up winding stairs until they reached the wing that hosted Vlad's study. Tristan led her to a high oaken door.

Myra stepped inside and gasped. Vlad had given her a book on art history, and she could easily recognize what she was seeing. Well-known impressionist paintings covered the walls—Monet's *Water Lilies*, Pissarro's *Old Chelsea Bridge*, Renoir's *By the Water*, and many more whose names she could not remember, but which she had seen in the book. Were those originals? Apparently the vampires had pillaged the world's finest art galleries, along with all the museums and palaces.

Large wardrobes with mirror doors stood against the walls. A massive crystal chandelier with lit candles hung from the ceiling. No carpet covered the stone floor, save for a single stag skin in front of the black leather sofa. "Is this your study?" she asked.

"My dressing room," Tristan clarified. "I have a separate study. I can show it to you, but I imagine you wish to hear the story first."

Myra nodded and took a seat. Her eyes wandered to the table next to the black leather couch, and she reached out to take a sheet of paper. She stared at the color pencil reproduction of the *Water Lilies*—crude blobs of pink and blue marked the flowers in the water, the pencil marks measured and precise, yet strangely lifeless and mechanical. "Tristan, did you draw this?"

He snatched the paper from her hand, walked to a desk and placed it in a drawer. "I am trying to fight nature." A sad smile graced his lips as he turned to look at her. "Unsuccessfully. I can somewhat make copies of existing works, but cannot paint anything new."

Myra's breath caught in her throat. Tristan needed to create art, to express himself. And he could not. She was starting to understand how he felt, trapped inside a prison, unable to express the emotions bubbling inside his heart. "I'm sorry."

He looked away. "I gained more than I lost. Let us not chase empty dreams. You said you would refrain from making mean comments about my lord's book in front of him. Will you keep your word?"

"I swear it."

He smiled slightly and leaned forward, reaching for the glass bottle on the white marble table. "Very well. It is time for me to uphold my part of this bargain."

Myra leaned back on the sofa, taking the goblet he offered. A gust of wind blew through the open window, extinguishing most of the candles. The vampire's steady voice carried through the darkness, and she held her breath, drinking in every word.

Chapter Twenty-Three

Origins

"I lived in a small, remote village in southern Norway, up in the mountains," Tristan started. "I was orphaned when I was thirteen and had to take care of myself. I always managed to get by, but on many days, it was a close call.

"I stayed at my father's hut, on the outskirts of the village. I had a small garden and could grow some vegetables, but that was about it. I had neither land nor animals, and had no means to produce any bread or milk or meat on my own. I had to buy those, and money was hard to come by.

"Anything I managed to grow in the garden was barely enough for myself, and selling my produce on the market was unthinkable. To get money I had to take on all kinds of jobs—plowing, weeding, and harvesting someone else's fields, cleaning barns, carrying wood and stone. I had to work from sunrise to sunset and beyond, and I hated it so much, every minute of it. It all left me so little time to write."

"This was in the Middle Ages?" Myra interrupted.

He nodded. "Fourteenth century. Why?"

Fourteenth century. Myra sometimes forgot how old he actually was. Perhaps it was his pale hair, or his always-clean-shaven face, or his pouty lips that made him look so young, but in truth Tristan had walked the earth for over a thousand years. Her head hurt just thinking about it.

"I'm surprised you could write," Myra admitted. "I thought that was uncommon."

"My parents were illiterate," he said, "and so was I, for a time. When I was a child, my mother often sang to me, songs she made up on the spot, both the lyrics and the melody. Years after she died, words started coming to my head—poems, rhymes. I would repeat them day after day so I would not forget, but as the poems grew in length and number, some slipped away from my memory. I needed to write them down. The priest was the only man in our village who could read and write, and I begged him to teach me.

"I spent so many sleepless nights by the candle, feverishly scribbling down words. Time was never enough. Words were flowing through my mind as I worked, and I would have to recite the verses again and again so I would not forget them before I got the chance to write them down. And when I went back home every night, I would write down everything I could remember, and so much more.

"On precious few evenings, I could afford to spare time for the tavern. At first, I had hopes someone would listen, someone would understand. I tried sharing my poetry with the other patrons, but their reactions varied from bored indifference to outright ridicule. Soon I learned I had to keep it all to myself, and it was only on wild drunken nights that I would share my innermost thoughts with my companions."

Tristan smiled. "I told you I did not like vampires. Well, I never liked humans either. I could not relate to any of the people in my village. I felt extremely out of place and soon became a loner. I stopped talking to anyone, unless it was for business. And so the years passed, and I neared my twentieth birthday. I was expected to take a wife and start a family, but what father would give his daughter to someone who could barely provide for himself?"

"Did you wish to take a wife?" Myra asked.

He shrugged. "I never gave it much thought. I did have a few affairs at the time. You see, I looked a bit different back then—my hands were chafed, my nails dirty, and my hair much shorter and messier, but my striking beauty was still obvious for anyone with eyes to see." He chuckled as Myra rolled her eyes. "Still, none of the maids I met during my human years was anything special. I could not truly talk to any of them."

"If you couldn't talk to any of them, maybe the problem wasn't with the maids," Myra pointed out.

"Whatever. I was strange, odd, abnormal, a weirdo, you name it. I have been called all that, and more, and I could not have cared less. All I wished from life was enough coin for bread and candles, and ink and paper. And I had it, until the Hungry Year.

"That year was bad for everyone. A terrible sleet destroyed over half of the crops. Most people managed to get by, but their means were severely diminished. No one would spare money to hire additional help, and I was left out of work.

"I thought I would not live through the winter. I lived on a loaf of bread for weeks, rationing every bite. And then, on one of the coldest nights, I no longer had the strength to write and just lay on the bed, staring at the low ceiling. I was so hungry that I felt dizzy, and my vision was starting to turn black. My mind was so muddled that when I heard the knock on the door, I first thought I had hallucinated it.

"I could not imagine who would be coming to my house at this hour, and I knew that even if someone wished to offer me work, I had no strength left to do it. And yet, I finally dragged myself out of the bed and to the door.

"As I opened the door, I almost closed it right away to stop the sudden gust of wind. I had almost no wood left and could not afford to reheat the house. I nearly swore as I saw there was no one there… and yet, there was something.

"In front of my feet lay a large stag, freshly killed. At first, I could not believe this was happening. I feared someone was playing tricks on me and if I ate any of the meat, they would come for me and want it back. I had no well-wishers in town, so I could not believe anyone wanted to help me. It was far more likely that someone wished to bring me trouble. The neighboring woods belonged to the local lord, and I knew he would have killed anyone hunting on his property. Yes, many villagers often set traps to catch rabbits or other small game, and the lord sometimes ignored this, but a stag was another matter. I was not at all sure how he would react. You see, something like this had never happened before.

"And then a sudden realization hit me. None of my fellow villagers had ever killed a stag in these woods because none of them possessed the skill to hunt such game. We were simple farmers. Hunting was a nobleman's pastime. And the kill was perfect—a single arrow straight through the heart. I knew no one who could make such a shot.

"At last, hunger won over caution and I dragged the stag inside. It was cold, even inside, so I was not overly worried about rotting, and yet this was a lot of meat and could sustain me through the winter. I had to start smoking or salting what I could not eat right away.

"As I skinned the animal, I thought about its magnificent hide. I knew the leather would bring me good coin if I took it to the market, provided that no one asked where I had it from. But for now, I would keep it, perhaps for a day or two. After tanning it, I would lay it in front of my bed, giving my small hut a single touch of luxury.

"My first meal off the stag made me sick. I was so hungry I thought I could eat half of it, but during the weeks of starvation, my stomach had shrunk and I was filled up by only a few bites. And yet, I could not bring myself to stop eating. I forced myself to go on and on, afraid that every bite could be my last.

"I survived the winter. Spring came, and then summer, and yet I could not bring myself to take the stag's hide to the market. On some days I was desperate for bread, and yet I never did it, never gave it up. I wanted to keep this small memento from the miracle that had happened that night, the miracle that had saved my life.

"Things started to pick up that summer. Crops grew, people were happy, and I was offered more work than I could take. One night I was returning home from a late errand when a large, strange man barred my path. You see, in our village everyone knew each other, and it was unusual to see strangers. And yet, I had never before seen this man or his two burly companions, and when they took out the clubs, I knew this would not go well.

"I tried to fight them, but I had neither the skill nor the weapons. Luckily, they were only interested in the money I had earned that day and left me alive, if badly bruised. I wished to go after them, to make them pay, but all I could do was drag myself back to my hut and bar the door.

"On the next day, I was almost afraid to go out. But when I opened the front door, there was something hanging from the knob. A pouch with money, all my money from the day before, untouched.

"I knew I probably should have been scared, but I was strangely calm. I took the money and went to the central market, only to find the village in an uproar. Three strange men had been found, dead. The manner of their deaths was unusual. They had all suffered severe blood loss caused by two puncture wounds on the neck.

"And then, as I stared at the bodies of the men who had attacked me the night before, I knew I would never need to be afraid, ever again.

"I was the only one not afraid, though. The people were terrified. There was talk of vampires—creatures of the night that wandered the world alone and killed people for food. And, believe it or not, I found the idea fascinating.

"From that night on, my poems had a new subject—a lone vampire, who walked under the light of moon and stars and hunted his prey. In my poems, I described his emotions—the instinct of a predator, the stalking, the hunt, the thrill of the kill. Yet my protagonist was more than a wild animal—he was refined, and different, and misunderstood. He was a loner, and a dreamer."

"He was a twisted version of you," Myra whispered in horror. "You *wanted* to be a vampire. Before you were even turned."

"For certain I did not want to be human," Tristan admitted. "I did not belong in my village. Any chance to be something else was more than welcome."

"You wimp," she spat. "Do you have any idea how many people feel like they don't belong, like they are misunderstood and meant for something different? And none of them decide to solve the problem by turning themselves into bloodthirsty monsters."

"You think I am a coward and chose the easy way out," he said indifferently. "And perhaps you are right. But there was more to it, so much more.

"I went on writing my poems. The fear of vampires in the village persisted for some time, though there were no new kills. I knew that if I shared my works with anyone, I would probably be burned alive, and so I kept them for myself. And yet, I do not know why, but every evening I would take my scribblings to the garden outside and put them underneath a stone.

"In a year or so the mysterious incident was all but forgotten, but I kept writing my poems. I took on less work because I wanted to have more time for writing, and my income suffered because of it. Often I had to choose between buying bread or ink, and I never made a wise choice.

"One evening I was returning home late, when my life changed forever. I had rounded the corner to the small, dark street leading to my hut, when I saw her. She was a vision under the pale moonlight and did not seem to belong on the dusty road.

"She was dressed like a noblewoman, with a midnight-blue fitted kirtle and overgown, and a fur-lined mantle. A silver belt circled her slim waist, and her small hands were covered in black lace gloves. The only thing that did not fit her noble lady image was her loose hair, falling freely around her shoulders and down to her waist.

"Her hair was black as night. You see, dark-haired people were very rare in my village, and with her pale olive skin and warm eyes, she looked definitely foreign. I could not explain what she was doing there. A strange woman all by herself at this time of night could only be one thing. And yet, she did not look like a harlot. She looked like a being from another world.

"'Are you a goddess?' I blurted out, before I could stop myself.

"She smiled. 'Something like that,' she said, and I could not help but notice the strange way she spoke my tongue. 'And you could be a god too, if only you choose so. You must be Tristan. He speaks so highly of you. I wished to see you with my own eyes.'

"Naturally, I wondered who 'he' was, but there were so many questions on my mind that I could not sort them out. 'Who are you?' I asked instead.

"'My name is Callisto,' she said. 'And you and I will meet again, beautiful one, and we will have enough time to talk. We will have all the time in the world.'

"She turned to leave, but I could not bear to see her go. 'When will I see you again?' I cried, unable to hide the despair in my voice.

"'Whenever he thinks you are ready,' she said, and before I could ask more, she was gone. One moment she was there, and the next she was away. I could not comprehend what had happened. All I knew was that she was a creature of another world, and that her world was in all likelihood better than mine."

Myra bit her lip, self-consciously fingering her golden gown. *A vision. A goddess.* Would Tristan ever use such words to describe her? Would anyone? She frowned. And why was this disturbing her, anyway? She did not wish to be viewed as 'a vision.' She was a person with hopes and dreams, not somebody's muse. And yet, she could not help wondering if anyone would ever look at her and think the same thoughts as Tristan had when he had seen Callisto for the first time.

"She was a vampire," Myra said.

He nodded. "The first vampire I ever saw. The first I talked to."

"And 'he' was the Prince, I assume? So this Callisto was—"

"His lover, centuries before Armida was born," Tristan supplied, his eyes taking on a faraway look. "She was his first, after the long mourning for his murdered wife. But more than that, she was his sire."

"His sire?"

"The one who turned him. There is a special connection every vampire shares with the one who created him or her. The bond works one way, though—some of us may choose to sire dozens and will naturally not feel connected to each of them. And yet, each vampire has only one sire, one who created them, who gave them life, and this is a bond one can never break."

"How many have you sired?" Myra asked, dreading the answer.

"Not a single one before the Nightfall," Tristan said. "After that, I lost count."

"So this Callisto was older than Vlad?"

"Much older. She used to be a hetaera in ancient Athens until one of her clients was so impressed that he decided to turn her."

"Hetaera?" Myra said. "That's something like a high-class courtesan?"

"More than that," said Tristan. "These women were educated in art and music, and were expected to be witty and refined, providing skillful conversation for their clients."

"And let me guess? After you met her, your poems took a different turn?"

He smiled, almost shyly. "Well, yes, they did. At the time I did not know she was a vampire, but I knew she was more than a mere human."

"I think we disagree on if a vampire is more or less than a human," Myra said. "So this was when you decided you wanted to be a vampire?"

"I had known it for a long time," he said. "But this was not when it all started to happen. This is just the beginning of my story.

"After that night, I kept waiting for Callisto to return, but she never did. I spent more time writing and less time working than ever. And then came the coldest winter I had yet to witness. I could still earn enough to survive, but the cold was so deep, it permeated your skin and flesh and bones. I would spend hours outside, chopping wood for someone else, until I could no longer feel my hands. And when I returned home, I would have no wood for myself, to build my own fire.

"It did not take long before I fell ill. I was bound to bed with fever for days, and even though work was offered to me, I could not take it. I could only lie down, bathed in sweat and the stench of death, not knowing dream from reality. I knew I was losing my mind, but it was not so bad at all. In my hallucinations I saw vampires, and death, and Callisto, come back to pick me and take me to her world. But she never came.

"I knew this could go on no longer. I had to get back on my feet and go to the woods to chop some wood, this time for myself. I had to build a fire and warm myself and drink herbal potions until this disease was washed out of my system. If I did not find the strength to do this now, I was practically lying down, waiting for death.

"I walked towards the other end of the village, where the woods were, but I had barely reached the central square, when I realized I could never make it. I was frozen to the core, shaking like a leaf in the wind. The sky was covered by impenetrable clouds, so that not a single ray of sunlight could come and caress my face. I had to get warm, or I would never make it back home.

"Fortunately, I knew the right place for that. The tavern was not far away, and the fire there was always burning. I stumbled forward and nearly fell on the floor when I opened the door. There were only a few men inside—it was still early and everyone tried to get some work done before nightfall—and every single head turned to look at me. They spared me a short glance and went back to their own conversations, and meals and drinks. It was only the innkeeper who never took his eyes off me.

"I approached the counter and leaned against the wood to keep myself from falling down. I asked the innkeeper for a hot toddy—it had been ages since I had drunk anything warm. He looked at me and asked if I had money to pay. I took out my pouch and let the coins spill on the counter. He counted them and pushed them back at me. They were not enough.

"I told him I would pay back later. He knew me, I lived there, I would not run and hide. I told him I would take up some new work after tonight and pay him back. And do you know what he said to me? He said I did not look like I would live long enough to pay him back."

"This is terrible," Myra murmured involuntary.

Tristan snorted. "Yes, they call vampires monsters. But some vampires possess more of what you would call *humanity* than any of you."

"What did you do?"

"I begged him. This is something I had never seen myself doing. I was proud and did not want anyone to see me on my knees, but Heaven and Hell help me, I begged him. I promised him anything, I would pay double, even triple when I got the money. I was so desperate, and he saw it, and he did not care. In the end, I simply asked him to let me sit by the fire. He said I could not stay inside unless I ordered food or drink. He told two of his men to kick me out—he did not want me dying in his tavern, he said. And then, my dear girl, is when this story begins."

"You took your time getting to the beginning," Myra said with a smile. "But I don't mind. I admit I wanted to know more about you."

"You will never learn all that there is to know about me, of course," Tristan said smugly. "I have many layers, and I am rich in fascinating stories. But for me nothing was more fascinating than the events that occurred in the following years."

"Years?" Myra echoed. "I thought we had gotten to the turning point. I mean, the literal turning point."

"We have gotten to a turning point, yes, but not *the* turning point as you mean it," he said cheerfully. "The men grabbed me and dragged me to the door, but before they could reach it, the gate slammed open.

"A gust of wind and snow entered the warm hall and everyone glared at the door. The innkeeper dropped the glass he had picked up and it shattered loudly on the floor, the pieces spilling everywhere.

"He entered then, and no one could take their eyes off him. It was only folks from our village who ever visited this tavern, but this man looked like a noble lord. It was not only his fine clothes, the jewelry, the leather boots, the long fur-lined cloak that gave this impression. It was everything about him—the way he stood tall and proud, the way he walked forward, the way he looked at us.

"He reached the counter and placed a few coins on the wooden surface. The innkeeper stared at the gold as if his eyes would pop out.

"'Bring me two bowls of stew and two cups of mulled wine,' he said, and even though he spoke our language in a strange way, there was an unmistakable authority in his voice, the kind that makes you want to obey every word he says.

"'Of course, my lord, right away, my lord,' the innkeeper stammered. 'Two bowls and two cups, you say? Do you have a companion joining you?'

"'I do,' he said then and looked evenly at the two men restraining me. 'And you would do well to release him.'

"I can barely remember what happened next. The blood was rushing to my head. It was all so unreal, so unbelievable. The innkeeper and his men seemed just as confused while I was led to a table and seated, and a bowl of steaming stew was placed before me.

"And then, all I felt was anger. I was no beggar. I was young and strong and capable, I did not need anyone to give me money or buy me food, and I told him as much.

"He smiled then, and there was a sparkle in his eyes. 'I am far from thinking you a beggar, Tristan,' he said, and I did not even find it strange that he knew my name. 'You are so much more than that. This is no charity, my boy. This is payment.'

"'Payment?' I echoed. 'I have never done any work for you, my lord.'

"'Oh, but you have,' he said. 'You have done more than I can ever pay you for.'

"And then, he told me that he had read some of my poems and wanted to repay me for the pleasure they had given him. Never before had I heard of anyone getting paid for writing poetry, but he told me that in some parts of the world it was common practice. He told me that in some societies poets were held in high regard, and I could barely stop myself from asking him to take me there.

"The warm food and drink made me feel much better, but they were no cure. A few violent coughs tore through my frame as we talked, and though I was ashamed to let him see me so weak, there was true compassion in his eyes.

"He then said that perhaps he could help. He told me how he had recently returned from a trip to the Far East—he had spent time in Kashmir, the Tibetan Kingdoms, China, had traveled south and witnessed the fall of the Khmer Empire, and the rise of the Mongols. At the time my knowledge of history and geography was nonexistent. I had no idea some of the events that he mentioned had happened last century. I could not guess that he was any older than midthirties. And then, he said that he had brought back something from the distant lands—medicines made of the strange plants of the jungle. He gave me a jar with a balm that would relieve the cough, and leaves I had to chew. They were no miracle cure, he said, but would help, and with proper rest and keeping warm, I should get better.

"And then, we talked about my poetry. He had much to say, and everything he said was meaningful. I had never talked to anyone about my works before; no one had ever been interested. Throughout the conversation, I could not take my eyes off him. There was something about the way he talked, the way he ate and drank, the way he behaved at the table, that was strangely dignified, in a way I had never seen before and could not explain. He was magnificent. He was everything I had ever wanted to be, and so much more.

"He dissected my poems, finding themes and meanings I had never thought anyone would notice. For the first time in my life, I was having a conversation that I enjoyed. For the first time in my life, I was happy.

"I did not wish this meeting to end. I did not wish to finish my food and drink and go back home as if nothing had happened. When we finished, he ordered another round of mulled wine, and then another, but then it was time to go.

"He asked me if I had any new poems and offered to buy them. He said he would pay me to write more. It was a strange notion for me, to be paid for something I would have done anyway. I saw that if this went well, I might not need to work ever again."

"Yes, I'm certain you could spend the rest of your life in comfort and happiness, living off the money stolen from Vlad's victims," Myra remarked dryly.

"My lord was never a common thief," Tristan said defensively. "He had other ways of getting this money. And when he made me the offer, my heart sang with happiness. Not because of the gold, no, even though it was also important. It was because I would see him again.

"I stood up to leave and asked him if he would accompany me home, so that I could show him more poems. He glanced through the window then and said he would have loved to, but had to stay at the inn for a while longer. I was disappointed, not knowing that the only reason he had refused my offer were the sunrays that had made their way through the clouds. It was not until much later that I realized he had made his way to the inn in the middle of the day, relying on the weather to remain the same. At the time, I had no idea he had risked his life to come to me.

"I returned home, feeling more excited than ever, but soon the effects of the warm food and drink wore off, and my misery returned. It did not help that the temperature at home was not much different than outside. At least I was away from the wind and snow, I thought optimistically as I covered myself with every single blanket I could find. I used the rub he had given me, and it helped for a time, but I knew I needed to get warm, and soon.

"Several hours had passed after the sun had set, when someone knocked on the door. I nearly ran to open it, my heart beating wildly in my chest. All this time I had worried he would never come.

"But he did. He was carrying a load of firewood and two rabbits. He assumed I would have trouble getting wood and food until I got better and that was the least he could do, he said. I was offended then; I did not want to accept help, I did not need any. But he said it was only a small part of the payment that I deserved for all I had done for him.

"There was another thing that bothered me. 'You are coming from the woods right now?' I asked in disbelief.

"He smiled then. 'What bothers you?'

"'It is dark,' I said simply, as if this explained it all.

"'I am not afraid of the dark,' he said. 'Are you?'

"I shook my head. 'There is a beauty and mystery in the dark that the light lacks. I would rather live in a world with no day, than in a world of no night.'

"He seemed to like my answer. I showed him more of my poetry, and we talked about it for hours. But he noticed I was not feeling well, and told me I had to rest. He said a warm soup would make me feel better and stood up to prepare the rabbits—what?"

"I… I am sorry—" Myra managed in between chuckles and pressed her hands against her mouth, trying to suppress her laughter. "But I just had a mental image of the Dark Prince of all Vampires, cooking soup. I don't know why, but this is hilarious."

"Make fun all you want," Tristan said. "But he is a good cook for someone who requires no food. To me, this was the best soup I had ever eaten. I felt much better afterwards, and we talked some more, but I was growing tired, and he stood up to leave. I could not believe he meant to go at this hour and invited him to stay over for the rest of the night. 'I know you do not fear the dark,' I said, 'but the woods are a dangerous place at this time. The wolves come out, and all kinds of dangerous beasts.'

"'The most dangerous thing in these woods at night,' he said, his eyes burning like flames, 'is me.'

"With these words he disappeared and did not come back on the following night. I feared he would not return; I feared something had befallen him, and I prayed that my weakness would pass so that I could go into the woods and look for him. I lay on my bed, staring at the ceiling, replaying in my mind all that he had said to me over and over again. Tears came to my eyes as I feared I would never speak to him again.

"He came back on the following night, and I wanted to weep with relief. I gave him more poems, we talked some more, and from then on, he would come almost every evening. I never wondered why he always came after nightfall—it seemed right.

"My sickness passed, thanks to his care. I felt it inappropriate that he, the lord, should wait on a commoner like me, but he seemed puzzled by my hesitance. I did not know my worth, he said. I did not know how much I deserved and what I would one day be.

"I often wondered where he went after he left my house, where he lived. The closest village was hours away, and the closest place with a proper accommodation for a man of his standing even further. I asked him once, and he said he lived in a cave up in the mountains. This surprised me; he did not look like someone who lived in a cave. He said he would take me there, but it would be too cold for me at this time of year. For some reason, I did not find it strange that the cold did not bother him.

"Once he commented on the stag skin I still had in front of my bed. He said it was beautiful, and indeed it was, with the single white spot on the neck that made it special. He asked if I was not afraid someone would see it and question me. 'Will your lord not be angry when he hears you have the skin of a stag killed in his woods?' he asked.

"'He is not my lord,' I said. 'You are.'

"Winter turned to spring, the nights grew shorter, and so did his visits. I had grown so used to his nightly stops that I grew anxious and restless any evening he would not show up. I spent my days reading the books he brought to me and thinking of all I wanted to say when I saw him again.

"As the nights passed, a suspicion grew in my mind, and I gathered the courage to ask him something I had wondered about for a while.

"'Do you know Callisto?'

"He smiled. 'Very well.'

"I should have known it. I had always known it in my heart. 'So you are also a god, then?'

"He laughed. 'A god? There is only one god, the god of the blue sky I will never see again. No, my boy, I am no god.'

"I stood up then and faced him, locking eyes with him. 'You are a vampire.'

"Not a muscle on his face twitched. 'Does that scare you?'

"'I think you already know the answer to that,' I said calmly. 'It is the answer to another question I find more interesting. Can you make me like you?'

"He said this had never been a question. The very reason he had sought contact with me in the first place was because he had picked me. He said I was perfect, he said I was born to be a vampire—"

"Oh joy," Myra said.

He grinned. "I know how you feel about that."

"Actually, I think the Prince did have a point," she said. "You were a vampire before you were even turned. You were a jerk to others, you were lazy, and you had no redeeming qualities—"

"No redeeming qualities?" Tristan cried. "Give me a break. I was poor and misunderstood, and felt out of place."

"These aren't redeeming qualities," Myra said. "They might count for excuses, although that is also open to debate, but they're not qualities. This was simply the hand fate had dealt you, and you did nothing to change it, nothing to fight it. You chose to sulk and wallow in self-pity and turn into a monster who could punish those who shunned him. You say you were unhappy? You have felt the sun on your face. My friends and I never experienced that. You had the freedom to grow your crops under the nourishing sun and without the constant fear that someone would hunt you down like an animal and drain your blood. You say you were poor? Your life was probably better than what my people are going through right now. Do you see any Resistance members rushing to the Palace, begging to be turned?"

"As if we would turn you," Tristan said. "Most of you humans are not vampire material anyway."

Myra fisted her hand. "How dare you."

"Well, I think *you* might be vampire material."

"What? Am I supposed to be flattered?"

He sighed. "I say you are not vampire material, you are offended, I say you are vampire material, you are offended. Is there a way to please you?"

"You arrogant fool," she said. "You never let me finish."

He raised an eyebrow. "Go on, then."

"I was saying that as a human you had no redeeming qualities. But as you were turned, you learned to care for others. You are a better vampire than you were a man. The Prince was right—you were born for it."

Tristan smiled. "Thank you."

"But I'm surprised by this story," Myra continued. "Are you saying that when a vampire wants to turn someone, they befriend them first and teach them about the ways of vampires, before turning them? I am quite certain that didn't happen during the Nightfall. There was no time, and people were turned by the hundreds."

"You are right, this was not done during the Nightfall," Tristan said. "Neither was it done before it. My lord told me that when a vampire liked someone, they turned them right there and then. There was no shared knowledge, no questions, no choice. But he said I was more than that. He said he respected me too much to turn me against my will. He said he would turn me only when I asked for it."

"And no doubt you asked for it on the spot."

"I did," Tristan admitted, "but he refused. He said I had to first think about what I was doing. I had to die first, in order to rise again. He said that once turned, I would never again see the sun. I was still young, he said, I had my whole life ahead of me. I had to enjoy it for a few years more.

"I told him this did not matter to me. I told him I had seen enough of sun, and of people. I told him I was ready.

"And then, he said there was one more thing I needed to know. He said that when I was turned, my soul would be damaged. I would be unable to create any kind of art. I would no longer be able to write poetry.

"I was terrified. I could not lose my talent—I was so used to writing, and it was a large part of me. It was who I was. I feared I would not be myself without it. Yet, I knew that being a vampire was what I was born for and I would choose it over my ability to write.

"But then another terrible thought occurred to me. My lord had approached me because of my poetry. He visited me every night because he wished to discuss it. Once I stopped writing, he would have no reason to talk to me ever again.

"Would he take me with him once I was turned, or would he leave and take his own path? Did vampires travel in groups? When I saw Callisto, she had been alone, and I had never seen my lord with another vampire. Legends said they were lone creatures, roaming the night by themselves.

"He would do me a great favor by making me a vampire, making me immortal. This would be his last payment, a payment for all the poems I had written for him. And then, this would be the end. I was certain of it. He would go his own way, and I would go mine. For what reason would he have to talk to me at all if I was unable to write?

"And then I realized with horror that I no longer wanted to be a lone creature of the night. You see, I had always been alone, but I had never been lonely. I had always enjoyed solitude, sought it, even. This was the first time I knew what it was like to be lonely. This was the first time I enjoyed someone else's company more than my own, and the thought of losing it filled my heart with terror.

"And so I told him I was not ready. I told him I enjoyed my poetry too much, and I did not wish to give it up just yet. I never dared tell him of my doubts and the true reason for my hesitance.

"He said he understood. He promised not to push me and said he would wait for as long as I needed." Tristan fell quiet. "And now I fear it is time for me to go. I will continue my tale next time."

"What?" Myra said. "But we never got to the actual turning point. I still don't understand why the Prince turned you, if you wished to keep your ability to write."

"There is still a long way to go before the turning point," Tristan said and gazed through the window at the castle wing that hosted the Great Hall. "My lord is hosting an Audience in a few days. I promised to help with the preparations."

"Can't we finish the story first?"

He shook his head. "Don't look so gloomy. I will tell you the rest next time."

"Of course," she said, forcing herself to smile. "You should go." *Next time?* she thought sadly. *If Armida and I succeed, there might not be a next time.*

Chapter Twenty-Four

The Devil You Know

A large mirror covered almost the entire wall in the royal dressing room. Myra reached out for her glass of fresh watermelon juice and stretched herself on the red velvet-covered canapé, gazing at Prince Vladimir's reflection. Some Old World legends claimed vampires cast no reflection in mirrors, and she wished that was true. It would have spared her hours of watching vamps admire their own images and painstakingly perfect minor details in their appearance. Tristan was by far the worst offender, but she had yet to meet a vampire who would not spend hours in front of the mirror.

Tristan walked to the fireplace to pick a few burning coals for the antique iron. "I think the red-rimmed woolen cape will match well with your waistcoat, my lord," he said.

Myra placed her glass back on the low blue marble table. "Aren't you *done*? You've been fixing Vlad's clothes and hair for the past hour."

The Prince turned to look at her. "Of course we are not done. The Royal Audience is an official event and I have to be dressed for the occasion. Every single vampire in my kingdom has the right to come and present a petition. As you have probably noticed, appearances mean a lot to our kind. I am their Prince. I need to outshine them all if I want to reaffirm my authority."

Tristan snorted. "My lord, you would outshine those idiots even if you walked into the Great Hall in your sleepwear."

Vlad glared at him. "I would have you show some respect for my subjects. Is that so much to ask for?"

"What I meant is, you are born to rule," Tristan said. "And it shows, no matter what you are wearing."

He's born to conquer, more like, Myra thought. *I'm not so sure about ruling.* She looked at Tristan, who was now busy ironing the cape. "So you *are* capable of manual work when it suits you?"

"Why does that surprise you?" Vlad said. "We are capable of anything."

"Then why was it so hard to maintain the world humans created?" she asked. "It's not like you had to build it from scratch. You had everything ready. All you had to do was keep it from falling apart, and you've done an appalling job."

"Do you know why people of the Old World did any work?" Vlad asked.

"Because they wanted to create a home for themselves?" Myra guessed. "To build a beautiful and a functional place, where things would work smoothly?"

"I am talking smaller scale here." He tapped at the canapé's carved ebony armrest. "The people who built the furniture you see in this room. Why did they work?"

"To get paid?" she guessed.

He nodded. "Payment was one of the many types of incentive people had. One way or another, they had motivation to work. How could I motivate vampires? In the Old World, vampires never had to work. They lived like nobles among the common folk. The humans labored and created, and the vampires exploited the system and plucked the fruits when they were ripe."

Myra raised an eyebrow. Vlad had often claimed vampires had lived poorly in the Old World, hiding from humans, and he had used this argument to justify the Nightfall. Did he realize his own hypocrisy?

The Prince walked to the window and pulled back the curtains, revealing a starry night sky. "And then I create a new world, in which they need to work and sweat. Why would any of them prefer my world to the one before? Vampires are proud and find most types of work degrading. It is hard enough to find decent servants, or guards, or sailors on the postal ships."

"So how do you motivate them?" Myra asked.

"By giving them rewards, as usual," he said. "For a month, they work as servants or guards, and for another month they can live as noble-vampires in one of the castles. Also, they get the best picks from the Farm. The system works for now, but is hardly sustainable."

"This is pathetic," Myra said. "You wouldn't work to make the world you live in a better place, and you are *proud* of it? You prefer someone else to do it for you, and have no respect for those who do. You are social parasites."

"Plenty of people in the Old World exploited the system and were what you call social parasites," Vlad said. "But I admit it is a problem I did not foresee when I planned the Nightfall. For a time I considered using the domesticated humans for work, but that meant educating them and teaching them skills, and the less they know, the better. Besides, I find slave labor disgusting."

"What?" Myra blurted out. "Seriously? You find it immoral to use people as slaves, but have no trouble *eating* them?"

"I eat them to survive," he replied. "I am a predator. They are game. But I do not need their labor for my survival. It would be immoral."

Myra thought it was pointless to argue. The vampire's statements were so absurd; she was not sure where to start. She stole a glance at Tristan, who was now rummaging through a chest of golden and gem-encrusted pins and brooches. "So does Tristan also get to rule a castle in exchange for being your valet?"

The blond vampire laughed. "I get so much more than that." He approached the Prince, holding the perfectly ironed cape and a sun-shaped golden pin. "Do you want me to join you at the Audience, my lord?"

"No, my boy," Vlad said as Tristan secured the cape around his shoulders. "Myra will be joining me. There is no need for you to suffer as well."

"So *I* have to suffer?" Myra said. "And why is an Audience such a torture for you? Ruling takes more than wearing fancy clothes and sitting on a cool throne, you know."

"I know that better than anyone. Which is why I am taking you with me tonight. Perhaps once you have seen how things are run around here, you will learn to appreciate my efforts."

He put on his golden circlet and left the dressing room, leaving Myra no choice but to follow.

***

The Prince swished his cape to the side and sat on the large black throne. He gestured at a chair next to him, and Myra took the seat. He then looked up, nodding at the guard at the door.

"Yong, could you please invite the first petitioner?"

Myra followed the guard with her eyes as he left the Great Hall. "How many petitioners are you receiving today?"

"As many as I can meet until the sun rises, then sets and rises again. You will, of course, be dismissed when you are tired."

"Speaking of the sun," she said and pointed at his sun-shaped pin, "that's not very fitting for a vampire, is it?"

"My people worshipped the clear blue sky. It is fitting for me."

The doors opened before she could ask him any more questions, and a vampire woman stepped in. She wore a pink silken kimono, decorated with white flower patterns, and her jet-black hair was held up in a complex bun. To Myra's surprise, Vlad stood up and bowed deeply.

"Countess Izumi. I was not aware of your arrival. My people have shown you to your accommodations, I trust?"

"Your people have been most kind, Your Highness," Izumi said, stealing a glance at Myra. "I arrived an hour ago. I wished to discuss my problem with you before I would rest."

"The road was not too tiring, I hope. Did you come by car?"

She shook her head. "We have little fuel left. I came by a cart."

"This must have taken you almost two days," said Vladimir as he returned to his seat. "This problem of yours must be serious indeed."

"It is," she said. "There was an outbreak in my Farm. Some sort of flu. We couldn't contain it. We lost nearly a fourth of our humans, and the ones left cannot sustain all my people. A few of us need to feed from the same human, and the humans often die or are unusable for a long time."

"You need to manage your resources better," the Prince said. "Here is what you will do. For a while, you and your people will survive on animals. Give your humans time to recover. The children need to grow, and the ones of breeding age need to produce more babies."

"This will take years," Izumi complained. "I will not spend years living on animal blood."

"This is what you need to do to let your Farm recover and grow," he said sternly.

She glared at him. "I never had to spend years away from human blood before the Nightfall."

He sighed. "What would you have me do, my lady? I want to help, but my own Farm is smaller than I would like. If you wish, I can send you fifty men and women of breeding age, to help your Farm recover. Would that be enough?"

"Thank you, Your Highness," Izumi said. "Your gift is much appreciated."

She made no move to leave, and the Prince raised his eyebrows. "Anything else I can help you with?"

Izumi broke her eye contact with him and stared at Myra. "So this is your infamous pet?"

Myra blushed and bit her lower lip, forcing herself to keep quiet.

The Prince smiled. "Why, yes, this is my pet. What bothers you?"

"She is from the Resistance. The same Resistance that has been terrorizing your people, and the same Resistance you stubbornly refuse to squash."

"And your point is?" he said calmly.

Izumi approached the throne and placed her hand over his. "Vladimir," she said softly. Myra looked up, startled. She had never heard any vampire besides Armida address the Prince without using his title.

"Mark my words," Izumi continued. "Your love for all things human will be your downfall."

He grinned at her. "Is that a threat, my lady?"

"It is a warning, my sweet prince. So many would love to take your place. The Duchess is ambitious, and so are Mizuki and Count Lucien. You know how much I like you. I would hate to see you assassinated and replaced."

"Of course," he said, his grin broadening. "Unless you are the one to replace me."

She frowned and pulled her hand back. "How can you say that?"

"You have thought about it," he said calmly. "You know it. I know it. Well, you are not the first. Get in line. I am giving you the Farm humans you asked for. Unless you have any other requests, I shall see you later at the feast."

She smiled and curtsied. "Of course. Thank you very much for the gift, Your Highness." She bowed to kiss the ruby ring on his index finger before leaving the hall.

Myra glanced at Vlad. "What was that about? Is someone trying to kill you?"

He raised an eyebrow. "Apart from you, you mean?"

She sighed. "Vlad, I'm not trying to kill you."

"Right. I can assure you that everyone else will have the same success you did."

She frowned. "You never take anything seriously, do you? And who are those ambitious vamps she mentioned?"

"Lucien is someone who will never be Prince," he said, his voice uncharacteristically strained. "The others are inconsequential."

Myra shuddered. *The Duchess is ambitious, and so are Mizuki and Count Lucien.* Myra knew nothing about Mizuki, but she remembered the Duchess from Franka's story. If she was of no importance, Myra did not wish to think about Lucien.

The double doors opened again. "Your Highness," Yong said. "The next petitioner is Casiel."

The Prince leaned his head against the backrest and momentarily closed his eyes. "Brilliant," he groaned and looked up at Yong. "Send him in."

The tall male vampire stepped in and Myra observed him curiously. His dark curly hair was cut short, unusual for the vampires at court, and he was wearing dark blue polyester trousers and a button-front shirt. "Your Highness," he said. "I'm afraid I have bad news."

The Prince smiled, but it did not reach his eyes. "Will you ever come with good news, my friend? Speak."

"Toni is missing. We believe this is the Resistance's work."

Myra suppressed a grin. It was good to hear Zack was still active and successful.

"Bad news indeed," the Prince said. "How long has he been gone?"

"Two days now. I tried to track him down, but found nothing."

Vlad nodded. "I will send search parties to look for him."

Casiel glared at him. "This is *all* you will do?"

The Prince stared back evenly. "If you have something to say, say it."

"You won't find him," Casiel said. "The Resistance is keeping him wherever they keep the rest of our people they've captured. We have tried to find the place with little success, though I wonder why. I wonder how it is possible to have the key right in front of us, and not use it. Your Highness, why are you so reluctant to ask your pet where the Resistance hides?"

Myra squeezed her armrests, her palms sweaty. Casiel was right. Their people were disappearing, and interrogating her was the vampires' most logical course of action.

"I have asked her," Vlad lied. "She will not tell me."

Casiel snorted. "Then give her to me and my guys. We have ways to make her talk."

"I have other uses for her," the Prince said. "She is my pet, not yours. This is out of the question."

"Right," Casiel spat. "And would your answer be the same if Armida or Tristan went missing?"

The Prince stood up, reaching Casiel in three quick strides. "If anything happened to them," he said, "I would find who was behind it and punish them in ways you cannot begin to comprehend. Are we clear?"

Casiel nodded stiffly. "How comforting. Too bad you won't give the rest of your people the same consideration."

He turned to leave, and the Prince cleared his throat. "Are you forgetting something?"

Casiel turned back, eyes blazing. He bowed down and kissed Vlad's ring. "Thank you for the Audience, Your Highness," he said, his voice acidic.

He stood up and stormed out, and Vlad collapsed in his throne, brow furrowed.

Yong's orange head popped out at the door. "Shall I invite the next one, Your Highness?"

"Give me ten minutes," the Prince called.

"I'm not your pet, you know," Myra said as Yong left. "And what happened here? Did you just tell him that if Armida or Tristan disappeared, he would be a suspect?"

The Prince nodded. "He is determined to make me destroy the Resistance. I would not put it past him to try to kidnap Armida or Tristan and make it look like it was the Resistance's work to force my hand. I made it clear to him that if this happened, he would be my first suspect."

"And what if the Resistance really captures them?" Myra challenged.

"They are not so stupid as to get themselves captured," Vlad said. "And I would never let anything happen to them. You know that."

But what if we do capture them? Myra wondered. *What if we succeed and threaten to kill them unless Vlad destroys the Wizard?* "I do," she said. "But hypothetically, let's assume the Resistance captures them. What would you do?"

He leaned back in his chair. "Well, hypothetically, I would get my hands on everyone involved and would break each of the two hundred and six bones in each of their bodies. Does that answer your question?"

It did, but not in the way she had hoped. "Why are you protecting me?" she asked.

"Don't take it personally," he said. "You know I need someone to finish my book. Besides, I am sentimental. I would not want to have human culture completely destroyed."

"Is this why Franka and other elders are still alive?" Myra asked. "I wondered about it at first. She is past her prime and can no longer reproduce. She is useless to you, and yet, you keep her alive. And then, I got it. You knew her. You pretended you didn't know who I was talking about when I asked you to bring her to me, but you knew her. You met her in London, and you remembered her. You ordered your people to spare her."

"And why would I do that?" he asked.

"Because you needed her. Not for food or babies. You needed her to teach the future generations. You didn't want to completely brainwash the Farm humans. You wished to preserve a spark of humanity."

He grinned. "Very good. I did not need Franka in particular, but I did wish to keep a few elders, and she worked just as well as anyone. You know my secret now. How are you going to use it?"

She frowned. "You wanted me to figure it out? You keep giving me more and more hints about your weaknesses and how to exploit them. You are insane, you know that?"

His smile did not fade. "Perhaps I seem irrational to you, but everything I do has a reason. Perhaps you will one day figure it out."

"Or perhaps I *have* figured it out," Myra said haughtily. She had no idea what reason he was referring to, but what she *had* figured out was a plan to defeat him. Vlad could underestimate her as much as he liked, but she was certain this would work and he would not see it coming.

***

Myra leaned against the white marble wall around the small basin, gazing at the water. Seven red-and-white koi fish were swimming around, merrily chasing one another. She followed them with her eyes, trying to calm her racing mind.

Everyone seemed to want her tortured and killed. The Prince was the one thing that stood between her and a painful death. She was not grateful—she was well aware he only kept her alive for his own selfish purpose, but she had seen enough to realize that if he died, so would she.

Was this why she was always escorted by so many guards? Myra had assumed the Prince considered her dangerous, but now she realized the guards were not there to prevent her from running away. They were there to *protect* her. She was in danger from practically everyone.

The Resistance had always believed that killing Prince Vladimir would further their cause. Myra now saw that it would have brought more harm than good and was glad they never succeeded. The Prince held back when fighting against her people, reluctant to completely destroy humanity. Whoever would potentially replace him would have no such qualms.

Myra looked at the cloud-covered sky and then back at the water, smiling as she watched the colorful fish. She could almost forget that her guards were just around the corner. She could almost imagine that no one was watching her.

The illusion went away as a pale hand grabbed the marble fence right next to her. She looked up, staring at Armida's smiling face.

"A beautiful night, isn't it?" the vampire said. "Will you miss the Palace once you leave?"

"I miss my friends more," Myra said.

"Of course. I can imagine you cannot wait to go back home. The story is going well, I trust?"

"Yes, I've already written a large part," Myra lied. She had not simply written a lot. She had nearly finished. However, she could not tell that to Armida just yet. The vampire would help her escape as soon as the story was done, and Myra first needed a chance to visit the library and find all she could on the WeatherWizard. "Any ideas how you'll help us escape?"

"Plenty," Armida said. "But first, where do you wish me to drop you off? Can you find your way home from the house in the woods where Yong captured you?"

Myra frowned, surprised. She had thought Armida would consider her part of the bargain done once she had helped her out of the Palace. Was the vampire really concerned about getting her home? Or did she wish to follow her to find the Resistance?

"Close to the woods there is a large, stony desert," Myra said. "Your people have placed traps, covered with dead branches. I can find my way from there." Or at least she hoped she could, but she did not dare ask Armida to take her to the woods around the Resistance.

"I know the place," Armida said. "Leave all the escape planning to me. The old woman should be easy—she is just another human. I can pretend to be taking a snack outside, and no one will wonder when I return without her. You are a different matter. Your face is widely known now, and I must make sure I am not the last person seen with you before you disappear."

"But Franka isn't unknown, is she?" Myra said. "She's one of the elders the Prince keeps alive on purpose."

Armida frowned. "You know that? He trusts you a lot, I see. Even so, you must know that almost everyone around here disagrees with this policy. If they believe I'm ridding us of Franka, they will thank me and keep quiet."

"Keep quiet about what?" a voice from behind interrupted them, and Armida turned around to flash a grin at Izumi.

"Countess," Armida cried and stepped forward, giving Izumi a kiss on each cheek. "It is good to see you. You are looking for the Prince, I imagine? Unfortunately, the Audience is still running."

"I was looking for you, actually," Izumi said. "I tried to warn Vladimir, but he didn't take me seriously."

"Warn him?" Armida frowned. "What about?"

Izumi threw a quick look around, apparently checking for other vampires but not caring that Myra was still there. "Many would see him fall. And now they are more than ever, and their voices are louder."

"That is not news to me," Armida said. "I have it under control."

Myra glanced between the two, half-annoyed, half-grateful that the vampires seemed to have forgotten she was there, listening. She dipped her hand into the pond, staring at the water and trying to remain inconspicuous.

"Are you certain?" Izumi asked.

"Positive. You know how things work in the Palace. No one is overthrowing anyone unless I say so."

"And you have no intention of saying so, I hope?" Izumi said.

Armida glowered at her. "What do you think? And why are you so concerned about this anyway?"

"Vladimir and I have our differences," Izumi admitted, "but I have far more significant disagreements with whoever may come to replace him. Look, I am not your enemy. If you need help, you can count on me."

Armida smiled. "How kind of you. I will keep that in mind."

Myra looked up when Izumi walked away. "Is it true? What's going on?"

"She is trying to win my favor, that is what is going on," Armida said. "Or, most likely, she is hedging her bets—I would not be surprised to hear she is going to the ones supposedly planning to overthrow my beloved, telling them she is on their side. That is how things work in court."

"It must be exhausting," Myra said. "Talking to so many insincere people, who try to win your trust but wouldn't hesitate to stab you in the back."

"Exhausting? No, not really. I love it."

"You must be good at this," Myra said. "Now, about my escape. You said Franka would be easy. How about me?"

"No need to worry," Armida said. "I have a very good idea how to get you out of the castle. I will leave it as a surprise—you will have to trust me and follow my lead."

Brilliant. Armida had just told her how much she enjoyed courtly intrigue and duplicity, and now she was asking Myra to trust her. "Very well," she said reluctantly. "But, as you can imagine, I find it hard to trust you with my life and Franka's. I would need a guarantee."

Armida smiled. "For shame, Myra. I thought we were friends. What guarantee are you talking about?"

Myra looked around. "Can we go somewhere private?"

"Of course," Armida said. "Let us go to my beloved's study. His notebook is there—he finished translating the rest of his book and asked me to give it to you."

Myra breathed a sigh of relief. She had feared she would escape before she had a chance to read the rest. "The Prince expects me to continue the book for him," she said. "He'll be disappointed when I escape."

"He'll survive it," Armida said as she led Myra across the courtyard, towards a narrow street between two high stone walls that led inside the castle. The guards followed at a not-so-discreet distance, and Myra tried to ignore them.

"Do you need any help with my story so far?" Armida asked as they walked.

"Actually, I do," said Myra. "I want to run it by you to make sure it sounds like something you could have written."

"I couldn't have written anything," Armida said. "But I know what you mean. Go on."

"The protagonist is an eighteen-year-old girl, Amalia," Myra said.

"No one was called that anywhere around my village," Armida said. "I would have never come up with that name. Try Francesca."

"Very well. Francesca's parents are simple shepherds, but she dreams of something more. She's planning to go to the sea and sail away. You knew you lived close to the sea, right?"

"Of course. I wasn't stupid," Armida said. "I had been there once."

"Did you see the fishing boats?"

"I did," the vampire said. They reached the end of the narrow street and stood in front of the wooden gate leading inside the castle. Armida placed her hand on the knob and turned back to look at Myra. "You can easily include fishing boats in your story. I had seen plenty of them before I was turned."

Myra smiled. "Perfect. That's exactly what I did. Francesca sneaks onto a larger fishing boat and hides underneath the blankets, hoping to see the open sea. A vicious storm sinks the boat and the crew dies, but Francesca survives, saved by mermaids."

"Mermaids?" Armida snorted. "There are no mermaids in Italian folklore."

"On the contrary," Myra said. "The Prince gave me a few books, and I've been researching. The idea of mermaids came from the sirens in Greek mythology, mixed with Nordic legends. These reached Italy during the barbaric invasions. In fact, many mermaid sightings had been reported along the coasts of Campania, Puglia, Sicily and Calabria. That's where you are from, right?"

Armida's eyes widened. "Well done, young lady." She opened the door and held it for Myra to enter. "Mermaids it is."

Myra walked down the corridor after Armida lit the torches on the walls. "My guards will want to follow," she said when the vampire closed the door behind them.

"This is their problem," Armida said. "So you were saying you did not trust my word?"

"I don't mean to offend you," Myra said. "But how do I know that you won't simply kill Franka and give me to the vamps who want to interrogate me? If you do them this one little favor, they will always be on your side."

Armida rolled her eyes. "Oh, please. They will be on my side no matter what I do." They reached the Prince's study and stepped inside. Armida took a chair and Myra followed suit.

"You may have no reason to betray me, but you have no reason to let me go either," Myra said.

"Oh, but I do," the vampire said. "Keeping you hidden in the dungeons is a bad idea. As soon as my love discovers your disappearance, he will send Tristan to have the Palace searched. That little brat will not stop until he has found you, and if they investigate further, the tracks may lead to me. It is in my best interest to have you far away from here."

"I will need something more than that," Myra said. "Do you have something sharp?"

Armida gave her a blank look, but then her face lit up in understanding. The vampire grinned. "You want a blood oath? I admit I am deeply hurt you feel this is necessary, but if it will make you feel better—" In one quick move Armida unsheathed a dagger from a scabbard at her belt and slashed through her palm. "Draw blood," she commanded as she pushed the blade in Myra's hand.

Myra took the blade, shaking, and stared at her palm, her hand frozen.

Armida grinned. "Having doubts? What do you fear, Myra? Is it the pain? It is but a quick sting. You do not think you can catch a disease, do you? I am dead. Viruses and bacteria cannot survive in my blood. Or do you fear that being my blood sister would corrupt you somehow?"

Myra took a deep breath and made a shallow cut across her palm.

"See?" Armida said. "It was easy."

Myra winced as the vampire clasped their hands together. Their blood mingled. Armida released her hold, brought her hand to her face and licked.

"What happens now?" Myra asked.

Armida halted her gruesome meal. "I swear I will not betray you. I swear to help you escape. No harm will befall you while you are under my protection. Can you trust me now?"

Myra nodded. "I admit a blood oath doesn't hold the same meaning to me as it does to you, but I too swear that I won't betray you in any way."

The vampire grinned. "Congratulations, Myra. You just became my blood sister."

Chapter Twenty-Five

Last Shred of Being Human

Myra closed the journal Armida had given her and gazed at the cover. She longed to keep reading, to finish all that Vlad had written while he had still been human, but there were more pressing matters. The time for her escape was drawing near, and she still did not have all she needed.

She placed the journal on the shelf, with the rest of her books. Her personal library was full now—books on history, geography, strategy games, art, chemistry, medicine—each and every one of them chosen by the Prince. She had no say in what books she would have in her room, and he would give her only the ones he thought she would need for researching his story. The best she could do was convince him she needed a certain book for writing one scene or another. Unfortunately, he would never believe a book on the WeatherWizard was necessary for her writing.

The information on the WeatherWizard was still there, in the library. She had to go and get it sooner rather than later. Her eyes darted towards a notebook on the desk, where she had Armida's story. Armida's *fully complete* story. Myra could not delay her escape forever, and she needed to get her hands on the WeatherWizard book before the time came.

She walked to the door and opened it with a quick, determined move. Not surprisingly, Yong, Natalia, and two more vampires whose names she did not know waited outside. "I'd like to go to the library," Myra said.

Yong grinned. A shiver ran down her spine. She had not seen him smile since before Tristan had found her in the dungeons.

"You may like or dislike whatever you wish," the vampire said. "You are not going to the library."

Myra's breath caught in her throat, and she tried to force a stern expression on her face. "His Highness ordered you to take me to any place in the Palace to which he has granted me access, whenever I liked."

"He did," Yong said calmly, his smile unfaltering.

Myra felt sweat break across her palms. "I would like to go to the library. Now."

The vampire sneered. "And I said you are not going to the library."

"But—"

Yong looked about to burst into laughter. "You may go to any premise where you are allowed, and nowhere else. His Highness has revoked your access to the library."

"What?" Myra froze, her throat growing tight. What had Vlad done? Why? This could not be; she *needed* the library. Her escape would be useless for the Resistance if she had no information.

"Are you daft?" he said. "I said, your access has been revoked. You cannot go to the library."

Myra took a deep breath. "Take me to His Highness."

Yong hesitated, and she frowned. "What? Has he revoked my access to his study as well?"

"No," the vampire said. "But I expect he will wish he had. Come."

Myra followed her guards along the now-familiar path, her thoughts running wildly through her mind. What was Vlad playing at? Had he sensed she was planning to look for information on the Wizard? Or did he simply wish to make a point of his power over her? Whatever that was, she needed to resolve it fast—Myra could not lie to Armida forever; the story was finished and the time to escape was drawing near.

Yong knocked on the Prince's door and stepped aside, allowing Myra to enter. Vlad sat in his armchair with a thick book in his hand, a pair of candles flickering at his sides. He moved no muscle when she entered; only his eyes shifted from the page and focused on her.

"Welcome, Myra," he said. "Please, take a seat."

She frowned and sat in the armchair opposite him. On the table between them was a beautifully carved wooden checkerboard, all the pieces laid out and ready. "You revoked my library access."

"Make a move," he said calmly, gesturing at the board.

Myra fixed him with a firm stare. "I'm not here to play games."

"Oh, but this is exactly what we are doing. Playing a game. Your move."

She sighed and moved a piece. He responded right away, barely lifting his eyes from the book. "Why did you revoke my access?"

"Keep playing," he said, and, reluctantly, she did.

What is he doing? Will he give me my access back if I beat him? She tried to concentrate. She had read a bit about checkers in one of the books he had given her, and she believed she knew the basics. Control the center. Focus on getting a piece on the opposite side. It seemed easy enough.

"You are impatient," he said and leaned forward to lift his piece, capturing three of hers with a single move. "Do you know what your problem is, Myra?"

"I'm sure you are about to enlighten me."

He smiled. "You think you are a player. And your move would have made sense… if you had no opponent, that is. You play as if you are playing alone. You pay no attention to my moves and do not adapt your strategy accordingly. Every move I make has a purpose. And each one is a part of a larger plan. Before you make your own moves, you need to figure out my reasons, so that you can come up with a counterstrategy of your own. You need to think a few steps in advance."

Myra leaned back in her chair. She had no time for his games. "Very well. Your move was to revoke my library access. Are you telling me that it's a part of a larger plan?"

"I am not telling you anything."

She stood up, crossing her arms across her chest. "Why did you revoke my access?"

He flipped a black checkers piece between his fingers. "Why do you think?"

"You want something from me," Myra guessed. "And you are using the library as leverage."

"Obviously," he said. "I admit I do need something from you. And if you deliver, you will get your access back. The question is, what are you willing to do for it?"

Anything. "Depends. What do you want?"

He sighed and put the piece down. "So impatient." He poured himself a goblet of dark, ruby wine and took a slow sip. "Very well. We had these two humans in the Farm, Serena and Bastien. This morning they escaped."

Myra's eyes widened. "How?"

"This is what I would like to know. We captured Serena, but her partner got away. I need to know what their plans were and where he went. As you can imagine, if we never retrieve him, this will give a very bad example to the other domesticated humans. We are interrogating Serena—"

"You are torturing her, you mean?" Myra paled, grabbing her armrests. The news was amazing. Some humans still had enough spirit to attempt an escape, and a few even succeeded. If Bastien indeed managed to get away, it would, as Vlad had said, send a clear message to the rest of the Farm humans and encourage them to attempt escapes of their own. But where would they go? The Farm humans knew nothing of the world outside.

"You could call it that," he said. "Though at the moment my people are focusing on causing maximum pain with minimum damage. Humans are valuable. I would prefer to keep her alive."

Myra hated it when he referred to people as a commodity, but she supposed this was something she had to accept. She had already seen that Vlad was the lesser evil. Anyone else in his place would have been worse. "So what do you need me for?"

"I want you to make Serena talk."

"What? How would I make her talk?"

"This is your problem. Figure it out. The interrogators are failing, and time is running short. I need to capture Bastien alive. If I find him thanks to your assistance, I will return your library access."

Myra stood up and stepped behind her armchair. "This is ridiculous. I'm not helping you capture a human."

"Fine," he said. "And you are never taking another step into my library again."

She ran her hands through her hair. "Vlad, why are you doing this to me? You know I can't help you. I'm grateful you gave me access to your library, and I appreciate it a lot. Why do you want to take it away now? Reading more helps me write better. I can't write a very good book if I've never been exposed to most of the literature and knowledge created by the humans before me."

"I have given you selected books for your personal library," he said. "If you believe you require another, let me know and I will think about it. Do you have a specific book in mind?"

She shuddered. *How much does he know?* "I can't have a specific book in mind if I don't know what's out there. Let me browse your library just one more time and make a list of books I'm interested in. After that, I'll only read the books you provide."

"I will let you in the library one more time," he said. "And one more, and many times after. If and only if you talk to

Serena and provide me the information necessary to capture Bastien."

Myra grabbed the armchair's backrest and looked down. There was no way she would do this. Bastien had the potential to become a symbol of freedom and to inspire other humans. And she needed the Farm humans spirited and ready to fight. She had few illusions that the Resistance could destroy the Wizard on their own.

"What will happen to Bastien if you capture him?" she asked.

He emptied his goblet and poured himself more wine. "That is none of your concern."

"You know that it is. Will he die?"

"All humans die."

"Vlad, please."

The Prince sighed and took a long sip. He put his goblet down and silently stared at the fire. "Of course he will die," he said after a while. "I need to set an example for the domesticated humans. I see this is hard for you, so let me make it easier—if we capture him, I will kill him, but spare Serena. If he gets away, I will kill her in his stead."

Myra turned away from him and paced to the fireplace and back. "How exactly is this making things easier for me? Am I supposed to choose between the lives of people I've never met? Vlad, if you want to torment me, do it, but don't use other humans as pawns."

"I have many reasons for the things I do. Believe it or not, tormenting you is not among them. This is bigger than you. You saw how things were at the Audience. My people want to see human blood spill. To be precise, they want *your* blood. I need to give them the next best thing."

"Oh, so now you are saying humans are dying because of me? Don't put the blame on me. You staged the Nightfall without giving any thought to the consequences. If you can't control your people, the fault is yours alone."

"Fair enough," he said. "But now things are the way they are, and we cannot change them. I give you this choice—either help me capture Bastien, save Serena and regain your access to the library, or do nothing, let Serena die and lose your access forever."

Myra's head hurt. She needed the library. It was the only way to find the information on the WeatherWizard and give the Resistance an opportunity to destroy it. She had to get her hands on those pages, and she needed to do it fast, before it was time to escape.

And yet, agreeing to the Prince's terms would doom another human being. Human lives were not comparable—each one was infinitely precious and it was impossible to say that one was more valuable than another.

And how was she supposed to accomplish that anyway? Gain Serena's trust and then betray her? Myra was human. In the past few weeks she had started to forget what this meant, but now she was beginning to remember. "I can't do it," she said.

"Of course you can," he said. "I will give you time to think on my proposal, but try to decide quickly. With every minute our chances of recapturing Bastien grow slimmer."

Myra had no desire to reconsider anything. "I need to talk to Franka."

"You believe she will help you decide? Very well. I will send someone to fetch her from the Farm."

Myra's eyes widened. "The Farm? I thought you gave her her own quarters to stay in."

He shrugged. "Yesterday she requested to spend the night in the Farm. Who am I to refuse? Come, now, your guards will take you back to your room, and I will find someone to bring Franka to you. Does that arrangement work for you?"

"It doesn't sound like I have a choice," Myra grumbled.

She opened the door and stepped outside. As expected, her guards were dutifully waiting. She followed them along the torchlit corridor, barely noticing where she was going. Franka had requested to go back to the Farm? And two humans had escaped? Were the two events connected?

Once she was back in her room and the guards had left her alone, Myra started pacing back and forth. She could not do as Vlad requested. If she did, she would give up a part of herself, a part of the thing that made her human. And yet, if she refused, she would lose her only opportunity to save human civilization. Was it worth it? Was she selfish to refuse? Was she refusing so that she would feel good about it?

But was there anything to feel good about? She was practically dooming humanity. She was throwing away her one single opportunity to learn more about the device that gave vamps so much power. What would Zack do if he were in her place?

And what did it matter? If Zack were in her place, he would have probably died long ago. He had chosen her for this mission because he believed in her. She needed to trust herself to make the right choice instead of wondering what anyone else would have done.

Alerie had died to give her a chance to destroy the vamps. And this chance was here and now. She would be a fool not to grab it.

I'm sorry, Bastien, she thought as she made her decision.

Just then, the door opened and Yong led Franka inside. The old woman was grinning madly, her eyes shining like sapphires under the torchlight. Myra had no idea why, but it scared her.

Franka barely waited for Yong to close the door behind him, when she clapped her hands, her grin growing broader. "Myra! Did you hear the news?"

So the humans in the Farm knew what was happening? "Two humans escaped."

The old woman nodded. "It's awesome. I've never seen the Farm like this. People are afraid to speak openly, but the whispers are everywhere. There is hope."

"Don't get your hopes up just yet. Serena was captured." Breathlessly, Myra told Franka all that she knew and all that Vlad had requested of her.

The old woman burst into laughter. "Oh, but that's great news. I never expected any of them to get very far. Now you are telling me that Bastien escaped, and His Evilness has no idea how to find him. That's hilarious."

"I wish it was," Myra said. "But I need to help the Prince find him. It's the only way I can get the WeatherWizard book."

Franka grabbed Myra's arms and shook her. "Are you insane? Something like this has never happened before. Bastien's escape sends a message. It gives us hope. Others will try to run away, and even if some die, many will succeed."

"I don't think it's so simple. In any case, if Bastien gets away, Serena will die."

The old woman released her and took a step back. "Look, Myra, I know how things work better than you. I know Serena. And I know she would have accepted death for the cause. It's sad, but it's for the greater good. Do you know how excited she was when I told her about you?"

"You told her about me?"

"Of course. That's why I went back. I told my people about you and about the Resistance. Many were thrilled to know humans still survived outside. I suspect that might have been the reason why Bastien and Serena decided to escape—perhaps they were planning to look for the Resistance."

"This doesn't make any difference," Myra said. "All your hopes are empty. After this, the vamps will tighten their security measures. Most probably, no one else will escape ever again. And they will retaliate. They'll kill Serena, and probably others, just to send a message."

"So you are suggesting we give in to terror? You are suggesting we should bend our necks and let them treat us like cattle instead of standing up to them?"

Myra walked to the door and placed one hand over the handle. "That is far from what I'm suggesting. I suggest we pretend to be defeated. Then, when the time is right, I'll get the info on the Wizard, and we'll escape and get it back to my people. And then, we'll be ready to strike."

Before Franka could speak and try to sway her, she opened the door and waved at her guards to approach. "Take me to His Highness," Myra said.

***

Vlad's triumphant grin nearly made her change her mind. She wondered if he was actually happy the humans escaped, giving him a chance to play with her.

"So you will help me?" he said.

"I will. But first, I need something from you."

He leaned back into his armchair and crossed his legs. "Another favor? On top of restoring your library access? That is not how things work."

"It's most definitely not a favor," Myra said. "Just something I need to get the information you asked for. I need your people to hurt Serena's leg."

His grin grew broader. "Interesting. And you believe this will help you get what you want?"

She nodded. "Yes. But I need the injury to be serious enough to prevent her from walking. A sprained ankle, or a stretched tendon, perhaps."

"I am sure my people will think of something," the Prince said and walked to the door. He opened it and whispered something to one of the guards outside. Then he walked back and sat in his armchair. "We never finished our checkers game."

Myra eyed the board, with the black pieces greatly outnumbering the red. "You've already won."

"I have not won until I have either taken all your pieces, or blocked all your moves. While the game is on, there is always hope." He reached out and rotated the board, slowly and carefully, making sure none of the pieces slid out of its place. "Come, now. You will play as black."

She sighed. "Are you trying to humiliate me?"

"Of course not. I am trying to teach you."

Myra had thought the game was unsalvageable, but he quickly proved her wrong. She bit her lip and ran her hand through her hair, pulling a few hairs out in the process. She was about to do the most inhuman thing in her life. She had no patience for his games.

"You really need to start putting a bit more thought into this," he said as he captured her last piece.

A knock at the door interrupted them, and Yong stepped in. "Your Highness, it is done," he reported.

The Prince smiled, stood up and bowed to Myra. "The scene is yours. Show me what you can do."

***

Vlad stopped in front of the cell door. "I will let you go in there alone."

Myra gulped and nodded. With shaking hands, she took the cold metal key and pushed it into the keyhole. The door opened with a creak, and she brought her torch forward, letting it cast light over the small cell.

The room was so small it was impossible to lie stretched out on the floor, which was covered in crumbs of food and something sticky. A large rat skeleton lay in the corner.

The prisoner was sitting down, leaning against the wall. Her face and bare arms were covered in cuts and bruises, and her dark eyes were bright with fever. Her brown hair was sticking to her sweaty face, and she was breathing heavily, but at first glance Myra saw no life-threatening injuries.

The woman's eyes widened as she looked up at her, and Myra dropped to her knees. "Serena," she said. "My name is Myra Andersen. I am a member of the Resistance. Franka has told you about me."

Serena paled and nodded. "So the Resistance is real?"

"It is. And you're going to meet them very soon. We are running away."

Serena gasped. "What?"

"I found a way to get out," Myra said. "I'm returning to my people. I learned you were here, and I stole the key. You are coming with me."

The prisoner leaned her head against the wall. "Thank you so much. I'd love to come with you. There's nothing I ever wanted more. You must have risked so much to come here."

"Think nothing of it," Myra said. "Come. We don't have time."

Serena shook her head. "Thank you for coming, truly, but you must go without me. I can't walk. They broke my leg."

They broke my leg. That was not what Myra had had in mind when she had asked for the vamps to hurt Serena's leg, but she supposed it worked. "I can't leave you here," she said.

"You must," Serena said. "You must go and find Bastien. Take him to the Resistance. Make sure he reaches safety."

Myra leaned forward and grabbed Serena's hand. "I will. How can I find him?"

"One of the vampires, Lucy, sympathized with us," Serena said. "She helped us escape. She had a safe house prepared for us. Bastien and I were supposed to meet there if we were separated. He must still be there, waiting for me."

Lucy. The vampire who helped her put on her ballgowns. Myra had never expected Lucy to be willing to help humans, but she had to admit she had never made an effort to get to know the vamp.

"Where is the safe house?"

"Not far from the sunlit clearing where vampires sometimes take us at night and leave us chained for the day to get sunlight," Serena said. "Lucy gave us a map. There is a path going straight north into the woods from there. We were supposed to follow it for about a mile and a half until we reach a lake. There is an abandoned cabin there."

Myra nodded. "That should be enough. I'll find it."

"Do you know the sunlit place?"

"Yes," she lied. Vlad would know where it was. "The vamps took me there once. I remember how to find it. Serena, I must go now. Be brave."

"Find him," Serena said. "Find him and bring him to safety."

"I will," Myra said and left the cell, heart clenched.

Once she had closed and locked the door behind her, the Prince took the torch from her hand and smiled.

"I heard everything," he said. "Well done. I am proud of you."

I am proud of you. She had hoped for these words so many times, and yet now she would give anything to erase this day from her life.

***

Myra watched from her window as the search party assembled in the courtyard. The Prince himself was leading it, mounted on a large black stallion. His hair was braided and adorned with his golden circlet. Tristan and Armida were at his side, each on a silver-white steed. About twenty vampires had assembled around them, preparing to ride out. Why did they need so many to capture a single fugitive?

It's a hunt. Myra shuddered, grabbing the windowsill. *They are enjoying it.*

The Prince rode in a wide circle, saying something to the assembled vampires, before turning to the lowered drawbridge. All the riders followed him in a line.

"Are you happy now?" Franka asked from behind her.

Myra could hardly remember being more unhappy. "It was necessary. This step might have won us the war."

"More likely, it has lost us the war," Franka said.

Myra frowned and tore her gaze from the window, looking at the old woman. "What do you mean?"

"The Resistance can't assault the Wizard on their own. You said you were less than five hundred people, many of whom not of fighting age. You need my people to help you, and they never will after this."

"They'll never know," Myra said. "You won't tell them, will you?"

"Of course not," Franka said. "But they will know. You never stop to think of the possible consequences of your actions, do you?"

"I do," Myra protested.

Of course you do, she heard the Prince's voice in her head. *But you only think one move at a time.*

Chapter Twenty-Six

Prince of Darkness

Myra sat on the bed, her knees drawn up to her chest, her arm wrapped around them. She could still see Serena in her mind, trusting her, thanking her, begging her to find and save Bastien. The vamps had ridden out after the fugitive, and Myra knew she had to hope they would capture him. Otherwise, Vlad would never allow her back into the library, and all would have been in vain. And yet, a part of her hoped Bastien would somehow get away.

Hours passed in uncertainly, before Tristan came to her room. Myra raised her pale face to look at him. "Did you capture Bastien?" she asked.

Instead of an answer, Tristan produced a long flowing white dress and threw it on the bed. "His Highness has requested your presence. And he requested that you wear this."

"Why?" Myra asked. "Is he throwing a ball to celebrate Bastien's capture?" And why white? Was it a cruel joke? White meant innocence, and she had none left.

Tristan was also dressed in white, she noted, like an angel of death.

"You will have all your answers when you join His Highness," Tristan said. "Now put it on. I will wait outside."

Myra obliged. The dress was light and comfortable, and she needed no help putting it on. Once she was ready, she came out.

Tristan was waiting for her, but all the guards were gone. He offered her his arm, and she silently took it. They walked to the end of the corridor, but instead of turning right on the way to the Great Hall or the Prince's study, they turned left and then started descending the winding staircase. Myra's heart sank. They were going to the dungeons.

Myra threw a glance at her old cell as they passed by it. She had been locked here, starving and afraid, what seemed like a lifetime ago. But was she any less afraid now?

Her reasons to fear were different. Back then, her conscience had been clean, and her goals and aspirations had been clear. Her only worry had been surviving another day. Now Myra no longer worried about survival. She only worried about everything else.

They walked to a wide corridor with one of the largest Farm cells on the left and a wall on the right. A set of black curtains hung against the wall, concealing something. Many vampires had assembled in the corridor, standing along the wall, their eyes fixed on the humans.

"What are we doing here?" Myra asked.

"Patience," said Tristan.

She tried to be patient, but every moment felt like hours. No one spoke, and the vamps never tore their gazes from the prisoners. Myra's eyes scanned the people in the cell, but she did not see Serena.

After what seemed like a lifetime, the door at the far end opened and Prince Vladimir stepped in. He wore black from head to toe, and his gleaming raven hair was loose and brushed to perfection, falling down impeccably straight.

He stepped forward slowly and deliberately, not saying a word, but his amber eyes never left the humans in the cells. The silence was deafening. Myra's heartbeat sounded loud and irritating to her own ears.

The Prince had walked about three-fourths of the way to her, when he turned around and started walking back. He had almost reached the far door when he turned around once again.

"I am sad," he said, his gaze fixed on the Farm humans. "Sad and disappointed. To me, you are my children. I love each and every one of you. I have raised you from small babes, and I have provided you with food, clothes, medicines, safety and comfort." He reached the middle of the corridor and paused, fully facing the cell and raising his hands. "I have hunted game for you with my own hands."

He took a torch from the wall and brought it closer to the cell, illuminating people's faces. "Do you have any idea how people in the Old World lived? Humans in some places had no food and shelter, no access to clean water, and no medical treatment or vaccination against easily preventable diseases."

The Prince lowered the torch, casting light over two toddlers, blissfully playing on the carpeted floor and paying him no attention. "In other areas people did not lack food, but they had other concerns. Taxes, bills, loans, mortgages, educating their children, having quality healthcare. Humans worked inhumane hours at jobs they hated but could never leave. They had no choice, drowning in loans they had taken out to afford petty comforts. People willingly sold themselves into slavery and had to repay the price all their lives."

The toddlers stopped playing and stared at him. He knelt down, reaching out through the bars and gently caressing the nearest one's curly hair. He then stood up, placed the torch back on the wall, and once again turned to the humans.

"I destroyed this world. And I created a new one, where you would want for nothing. You have all you need, and you have no worries. I could have easily made you my slaves and forced you to work for me. Instead, my people and I are working hard to provide you with any comfort you might desire. All I asked in return was a small sacrifice—a few drops of blood every now and then, so my people and I could stay alive and continue serving you. Was it too much to ask for?"

He looked up, and to Myra's horror, he was staring straight at her.

"Myra, my dear, please come and join me," Prince Vladimir said and stretched out his hand.

Hearth pounding, Myra walked to him, feeling numerous eyes on her. The Prince took her hand in his and raised it high.

"You may or may not know this, but Myra is a member of the Resistance," he said. "It is a group of humans that lived outside the Palace and opposed my rule. However, Myra came here and saw how you live compared to her people. The Resistance changed their minds. Now they believe that living in my Farm is what is best for humanity."

When he released Myra's hand, she was shaking. He winked at her and his eyes darted downwards, towards the toddler he had caressed. Myra's blood drained from her face. Was that a warning? Was he telling her he would kill the baby unless she kept her mouth shut?

The Prince turned back to the cells. "You are well aware that a few hours ago two of my children ran away. Myra knew they were making a mistake and wanted to do them a favor. She knew they would be better off back here, back home. This is why she helped me recapture them."

Vladimir grabbed the black curtain and pulled it down, and Myra's gasp was echoed by all humans in the cells. Two wooden, X-shaped structures stood against the wall, a human tied to each with arms and legs spread out. One was Serena, the other a man in his late teens or early twenties. Both were blindfolded and gagged.

"I have done so much for you all," the Prince said. "And yet you run away from me. I love all of you equally, and yet, when children disobey, it is the parents' duty to discipline them, no matter how painful." He sighed. "It hurts me to do this, but I must. Yong, please show my children what happens if they run away."

Yong approached, carrying a long box and a foldable table. He positioned the table next to the male prisoner, who had to be Bastien, and placed the box on top. He then walked to Serena and undid her blindfold.

"Watch carefully what happens to your friend," Yong said. "And remember—you will be next."

Serena glanced at Bastien, but her gaze immediately moved away and focused on Myra. Myra looked away, feeling the blood rush to her face.

"How shall we start?" Yong said in a low, singsong voice.

Vladimir looked away from the scene, but Myra stared at Bastien, transfixed, unable to tear her eyes away. Yong reached inside a box and produced a long, thin knife. He placed the tip against Bastien's temple and grinned. The man shuddered and made a sound around his gag. Myra fisted her hands. The poor man was blindfolded; he had no idea what was happening around him. He would have no warning for whatever pain was to come.

"You have a well-shaped face," Yong said, sliding the tip along the prisoner's temple, down his cheekbone, cheek and jaw. "I would hate to destroy it."

The blade slid down Bastien's neck and chest, and Myra noticed in surprise that it was barely scratching the skin, not even drawing blood. She did not know whether to be relieved or scared. In all likelihood, Yong was toying with his prisoner, building the fear and anticipation.

The knife traveled down Bastien's stomach until it reached his navel. Yong lifted the knife, placed it back at the human's temple, and started slowly tracing the same path down, this time going deeper and drawing blood. A small whimper escaped around the man's gag, and the vampire smiled.

Once the knife reached the navel again, Yong put it away. Myra expected him to take another device from the box, but he took nothing. Instead, he stared at the prisoner and then placed his fingernail against Bastien's temple, at the place where the cut began.

Myra hissed as the vampire sank his nail into the cut and trailed it as he had done before with the knife. More sounds escaped the captive's throat, and Serena struggled in her bonds, her eyes wide. Once Yong's nail reached the prisoner's chest, he pushed it deeper, the tip of his finger sinking into the human's torn flesh. Even the gag could not block the sounds of agony.

Myra's heart was about to burst out of her chest. She glanced at Vlad, seeking help, hoping he would somehow stop this, but he had turned away. Her eyes moved to Tristan, standing at the door she had come from, but his face was a stone mask of calm. Armida was not around. She had no idea whom to turn to.

Yong finished trailing the long cut and raised his bloodied finger to his lips, giving it a slow lick. He then returned to his box, taking out a sharp wooden wedge and a hammer. Myra gasped when he placed the wedge underneath the nail of the prisoner's right index finger.

Bastien's whole body shook as Yong struck the wedge with the hammer. The vampire continued hammering further and further until the nail was completely detached from the nail bed. Yong took the nail between his fingers and pulled it out.

Serena struggled against her ropes, shaking and weeping. Bastien was breathing heavily, his body twitching, his bare torso covered in sweat. Some humans from the cell stared mutely at the scene, while others had their heads turned away. The toddler whose hair the Prince had stroked was observing the torture, his eyes wide.

Myra could not look away as Yong removed all of Bastien's fingernails, and two of his toenails. *I did this. And they all know it.* Tears streamed down her face, but she did not close her eyes. These were the consequences of her choices, and she had to face them.

"Stop," Prince Vladimir said, finally turning around to look at the tormented prisoner. "Yong, this is ugly. I cannot bear to see one of my children suffer so. He deserves a quick death."

He approached the box, took the blade Yong had used at first, and ran it through Bastien's heart. The man twitched and went still in an instant.

The Prince took a step towards Serena and undid her gag.

"Your Highness," she sobbed. "Please don't hurt me!"

He gave a dramatic sigh. "My child, your escape caused me a lot of pain. But I know that you are young and naive rather than ungrateful. I know you love me and would not hurt me on purpose. I forgive you."

Myra threw him a disbelieving look. Seriously? Did any of the humans believe any of this farce?

Vladimir nodded at Tristan, who approached with a small suitcase. The Prince opened it, and to Myra's surprise she saw that it was filled with medical supplies.

The Prince cut Serena's bonds and gently laid her down on the ground. He then gave her painkillers and deftly cleaned, set and splinted her broken leg. Once he was done, he took her into his arms and walked to the cell door.

Myra expected him to order the guards to take her inside. Instead, he unlocked the door with his free hand and stepped in.

Myra's eyes widened. What was he doing? He was going in there all by himself? Yes, the humans were not as strong as him, and were unarmed, but they were hundreds. They could tear him apart piece by piece.

Instead, all humans dropped to their knees, clearing a path in front of him. The Prince walked to a sofa and laid Serena down. He then turned to walk to the door.

"Your Highness!" a woman in her forties cried. She ran to him, collapsed on her knees, grabbed his right hand and kissed it.

Vladimir stretched out his hands as more humans flocked around him, trying to touch him, to kiss his ring. "Long live the Prince!" many cried, their eyes wide and bright.

Myra stared, not sure what she was seeing. Were any of the humans sincere, or were they just terrified? Whatever this was, it worked.

Vladimir finally made it to the door, but before he stepped out, he took the toddler he had caressed before and lifted him in his arms. "Just remember that I love you," he said, looking at the humans. "Each of you has a place in my heart. When you show ungratefulness, it makes me very sad. But when you show me that you appreciate all I have done for you, it fills my heart with joy."

He placed the baby down and walked out, locking the door behind him. He walked to Myra and took her hand in his. "My lady. Please allow me to escort you to your room."

Shaking, Myra followed. She waited until the two of them were alone in the corridor and turned blazing eyes at him. "How could you do this?"

"I did not do anything," he said. "You did."

"Oh no, don't you dare try to put the blame on me," she cried. "And what is wrong with all these people? That can't seriously believe your mumbo-jumbo about doing what is good for them."

He smiled. "You saw it yourself."

"What I saw was you being a complete monster. Why did you tell them I helped with the capture? Now they'll never trust me."

"Precisely," he said. "I knew you were planning to bring the domesticated humans to your cause, and I had to make sure that never happened. There is unrest in the Palace. If it comes to war, the domesticated humans will be in my army, not yours."

"Oh, so you'll use them as cannon fodder now? What happened to 'I do what is best for you'? And did you honestly torture this poor man only to turn the people against me?"

"I said I would kill him and keep Serena alive. I never broke my word. Stop blaming me for your failings. I told you to think a few moves ahead and to try to figure out my long-term strategy. You did not think my end goal was capturing and killing Bastien, did you?"

"So your end goal was to turn the humans against me?"

"Again, you are only thinking one move at a time. You are nowhere close to my end goal."

They reached a point where the passage divided in three and turned left. Myra frowned. This was not the way to her room. Where were they going?

"You are a beast," she said. "Whatever your final goal is, what happened today wasn't worth it. I'll never forgive you."

Nothing in his face changed. "I never asked for your forgiveness."

She pressed her lips together and looked away. Perhaps she had to reconsider her plan not to kill him. The sharpened stake and the sleeping powder were still under her bed, ready to use.

"What did you do to Lucy?" she asked. "She helped the humans escape. I can't imagine you didn't punish her."

"Of course I did. I made an example of her for the rest of my people. Naturally, I did not do it in front of the humans; it is unwise to show them our vulnerabilities. I also decided to spare you the scene. Did I make a mistake?"

"Do you expect me to be grateful?" Myra asked.

They came to a halt in front of a staircase, and he started going up. Myra froze in her tracks, blanching.

He turned back. "Is something wrong?"

"We're going to the library?"

"Of course we are going to the library. A favor for a favor. You kept your word, and now I will keep mine."

That was the first good news Myra had heard all day. Finally, she would get her hands on that book, and the whole horror would not be in vain. If one day the Resistance destroyed the Wizard thanks to the information in the library, perhaps she would learn to live with herself.

The Prince opened the large door for her. "Take as long as you need. I will send guards to wait for you at the door and take you back to your room whenever you would like to leave."

Thank you, she nearly said, but swallowed her words. She would never thank him again for anything. "Sure," she said instead and stepped inside.

Myra took in a deep breath, savoring the smell of old paper and leather. But as much as she wanted to run her hands over every book, flip through the pages and read it, she had a more important task.

She nearly ran to the meteorology section, her eyes immediately going to the spot where she had seen the book the last time. And there it was—the book on deadly hurricanes she had seen last time, and right next to it the book on types of clouds.

The WeatherWizard book was missing.

Myra stared at the shelf, frozen still. She reached out for the first book on the shelf, flipped through the pages as if the missing book would miraculously pop out from there, and put it back, pulling out the second and the third and doing the same. After she had gone through the shelf twice, the answer was clear—the book was not there.

Tristan had seen her in this section. He had guessed her intentions and had reported to the Prince. All this time Vlad had known she wanted to see the book again. He had known that going back to the library was important to her for more than reasons of mere curiosity, and he had used it against her, never meaning to let her have the book. All this time he had been deceiving her. All had been for nothing.

Myra fisted her shaking hand, her lips pressed together. Perhaps she would find a use for that stake and sleeping powder after all.

Chapter Twenty-Seven

Predators and Prey

The beast underneath her moved, and Myra clutched at the pommel, heart pounding. The horse hated her, she was certain of it. She closed her eyes and took a deep breath. It was necessary. She no longer had access to the information on the WeatherWizard. There was only one way to destroy the Wizard now, and it involved learning more about the woods where the vamps went hunting.

"Whoa, slowly!" Myra yelped as the beast trotted forward, and Tristan laughed.

"You need to learn to move your body with the horse's pace to keep yourself from being thrown up and down," he said. "That takes time to get used to. Do not be afraid—Alba is the most well-behaved mare I know. She will not throw you down or go any faster than you want her to. My lord selected her especially for you. And also," he added with a grin, "he selected me especially to babysit you."

He could smile at her all he wanted, bright grey eyes and angelic face framed by a halo of silver hair. She had seen him.

She had seen him watch Bastien's torture, doing nothing to stop it or to show disapproval.

"Great," Myra grumbled. "I have nothing to fear, then."

She looked up as the Prince approached them. Vladimir was riding a large black stallion without a saddle or a bridle. He was clad in clothes of tanned leather, a bow and a quiver at his back and two swords hanging from his belt. His long raven hair was braided on the sides to keep it away from his face, and a large falcon perched on his forearm, a hood over its head.

"Myra," the Prince said once he reached them. "Did you finish reading my book?"

"I did," she said. *And I'm so happy you can never finish it. I know that it pains you, and my heart sings.* Too bad she had promised Tristan to behave when it came to Vlad's book. Now was not the time to break her vow—she would need Tristan's trust before this was over. "I enjoyed it. Actually, I already started writing the next chapters. When you have time, I could read them to you."

A small smile appeared on his face. "I would love that," he said and rode forward, leaving them behind.

Myra and Tristan rode on and soon fell far behind the Prince. Vlad was not going to accommodate her pace, but at least he had spared Tristan to stay behind and make sure she was safe. *Or make sure I don't run away.* As if she could run anywhere on top of this beast.

After a while, the Prince seemed to spot something in the distance and galloped forward. Myra followed him with her eyes as he disappeared far ahead. She had a hard time staying on the horse even with the help of a saddle and a bridle—how he could *gallop* without any of these was beyond her. "So when he said he would take me hunting, he meant he would be hunting, and I would be taking a leisurely walk with you?"

"Precisely," Tristan said.

"And I thought he was to teach me how to ride?"

"He is letting me teach the boring basics," Tristan said. "He will show you the advanced tricks once you have progressed."

"Why do you need horses anyway?" she asked. "I thought you could run fast."

"If we have recently fed on human blood, we can run as fast as a horse, and we have more stamina," said Tristan. "But riding gives you more freedom. For example, you can shoot an arrow while on horseback, but shooting while running is tricky. Besides, riding is fun, or at least my lord thinks so."

"So you are faster and stronger than humans," Myra said. "This is so unfair."

"And we can also count quicker than you can think," Tristan said with a grin. "Right now I can tell you there are one thousand, three hundred and seventy-two visible trees ahead of us."

"Now you're making that up."

"Count them if you wish," he said with a shrug.

They reached the forest the vampire had told her about, and Myra looked around in awe. Green grass, fresh leaves. Myra had only seen living plants in the Rose Gardens, and that had been at night. Now for the first time she could admire them under the meager sunlight that made its way through the thick clouds.

"Could you help me to get off this beast?" she asked. "If we are to take a walk, I may as well at least try to enjoy it."

"Sure." Tristan gracefully slid off his own steed and hurried to help her down. Myra breathed a sigh of relief as her feet touched solid ground.

"You have no idea how much safer I feel right now," Myra said happily and breathed in the crisp air.

Myra took a step. The grass was fresh and soft under her feet. It felt like stepping on a thick carpet, and yet somehow better, more natural. The grass was *alive*, each blade a living organism that had absorbed sunlight and had grown long and green. She filled her lungs with the cool air, breathing in the heavy aroma of flowers. Leaves moved with the wind, whispering secrets, but that was not the only sound she heard.

"What are all these sounds?" she asked, and her heart swelled with excitement.

"Chirping crickets, croaking frogs," Tristan replied. "You will learn to distinguish them. I can teach you."

A grin spread across Myra's face, and then laughter broke from her lips. She ran towards the woods, momentarily forgetting all fear and pain. All she felt was the ground underneath her feet and the wind in her hair. Suddenly she stopped in her tracks and gasped.

A fluffy four-legged creature stood in the grass. It was small, barely tall enough to reach her knee. Its wide, round head, topped with two small ears, looked almost too big for its body. Dark brown fur covered it completely, making it look like a fluffy stuffed toy. Myra grinned. She had seen bears only in pictures, and had feared they were extinct.

"Come here, beauty," she cried and knelt by the small fluffy animal, stretching her arms forward in a gesture of invitation. The cub gave out a soft roar and ran back into the woods.

"Myra, get back here right now!" Tristan cried. "Get back on the horse!"

She looked at him, confused, before a sudden realization hit her. "If there is a bear cub here—"

"Then the mother is close," Tristan finished impatiently. "And she will be overprotective and dangerous."

Myra rushed back to the horses, her heart hammering. How could she be so thoughtless? Would she never learn to think before she acted?

She was still far away from the horses when an earth-shattering roar made her heart skip a beat. She turned around, and all blood drained from her face.

The bear was as tall as a horse, but much more massive. She was the largest living creature Myra had ever seen, her claws sharp and her paws enormous enough to knock down a tree. The beast was running towards her at an alarming speed, and Myra heard the horses behind her neighing in panic and trying to get away. She had nowhere to run.

And then, Tristan was in front of her, a sword in his hand. "Stay behind me. She is only interested in you and the horses. Bears do not eat dead flesh."

Myra knew the bear was not hunting for food. She was fighting to protect her cub, and she would not differentiate between her and the vampire. She wanted to tell Tristan this, but her voice froze in her throat. All she could do was watch in panic as the bear barely flinched at the sword cut across her upper front leg. Her gigantic paw sent the vampire flying backwards, as if he was a tedious fly.

Suddenly the beast stood on her hind legs, roaring in pain, an arrow sticking from her shoulder. She turned around, facing the raven-haired vampire who had already nocked a second arrow. Vladimir smiled and nodded at the animal, as if saluting a rival before a duel.

The second arrow embedded itself into the animal's thick hide, flying true and yet doing minimal damage. The beast was outraged now and snarled viciously at the vampire who had dared attack her. Vlad released a third arrow, which missed the bear's left eye by an inch, before letting his bow drop to the ground and unsheathing his twin swords.

The blades slashed dangerously, going for the animal's throat, but the bear moved to the side and raised a paw to defend herself. She roared then, sending a strong current of her breath into the vampire's face, making his long hair wave, and tried to knock him down. He raised his right-hand sword in a defensive move, but he barely delivered a superficial cut as she sent him sprawling backwards.

Vlad quickly recovered and prepared himself for another attack. The bear lunged at him, but he ducked, going underneath her front paw and slashing at her chest. The bear sidestepped his move at the last moment, her instincts surprisingly quick for an animal of that size. As the vampire was carried forward from the momentum, the animal used the opportunity to slam her body into her enemy, sending him falling to the ground.

The vampire regained his balance before hitting the ground and dropped to one knee, raising his sword to let the bear impale herself on it. This delivered only a glancing blow as the animal moved quickly and stood up on her hind legs once again.

Vlad held both swords tightly and jumped forward, plunging them deep into the beast's shoulders. Before he could pull them out, the animal twisted to the side and moved out of his reach.

The two swords were sticking from the bear's shoulders, but she was as strong and vicious as ever, and Vlad was now facing her empty-handed. The vampire snarled then—an animalistic, predatory sound—and jumped forward, grabbing tufts of the animal's chest hair into his fists and sinking his teeth deep into the bear's skin, sucking her blood.

The animal pushed him away forcefully, removing him from her skin like an annoying tick. The vampire's body flew through the air and collided with a protruding rock with a sickening crunch. Vlad lay there, momentarily stunned, before he stood up and shook his head.

The bear's paw shot towards him, sharp nails slashing through the air, and the vampire jumped back, at the last moment saving himself from being cut in half. He was not fast enough, though, and the sharp claws left five deep, angry slashes on his chest.

Myra watched helplessly, unsure what she could do to help. And, most of all, she was not certain why exactly she wanted to help anyway. A part of her hoped that the bear would somehow decapitate the Prince, but if the bear won this fight, she would be the next one torn to pieces.

No matter what, Vladimir was in this position now because he had come to her aid. Perhaps he had done it to help Tristan, or the horses, or perhaps merely for the thrill of hunting and fighting a bear, but the fact remained.

If he dies, he'll never read the new chapters I wrote for his book. He'll never give me his feedback. Myra blinked. What the hell was she thinking? This monster had cold-bloodedly tortured and murdered a young man just to keep her in line, and her first concern was whether he would give her advice on her writing. What was wrong with her?

And why did such petty concerns matter? She could hardly close her eyes without seeing Bastien's bloodless face or Serena's shocked, listless eyes. She feared the silence because then she heard their screams again and again. She wished to punish Vlad for what he had done to them, to hurt him, and yet she also wished to hear his feedback on her writing.

A hand grabbed her arm. "Stay back," Tristan said. "He knows what he is doing."

Only now did she notice that the blond vampire was busy trying to calm down his horse. Alba had apparently run off into the woods, but Tristan's horse was still here, thrashing wildly around and foaming at the mouth as his eyes rolled back into his head. The vampire tried to hold him down and speak words of comfort, but the animal was too fearful to listen.

Out of the corner of her eye, Myra kept watching the fight. Vladimir growled at the bear, blood flowing down his chest and from his mouth. His sharp white teeth glistened like silver, and the sight would have sent any sensible animal running for its life. But the bear was beyond sense now. She was fighting to protect her cub, and she was injured and enraged. She would fight to the death.

The vampire jumped up, one hand grabbing the handle of the sword still protruding from the animal's shoulder while the other held on to the bear's huge head. Once again, he sank his sharp teeth into the bear's thick neck, drinking deeply. The animal fought him wildly, trying to push him away and running her sharp long claws along his back, but Vlad did not flinch. Finally, the bear collapsed, crushing the vampire beneath her.

Tristan bolted forward, abandoning his thrashing horse, and Myra ran after him. A vampire could not be killed by a bear collapsing on top of him, right? Beheading—yes. A stake—yes. Fire—sure. But a bear? She doubted anyone had tried it before.

Before they reached him, Vlad crawled from underneath the bear and stood up in one fluid motion, casually brushing some dirt off his clothes. It did little to improve his appearance, though, as nothing could brush away the numerous cuts and bruises covering his exposed skin, and the multitude of bloodied tears in his clothing.

"My lord," Tristan said, scanning the other vampire up and down. "You look dreadful."

"I prefer 'rugged and manly,' but 'dreadful' is also good," Vlad said with a shrug, and the younger vampire rolled his eyes. "Now, let us calm the horses down and go back to the hunt."

"Go back to the hunt?" Myra stared at him. Had he lost his mind? "After *this*?"

"Such things happen during hunts all the time," Vladimir said. "It is no big deal. You cannot return home every time a bear attacks you. Come, now, we will have enough time to catch more game and return home in time to wash up and change for the ball."

"Another ball?" Myra asked, falling in step with him as he walked towards Tristan's horse.

"I believe you enjoyed the last one," he said.

Yes, that was before I knew what a monster you were. But had she really not known that? She had known he bred humans for food. She had known he had caused the death of millions and destroyed human civilization. She had known he had killed a child to control her. Yet, she had chosen to look the other way and pretend none of this had ever happened.

The Prince looked around. "Where is Alba?"

"She bolted and ran into the woods when the bear arrived," Myra said.

"Smart girl," Vlad said and whistled softly. The chestnut mare appeared, still looking shaken.

The vampire approached her slowly, all the while muttering words in a language Myra did not understand in a singsong voice. When he stood a pace away from the mare, Alba tried to pull back, but he gently reached out to her, rubbing first her neck, and then her back. He then moved to the horse's head and stroked the middle of her forehead, never stopping his flow of comforting words.

"Is that Old Church Slavonic?" Myra asked.

The vampire snorted. "Your linguistic skills are severely lacking. And why would I be speaking Church Slavonic to a horse? No, Myra, this is my native tongue. It has been dead for many centuries now, but I still use it to talk to the horses."

"Of course my skills are lacking; I have no experience at all with spoken languages, for obvious reasons," Myra said. "And I thought Church Slavonic was your native tongue. Tristan said it was the original language of your book."

"Ah, that?" The vampire shrugged. "I merely thought it would be good practice for my children to master the language of the slaves. It was not called *Church* Slavonic at the time, of course."

Tristan cleared his throat. "The language of the *Slavs*, you mean," he said pointedly.

"Yes, that is what I just said," Vlad said innocently, and Tristan rolled his eyes.

"See, Myra, this is my lord's definition of 'we did not *conquer* the locals, we *liberated* them.'"

"Oh, but you know very well that we did liberate them," said Vlad. "They were worse off before. We made them rightful citizens of the realm, even encouraged our people to mix with them, until we dissolved among them. Our language, our culture, our looks, our beliefs, it was all gone. They took it all."

Myra sighed. A few days ago she would have been excited at the new information and planning to put it all together once she had access to a good encyclopedia. Now she no longer cared. Whoever the Prince had been as a human no longer mattered. Now he was a beast.

"I thought your name was Slavic," she said.

"I have been telling him the same thing for centuries," Tristan muttered under his breath.

Vlad ignored him and nodded at Myra. "I see you do have some minor understanding of names and languages after all," the Prince said. "You are correct, it is. Let me tell you one thing, Myra—the origin of a name matters not. When you choose a name, what matters is who bore it before you and what they did with it."

"Are you saying you chose this name for yourself?" she asked. "That it's not the name you were born with?"

"Does that surprise you?"

"I'm just surprised by your choice," Myra said. "A vampire called 'Vlad'? That's not especially original. People might confuse you with Dracula."

"First of all," he said, "I took that name and made it known among our kind long before that whelp's grandparents were conceived. I had a specific reason to choose it, and I would not change it just because he became famous among humans. Besides," he added, "you are the only person to call me Vlad. As I have told you before, this is not even the proper way to shorten my name."

"Fair enough," she said. "What is the proper short form, then?"

"'Your Highness' works. I will leave you now; I need to find my horse if you do not mind. There is still some hunting to do, and, of course, I need to find that bear cub and bring it to the Palace so we can take care of it until it is older. You two will be fine on your own, I trust? I can sense no other dangerous animals around."

"Let me at least bind your wounds, my lord," Tristan said, exasperated. "You will bleed yourself out."

"Do vampires' wounds heal fast?" Myra asked.

"Yes," Vladimir said.

"No," said Tristan at the same time.

The two vampires glared at each other. Vlad broke the eye contact first and looked at Myra. "If a vampire is in a bad shape already, injured or starved, the wounds will take longer to heal. Yet a vampire in good health heals much faster than a human. A good meal and a good day's sleep are enough for most wounds."

"You sleep during the day, then?" Myra said.

"We used to, in the Old World," the Prince said. "A healthy vampire needs about four hours of sleep per day. We would usually take them during daylight, so we would not miss the night, but after the Nightfall we do not need to worry about that and can arrange our schedules any way we please."

"So whenever you are hurt, you just need to drink some blood and get a few hours of sleep, and you get better?" Myra asked.

"Exactly," Vlad said.

"Not at all," Tristan said simultaneously as he took some supplies out of the saddlebags. "Even for a vampire in perfect health, the healing is not instantaneous. My lord—please."

The Prince sighed in resignation and allowed the younger vampire to bandage his cuts. "Are you in much pain?" Tristan asked as he worked, and Vlad glared at him.

"My boy, I cannot bear you of all people to ask me this question. Whatever pain I am feeling must be nothing compared to what you have to face every day."

"I am used to my pain," Tristan said. "I barely notice it anymore."

"What pain?" Myra asked.

Vlad took two steps, placing himself between her and Tristan. "Nothing of concern to you," he said. "I will take my leave of you and resume the hunt. You two are welcome to go home if you are tired. I will see you at the Palace."

He turned back to the south and whistled, until his black stallion reappeared and ran to his master. Vlad pulled himself onto his steed's back in one fluid motion, and the horse and rider galloped away. Myra watched them as they passed by the fallen bear and, without slowing down, Vlad dropped to the side to retrieve his fallen bow and then straightened himself right away.

"Show-off," Tristan murmured under his breath.

Myra gazed at the Prince's retreating back, fighting her own frustration. She would not need to put up with him for much longer, she reminded herself. If Armida was true to her word, she would be out of here soon. And once she was free, she knew exactly what to do.

"Do you want to go back?" Tristan asked.

"Let me stay here for a while," said Myra. "It's not often that I see living plants. Unless you think there might be more bears?"

Tristan sat on the grass next to her. "I think we should be safe."

"I'm surprised to see a bear here. I thought there were none around these parts, even before the Nightfall."

"Brown bears lived here a long time ago, but died off around the ninth century," Tristan said. "After the Nightfall, my lord decided to reintroduce them."

"It must have been a lot of work," Myra said and ran her hand through the grass.

Her mind was working furiously. Once she was back home, she would tell the Warriors' Council about this place. It was perfect for her plan. The only problem was, she had no idea how to reach these woods from the Palace. She had tried to remember the road, but she had seen only cloudy skies, barren ground, dead trees, and then living trees. There were no landmarks to show her the way.

"Tristan, may I ask you for a favor?" she said.

The blond vampire turned at her and smiled. "Of course. As you well know, I am highly skilled in a variety of fields, and can help you with almost anything. You already know how this works. A favor for a favor. We are not friends, as you said yourself. If you wish me to help you, you will have to do something in return."

Myra looked down. "You already asked me to refrain from hurtful comments about the Prince's book, and I've done it. What else can I do for you?"

"Let's see," he said. "What can you offer me?"

Myra considered her answer. She hardly had anything she could give him. "I can spy for you."

He laughed. "You are hardly inconspicuous."

"I might be conspicuous, but it makes no difference. Vampires underestimate me. Everyone talks freely in front of me."

Tristan leaned back on the ground and ran his fingers through the grass. "Let us say that is true. Why would I need a spy? What information can you get for me?"

"Things are going on in the Palace," she said. "You know it. And if you don't, then you need my help more than you think."

"What things?"

"I attended the Audience for a few hours. I listened to several petitioners. A few veiled threats were made against your life, and against the Prince's. I don't know how much he tells you about these—"

Tristan stared at her, his lips pressed together. "I am well aware of that."

He wasn't, Myra realized with a start. Vlad had known what to expect at the Audience. He had refused Tristan's offer to join him and most likely planned to keep him in the dark. Perhaps he had done it many times before. "Help me," she said, "and I'll tell you all that happened at the Audience while I was there. I will report to you all I've seen and heard of anyone suspicious."

Tristan stood silent for a moment, still as a stone statue. "Speak," he said.

He listened with an expressionless face as she told him all that had transpired at the Great Hall, and what had followed in the courtyard with Izumi and Armida. If he was surprised, he did nothing to show it. When she finished, he nodded slowly and pulled one leg to his chest.

"Thank you for sharing this," he said. "I will ask you to come to me whenever you see or hear something else relevant."

"I will."

His smile reappeared. "Good. Now, what can I do for you?"

"I have a terrible sense of direction," Myra admitted. "I don't know if it's genetic or if it's because I've spent all my life underground, but I want to develop it. I tried to remember the road when we came here, but now it's all a mess in my mind. Could you explain me how we got here? How long we rode in each direction and what landmarks you used to remember it all."

"I can do better than that," Tristan said, "but only if you tell me why you really want to know how to reach this place."

"I told you," Myra said. "I want to practice my sense of direction. Tristan, you agreed to this. A favor for a favor. I told you all I knew about the discontent in the Palace. Now it's your turn."

He snorted. "Right." Tristan stood up and walked to the horses. He took a notebook from the saddlebag and sat back on the ground. "I can draw you a map. See, the Palace is here. Then we rode northwest for three miles. This is where we came to the dead forest, turned left and rode for another mile. When we ride back, I will show you each point and where we are on the map."

He kept on talking, meticulously drawing the route, marking the distances and every point where they had taken a turn. Myra stared at the map, feeling a twinge of guilt. It was unfair to cheat Tristan into drawing the map for her, given what she was planning to do with it.

Myra bit her lip and pushed her guilt aside. There was no time for this. This was war, and if she wished to win, she could not hesitate.

Chapter Twenty-Eight

A Wicked Game

"There isn't a single thing I like about this," Franka said.

"What is bothering you?" Myra asked.

"Apart from *everything*?" the elderly woman cried and stood up from the bed, pacing back and forth. "For starters, you are abandoning your mission. You are supposed to kill the Prince, and now you are leaving even though your life is in no immediate danger. You'll never get another opportunity to be so close to him, and you're throwing it away."

Myra sighed. "Honestly, after the horror in the dungeons I've been sorely tempted to kill him, but that would be irrational. The Resistance's final goal is to destroy the WeatherWizard, and now, for the first time, I have a plan that might actually work. And my plan involves me getting out of here and back to my friends."

Franka stopped her pacing and stared at her. "Right. And I'm going to take a wild guess and assume the plan doesn't involve killing the Prince."

Myra gave her a sharp look. "What is that supposed to mean?"

"You're way too friendly with the vampires," said Franka. "You're discussing stories, dancing, hunting, and whatnot."

"Can you even hear what you are saying?" Myra said. "Do you have any idea how much I hate the Prince after what he did to Bastien?"

"Honestly, I don't," Franka said, turning away. "And anyway, this idea is stupid."

Myra bristled. "What is stupid, exactly?"

"Oh, many things," said Franka. "But, most of all, trusting Armida. She's a vampire. Best case, she will simply drink us and dump our bodies somewhere. Worst case, she will take you to a cell no one will ever find, and she will torture you for information about the Resistance."

"We struck a blood oath."

"Indeed. Are you so familiar with vampire customs to know what exactly such an oath means? It may force Armida to keep her word, or it may not. Vampires can't be trusted."

"All vampires are evil," Myra agreed. "Yet some are less evil than others. Armida strikes me as unconfident rather than menacing. And she clearly loves the Prince. She's not a complete monster."

Franka shook her head. "All vampires are evil," she echoed. "And some are more evil than others. I believe Armida is one of them."

Myra frowned. "What are you talking about?"

"I told you about her and the Prince visiting the dungeons," Franka said. "She was always the one to insist on persecuting all free humans, while he tried to keep a shard of the Old

World alive. No matter what His Evilness says and does, he likes the Old World and he would never destroy it completely. She only cares about absolute power and has no such qualms. I wouldn't be surprised to learn that the Prince staged the Nightfall because of her."

"These are conjectures," Myra protested. "You don't know Armida and the Prince. You can't make guesses about their relationship."

"And you do?" Franka challenged. "Sorry, I forgot the vampires are your friends now."

Myra's fists clenched. "As you said yourself, I've been spending a lot of time with them. I know them better than you, and I believe we can trust Armida."

"Yes, about that," Franka paused. "There is something else. I didn't want to tell you because I feared it would upset you."

Myra's heart went cold. "Tell me."

"I've given up keeping track of time," Franka said, "so I'm not certain when it happened. Perhaps it was ten years ago, or perhaps more. One night the guards dragged a young woman to our cell. The vampires had captured her outside. She spent a day in the cells until they dragged her somewhere else. I heard the guards talking—they were interrogating her about the Resistance. After two weeks, she died. She never told them anything."

Myra struggled to draw breath. She grew pale, and a cold sweat broke out across her forehead. The room was swimming in front of her eyes, whirling, rotating, shaking in a crazy dance. She opened her mouth to speak, but the words would not come out. She clenched the armrest and tried again. "Why are you telling me this?"

"It was a few days before her death," Franka continued. "Armida came to the dungeons. I still remember it clear as day.

"'My dear friend,' Armida whispered as she wrapped her arms around one of the guards. 'What is it I hear about you keeping a pet in the Dark Cell? Surely, you know the orders. You must deliver all wild humans to the Prince.'

"The guard scolded. 'I know the orders better than anyone, my lady. It does not mean I agree. His Highness will have his fun with her and eat her before we have learned anything. Right now she is the only one who can tell us more about the Resistance. These humans have opposed us long enough.'

"'There is exactly one way to destroy the Resistance,' Armida replied. 'And this is not it. But now is not the time to speak of this—we are not ready.'

"'What would you have me do, my lady?' he asked. 'Should I hand the human over to His Highness?'

"She shook her head. 'Keep your pet. Have your fun and learn what you can, if you think it will be of use. But next time—' She paused and gave him a stern look. 'Next time you will let me know what you are doing.'"

Franka fell silent. For a long while, no one spoke. Myra tried to draw deep, slow breaths, but she could not stop shaking.

"The captured woman," Franka said. "She was short. She had long, light brown hair. Hazel eyes. Chubby face, pale skin, and a small dark mole on the right cheek. She was wearing a purple shirt when the guards brought her to the dungeons. Did you know her?"

"My aunt Sandra," Myra choked. "My dad's sister. She disappeared eleven years ago. I was eight. Her daughter—my cousin Thea—was just a baby."

Franka knelt in front of Myra and grasped her hand. "I'm so sorry. No one deserves what you and your cousin have been through."

Myra said nothing. She stood up and went to the fireplace to place another log on the fire, then sat cross-legged on the floor, staring at the flames.

"Do you wish to talk about it?" Franka asked at length.

"Death is common at the Resistance," Myra said. Her voice sounded hollow even to her own ears. "Many of our own were killed while hunting or spying. Often we would find the bodies. Sometimes we would even kill or capture the vampires and get revenge."

Myra fell silent. The flames were dancing before her, consuming, destroying. "This was what happened to my parents," she continued softly. "I was so happy and relieved when they survived the Great Massacre, which took hundreds of lives, including Thea's dad's. And then, five years ago, my parents joined an expedition to the ruins of a nearby town to look for supplies. On the way back, they came across two vampires. Out of the fifteen humans, only three survived, but they managed to kill one of their attackers and capture the other. They brought him back to the caves, so that—" She paused and took a deep breath. "So that I could kill him myself."

"Did you?" Franka asked.

Myra raised a hand to brush her tears away. "I did. I drove a stake right through his heart. It didn't help."

She placed another log on the fire and stood up. "Many of our people died," Myra continued, "and almost as many simply disappeared. We never found the bodies. We never learned what happened to them. One day they would go outside on a simple task, and would not come back. Aunt Sandra was one of them. We never heard anything of her again and never found any evidence that she was dead. Until now, I had held out hope. Stupid, I know."

She collapsed to her knees, her body wracked by sobs. Franka knelt next to her and squeezed her hand. "And to know that her death was slow, that she suffered for two weeks," Myra muttered. "Can you imagine how scared she must have been? And knowing she would never see her baby again. She was barely twenty."

Images flashed before Myra's eyes. Bastien, tied to the X-shaped wooden structure, shaking, scared and in pain. Only this time, it was not Bastien's face there. It was Aunt Sandra, trembling and begging for mercy. They had tortured her just like they had tortured him. She had been scared, just like him.

"I shouldn't have told you," said Franka. "I am sorry."

Myra shook her head and brushed her wet face with her sleeve. "No. You did the right thing. I had to know."

She heard a scream in her head, muffled by a gag. Only this time it was a woman screaming.

"I want to kill them," Myra said, her voice breaking. "I want to kill them all."

"Then do it," Franka said. "Start with the Prince. Take your stake and the powder. You said he was injured. That's perfect—he'll be weaker and more vulnerable. Go for it. I know you're ready."

Myra shook her head. "I can't. We are so close to getting away. Armida's story is finished. Once I tell her that, she'll help us escape."

"Didn't you hear a word of what I just said? The reason I told you this story was to show you Armida can't be trusted. She clearly wants the Resistance destroyed."

"Or she wanted to throw a bone to the guard and gain his trust," Myra countered. "For all we know, the Prince may be aware of her visits to the dungeons. He may be sending her there himself to spy on the guards. Armida will help us escape—I know it. We can't throw this away."

"You don't have to throw away anything," Franka said. "You can still escape. Lure the Prince somewhere outside. Perhaps to those Rose Gardens you told me about. Tell him you want to read him what you've written for his book and you want to do it there. Then drug him and kill him as planned and make a break for it."

"I don't even know how to get home from the Rose Gardens," Myra said. "And I can't just kill the Prince and run away. They'll kill you if I leave you behind."

"And I'll die happy, knowing that I'm taking His Evilness down with me."

A knock sounded on the door, and they fell silent. Myra took a deep breath to steady her heart. "Come in."

Tristan entered and bowed. "My ladies," he said. "Forgive my intrusion, but it is time for the ball."

Was he mocking her? With a faked smile, Myra took his offered hand.

"Goodbye, Franka. I'll see you later," she said and left the room.

***

The silence stretched between them as they walked down the corridor. Did he know she had no desire to talk? Did he feel how much she hated them all?

Tristan never broke his stride as he raised his hands, braiding his silver hair away from his face. Myra stared at his long pale fingers as they deftly weaved thin strands into intricate formations. The fingers that had played the flute to elicit heartbreaking sounds. The fingers that had tortured and killed.

"Ready for the ball?" he asked. His lips curled into a smile, but his constant perma-frown stayed on his face.

A ball was the very last thing she had the patience to deal with right now. "Will it be like the last?"

"Different music, different clothes," he replied. "If you mean whether you'll spend the night dancing with me—that depends on you."

"I thought you hated dancing?"

He smiled. "I love music and dancing. Music was never a part of my life before my lord and Lady Callisto came along and opened my eyes to a world I never knew existed. What I hate is dancing with vampires or humans I dislike."

"Which covers most of the world's population," Myra said. Would he continue his story? She ached to ask him, but stopped herself. She no longer cared. Why would she want to hear the story of how a monster became who he was? And yet, she could not help but wonder.

"Precisely," he said. "Now that I have shared my love for music, perhaps you can tell me why you have been crying."

She blushed. "You're mistaken. I haven't—"

"Oh, please, spare me the theater," he said. "I recognize red puffy eyes when I see them."

"My eyes have been itchy after we returned from the hunt," she said. "Perhaps I have some allergy and the trip to the forest triggered it."

He grinned. "I hear my lord has been teaching you how to be a better liar. All I can say is—he seems to be a poor teacher."

Myra glared at him. "Why don't you mind your own business? You and the Prince didn't want to tell me what the deal was about you feeling pain every day—fair enough. I took the hint and never asked again. Is it so much to ask the same in return?"

"I did not mean to pry," he said. "All I meant to say is—I understand that living here, with us, is hard for you. If there is anything that would make you feel better, let me know and I will do what I can."

Right. And what could he give her exactly? Good food? Fine clothes? Books? Could he restore what the vampires had destroyed? Could he give back the lives they had taken? "There is nothing you can do for me," she said.

Tristan raised an eyebrow but said nothing until they reached the hall. Myra took a deep breath before she stepped inside. A flurry of colors assaulted her senses, and she sighed.

She could no longer see beauty in the intricate dresses flying all around her as the vampires danced. She had seen all the blood on top of which this lovely empire had been built. Everywhere she looked, she saw Bastien's face, his horror palpable in spite of the blindfold. And whenever she pushed the image away, she saw Aunt Sandra instead.

She blinked and raised her eyes, catching a glimpse of the Prince and Armida, talking and laughing. She had to admit she was impressed he had cleaned up so nicely after the hunt in such a short time. He had returned a few hours after Tristan and her, and his appearance did not betray that he had been battling a bear not long ago.

But he had. The impeccable clothes concealed cuts and bruises that no makeup could erase. *He is injured and more vulnerable*, Franka had said. Myra shuddered. She wished to hurt him so much, and yet that would burn all her plans to dust.

Myra stared at Vlad and Armida for a minute, but they did not look back at her. She breathed a sigh of relief. Good riddance.

Tristan invited her for a dance, but she shook her head and retired into a dark corner, nursing a glass of wine. Dancing couples and triples flew all around her, in bright red, blue, orange and purple clothes. Myra averted her eyes. It was all so ugly.

The hours dragged painfully slowly. Myra wished for nothing more than to be left alone, so that she could cry until her tears ran dry and no one would bother her with questions. It seemed as if a full day and night had passed before Tristan came to her and gave her a small bow.

"Shall I escort you back to your room, my lady?" he asked, offering Myra his hand.

"No," a deep voice from far away chimed in, and she looked up as Vlad approached them, with Armida at his side. "Myra, please stay. I wished to speak to you. Alone," he added, giving Tristan and Armida a pointed look.

Armida paled, and a flash of pain sparked in her eyes. Myra bit her lip. What was Vlad doing? Was he blind? Once again, he was choosing to trade stories with a human rather than spend time with his lover. And even though Franka thought that Armida was a monster, at that moment Myra saw only a woman terrified of losing her beloved. Armida could be trusted to help them escape, she was sure of it. But was escape worth giving up the sweetness of revenge?

On her way out, Armida paused and cupped the Prince's face with one hand. "How are your injuries, my love?" she asked.

"Practically healed," he replied. "You should not concern yourself."

"Right," Tristan mumbled and gave the Prince a light punch in the ribs.

Vlad's eyes widened, but he made no sound and grinned at Tristan. "See? As I said, practically healed."

Tristan grinned back and rolled his eyes before Armida dragged him out of the hall.

"You wished to speak to me," Myra said when she was alone with the Prince.

He stared at her, his gaze deep and piercing. "Are you happy here, Myra?"

What? Was he serious? *I'll be happy once I finish the job the bear started.* "What do you mean? You know that I'm a prisoner."

"Yes, you are," he agreed. "But your life here must be better than it was in the Resistance. You have books, hunts, operas, music, culture. I am certain you had little of those before."

"Next to none," Myra admitted. "But you surely see that I'm nothing more than a bird in a gilded cage. I desire my freedom. Freedom is a basic human need, like food to eat or air to breathe."

"Your freedom is something I will not give you, I fear," Vlad said. "But I would make your captivity easier to bear, if it is within my power. Tell me, what is bothering you the most about your imprisonment?"

Seriously? Don't try to be kind and gentle with me. I've seen your true face; you made sure of it. "What weighs on me most heavily is the thought that my friends have no idea what happened to me," she said. "I've been here for nearly two months now. My cousin and everyone else in the Resistance probably think I'm dead. I wish there was a way to let them know I'm well."

"I could give them a message," Vlad suggested, and smiled as she stared at him wide-eyed. "You could write a letter, and I can deliver it. Of course, you will be unwilling to tell me where the Headquarters are, but I am certain your people sometimes go out hunting or gathering supplies. You could tell me where, and I could go there when they are not around and leave your letter for them to find. Don't look at me like that. You know I do not plan to bring down the Resistance."

"Yes, but this doesn't mean you wouldn't hunt down a few Resistance members, just for fun," Myra said, eyes blazing.

He sighed dramatically. "So little faith in me. What have I ever done to deserve it? I give you my word that I will not harm any of your people."

"And I'm supposed to believe you? You said you wouldn't kill the boy if I finished the story, but you killed him nevertheless."

He gave her a hurt look. "But my dear girl, I said no such thing. I said I *would* kill the boy if you did *not* finish the story. I never said what I would do if you did. I am many things, but I am no liar."

"Oh, how comforting," Myra said wryly. "You're a mass murderer, but you're not a liar. There is no way I'm telling you where my people go."

"What is the matter, Myra, are you afraid I would read the contents of your letter?" the vampire asked with an annoying grin. "You do not think I would be overly disturbed when I read, 'I haven't managed to kill the Prince yet, but I'm working on it,' do you? It is not like I have not figured out why you were sent here. Unless…" His eyes narrowed to mere slits, and his grin broadened. "Unless this is not at all what you are going to write. Unless you are planning to write, 'Forgive me, my friends, but now that I have met His Highness, I cannot bring myself to do it. He is the most magnificent, admirable and wonderful vampire, and I have grown to—'"

"Enough," Myra said. "I'm not giving you any information, and that is the end of it."

"As you wish. I could tell your friends you are well, but if you do not want me to, I am not going to beg."

There is no need for that, Vlad, she thought. *I can tell them myself.*

Vampires kept leaving the hall one by one or in groups as they talked, and a large pink dress caught Myra's attention. Spiral-shaped auburn curls spilled on top of the wearer's slender shoulders. Myra's head swam, and she blindly reached out, searching for something to grab.

Lucy. Lucy was alive and well.

One of the vampires, Lucy, sympathized with us. She helped us escape, Serena's words echoed in her head.

I made an example of her for the rest of my people, Vlad had said.

Myra's heart pumped wildly, and sweat broke across her forehead. Vlad had lied.

At first, it made no sense at all. And then, it made all the sense in the world.

Serena had said Lucy had helped her and Bastien escape, and Myra had believed her. She knew it now. Lucy had indeed helped the humans. Under the Prince's orders.

Vladimir had staged the whole thing. He had given two innocent humans hope, only to shatter it into pieces. And then he had used the poor people as pawns in his twisted game against Myra.

Something snapped inside her then, and her rage spilled over her heart like water breaking over a dam. She took in slow, deep breaths, trying to calm her racing heart. She needed to compose herself for what she was about to do.

Once Myra was certain her voice would not break, she put on a sweet smile and turned to the Prince. "My lord? I have started work on continuing your book, but I have a few questions. Would you have some time to discuss them?"

His amber eyes brightened. "Of course. Anytime."

Was she imagining it, or was his voice shaking? "Right now is good," she said. "Do you mind if we go outside? I spent so many hours in this huge crowd. I need a breath of fresh air."

"Outside?"

"To the Rose Gardens, perhaps," she said. "I loved them and hoped to visit them a second time. Starting the new chapters of your book seems like a good occasion, don't you think?"

He smiled, his eyes shining. "Of course. I would love that."

"Bring the wine."

"I will bring more than that. Shall we go? I will ask the servants to prepare the carriage."

She shook her head. "The carriage will take us forever. Let's ride there."

"You feel up to it?"

"Absolutely," she said. "Let me go back to my room and change into the clothes you gave me for the hunt. I can't ride in this gown."

He grinned. "To be fair, you cannot ride in hunting clothes either."

She rolled her eyes and allowed him to escort her back to her room. Her heart hammered as she stepped inside. Franka was still there, waiting. Myra was glad for it.

"Give me the stake and the powder," she said once the door behind her closed. "It is time I complete my mission."

Chapter Twenty-Nine

Victory

The horse's pace was slow and even, and Myra was no longer afraid of falling down. All her thoughts were focused on the uncomfortable weight at her belt. Her tunic was long and wide and concealed the stake and the powder bag from prying eyes, but she was constantly aware of the strange objects pressing against her waist.

Vlad rode next to her, obviously fighting an urge to gallop forward, unconstrained by her slow pace. Every time he spoke to her, his voice was soft and strained. *He is scared*, Myra realized. *He has waited for centuries to see his book continued. He doesn't know what to expect.*

Too bad he would not live long enough to see his book finished. Myra bit her lip and stared forward, swallowing against the lump in her throat. She had no sympathy left for this monster. All her pity was spent on Serena, Bastien, and Aunt Sandra.

When they reached the Rose Gardens, Vlad slid down from his horse and helped her dismount. She froze when his hands closed around her waist. He was shaking.

The vampire tied the horses and took off the saddlebags, slinging them over his back. He lit the torches as they walked down the familiar path. Myra stepped forward, her knees weak. That was it—the end of all things. Here she would kill him and finally accomplish her mission.

Vlad dropped the saddlebags on the ground, and they sat down, underneath the large oak. Myra breathed in deeply, the smell of roses making her dizzy. The silence stretched between them and Myra started to shake, her pulse accelerating. The end was so close now. It seemed like years ago when she had left the Resistance, with Alerie by her side, looking for this very place. It made perfect sense that all would end here, in the Rose Gardens, just like Alerie and she had imagined.

She looked at him. He was silent, staring at the ground, his brow furrowed. Did he know? Had he sensed anything, or was he simply thinking of his book? He looked up and their eyes met. Myra shivered.

"How much have you written?" he asked. His voice was strained, as if it hurt to talk.

"Two chapters," she said. "And I have some thoughts on what happens next, but I wanted to ask you some questions first."

A lopsided grin appeared on his face. "I have waited for this day for dozens of lifetimes. I suppose this moment calls for something special."

He stood up and walked to the place where he had dropped off the saddlebags. When he returned, he had a bottle and two tall crystal glasses in his hands.

Myra frowned at the golden liquid. "That's not wine."

"I drink wine every day," he said. "Today is not every day."

He shook the bottle and twisted the metal loop around the neck. Myra yelped and pressed her hands against her ears as the cork flew away with a loud pop, and pale golden bubbly liquid poured out like a fountain. Smiling, Vlad poured two glasses, and Myra stared as the liquid sparkled under the torchlight like thousands of stars.

"My notebook is in the saddlebags," Myra said once she found her voice. "Can you please get it?"

He nodded and put down the glasses. Myra's heart jumped to her throat as he turned around. He had his back to her now. He would not see her. He would not hear her. He would never know.

Or would he? His hearing was better than a human's. What if he heard the shuffling and wondered what happened? What if he smelled the powder? What if he detected a subtle change in color?

And would the change be subtle at all? Myra had only tested the powder in water and red wine. What if it reacted with some chemical in this liquid and changed color or smell, or even exploded?

And what would he do to her if he caught her? Would he kill her? Torture her as he had Bastien? Would he never read her stories again and give her advice on how to be a better writer? She shuddered, realizing that the last scenario scared her no less than the others.

Shaking, Myra reached to her belt and took out the bag. She brought it over one of the cups and started pouring. A few bubbles appeared and Myra's hand started trembling violently, spilling powder all over the grass.

Oh no. No, no, no. The white powder stood in stark contrast against the dark grass. Even she could see it clearly under the torchlight. Myra reached out and frantically brushed the powder across the grass, spreading it around. Great. Now the grass looked crumbled and tramped on, and the powder was still visible everywhere.

She tried to collect as much as she could with her hands and put it back in the bag. Her hands were covered in the white thing now, and she brushed them against her clothes, leaving traces. Paling, she looked at the glass and her eyes widened as she saw the powder accumulated at the bottom. She stirred it with her finger until it dissolved and looked at the grass around her.

No, that would not work. They had to change location. She took the glasses in her hands and followed the Prince.

He retrieved the notebook from the saddleback and turned back around. Myra met him on the way and handed him the spiked drink with a smile on her face. "Let us toast, my lord," she said. "To your book."

He smiled back and took the glass in his hand. Their fingers brushed. Did he feel that she was shivering?

He sniffed at his glass and Myra froze. Did he smell the powder?

"To my book," he echoed, "and to its two authors." He raised the glass and took a sip.

Myra stared at him as he drank, her breath caught in her throat. Did he taste something wrong? Suddenly, she realized she was expected to drink too.

She took a sip and gasped as multitude of tastes exploded in her mouth. Spices, leather and smoke, wood, fruits and pure sweetness. "What *is* that?"

"You know what it is," he said.

"Champagne?"

He smiled. "And a good one too. It tastes even better when properly cooled, but this will have to do."

It's a shame I have to waste it as a drug carrier, she thought. *Or perhaps not. After all, he deserves a classy end.*

They sat on the grass, a few feet away from the place where she had spilled the powder. He twirled his glass. "Every era in human history was different," he said. "The Enlightenment was the time when your people broke away from the Middle Ages and entered a period of unmatched breakthroughs in science. A period when champagne was discovered."

"How was it discovered?" Myra asked.

"By accident. The monk who created it was frustrated his wine would keep aerating. Champagne is a symbol of enlightenment in more ways than one. It is a triumph of humankind over nature. It is a way of saying, 'I do not exist to eat and sleep and survive. I exist to live, to enjoy, to create.' It is a way of showing that humans can bend and twist nature and create *this*." He raised his glass. "Without enlightenment you cannot have champagne. It requires greater human intervention than wine does, but most of all, it requires a triumph, a victory big or small, so that you can open your bottle in celebration. A triumph like the one we share today."

Myra shuddered and raised her glass in a toast. Their glasses met in a crystal kiss, the cling resonating through the Gardens, and Myra's heartbeat accelerated.

"You said you had questions?" Vlad said and took another sip. How long would the drug need to start acting? And would it even affect a vampire? He was still recovering from his wounds; hopefully that would be a factor.

Myra nodded and flipped through her notebook's pages. "I was preparing for the scene where Theodora kills the Emperor, and wanted to see what you thought of my ideas. I believe poison suits her best. I was thinking doll's eyes berries."

"That would not work," he said. "The doll's eyes plant is native to North America."

"You're right. I never thought about that," Myra said. "Belladonna, then?"

"Possible," he said, "though it was not called belladonna at the time. Nightshade is a better way to name it, or you could just use wolfsbane instead. Do you know why the plant was called belladonna?" He smiled as she shook her head. "Ladies of the past took small doses to dilate their pupils. Larger pupils were considered more beautiful."

"Oh," she said. "That's a bit extreme."

"They did not see it as extreme at the time. Throughout every period of history, human women and men have done extreme, often damaging, things to their bodies to fit some ridiculous beauty standard. I tolerate no such shenanigans among my people."

"Yes, of course, you're such a good and a just ruler," Myra said. "Your beauty standard is all natural—just a bit of dark magic and lots of blood and death."

"You are angry at me?" He sounded tired, and his moves were slow when he rubbed at his eyes. Was the drug working? Or was it merely his wounds?"

"What does it matter?" she said. "It's not like you ever cared what I thought."

"Of course I care what you think. I may disagree with you, but your opinion is taken into account." He sighed. "Myra, have you decided for certain that Theodora will kill the Emperor, or are you still debating?"

She frowned. "Of course she's going to kill him. What else could she do?"

"She could forgive him."

Myra snorted. "Right. Everyone she loves is dead because of him."

"It was not his fault. His influence was indirect. Their deaths were never his intention."

"But they were the result of his actions," Myra said.

He ran a hand through his long black hair, staring at the ground. "I was under the impression forgiveness was an inherent part of the human experience."

I'm not sure what it means to be human anymore. "There can be no forgiveness without remorse," she said. "Do you want me to read you what I have so far?"

"Of course," he said. "Please, go on."

She started reading, her voice hushed in the darkness. There was a pained look on his face as she went through the scene where Theodora discovered her family's deaths and revealed the events leading up to it. He listened, but said nothing. Myra frowned. It was unlike him not to interrupt her with comments and suggestions.

"Vlad? Do you dislike the story?"

He gave her a tired smile. "I like it very much. Forgive me, Myra, I was just thinking."

"About what?"

"My wife and children never had the chance to hear the end," he said. "I was just wondering what they would think of the new chapters." He smiled. "Ernike, my firstborn daughter, always thought Theodora would forgive the Emperor. I just… I wish she could hear the end of the book."

Oh no, you don't. You don't get to give me sappy stories about your murdered family and make me feel sorry for you. You are dying tonight, my Prince, and nothing will change my mind. And if Ernike thought Theodora would forgive the Emperor, it means she had never lost anyone in her life.

That was not the appropriate thing to say, of course. "I'm sorry," she said instead.

He sighed. "So am I."

"Were you planning to spare the Emperor? Do you want me to change this?"

He shook his head. "I had not made up my mind at the time. And please, do not change the story. It is your book now. I trust you."

Myra swallowed hard and kept reading. This time he interrupted her every now and then, giving comments and suggestions, and she made notes in the margins. After a while he fell silent once again, and Myra stole a glance at him.

His eyelids were drooping, and he was keeping them up with an obvious effort. She swallowed hard. The drug was working, but was the dosage enough? She needed him to be completely out when she plunged the stake through his heart.

He closed his eyes, massaging them with his thumb and index finger. She reached out to the bottle and poured him another glass, adding the white powder with a steady hand.

A pit opened in her heart, ready to swallow her whole. He was a monster, but were her actions any less monstrous? This was all so sneaky, so low. She had wished to destroy him, but not like this. Not by turning into a monster herself. But was there any other way?

He opened his eyes and she handed him his glass with a smile. He smiled back and took it, taking a long sip. Myra bit her lower lip, drawing blood. Vlad had done terrible things, but would he ever do something as low, something as despicable as what she was doing at the moment?

What was she thinking? He had devised an elaborate plan to turn the Farm humans against her, involving the painful death of a young man. He had done the lowest of the low, and worse. And yet, this was somehow different.

I trust you.

He had meant her writing skills, and yet the words burned her. *I trust you.* Myra sighed and went on reading.

After a while he stood up. "Forgive me, my dear. I enjoy your tale, but I need to return to the Palace. I have a meeting with one of the noble-vampires who arrived for the ball."

He did not have a meeting, Myra realized. He knew he was very tired and probably attributed it to his injuries. He wished to go home before he collapsed. And she had other plans.

"Please, my lord," she said and stood up, holding his hand in hers. "Let me finish the chapter. There is only a little bit left. I worked so hard and was looking forward to showing it to you."

He smiled. "I see. Well, then, let us hear the end."

He stretched out on the ground, his face turned to the stars. Myra kept on reading. Her heart clenched when she reached the last written word and he was still awake. Myra kept on speaking, making up the next sentence in her head, and flipping the pages, pretending she was still reading.

His eyes would fall closed for a few seconds, and then he would open them with a jerk. As Myra kept on speaking, this would happen more and more often, and his eyes would stay closed for longer. Her words and sentences turned into a random mess and she was glad he was not concentrating enough to notice.

At last, his eyes fell closed and stayed that way for a few minutes. "My lord?" Myra said and grabbed his shoulder, shaking him. He did not move.

Myra's stomach was tied in a knot. It had worked. The drug had worked. Then why was she not happy?

With a start, Myra realized that she had hoped it would not work. She had hoped she could tell herself that she had tried everything in her power, but that things had been out of her control. But this was not the case. She was in control now and she had to act.

Goodnight, sweet prince.

She took out her stake and pressed it against his heart. He would never again talk to her about history or art. Never again would he read one of her stories and give her advice. And although her writing had improved, there was still so much room for growth. She needed him to be a better writer.

What is wrong with you? People are dying, and all you care about is being a better writer.

She unbuttoned his thick leather vest to make it easier to push the stake down. Now his thin silken shirt was the only armor that separated his heart from the sharp wood. Myra pressed the tip down and frowned. There was something else underneath that shirt.

Bandages. The bandages for the wounds he had received defending her from the bear.

He killed the bear for sport. He doesn't care about you.

But he did care. He had gone to such great lengths to keep her alive, going against his people's wishes.

That's because he needs you to finish his book. Not because he cares.

Her grip around the stake tightened. *Can you see me now, Alerie? That's what we set out to do. You thought I couldn't do it. You thought I wasn't suited for the mission. Look at me now.*

His murdered family would never hear the end of his book. And neither would he.

Myra pressed her eyes tightly shut, feeling hot tears behind her eyelids. He deserved to hear the end of his book. He had waited for it for so long. Or did he really deserve it? He had caused so much pain. His deeds were unforgivable.

I was under the impression forgiveness was an inherent part of the human experience.

But was she human anymore? After what she had done to Serena and Bastien, so that she would have her library access back? After what she was doing to the Prince? Was she closer to being a human or a vampire?

Was this small victory worth selling her soul to the devil? Myra closed her eyes.

I have nothing left to sell.

Her grip around the stake tightened until she thought her fingers would break.

Look at me, Alerie. I accomplished the mission. I won.

Myra let the stake drop. She had won nothing. On the contrary, if she did this, she would lose it all.

Her final goal was to restore human civilization. But if humans lost their humanity in the process, if they became no better than the monsters they were fighting, it would be no victory at all. It would be total defeat.

Myra stood up, brushing the dirt off her knees. "Goodbye, Prince Vladimir. I hope you find someone to finish your story."

Yet as she walked back to the horses, mounted Alba and rode off in the darkness, with only the stars to guide her, she could not stop the tears from streaming down her face. She wished she could be the one to finish his book.

Chapter Thirty

Scheherazade

Myra had no idea where the horse was taking her or how to find the Resistance from here. Running like this was probably stupid. If she simply returned, Armida would help her escape as promised. Then both she and Franka would be free, and they would be close enough to the Resistance to find the way. The sensible thing was to turn back and continue with the plan as usual. Right now she would most likely ride on until she starved to death, or until some animal or a rogue vamp gave her a quick end.

And yet, if she returned, Vlad would most likely figure out what she had done. She would lose her freedom, if not her life.

And she had so many ideas for his book. She wished to share them with him, to hear his feedback.

Get a grip. You are not finishing his book. You will never see him again.

At least at first the sky had been clear and the stars had provided some guidance. Now thick clouds had come and concealed them all. Why did vamps need clouds in the middle of the night, anyway?

Myra froze in the saddle, a soft cry escaping her lips. The vamps needed clouds because the night was coming to an end. The sun would come up soon, and then the clouds would cover everything.

Everything except the Rose Gardens.

The Rose Gardens were one of the few places the vamps left sunlit during the day. And she had left Vlad there, drugged and helpless, waiting for the sun to come and burn him to dust.

"Stop!" she cried and pulled at the reins. Alba whinnied and bolted, standing up on her hind legs. Myra shrieked and slid down the animal's back. She hit the ground hard, and a sharp jolt of pain shot through her shoulder. She stood up slowly, massaging her injury and staring at the place where the horse had disappeared in the darkness.

Great. Can any of this get any worse?

Myra turned back and ran the way she had come from. Or at least she hoped she did. In this darkness it was impossible to say which way was which.

I need to find the place with the clear skies.

She ran on and on, tripping and falling, and standing up once again. She was certain that once the adrenaline left her system numerous cuts and bruises would make themselves known, but for now none of that mattered.

Her heart beat faster and faster and her breaths came out in short, ragged gasps. She had never run for so long in her life. Was she even running in the right direction, or was she getting further and further away?

Her head hurt and her ears rang. A sharp pain appeared to the right of her belly, and she placed a hand on top but kept on moving.

A pitiful sound made her stop in her tracks. A horse's whinny. Had Alba returned? Or had Myra unwittingly followed her? Had she been going in circles, returning to the place where she had fallen?

She looked up and tears streamed down her eyes as she saw the North Star.

Myra kept on running, her strength returning with the newfound hope. Soon she could see the torches burning not so far away. She passed by Vlad's horse, struggling against his bonds, but did not stop as her feet carried her down the familiar path to the old oak.

The sky was changing from pitch black into deep violet when she reached the place where she had left the Prince. He was still lying there, in the same spot, her discarded stake in the grass next to him. Myra grabbed the stake and threw it into the rose bushes. She knelt next to him, shaking him with all the strength she had.

"Vlad!" She slapped his cheek. "Vlad, wake up! The sun is coming up!"

She knew he would not wake up because of noise or disturbance. He would wake up only once the drug wore off, and Myra had no idea how long that would take. Still, she shook him violently and she cried until her throat was raw.

His eyelids fluttered and she sobbed with relief. He frowned and raised himself up on his elbow. "What happened?"

His eyes were clouded, but he seemed alert enough to ride. Myra grinned in relief. "You fell asleep. It looks like your injuries took their toll on you."

"Indeed?" He raised an eyebrow, his eyes suddenly clear. "Interesting. I have been injured many times, and it feels nothing like this."

Myra froze. "Vlad, the sun is coming up. We need to get going."

He reached out to his empty champagne glass and twirled it in his hand. "You drugged me."

All blood drained from her face. "Don't be ridiculous. Come on, we need to leave."

"Yes, you did," he said calmly. "The question is why."

He slid his fingers down his chest, trailing his unbuttoned vest, until his fingertips caught at the tear in his silken shirt, right above his heart. "I see."

"Vlad, I—"

"You drugged me so that you could kill me. That is why you brought me here. You lured me into the Gardens, and you used my desperation to see my book finished to control me. You kept me here with your tale and made me stay even when I wanted to leave."

Myra was shaking all over. She took a step back and tried to speak, but she could get no words past the lump in her throat. Perhaps it was for the better. What could she say to make things right? Now that he said it out loud, it all sounded so terrible. What had she been thinking?

His lips curled into a grin. "And I never saw it coming. Very well done, Myra. I am impressed."

She blinked. "You are not angry?"

"Of course not. That is what I wanted all along. I wished to turn you into a cunning enemy, into an equal. I wished to be able to feel fear once again."

Myra was relieved… and strangely disappointed. Did he care so little that she had tried to kill him? Did it mean nothing to him?

"And are you afraid now?"

"Sadly, no. I know you could never kill me. After all, I am your Scheherazade."

"What?"

He smiled. "Is it not ironic? When you first learned about the Farm, you were angry and tried to come up with a way to control me. You tried to become my Scheherazade. In the end, I became yours instead."

"It's not true," she said.

"Admit it," he said. "You want to be a better writer, and you need my guidance. You need me as much as I need you."

She sighed. "Vlad, we really need to go unless you want to burn to dust."

He laughed. "You put so much effort into killing me, and now you are working even harder to save me. Ironic indeed. Relax. The clouds start right outside the Gardens. We will be there in no time. Come."

"Alba ran away," Myra said as they walked to the place where they had left the horses.

He raised an eyebrow. "What exactly have you been up to? I will return at next nightfall to look for her. For now we can ride on one horse."

The vampire mounted his steed and pulled her behind him. She wrapped her arms around him and threw one last look at the Rose Gardens before they rode off into the night.

The adrenaline slowly left Myra's system, and then it hit her all at once. Serena, Bastien, the missing book from the library,

Lucy, Aunt Sandra, almost killing Vlad, and then the very physical pain of all the recent injuries she had sustained. Her body started shaking as tears streamed down her face.

"Come, now," the Prince said. "Tell me what happened."

"I had an aunt," Myra said. "She disappeared eleven years ago. I learned just before the ball that your people had captured her and tortured her to death."

"I am sorry," he said. "I am not in full control of what happens in the Palace. I value wild humans. If I had known about her, I would have kept her alive."

"How can you say that?" Myra cried. "I saw what you did to Bastien. And I saw Lucy alive and well. I know that you staged the escape. You play with people as if they are your pawns."

"It was necessary," he said.

"Necessary? You cheated two young humans by giving them a false taste of freedom, only to snatch it away and torture one of them to death! How exactly was it necessary?"

He turned back to look at her. "Myra, I need you alive. Not just because I like you, or because I need you to finish my book. I need you for something much bigger."

"What are you talking about?"

"I have a larger plan, and you are an important part of it. You will learn it all when you are ready."

His words sparked her curiosity, but she had no intention of sticking around long enough to learn what this was about. "If you tell me what it is, perhaps I can help you."

"I will tell you when it is time for you to know."

She sighed. "Fine. Play your games. I still don't see how this has anything to do with Bastien."

"I said I need you alive," he said. "But it is hard to keep you safe. Do you know why I always assign you at least four guards? I need them to protect you not just from outside attackers, but from each other. Many of my people want you dead, Myra. If I assign you a single guard, chances are he or she would be one of them and would be reckless enough to kill you. If I give you multiple guards, you are in danger if and only if all of them are ready to act against you and, more importantly, they all need to trust each other enough to share their plans."

"So I'm in danger," she said, "but you can't give me to your people, and so you gave them Bastien instead. You used him as a scapegoat."

"My people wanted your blood," he said. "I gave them a human torture to pacify them for the time being. You will be safer for a while."

"I never asked for any of this," Myra cried. "I never asked you to sacrifice people because of me. And it's a stupid plan anyway. Are you planning to stage an escape and torture and kill a human every month or so to keep your people in line?"

"Of course not," he said. "The current situation will not last for more than a month. I told you, I am planning something, and if I succeed, everything will change. I was merely buying myself more time."

"Next time you buy something," Myra said, "don't pay for it with human lives."

"Next time," he said, "I plan to lose as few lives as possible."

Myra frowned. This did not sound good at all. Whatever Vlad had in mind, it sounded like it involved people dying. Then perhaps if she got away, his plan would fail and none of it would come to pass. Of course, Armida would never help her get away if she heard what Myra had almost done. "Are you going to tell Tristan and Armida what happened?" she asked.

"Of course not. I said I needed you alive. Besides, this is not the first attempt on my life they will hear nothing about."

"Are there that many attempts on your life?"

He grinned. "Not nearly enough to make it exciting."

***

Franka stared at her, eyes blazing. "What the hell is wrong with you? I'll be blunt—I hoped never to see you again."

Myra tried to meet her eyes. "The drug didn't work."

"Are you kidding me? How exactly could it not work? What did you do?"

"I tried. I failed. What more do you need to know?"

The old woman threw her hands in the air and started pacing across the room. "Details. I want to know details. What did you do exactly? Did you give him the drug at all?"

"I did," Myra said. "I dissolved the powder in his champagne. All of it. He didn't react."

Franka stared at her long and hard, and Myra's breath caught in her throat. Was it better to tell Franka the truth? No, she would never understand. Yet, Myra was being open and truthful with Vlad and then lying to her fellow humans. What did that make her?

"We need to get more," Franka said.

"No," said Myra. "It's over. We can't kill the Prince. I talked to Armida. She knows that her story is ready now. She'll take us out of here in two days."

"Two days is plenty of time to kill the Prince," Franka said.

"I said drop it," Myra cried. "I don't have time for revenge. We need to destroy the WeatherWizard, and if I wish my plan to work, I need the Prince alive."

Franka looked away from her. "Do you remember the day when I told you how I ended up in the Farm?"

Myra stood up from the bed and walked into the old woman's line of sight. "Of course I do."

"And do you remember what you told me then?"

Myra ran a hand through her hair. "Yes. I said I would kill him. Well, I was wrong—it turns out that's not our best course of action."

"And what *is* our best course of action? Trade stories with him? Finish his book so that he can get closure? You are pathetic. You know he is a monster. You know how many lives he has destroyed, and you still don't want to kill him."

Myra grabbed Franka's arm and pulled her, so that the old woman would look at her. Franka's pale blue eyes stared at her unflinchingly. "That's right," Myra said. "He is a monster. I am not like him. I *will* destroy him, and I will do it the right way."

Franka started to laugh, and Myra shuddered, taking a step back. "The right way?" the old woman said. "This is war. The right way is the way that works. Your pseudo-conscience will one day doom mankind."

Chapter Thirty-One

Metamorphosis

As the last hues of orange and pink died down, the thick clouds started to disperse, revealing multitudes of constellations that Myra now recognized. She stared at the night sky through the large window in the Prince's study, before her gaze moved along the piano, the tapestry, the games on the table, and the shelves heavy with books, silently bidding goodbye to the sights around her. Her eyes then moved back to the notebook in her hands.

"Theodora knelt on the dusty ground and lifted a mossy stone to place the incriminating vial underneath," Myra read, her soft voice carrying in the darkness. "The magister would order her rooms searched once he discovered the traces of wolfsbane in the Emperor's wine. She stood up, brushing off the dirt from her green velvet gown, and with a last look to the woods headed back to the castle." Myra paused and put her notebook down as Vlad stood up.

"This should be enough for today, my dear," he said. "I am afraid my presence is required elsewhere. We can continue tomorrow."

Myra tried to suppress her disappointment. "You have no comments?"

"I do have a thought or two," he said. "But we can discuss them tomorrow, when you read me the rest of the chapter. Out of curiosity, have you planned the ending yet, or are you making this up as you go?"

"I have," she said. "Do you wish to hear it?"

"I prefer to read the chapters one by one and be surprised," Vlad said. "I admit I am eager to learn where my book is going, but I have waited for centuries. I can wait a few more weeks."

But if I don't tell you the ending now, you will never hear it, Myra wanted to scream. *Can't you see? If Armida's plan goes through, this will be the last time we talk. You will walk out of this door, and I will never see you again.*

"Are you certain?" she asked in a small voice. "Perhaps you won't like it and will ask me to change it."

Oh, but he *would* like it, Myra knew. She was proud of the plot twist she had come up with. She wished to share it with him, to see his admiration, to hear his approval, but now that would never happen. She had come up with the story of her life, and he would never hear it.

"I am certain," he said. "I trust you. I have written the first half of the book—the second is all yours. I can give you small suggestions, but I have no right to ask you to alter your story in any significant way. I have to admit I am glad to hear you know the ending. Now if I choose to turn you before the book is finished, the story will not be lost forever." Her expression must have been rather comical, and Vlad smiled. "No need to worry, I have no plans to do that anytime soon. Thank you again, Myra. You know this means a lot to me. Goodnight for now; I will talk to you tomorrow."

"Goodnight," Myra whispered, watching his back disappear through the door frame. The moment the door closed, she took in a shuddering breath and squeezed her eyes shut. That was it, then. This had been her very last conversation with Prince Vladimir.

***

Myra stared at the first page. The story was ready now; it had been finished for some days. She had been delaying giving it to Armida, telling herself that she needed to edit, and then re-edit again and again. However, it was over—the story was as perfect as it would ever be. In fact, it was as perfect as anything Myra would ever write. It was her masterpiece, her magnum opus. And Vlad would read it and think Armida had written it. He would never know it was hers. He would never know that thanks to his feedback, she had improved so much.

A sudden thought struck her, and she flipped through the pages until she found the passage she was looking for. Swiftly, she grabbed her pen and scratched over a few lines, inserting a couple of new sentences above. It looked inconspicuous enough—she had done such corrections throughout the story, sometimes on top of each other. If Armida did not get rid of her newest addition as she was translating, it was her own fault, Myra told herself in an attempt to silence her guilt.

Myra sighed and flung the notebook across the room. Why did the escape have to be today? Vlad would never hear the rest of his book. She would never decipher his past, or learn his mysterious future plans. She would never hear the end of Tristan's tale. It was so unfair. For weeks she had hoped to escape, and now that the day had come, she wished she could stay one more day. And then perhaps one more.

Tristan's story had left so many questions. Why had Vlad turned him if he had initially refused? And why had Vlad chosen him in the first place, among all other humans? What was so special about him? And what had happened to Callisto? Was she alive, and where was she now?

Myra gasped as her window's shutter opened and Armida crawled in. She was wearing light suede pants and flat leather boots, perfectly suited for climbing.

"What did you expect?" Armida asked cheerfully. "It is easy to get you out of here. What is hard is to get you out and to keep my involvement a secret. I have no intention of being the last person seen going in and out of your room right before you disappear."

"And how am *I* going out?" Myra asked, dreading the answer.

"Obviously the same way I came in."

"All the way down?" she asked incredulously.

"Of course not," Armida said. "We are going to a nearby room, and then I have to employ my cunning plan to get you out of the castle. Franka is already out, waiting for you. With you, though, it will be harder. To get past the guards, you must change. You must look like a vampire."

Armida took her large handbag off her shoulder. "I have brought you some clothes, practical, yet vampiric enough."

Myra changed into black leather pants, a white long-sleeved blouse, and a red brocade corset with steel boning on top. She sighed as she slipped on the black silken gloves. It seemed she was not going to escape that vampire makeover Tristan had offered after all.

"Where's Franka?" she asked.

"In my hideout, close to the stony desert you described," Armida said. "Since you are unconfident with horses, I have provided a tandem bike for you two. You can ride it down the road until you reach the place you mentioned, and from there you should know how to get home."

"A bike?" Myra asked incredulously. "You do know I've never been on a bike, ever?"

"Franka claims she used to bike a lot before the Nightfall, and she says this is something you never forget. She will give you a quick lesson. Do you have my story?"

Myra went to retrieve the notebook and handed it to Armida. The vampire quickly flipped through the pages. "Good. Come, now, follow me. It is not far."

Myra cautiously climbed out of the window and followed Armida along the stone sill. She tried not to look down and for once was grateful for the darkness. At least she could not see the ground far below. Armida seemed more confident at this, and no wonder—if worse came to worst, the vampire would survive the fall.

Franka's words came back to her. Was Armida to be trusted? What if Franka was already dead? What if the vampire pushed her down? They would discover her broken body on the ground and everyone would assume she had fallen to her death during a failed escape attempt. No one would connect her death to Armida. The vampire already had her story—she had no more need of her.

After what seemed like hours, they reached an open window, and Armida jumped in. Myra followed her cautiously, her legs trembling with exhaustion. She nearly collapsed on the floor but managed to stand up straight, finding herself face to face with a tall female vampire.

The stranger had dark skin and sharp features, with thick jet-black hair falling beyond her waist, perfectly straight and impossibly shiny. She was dressed in a bright orange sari, and floral patterns were painted all over her hands with henna. But there was one thing Myra noticed before all else.

She did not know this vampire. She was on her way to escape, and this woman was here, barring her path. Had Armida miscalculated and led her into an occupied room? Or had the vampire betrayed her? Had Armida never planned to set her free, but instead meant to eat her?

"Oh, relax," Armida's half-annoyed, half-amused voice sounded from behind her. "This is Indira, my most trusted friend. She can make you look like a true vampire."

"It will take some work," Indira said, reaching out to grab a strand of Myra's hair. "Your hair is weak and brittle. I attribute it to poor nutrition and negligence. It will take years to grow it strong and healthy."

"I am sure you have some tricks up your sleeve," Armida said. "I guess a dye could temporarily hide the damage."

"I have something better," Indira said. "Let me get my supplies. We don't have all night."

Great. Trusting Armida was hard enough, but trusting a random vampire she had never met before was even worse. Myra's eyes traveled across the room they were in. Thick, soft carpets covered the floor, and large and small pillows lay along the walls and in a circle around a low wooden table. Armida lowered herself to the ground, leaning against a huge red pillow, and Myra followed.

"Thank you for doing this," Armida said.

Indira narrowed her eyes. "Don't thank me. The fact that I am helping you doesn't mean I approve of any of this madness."

"I told you, the girl is harmless."

Indira pulled an ottoman in front of the blue-and-white ceramic fireplace and climbed on it, reaching for a shelf high above. "I am aware she and the Resistance are perfectly harmless," she said. "I could not care less what she does with her life once she leaves the Palace. No, Armida, that is not the point. The point is that you feel the need to do this in the first place. You must put an end to this lack of self-esteem; it's getting ridiculous."

Armida glared at her. "I do not have low self-esteem."

Indira retrieved a large wooden box and turned around to look at Armida. "That is what you want everyone to believe. That is why you keep up this charade in front of the guards. You are always so cocky, and you think cockiness is the same as confidence. Well, it's not. The truth is you have so many complexes that Freud could have a field day with you."

Myra sighed. Once again, vampires were discussing private matters in front of her as if she was not even there. Armida and Indira did not regard her as an equal. Talking in front of her was like sharing their secrets with a puppy or a teddy bear. So be it. They could underestimate her as much as they wanted, but she would listen and remember.

"What gives you that idea?" Armida challenged. She rose up and sat cross-legged on top of the red pillow. "I am beautiful and skilled in many things, and the Prince himself is in love with me. Why would I have low self-esteem?"

Indira walked to them and lowered herself on the carpet besides Myra. She opened the wooden box and looked inside. "Oh, please," she said, sounding bored. "I am a princess by birth, and His Highness is a nobleman by birth and a prince by right of conquest. And you yourself are a peasant by birth and a noble lady by right of… what again? Being the Prince's paramour? It makes you feel inferior among us. What you fail to see is that none of this matters to me or to the Prince. You are the only one who cares."

"How could I not care?" Armida said. "Everything I have right now, I owe to the Prince's love for me. I have nothing of my own. If I ever fall out of grace, I lose it all. I need to gain wealth and power on my own; only then will I feel secure."

Indira took a set of makeup brushes out of the box and examined them, before putting them back in. "Manipulating the Prince into believing you used to be a writer is hardly a step in that direction," she pointed out, and Armida smiled.

"Oh, but it is. It is only the first step in my plan, but I know exactly where I am headed and how to get there."

Indira arched an eyebrow. "So you do have a plan after all?"

Armida seemed about to reply, but bit her lip and gave Myra a pointed look. Ah, so at last someone realized she was more than a piece of furniture. Myra had to admit she would have lived with the vamps ignoring her for a while longer—she was curious about Armida's plan, not to mention worried. But since they had noticed her already, she might as well raise her question.

"Tristan was also a commoner," Myra pointed out. "And he shows no signs of fear or insecurity."

Armida snorted. "Well, yes, that is because our dear pretty boy is in no danger of falling out of grace, ever."

"And neither are you," Indira said.

"Wouldn't Tristan help you keep your position in court?" Myra asked. "He seems fond of you." She was blindly fishing for information. She had seen affection between the two vampires, but she had also seen rivalry. If there was any animosity between Armida and Tristan, she needed to know about it.

Armida stared at her for a moment before bursting into a fit of wild, hysterical laughter. "Tristan?" she managed in between gasps. "Fond of me? My dear, you must be blind indeed. Tristan loathes me."

Ah, so she had been correct. "But why would he hate you?" Myra said, feigning surprise. "Is he jealous of you? He's not in love with the Prince, is he?"

Armida laughed. "Not at all. Their relationship is of a different kind."

Indira continued rummaging through the contents of the wooden box, frowning. "Even if he was, it wouldn't be a problem," she said without looking up. "Most vampires are polyamorous. It's not uncommon to be in love with a few at the same time."

Myra sighed. "Why does everything I learn about vampires involve either blood-drinking or orgies?"

Indira laughed. "It is not either one or the other. The blood-drinking is a part of the orgies."

Armida cleared her throat and glared at her friend. "Dearest, could you please try not to scare the human?" She turned around, flashing Myra a bright grin. "To be honest with you, I doubt Tristan could ever be in love with anyone but himself. Not that I blame him, of course. He is one fluffy cupcake, and his blood tastes of wild strawberries dipped in dark chocolate, and—"

"Oh, he has been in love," Indira chimed in and stood up.

Armida threw her a sideways glance. "You don't mean his crush on the vegetarian bimbo, do you?"

"Of course not," Indira said. "I am not sure about anything recent, but there was one incident with a certain vampire woman, a few centuries before you were turned."

"What?" Armida rose from her seat. "Do I know her? You have such information about Tristan and you have told me nothing?"

"I had met Tristan and Vladimir only ten times or so before the Nightfall, and for not more than a few months at a time," Indira said and walked to a cabinet, returning with a brush and a jar of powder. "I cannot claim to know all the gossip. Yes, you do know her, but let us not speak of this now. Honestly, I find your obsession with Tristan unhealthy."

"If he's not jealous, what reason would he have to hate you?" Myra asked.

"How should I know?" Armida said. "He thinks I am not good enough for his precious Prince, I suppose."

"You are paranoid, that is what this is. Tristan is nearly as smitten with you as His Highness is," Indira said. "Come, now. I have everything I need."

"You have nothing for the hair," Armida said, and Indira rolled her eyes.

"I know what I am doing. Come."

They walked through a small chamber connecting the larger rooms. Myra's gaze wandered to a tiny cup of steaming coffee next to a few burning scented sticks in front of a foot-high stone statue of a cross-legged deity. "I see the Prince isn't the only vampire who has kept his traditions."

"Ah, that?" Indira gestured at the statue. "I have not kept them, not truly. Still, I do my best to preserve my culture and my roots, in a world where so many cultures are forgotten one by one. It makes me feel at home. The Prince is doing the same, with his horses, and falcon hunting and all, but I can imagine it must be harder for him."

"Why?" Myra asked.

"His culture disappeared over a millennium ago," Indira said, "while mine survived up until the Nightfall. The main difference between us is that I do this to keep some sense of identity and not let the beliefs of my ancestors be forgotten, while Vladimir truly believes in his god."

"God, you say," Myra remarked. "And not *gods*. What religion is that?"

Armida smiled. "If my love never told you, he did not want you to know. I will not break his trust."

"Says the woman who helps his prisoner escape," Indira muttered under her breath, and Armida shot her a dark look.

"I'm just surprised you used the singular form of god," Myra said. "I can't think of any monotheistic pagan religions."

"Why would you say the Prince's religion is pagan?" Indira asked.

"I understand the definition of 'pagan' is vague," Myra admitted, "but I don't see what else it could be. With the animal sacrifices to predict the future and all, and the Prince said the man who killed his family was canonized as a saint. This leads me to believe that he was some missionary, who converted the Prince's people to Christianity."

Indira snorted. "Missionary? That man was much more than that. But I fear you are trying to learn more than you deserve to know." She placed her hand on a golden doorknob. Come, now, why don't we go on and turn you into a proper vampire?"

The dream of my life, Myra thought darkly as she followed the vampire into the adjacent room.

"I said I had something better than hair dye," Indira said proudly as she stepped inside, letting Myra look into the room for the first time. "And indeed I do."

The large room was downright creepy. Faceless mannequins stood in neat rows, each wearing a different wig. There were wigs of every variety—from pixie length to below the knee, from perfectly straight through wavy to curly, layered or equal length, covering all natural shades of blond, red, brown or black, including white and greying, and a large selection of unnatural colors, such as blue, green, purple, or pink.

"I need to wear one of these?" Myra asked, curiosity, excitement, and disgust warring in her. She tried to imagine herself in some of the wigs, and she had to admit she liked what she saw. When had she turned so superficial and embraced the vamps' beauty ideal?

"Oh, this is brilliant," Armida cried and clapped her hands. "How come I have never seen your collection? I think something brown, bra-strap-length and inconspicuous would be best."

"And this is where you are wrong," Indira said with a smile. "We need a glamorous wig that gets the attention, so that everyone who sees her will remember the hair and not the face. I say something blond and long." She looked at Myra critically. "Your face is mostly in cool colors, except for your brown eyes, but I am thinking lenses anyway. We should look for something ash or platinum, and we want to go beyond waist-length."

"Yes, that's right, turn her into a female Tristan," Armida grumbled.

"Enough," Indira said. "If I hear Tristan's name one more time, I'm not doing this. Now be quiet and let me think."

Indira strolled past the mannequins, looking at each critically until she halted in front of a long, wavy, pale blond wig.

"It's gorgeous," Myra could not help saying, and Indira grinned.

"Of course it is. All the wigs here are made of real human hair and are of the highest quality. Still, some are better than others. Most of what you see here was meant for women who had trouble with their own natural hair. But this baby," she said, running her hand lovingly along the silky tresses, "was used as a movie prop and is more intricate. I had my eye on this wig ever since I saw the film and finally got my hands on it shortly after the Nightfall."

"So you wish me to return it to you once I escape?" Myra asked.

The vampire shook her head. "Consider it a present. For you and mostly for Armida. No, don't worry—I love this wig, but it is not my favorite. You can keep it. Sit down now, and I will put the wig on you before I apply makeup."

Myra took a seat, and Indira stood behind her and started braiding her hair very tightly so that nothing would show once the wig was on. Finally, Indira secured the wig on her head, and Myra stood up to look at herself in the mirror.

Whatever she had expected to see, it was not this. She looked at what she knew to be her own reflection and for a moment felt like a completely different person. She was no longer Myra, a member of the Resistance, born and raised in darkness and fear. For the next few hours, she would be a princess, or a fairy, or an elven queen, or a vampire…

The thought startled her and she snapped back to her senses. She was pretending to be a vampire and she found it to be… *fun*? She had imagined being a vampire to be many things—horrible and disgusting and unnatural, and still maybe interesting and exciting, but most definitely not fun.

"How do you like it?" Indira asked.

Myra gave the vampire's reflection a tentative smile. "I look like a vampire now," she said, and let the implications remain unspoken. "You know, there used to be an Old World superstition that vampires cast no reflection in the mirror."

Armida sniggered, and Indira gave her a raised eyebrow. "And what is so amusing about that?" she asked.

"Oh, nothing," Armida said sleekly. "I was only thinking that if a certain silver-haired bimbo, whose name I am forbidden to speak, was unable to see his reflection, he would have staked himself long ago."

Indira rolled her eyes. "We really need to do something about this obsession of yours. You make me wonder if you are more in love with the Prince or with his puppy."

"What I feel for the pretty boy is far from love, believe me," Armida said. "Thankfully, the shade you picked for Myra is far darker than his. I like it. It might go well with green or blue eye shadow."

"Yes, let us pick the eye shadow and lenses," Indira agreed and reached out to the makeup inside the wooden box.

"When was all this produced?" Myra asked, dreading the answer. "Isn't it expired?"

"Perhaps," Indira said. "But it still works, and you will only wear it for a few hours, so it won't destroy your skin. I have no fake teeth to give you, though. If you have to speak, try to keep your own teeth hidden."

Putting the makeup on took no longer than ten minutes, and once Indira was done, Myra stood up again and looked at her reflection. A small smile crept on her lips when she realized that, yes, this was fun, but not for the wrong reasons. She did not enjoy pretending to be a vampire. What she did enjoy was playing a role. This was not much different from the plays she used to stage at the Resistance, only this time her costume was more elaborate. She could pull this off. Her acting skills were good enough for the Resistance standards, which admittedly were not high, but she felt ready.

"Thank you so much, my friend," Armida said and kissed the other vampire on the cheeks. "Thank you for everything."

Indira smiled. "Thank me when this is over. I only hope you know what you are doing."

"I do," Armida said, and Myra took a deep breath as the vampire took her hand and led her outside the room.

Chapter Thirty-Two

Fear

They passed by the room Myra had occupied earlier and past the guards stationed in front of it. It would be a few hours before anyone came to visit her, and she hoped to be far away by then.

Armida held her by the elbow, and the two walked forward calmly, as if taking a leisurely stroll. They smiled and nodded at the vampires that passed them by, and Myra started to think this could actually work.

"Lady Armida?"

The voice came from behind them, and Myra's heart dropped. That was it. If she had to speak, this was the end.

Armida turned around, the smile never leaving her lips. "William. I thought you were still exploring the Pacific. When did you return?"

The vampire, who was now bowing to them, was one of the few short-haired vamps Myra had seen. His doublet and breeches placed his fashion taste in early-seventeenth-century Europe, and his thick golden chain was the only item that did not fit. His thin moustache was also atypical for vampires, and yet this one looked as if he belonged here.

"My ship set anchor at the harbor three nights ago," he replied. "I took a horse from the inn and rode straight here. It is a pleasure to lay my eyes upon your lovely face again, my lady, but I do not have the pleasure to know your beautiful companion."

"I don't believe you have ever met her before," Armida said smoothly. "This is my friend, Micaela. She resides on the Mainland. This is her first visit to the Capital."

To Myra's dismay, William's eyes brightened. "Ah, the Mainland. I have barely traveled there after the Nightfall. Tell me, Lady Micaela, have you settled anywhere?"

The vampire's eyes were on her, and Myra forced herself to return his gaze. Her heartbeat was so loud she wondered how William could not hear it. If he did, she would be in trouble. Vampires' hearts were not supposed to do that.

She had no idea what places in former Europe were settled by vamps, and her mind worked furiously through books she had read and pictures she had seen, trying to come up with something feasible. "I have been living in the same castle for the past thirty years. It is a small place, called Chateau de Gisors," Myra said, trying to follow Indira's advice and keep the blunt edges of her front teeth out of sight. "It is not too far away from the channel."

William's hazel eyes lit up. "Ah, I know the place. An octagonal shell keep, flanking towers on the outer wall, a chemise around the keep? I have been to this castle, but only long before we inhabited it. It is under Baroness Maria's rule now, right?"

"Yes, you are right," Myra said, hoping this was not a trap. She had learned that there were many vampire settlements around the world, each with their own self-appointed noble-vamp to rule over them. Still, the only vampire rulers Myra knew by name were Countess Izumi and the few ambitious vamps she had mentioned—the Duchess, Count Lucien, and someone else whose name she had already forgotten. Even basic questions could give her away.

"I haven't seen Maria in five centuries or so," William said. "How is she doing?"

"All is well in the Chateau," Myra replied. "The Baroness manages her affairs well. We did have some trouble with not enough game last year, but after reallocating the hunting parties, things went on better. And Lady Maria is as radiant and lively as ever, throwing balls nearly every week."

She was going out on a limb here and hoped she had not said something that would raise an alarm, but she needed to give details to quash any suspicion before it had arisen. To her immense relief, William grinned.

"It is good to hear news of old friends. I see them so rarely nowadays. I always thought that after the Nightfall, traveling would be easier for us, but it turns out our means of transport are even more limited than before."

"Are you saying the Nightfall was badly organized, my dear?" Armida asked.

"Not at all, sweet lady," William cried. "His Highness is a visionary. Our lives improved in many ways, and the pros greatly outnumber the cons. Only a fool would complain."

"This is good to hear," Armida said. "I will see you later, William. I assume you will be playing bridge tonight with Laura and the others?"

"You know my habits far too well, my lady. Of course, you and Micaela are welcome to join."

"I will join you," Armida said. "But I fear Micaela is returning back home tonight."

"That is too bad," William said, sounding sincerely saddened. "I hope our paths will cross again in the future, my lady," he said and bent down to kiss Myra's gloved hand.

Myra froze. Only the thin silk separated the vampire's lips from her skin. Like every predator, vampires had a keen sense of smell. Could he scent that she was a human?

William stood up and flashed her a grin. "Until next time," he said and disappeared around the first corner.

Shaking, Myra turned around to look at Armida. "Did he know?"

Armida frowned. "I am not sure."

"Did he smell me?"

"Not likely," Armida said. "What we smell is blood. A vampire, recently fed on human blood, would not smell much different from a human. Yet there are other ways he could have figured out you were lying."

"What should we do? Do you think he'll go and tell someone now?"

"He will not," Armida said. "If he indeed knows one of my secrets, he will use it rather than give it away. I need to talk to him once I return and make sure he stays quiet."

Myra paled. "Use it? Did I get you into trouble?"

Armida laughed. "Trouble? Not at all. I can handle him easily." She froze, grabbed Myra's arm and yanked her backwards.

Before Myra could realize what was happening, Armida had dragged her into a dark room and closed the door behind them. "What are you doing?" Myra whispered. "I thought if we met any more vamps, we would play our—"

Armida put a hand over her mouth, cutting off her words. The vampire pointed at the keyhole, and Myra knelt down to take a look at the corridor.

This explained Armida's desire to hide. Tristan. Myra frowned. Something in the way the vampire moved seemed off. There was no trace of his usual haughtiness, and his steps lacked any grace. His back was slouched, his head bent down, and his arms wrapped around himself. His long tresses were falling unbraided down the sides of his face, hiding his eyes from view.

Tristan turned to face the door they were hiding behind, and for a long, torturous moment, Myra feared they were discovered. Then she realized the vampire had merely wished to rest his back against the opposite wall. Tristan slid down listlessly, until he was sitting on the hard stone floor. He drew his knees up to his chest and wrapped his arms around them with a soft whimper. His face was contorted, and his breathing was fast and shallow.

Tristan reached out to his pocket with a pale and shaking hand and took out a small bottle, filled with round pink pills. It took him a while to uncork it, and then he poured over a dozen of the small pills into his palm. *That can't be a healthy dose*, Myra thought, but the vampire seemed to disagree as he hungrily pushed them all inside his mouth. He swallowed the pills and pressed his eyes tightly shut, forcing himself to draw slow and deep breaths.

A raw cry escaped his lips, and he bit down on his fist to stifle it, drawing blood. As soon as Armida heard the cry, she pushed Myra aside and pressed her face against the keyhole.

Myra leaned against the door, her heart beating wildly. What was wrong with Tristan? Few things could harm vampires, and she could not imagine that any of them would have such effects. And were they supposed to go and help?

She heard fast footsteps down the corridor, and soon someone was speaking close to their door. It was Vlad's voice, low and soft and soothing, but firm and commanding at the same time. The Prince was speaking in a language she did not recognize. There was a quiet authority in his voice, and Myra felt the strange urge to obey even if she did not understand the words.

She could no longer take the uncertainty and gently pushed Armida away from the keyhole. The view that met her gaze was even more confusing. Tristan had not moved from his position on the floor, and the Prince was kneeling in front of him, his hands on Tristan's shoulders, speaking in a low voice. He did not seem to reach the other vampire, however, and Tristan appeared lost inside his own world, not hearing a word the Prince spoke.

Vlad seemed to rethink his options and swiftly unbuttoned the cuff around his left wrist. He rolled his sleeve up above his elbow, and Myra could see the Y-shaped tattoo she had glimpsed before. The Prince unsheathed his jeweled dagger, the blade making a sharp swishing sound as it left the scabbard. The raven-haired vampire did not hesitate for a second before he ran the sharp knife along his exposed forearm, the blade cutting easily through skin, flesh, veins and arteries and letting dark crimson blood flow freely.

The Prince brought his cut arm close to Tristan's face, never stopping the flow of comforting words, and for the first time the other vampire seemed to break out of his trance. Tristan stared at the bleeding wound before he grabbed Vladimir's arm and brought his face down, devouring the lifesaving liquid. Tristan drank as if he would never drink again, as if nothing else in this world mattered. He had grabbed Vlad's arm so tightly that his knuckles turned white, and his nails were boring down into the Prince's skin, leaving small cuts and bruises.

Vlad had winced the moment Tristan had started to drink, but now he stood silent, giving no outward sign or sound of pain, his face hard as if made of stone. Tristan drank deeply until the Prince's face lost all color, and yet he made no sound. Finally, with seeming reluctance, Vlad pulled his arm away, closing his eyes at the small whimper that escaped Tristan's lips when the blood was taken away from him. The Prince stood up in one fluid motion, holding and lifting the other vampire as if he was no heavier than a feather.

Vlad briefly turned to the door Myra and Armida were hiding behind, and for a moment, Myra had the terrifying feeling that the Prince's red-rimmed eyes bore straight into her. But then he walked into another room, bringing Tristan with him and closing the door behind them.

Shaken, Myra slid down on the floor and stared at Armida. "What just happened?" she asked, her voice trembling.

Armida ran her hands through her slightly disheveled hair. "If I had known Pretty Boy was in one of his phases again, we could have tried to go past him before my love arrived. He most likely wouldn't have noticed us."

"What phases? Has he lost blood?" Myra asked. "The Prince seemed to think drinking blood would help him; perhaps he hadn't fed in a while? Or—" A sudden thought struck her. "The pills. Is he on some kind of drugs?"

"Blood deficiency looks nothing like this," Armida said. "And he is most certainly not on drugs. No, my dear girl, what Tristan is suffering through right now is the consequence of a stupid choice he made centuries ago. He can never be free of this now. Yes, it is unpleasant, but he should have used his brains at the time."

"But what is it?" Myra kept asking. "What is wrong with him?"

"That is his business and the Prince's. You should stop sticking your nose into affairs that do not concern you."

"And nothing can be done to help?"

"No," Armida said. "The damage is permanent. He will have to suffer the consequences of his bad decision until the end of time or until someone is merciful enough to put a stake through his heart."

"Why did he make this decision?" Myra asked. "Was it to help someone?"

"Do not expect altruism from Tristan. He did it because he was afraid. Come, now, I think the way is clear."

A few vampires greeted them on the way out, but no one engaged them in a lengthier conversation, much to Myra's relief. After what she had seen, it was hard for her to muster the concentration to come up with backstories and play her part.

They took horses from the stables and left the castle. Much to the vampire's annoyance, Myra could go no faster than a trot, but it mattered little. Armida's cave was not far away, and soon enough they dismounted and stepped inside.

Franka shot Armida a murderous look before turning to Myra. "It's about time. Did you run into any trouble?"

"Nothing serious, and we handled it well," Armida replied. "I would expect some more gratitude from you, human, but it matters not to me. Take Myra and get as far away as possible."

"Lady Armida," Myra said. "Perhaps you should give the wig back to your friend."

Armida shook her head. "Keep it. In case you run into vampires, you can pretend that you are one of us, and the old woman is your snack. I will go back now, in case I am missed, but I think the two of you should manage on your own. The field with the traps you mentioned is just down the path."

"We'll be fine," Myra said.

"Goodbye, then," Armida said. "If all goes well, we will never see each other again."

"Lady Armida," Myra called, and the vampire turned back around. "Thank you."

Armida smiled. "I did not do it for you."

"I know," said Myra. "I wanted you to know that I'm grateful nevertheless. And one more thing, my lady. You said Tristan made a bad decision because he was afraid. Don't make the same mistake."

"I am not afraid," the vampire said. "Whatever gave you that idea?" With those words, she disappeared, leaving the two humans alone.

Myra breathed a sigh of relief. Armida had not betrayed them. Franka thought she was pure evil, but Myra saw something else.

Armida must have been in her early twenties when she became a vampire. Had the Prince been the one to turn her? Myra could picture it clearly—the young, uneducated woman, and the sophisticated, centuries-old vampire. The thought made her shudder. Had Vlad turned Armida without asking, or had he befriended her first? Had he approached her and brainwashed her, using pretty words and empty promises? Was Armida his victim?

But by that logic, was Vlad also a victim of his own sire? Were all vampires twisted, miserable creatures, who deserved pity rather than hatred?

Oh no, Myra thought. *I still hate them well enough.*

Yet, she could not push away the pang of guilt as she thought of the story she had given Armida. The hint she had left for Vlad was easy to spot, unless Armida changed that part while translating. The Prince would know his lover had not written the story, and it would not be hard for him to figure out what had happened. Myra bit her lip. It was done now, and nothing good would come from dwelling on the past.

"I didn't trust her until the last minute," Franka said.

"She has no interest in keeping us nearby," Myra replied. "Or in killing us for that matter. She has plenty of humans to feed on, and we are no threat to her, or so she believes."

"You were friendly to her," Franka remarked. "Giving her life advice and all."

"I have to play my part," Myra said, annoyed. "I hate vampires as much as you do—when will you finally believe that? Come, now, it will be a long and hard way home."

Franka showed her to the tandem bike and briefly explained to her what to do. To Myra's surprise, keeping her balance came naturally as she took the backseat, and Franka did not seem to have forgotten anything. They flew down the road, and Myra could not stop the joyous laughter that spilled from her lips. It felt similar to horseback riding, with the wind in her face and hair, but she was more in control and could go faster. The open field would soon end, and they would enter the forest of dead trees that presented a better hideout in case vampires appeared.

"Do you think your friends will be disappointed you failed in your mission?" Franka asked.

Myra sighed. Here came the why-is-the-Prince-alive speech. "I don't think anyone ever believed I would succeed. They'll just be happy to see me back alive. And they'll be even happier when they hear I have come up with a way to destroy the WeatherWizard."

"A way that doesn't involve killing the Prince," Franka remarked dryly.

"Enough," Myra cried, but just then she had to duck to avoid a flying rock. Rock? What—

"Jump!" Franka called, but it was too late. Another rock hit the bike's tire and they came crashing down. A sharp pain shot through Myra's arm and for a moment left her unable to move.

A heavy weight was on top of her, pressing her down. "I would stay still if I were you," a low voice whispered in her ear, seconds before a cold blade pressed against her neck.

Chapter Thirty-Three

The Survivor

The blade pressed against her skin, almost drawing blood, and Myra wanted to smack her attacker. "Thomas, you idiot, get off me!"

He froze and then jumped away, like a vampire touched by sunlight. Myra stood up shakily, brushing the dust off her clothes, and glared at the wide-eyed, red-haired man.

"Not exactly the welcome I was hoping for," she said, but Thomas raised his knife again, reaching with his free hand for the stake at his belt.

"What… how…?" he managed, his fingers curling around the sharpened wood. "They… they turned you!"

Myra rolled her eyes. "Yes, that's exactly how it works. They turn me, and I grow long and shiny hair in weeks. This is my disguise, you dolt."

She spotted another person, running through the dead woods and caught sight of a few dark curls spilling from underneath a blue hood. Lidia stood in front of her, for a few moments staring as if she had seen a ghost. Then the spell broke and she pulled her into a hug.

"Myra! We never hoped to see you again." Lidia looked her up and down. "You look better than when you left."

"There's so much I need to tell you," Myra said. *Alerie is dead.* She opened her mouth to speak, but her throat tightened and no words came out. She exhaled slowly and swallowed hard. "It's good to be home," she said instead.

Lidia frowned. "Alerie?"

Myra pressed her lips together and shook her head.

Lidia sighed. "We thought you were both dead. I'm glad at least you made it."

"I know where her remains are," Myra said softly. "We should give her a proper burial."

"We will," Lidia said, and her eyes focused on something behind Myra's back.

Myra suddenly remembered her companion. "That's Franka. We escaped together. She—"

"She must be from the human farm," Thomas said.

Myra looked up sharply. "How do you know about the Farm?"

Lidia smiled. "We have also had some updates since last time we met. Turns out we're not the only humans who escaped the purge."

"There is another Resistance?" Myra asked. As far as she knew, even the vampires were unaware of that.

"No, not a Resistance," Thomas said. "They are *the Survivors.* They don't actively fight vamps, but rather focus on running and hiding. They've captured and killed a few vamps in the past years, but mostly they try to stay safe and avoid conflict."

"And they call themselves the Survivors?" Myra asked, raising an eyebrow. This was even more ridiculous than Zack's terminology.

"They don't call themselves anything, really," Lidia explained with a wink. "Zack came up with the name to distinguish them from us." Myra smiled back. She should have known. Ah, she had missed Zack these past couple of months.

"The name is fitting," Thomas commented defensively.

"Not really," Lidia said. "They do much more than running and hiding, and their intelligence is better than ours. See, they knew about the Farm and we didn't."

"Now you'll know more than anyone," Franka said. "We know much about the Palace, the Prince, inside structures, plans, and everything else."

"Zack will be thrilled to hear that," Lidia said. "Come, now, let's go home, you must be tired. And, wow, I can't believe you rode a bike. Can we take it?"

"Of course, that was the idea," said Myra. "Tell me, how did you learn about these Survivors? Did you meet them? Are they here?"

"One of them," Thomas said. "This girl, Sissi. Apparently she went out to search for other survivors and found us. She's been staying with us for three days now, and we've exchanged knowledge. She plans to travel back home tomorrow, but now that you're here, it makes sense that she hears your story first."

"And there's another piece of good news," Lidia said with a grin. "We tried Estella's rat farm idea, and it worked out. The farm is flourishing."

"Really?" Myra said. "Estella must be very proud."

"She is," Lidia said. "It's good for all of us. Our meat supplies have never been better."

Myra's stomach turned at the thought of rats. In the past couple of months, she had eaten fresh pears, peaches and strawberries, roasted boar, venison and rabbit, juicy steaks and grilled fish, served with mushrooms and vegetables. She had fed on chocolate truffles and drunk rich red wine and sparkling champagne. At the same time, her friends had been fighting to survive, and a few baked rats had made them happy. Just two months at the Palace and she had nearly forgotten what it meant to be hungry.

They walked on, going around and underneath protruding rocks and crawling through low tunnels, until they entered a spacious cave. The path led underground, and the air grew stuffier with every step they took. Myra had forgotten how bad the stench was in this place.

The guards stationed in front greeted them, amazed at Myra's return. Hundreds of questions were thrown at her and Franka, and the news of her return spread like wildfire. More and more Resistance members were rushing forward to greet her, talk to her, and welcome her back.

"Make way, you fools. Make way!" Zack approached them in long, determined strides. He froze in front of her and, to her surprise, pulled her forward and kissed her on the cheek. "I am so sorry," he said.

Myra was startled at her leader's uncharacteristic behavior. "Sorry about what?"

"It was a suicide mission. You said so yourself. I nearly got you killed. For many weeks I thought that I had."

"There's nothing to regret," she said. "The idea might have been bad at first, but all turned out well. The mission wasn't a failure."

His eyes widened. "You don't mean to say you've killed Prince Vladimir?"

Myra ignored Franka's snort at that, and smiled. "No, the Prince lives, but it doesn't matter. I think I know how we can destroy the WeatherWizard."

"If that's true, it's even better than what we hoped for," Zack said. "Come, let's go to the Headquarters. You must tell me everything."

Myra suppressed a grin. She had missed hearing the word 'Headquarters'. "And I will. But first, I must go and see my cousin."

"Of course," her leader said. "We can wait. Go."

***

Excited youthful voices greeted Myra as she stepped into the school area of the caves. Children ran out of the classroom, talking to her, laughing.

They know I'm back, she realized. *The news reached them. Thea must know too. Then where is she?*

Her throat tightened. She had been gone for two months. Had Thea fared well all this time? Had anything happened to her?

She pushed the dark thoughts aside. Lidia or Zack would have said something. She had told Zack she would go see Thea, and her friend had not indicated anything was wrong. Children ran past her, and she saw everyone—Monica, Erik, Anastasia. The one person missing was Thea.

"Myra!"

She turned at the cry and met Grandma Pia's smiling face. The old woman grabbed her by the arm, her eyes bright. "It's so good to see you back! I had nearly lost hope."

"Nearly?" Myra asked with a smile. From what she had seen, everyone had given up hope completely.

"Yes, nearly," Grandma Pia said firmly. "I never stopped believing in you. Come, now, you must be dying to see Thea."

Myra's breath caught in her throat. "Where is she?"

"In the classroom. When the news came, everyone went out to see you, but she stayed. Myra, be gentle with her. She hasn't been well after your disappearance."

Myra nodded. Of course her failure to return must have been hard for Thea. What else had she expected? With a clenched heart, she stepped into the room.

Thea sat on top of a desk at the far end of the room, facing the door, her arms crossed in front of her chest. She looked taller and thinner than when Myra had last seen her, and her skin was paler. Had so much changed in two months? Or had Myra forgotten what her cousin looked like?

Thea's dark blond hair fell freely around her shoulders, over the faded blue T-shirt that was way too big for her. Her blue eyes were moist and glistening. Myra smiled. Thea was alive. She was healthy. And she was right in front of her.

"So," Thea said, her voice cold. "You're back."

A shiver ran down Myra's spine, but her smile grew. "Yes. I'm back. I'm here now, and I'll stay here."

"You lied to me."

Myra frowned. "Thea—"

"You said you would return. You never did."

"Well, I'm returning now."

Thea's eyes widened and she stood up from the desk. "Are you joking? You were supposed to return in a few days!"

"And I wanted to," Myra said. "I tried. It doesn't matter now. I'm back."

"Maybe it doesn't matter to you, but I was the one waiting," Thea said, scolding. A tear broke from her eye and slid down her cheek. Myra took a step forward, but her cousin pulled back. "You say you tried, but you didn't come back. If you didn't know if you'd return, you shouldn't have gone in the first place."

Myra frowned. "You are angry at me for volunteering."

"Of course I'm angry at you! Why did you volunteer, anyway? You were the least suited person for the task! We have enough good fighters."

"Yes, we do," Myra agreed. "Alerie was one of them. And now Alerie is dead. Another fighter in her place would have been dead too. Prince Vladimir let me live because of who I am and because of what I can do. I doubt he would have spared another. Anyone else in my place would have died. And now, because of what I went through, for the first time since the Nightfall we have a real shot at defeating the vamps and destroying the WeatherWizard. Thea, I'm truly sorry I hurt you. But I'm not going to apologize for volunteering. I did the right thing. It was my duty."

"Duty?" Thea said. "To whom?"

"To Zack, to the Resistance, to humanity."

"And what about your duty to *me*? My parents are gone. You are my only family, and you left me all alone, without help or guidance."

"Thea, I had to do it for the good of everyone."

"You think you are a hero?" Thea said. "You think you are brave and fight for what's right? And then you abandon your own family?"

Thea's body started to shake. Myra approached her, and this time she did not pull back. Myra pulled her cousin into her arms, stroking her soft hair. "Shh. I'm back now. I am back. And I'm not going anywhere."

"I thought I wouldn't see you again," Thea sobbed.

Myra swallowed hard, suddenly guilty. While captive, she had spared little thought for her cousin. Her mind had been preoccupied with stories, dances and plays, and, of course, finding a way to defeat Vlad. What she had been a part of was so much bigger than her, than Thea, than any of them. Or was it? Was the fate of the world truly more important than the weeping child in her arms?

If she had the power to take away Thea's pain, would she do it? If she could go back in time and choose not to volunteer, would she take the chance? Would she give up all the wonders she had seen, learning to write better, meeting Vlad, Armida and Tristan? Myra pushed away her guilt as she realized she would not.

Thea pulled back and wiped away her tears. "I have something for you," she said. "Come."

Myra followed her into the children's quarters, to the room which Thea shared with five more girls. None of Thea's roommates were there, and Myra sat on a cot, waiting for her cousin to show her what this was about.

Thea knelt on the stone floor and lifted a blanket, pulling a very small packet wrapped in brown paper from underneath.

She unwrapped it and held it up for Myra to see. "I saved it for you. So that we could share."

"Thea—" Myra stared, stunned. In her cousin's palm was a small piece of chocolate. The same chocolate that Alerie had brought for the children what seemed like lifetimes ago.

"I kept hoping you'd come back. I kept it for you."

Myra could not speak around the lump in her throat. How much chocolate had she eaten at the Palace, while her cousin had been here, waiting for her and saving this one piece?

"I was planning to save it for my mom in case she comes back, but I think now that you're here, we can eat it," Thea continued. "Did you learn anything about my mom while you were with the vamps?"

"No," Myra said, surprised and somewhat disturbed at how easily the lie came to her. "I heard nothing about her."

Thea smiled. "Well, she could still be alive, then. You came back, after all. Perhaps she will too."

Myra swallowed hard and smiled back. "Yes. Perhaps she will."

***

Myra stood in front of the door, afraid to knock. This encounter would be much more unpleasant than meeting Thea. *Don't be a coward*, she told herself angrily and opened the door before she could rethink it. *He deserves to hear it from you.*

She gazed sadly at the burly man sitting on the cot. His unkempt dark hair fell haphazardly around his round face. His too-small shirt had been white once, but was now covered in stains of every possible color.

Drigo had been a part of the Warrior's Council for over eight years, but he had never shared his sister's skills for patrolling and fighting. Many Warriors with little skill in combat would try to develop other knowledge and abilities that could aid their community, but Drigo was still searching to find where his talent lay. Myra doubted the news would help him.

He looked up, fixing dark brown eyes on her. "I suppose you're here to tell me how my sister died?"

Myra sighed. So much for hearing it from her. "Alerie fought bravely. It's thanks to her that I'm still alive. Drigo… you probably wish our places were reversed, and I understand."

"Don't be stupid," he said. "Just tell me one thing—did she suffer?"

She was wounded in the stomach, Myra thought. *Her death was slow. She knew that she was dying and was in a lot of pain. The vampires drank her alive, as if she was nothing more than a meal.*

Myra raised her head and looked him evenly in the eyes. Not a muscle on her face twitched as she spoke. "We had a skirmish with a few vamps and defeated them, thanks to her. She was magnificent. After the fight, we found a safe house. We didn't expect an attack. We were planning our moves for the next day. We were talking and joking around. She was laughing. A bullet came through the window and hit her in the head. She never felt a thing."

Drigo gave her a small smile. "Thank you."

Myra forced herself to return the smile. When had she become such a good liar? Perhaps Prince Vladimir had gotten what he had wanted after all. Perhaps he had succeeded in turning her into the enemy he desired. *Very well*, she thought. *I'm ready to fight.*

***

On the way to the Headquarters, Myra froze in her tracks, pressing a hand against her mouth. What was that hellish stench? The foul stink of burned fur assaulted her senses before she remembered. She had smelled it so many times before.

Resistance members baked rats whole, in an attempt to use all the meat. The fur was scorched until it turned to coal, and the rodent was ready to eat. She closed her eyes and pushed down the bile in her throat.

Myra opened the door to the Headquarters and peeked inside. Numerous expectant faces stared at her from all directions, and she swallowed hard.

"Please come in, Captain Andersen," Zack said, back to his usual self. "How is Thea doing?"

She sighed. "Mad at me, as expected. She still can't understand why I chose to go, and she can't forgive me easily."

"She was worried," Zack said. "She will forgive you in time. Please take a seat. I'm sure there is much to talk about. Should we invite Franka to our meeting?"

"No," Myra blurted out before she could stop herself. She did not want Franka here while she told Zack of her plan. The last thing she needed was the old woman commenting on her suggestion that the Prince's death was unnecessary. "I trust her, but this is between us. This is Resistance business, and she is a civilian."

Only then did she notice there were not only Resistance members there. Thomas and Lidia and everyone else had come, but there was also a girl she had never seen before. In fact, she had never seen a human such as this one.

The girl's fiery red hair fell past her shoulders in two neat braids, framing her pale, freckled face. Two blue ribbons, holding the braids together, matched the color of her large eyes. She was dressed like the other humans—in whatever rags she had managed to find—but with a stitch here and a cut there, she had obviously made an effort to have her clothes fit her willowy figure better.

Apart from Thea's experiment with the scavenged red ribbon, Myra had never seen any human do anything to their hair, besides a quick combing or a ponytail. Never before had she seen a human try to fit their clothes, not because of practical reasons, but to make them look better. It all seemed so strange, so unnatural, so *vampiric*.

And then, she realized something. Beauty, and the desire to be beautiful, was not something inherently evil. Vampires were known for their vanity, which was why she had learned to associate vanity with the creatures of the night. All members of the Resistance avoided caring for their appearance in an attempt to be different, to be better. But the desire to look good was not something only known to vampires—it was human, and nothing was wrong with it. And she would be a hypocrite if she denied that when she had removed the golden wig, unbraided her hair, and looked at the mirror, she had felt a painful longing to put it back on.

"You must be Sissi," she said.

"And you must be the one who saw the Dark Prince and lived to tell the tale," the girl said, her voice tense.

"Sissi shared a lot of information with us," Zack said. "The Survivors have been luckier with their interrogations. It's true, then? More humans are still alive?"

"Yes, I saw them myself," Myra said. "Most have been born and raised in captivity. They know nothing better."

"This is disgusting," Thomas stated, and Zack nodded.

"Still, having so many humans can tip the scales in our favor. Even if we do manage to destroy the WeatherWizard, the vampires are much more numerous than before the Nightfall. They won't give up without a fight, sun or not. We would need every fighter we can get," Zack said.

Myra swallowed hard. That ship had sailed forever. She could never ask the Farm humans to join forces with the Resistance after the incident with Serena and Bastien. She shuddered, wondering if Zack would ever find out what she had done, and how he would react if he did.

"Forget the Farm humans," she said. "They can't help us. There is only one way to destroy the Wizard."

Zack nodded. "Speak."

"Killing the Prince will achieve nothing," Myra said. "Even if we succeed, the Wizard is well guarded, and any commotion that might ensue won't be enough to make them let their guard down. Our only chance is to force the Prince to destroy the Wizard for us."

"There is a way to force him?" Zack asked.

Myra nodded, noticing Sissi's intense gaze on her. "We need to gain leverage over him. We need something he values more than ruling over the world. There are these two vampires, Armida and Tristan. They are very close to him, and he would do anything to keep them safe. If we succeed in capturing at least one, we can demand the Wizard's destruction in exchange for the prisoner's life."

"Doesn't sound promising," Zack said. "We've captured some vampires alive, but they have been random. To target a specific vampire, who is close to the Prince, and capture him or her alive might be harder than killing the Prince himself."

"You can't seriously think that would work," Thomas said. "Vampires care about no one. They don't care about humans, and they don't care about each other. They cannot love. Why do we think that the Prince would give up the Reign of Night to save anyone?"

"They can love, I've seen it," Myra said.

"Still, Thomas has a point," said Zack. "The Nightfall came at the expense of many lives, human and vampire alike. The Prince has worked hard and sacrificed much to achieve all this. Why do you think he would give it all up to save one single life?"

"Because his immortal life, his reign, his castles, his servants, the eternal night, all this will be meaningless to him if Tristan or Armida are dead. If we capture either of them, he would do anything to get them back."

"Why?" Sissi asked softly. The girl was staring at her with wide eyes, filled with some strange emotion Myra could not place. "Why would the Prince do that? What are these two vampires to him?"

"Armida has been his lover for eight centuries or so," Myra said. "And Tristan… I guess you could call him his protégé, or his closest friend, or something."

"Or something?" Sissi prompted.

"It's hard to explain," Myra said. "Vampire relationships are different from human. I'd say the two of them act like something between friends, master and servant, father and son, a puppy and its owner, and an old married couple. Ah, yes, and Tristan is involved in weird bloodsucking rituals with Armida, and the Prince doesn't mind. In any case, I am certain the Prince would give away his kingdom for Tristan."

"Even if this is true, how do we capture them?" Lidia asked. "If these two are so precious to the Prince, he would keep them safe."

"He underestimates us," Myra said. "His opinion of the Resistance is low, and that will be his downfall. He would never expect us to try something like that. And now I have a map of the forest where they go hunting. We could send scouts there to look around and set up traps."

"And what happens if you capture the Prince instead?" Sissi asked.

"We kill him, that's what happens," Zack said. Myra was about to protest, but he shot her a warning glance. "All this is too convoluted. I'm sorry, but I can't see how the Prince would agree to destroy everything he has fought for just to save a single vampire. You say he would do that? You know it for certain? What, you spend two months as his prisoner, and you are best pals now? You know his heart and soul? I doubt that. What I do know is that this creature has murdered millions. What I do know is that he is breeding humans for food. What I do know is that he took you prisoner and held you locked away against your will. No, Myra, I am certain you think your plan might work, but there is only one course to follow. The Resistance's primary goal is the same as before—to kill the Prince."

Myra looked down, knowing that when Zack was in this mood, there was no point in arguing. She would wait for him to calm down and would broach the subject again in a few days.

Why did he have to be so stubborn? Killing Vlad made no sense at all as a plan. She supposed it never had, but she had never properly questioned Zack's determination. She understood it somewhat—everyone in the Resistance had lost friends and family in the fight against the vamps and thirsted for revenge. Many humans would find killing Vlad satisfying, but it would bring them no closer to their goal. If anything, it would take them a few steps back. And Myra had found out the hard way that she could not bring herself to kill the Prince if given the chance.

"Still, there is more you can tell us, isn't there?" Sissi said. "Why did they let you live? How did you escape? Were you locked in the Farm?"

"Yes, please tell us," Zack said, real interest in his eyes. "Unless, of course, the memories are too painful and you would need some time?"

"Not at all," Myra said. "I'll tell you everything."

She started her tale—how she was captured and learned of the Farm, how she met the Prince, and he left her alive so that she could finish his book. She skipped over details she deemed unnecessary, or that she thought they would not understand. And when she told them how the Prince had threatened to kill a boy if she refused to finish her tale, she skipped the fact that the vampire had killed the child anyway. Myra made no mention of Serena and Bastien. Instead, she put an emphasis on how the Prince always held back when fighting the Resistance, and how she feared that if he were replaced, their enemies would grow more ruthless.

"So Armida actually helped you escape?" Zack said.

Myra nodded. "I was worried she would betray me, but she proved to be trustworthy."

"It was disgraceful of her to mislead her beloved like that," Sissi commented, and Zack gave her a sharp look.

"Yeah, that certainly tops her killing scores of humans. She is a vampire, what did you expect? And if she herself is so unconvinced of the Prince's love for her, why should we believe he would give away his kingdom for her?"

"Because she was wrong," Myra said. "The Prince loves her. But I suppose it doesn't matter. You dismissed my plan already."

"Yes, I did. For now," Zack said. "You know me, I never dismiss an idea completely, and I would be a fool not to trust you after all you've seen."

"Thank you," Myra said with a smile. Perhaps there was hope after all.

Chapter Thirty-Four

Madness

Myra put down her diary and crawled out from underneath the moth-eaten blanket. She had forgotten how hard her bed was, and how poorly the flimsy cover warded off the everlasting cold, but she was not complaining. She was free now. There was no need to fear, to hide, to pretend, to play a role day after day.

Only, she was still playing a role. She could still not tell anyone everything she had been through, everything she had felt. She was still walking on eggshells, careful with every word, afraid to let too much slip out.

With a sigh, she blew out the candles and walked out of her room. Sissi planned to leave the day after tomorrow and return to her people, and Myra wanted to talk to her before she left. She wished to learn more about these so-called Survivors, who they were, what they were like, if their society was much like the Resistance or completely different. The Nightfall had created unique conditions for a social experiment—how would isolated human settlements develop in a postapocalyptic world? Studying the differences and similarities could reveal so much about human nature, and it fascinated her, even if Zack would probably call it impractical.

She reached Sissi's cellar and knocked on the door. Myra heard a hurried shuffling of papers, followed by an invitation to come in. Sissi's face brightened when she saw who her visitor was, and she invited Myra inside.

Myra looked at the bed Sissi was sitting on and smiled. Empty sheets of paper and colored pencils were scattered around, but there were no drawings.

"You are an artist?" Myra asked, and the red-haired girl blushed.

"Oh, no, I'm not good at all. I try, but I have zero talent."

"There's no need to be shy," Myra assured her. "I've also tried, but I was born with no talent. Still, you can learn a lot with practice. While I was a prisoner, the Prince gave me drawing utensils and books with art lessons, and I made a lot of progress. If you show me your works, I could give you some tips."

Sissi's face was white as a sheet. "Thanks, but they're bad, really. I'm not ready to share them."

Myra decided not to press her. "As you wish. I came because I wanted to talk to you before you leave. Do you have a minute? I don't want to disturb you."

"Of course, you may stay as long as you like," Sissi said, a little too enthusiastically. "I also wanted to talk to you, so this works out nicely."

"It does," Myra said with a smile. "I can't tell you how happy I was to hear there were other free humans. We could learn so much from each other."

"I fear we can learn more from you than you from us," Sissi said. "There are not many of us; we are just nineteen."

"That is not many," Myra agreed. "Are you doing fine with food and all? Perhaps you can move to live with us. We don't have much, but the place is safe against vamps, and we have set up a school system for the kids."

Sissi shifted on the bed, putting herself between Myra and an open backpack filled with papers. "I'll certainly suggest that."

"Perhaps your people would like it better where they are, of course," Myra said. "I know we're not perfect. Who is the leader among your people?"

"We have no leader. If we need to make a decision, we get together and discuss it."

Myra considered this. The way she had been raised, it seemed natural as breathing that every society should have a leader, or at least some system of governance, but she supposed for a group so small, getting together and discussing things could be a fair way to settle decisions. Would the Resistance have been better off following a similar model, instead of blindly obeying Zack?

"I would love to see it and meet the rest of your people," she said. "Do many of them also draw?"

"No, not many. Only this girl, Zuri," Sissi said and looked down. "She draws normal stuff, though."

"Normal stuff?"

"What I mean is, she draws well. Mine are just scribblings."

"Does anyone write, or sing, or play an instrument?" Myra asked. "And do you have a library?"

"We do, but it's smaller than yours," Sissi said. "And we have no musical instruments, unfortunately. As for writing, a few of us are involved in writing the history of the Nightfall, collecting all we have managed to learn from different sources. Ikram is old enough to remember it, so he has written the most, but we all add what we can."

"And no one writes fiction or poetry?"

"No, not really," Sissi said, a bit too quickly.

Myra sighed. "Let me guess. You do write, but it's horrible, and you would never show it to anyone?"

Sissi blushed. "Something like that, yes."

"And offering to give you tips would prove useless?"

Sissi bowed her head. "I see we understand each other."

"We do," Myra confirmed, even though she felt there was something about that girl she could never begin to understand.

***

Myra flipped through her notebook's pages, scanning through everything she had written in the past hour. *Why am I doing this? I'll never see Vlad again. He'll never read this.* And yet, she felt the need to continue working on the Prince's book from the point where she had left off. So many questions still remained unanswered. Would Theodora be caught? Would she regret the Emperor's murder? Myra needed to come up with all the details and write the story down, or she would go insane. How had Vlad lived like that for centuries?

Her eyes widened at the sound of approaching footsteps, and she pushed the notebook under a blanket, heart pounding. Myra frowned. Since when did she have to hide from her friends? And yet, the thought that anyone would discover her secret made her heart clench.

She smiled as Thea entered. "Hey. How was your lesson?"

Thea made a face. "I'm starting to wonder if anything we learn at school is useful in the fight."

"The fight isn't the only thing that matters," Myra said. "What you are learning is important, and it's very insufficient. I wish I could teach you more."

"Sure," Thea said. "I came to tell you Zack is looking for you."

I wonder if Zack is ever not *looking for me.* "How many times do I need to tell you? You're not his messenger. Is it urgent?"

"He didn't say."

"Then it isn't," Myra said. "Come, Thea, sit down. We haven't talked in a while."

"Yes, in the two months you were gone."

Myra winced as if slapped. She had hoped her cousin had let it go already. "Remember before I left, I showed you a play I'd written about two baby pandas? I asked you to stage it if I was late. Did you do it?"

Thea snorted. "Are you serious? You were missing. I obviously wasn't going around staging plays. It didn't matter anymore."

Myra frowned. Theater always mattered. Culture needed to go on no matter what. What would have happened if she had never returned? Would no one at the Resistance have staged another play ever again? "Did you at least read it?"

"Yes."

Myra waited for her cousin to elaborate, but Thea said nothing. "And? Did you like it?"

"Sure. It was fun."

"You didn't see any problems with it? Anything I could have improved?"

"Not really. It was very good."

Myra sighed. The play was a mess. She recognized it now—the plot had no structure, no inciting event, no climax, no resolution, no anything. It started in the middle of nowhere, and ended in the middle of nowhere, with only pointless filler in between. And yet, there was not a single person in the Resistance who would tell her that.

She stole a glance at the blanket, hiding her notebook underneath. She had to finish that story. She was as good an author as she would ever be. From today on, she would never learn anything new.

***

"Zack, this is insane," Myra cried and forcefully slammed her glass on the table. "I've barely returned home, and you already want to send me away?"

"I don't *want* to send you away," Zack said. "This is what makes the most sense. We've been planning to send one of us with Sissi all along. It makes sense that it should be you, so that you can share your experiences with the Survivors."

"And what am I to tell Thea? She is nowhere near forgiving me."

"You can tell her that this is my order. She for one understands orders. Besides, this is different. Last time it was clear from the beginning that the mission was dangerous. Now you are perfectly safe. You will travel with Sissi, and she knows the paths to her home. Her people live no more than a two-day walk from here, and their place should be safe."

"I'm not afraid," Myra said. "It's just that I wanted to spend some time at home."

Truth be told, all she wanted right now was to stay close to Zack and observe his moves and moods. Perhaps if she found the right time, she would be able to sway him and convince him her plan would work, but that would never happen if she was away.

"And you will," he promised. "Two days getting there, a day or two at the Survivors' headquarters, then two days for the journey back—you will be back home in no time and you can stay as long as you want. But I find it important that our brothers and sisters learn firsthand from your experience."

She ran a hand through her hair and stood up. It was better not to antagonize Zack about this if she wanted to get on his good side for the more important matters. "You are right, of course. I'll start packing right away."

He thanked her, and she knew that under normal circumstances she would have been thrilled to meet the other humans. But right now, all she could think about was getting back home.

***

Dead, rotting trees and fallen branches surrounded the narrow, stony path. Thick, dark clouds hid the sun completely, and Myra was thankful there was no rain. She stared at Sissi's back as the girl jumped over a small stream. Sissi's fiery red hair was loose this time, falling down in thick curls. The color contrasted against the girl's green sweater, and Myra guessed Sissi had chosen her clothes on purpose, to make her hair stand out.

She would make a good vampire, Myra thought. The idea startled her. It was not vanity that made one a vampire. It was the desire to kill, hurt, and destroy, and as far as she had seen, Sissi possessed none of those traits.

"So we'll reach your home in two days?" Myra asked and jumped over the stream.

Sissi stopped walking and leaned her back against one of the rotten trunks. "It depends," she said.

"Depends? On what? Your camp isn't moving around, is it?"

"Depends on you," Sissi said.

"I can walk fast enough," Myra assured her. "Where are we going to spend the night?"

"There are a couple of shelters on the way. They should be safe. We are going farther away from the Palace, and vampire encounters are rare." Sissi paused. Her blue eyes darted left and right before fixing on Myra. "Myra, I need to talk to you, and I think the sooner I do it, the better."

Myra's heart skipped a beat. She did not like the sound of that. She had been strangely worried ever since her return—as if she had a big secret to hide, and something terrible would happen if it was discovered. Which made no sense at all—she had nothing to hide.

Or did she? It was true—she wished Zack would stop targeting Vlad, but that was because she believed her own plan would work much better. The Prince was someone they could negotiate with. Replacing him with another vampire would forever doom their chances of destroying the Wizard. Yet, she felt a heaviness in her chest at Sissi's words and hoped what was to follow had nothing to do with the Prince.

"Sure, go on," she said and tried to force a smile.

Sissi hesitated. "Maybe we should sit down."

Great. This sounded worse and worse with every word Sissi said. "You have bad news?"

"Oh no, not at all," Sissi assured her. "It is… a bit of a complicated subject."

Not getting better, Myra thought with a sigh. "I guess we can talk on the way. We have a long road ahead of us."

"As I said, that depends."

Now, that was unexpected. "You mean it depends if we have a long road ahead of us? Are we… are we going to your home?"

"I'm not sure," the red-haired girl admitted. "I have no idea what we should do, to be honest. Shall we sit down?"

This time, Myra could do nothing but comply. The two sat in uncomfortable silence for a few moments, until Sissi spoke first. "This question might seem random, but it matters. How would you describe the Prince? What is he like?"

So much for hoping this had nothing to do with Vlad. Myra tried to keep her face neutral. "In what way?"

"You know, what is he like as a person? You spent so much time in the Palace. You must have some impressions."

Myra wondered what the right answer was supposed to be. The truth was most definitely not. "I thought I made it clear from the stories I shared. He is a monster."

"So you want to see him dead?"

She shrugged. "I think killing him would be a mistake. Kidnapping one of his loved ones has a greater chance of success. Also, if we remove him from power, his replacement will likely be more vicious. But if Zack thinks killing the Prince is our mission, then that is the way to go."

"That is not what I asked," Sissi said. "Do you *want* to see him dead? Not as a part of the mission, not as a means to a goal, but on a personal level. Do you wish for it?"

Where was all this coming from? "I wouldn't care one way or another."

"But that doesn't make sense," Sissi said, wrapping her arms around herself. "He captured you and held you prisoner. You must hate him. And Zack said that before your capture you hated all vampires."

Zack. Of course. He had to be the one to put Sissi up to spying on her. "Well, of course every vampire is better dead rather than undead, and the Prince is no exception. I just don't care that much what happens to him either way."

Sissi smiled. "Myra, I'm not asking these questions to put you in a tight spot. I'm simply asking because I want to know if I can trust you."

"And what makes you think you can't trust me?"

"The better question is what makes me think I *can* trust you. No, please don't be offended—I hardly ever trust anyone. But I've been wondering, and I heard something yesterday."

"Heard what?"

"Franka was speaking to Zack. I heard her saying she wanted to talk to him in private, and they went to the Headquarters. I remembered how much you feared having her on the Council, and so I followed."

Myra wanted to smack herself. Had it been so obvious? "I didn't fear having her there; I just didn't think it was the right place for her. And you—what, eavesdropped on their private conversation?"

"Condemn me if you will, but I had your best interests in mind. I heard Franka tell Zack that she was worried about your motivations. She said she had noticed you being too friendly with the Prince, and you refused to discuss assassination plans. This was when Zack told her you used to hate all vampires before you left, and the two speculated on your behavior."

"Yes, Franka did believe that," Myra said. "But she is wrong. I escaped the Prince, didn't I? Isn't that proof that I didn't enjoy my time with him as much as she believes?"

"Zack wasn't sure what to believe either. But he had enough doubt to do what he did."

Myra's blood froze in her veins. "Do what?"

"Haven't you wondered why he sent you with me?" Sissi asked.

"He said he wanted your people to hear firsthand of my experience."

Sissi stared at her. "He sent you here because he wanted you out of the way."

"Out of the way of what?" Myra asked, her voice suddenly breaking.

"He plans to assassinate the Prince. He didn't want you around."

Myra laughed. "He's been planning to assassinate the Prince ever since he learned how to talk. He may try as much as he wishes. It's not happening whether I am in his way or not."

"Not this time," said Sissi. "This time he has information he didn't have before."

"What are you talking about?"

"On my way here, I came across a sunlit forest," Sissi said. "It was incredible, and I barely found the willpower to leave it behind. Naturally, I told the Resistance where to find it. Then you told us about the forest where the Prince would hunt at night and keep it sunlit during the day."

"It must be same one," Myra said. A heavy weight formed in her stomach, twisting her innards into a knot. "I didn't give Zack the map, but you've told him about it. So now he knows where to find it?"

Sissi nodded. "And he knows that vampires wouldn't go there if the sun is up. He has sent scouts, and they are investigating the terrain as we speak. He knows the Prince goes hunting almost every night, often alone or with only one or two companions. He is planning to set traps during the day to capture him or slow him down, and attack full force at night. It is a large part of the full-grown Resistance Warriors, against a single vampire, or two or three at most. I know the Prince must be good, but I wouldn't say Zack is as clueless as he used to be."

Myra blanched. "What do you expect me to do?"

"This is what I'm trying to find out. You don't have to fear me. I am on your side."

"How do you even know what side I'm on?" Myra asked. She was not sure about it herself.

"I only know that you don't wish to see the Prince dead," Sissi said with surprising conviction. "And neither do I."

This made no sense. No sense at all. The only explanation was that this was a test. That Zack had instructed Sissi to play this role and test Franka's suspicions. "And why would you say that?"

Sissi smiled sadly, and there was a strange longing in her eyes. "You wouldn't understand."

"Try me."

"It's not so simple," the red-haired girl said. "I haven't told this to anyone. For many years, I've kept it inside. If I tell you, you'll be the first to know."

"Why haven't you talked about this?" Myra asked. If Sissi was acting, she was very good.

Sissi looked away. "I am embarrassed. This means so much to me and goes too deep inside my heart. Talking about it would be like baring my soul. And the worst part is, no one could understand. They would condemn me, or they would think that I am insane, that I am a freak."

Myra gave her what she hoped was an encouraging smile. "I've spent the last two months among vampires. You cannot imagine the things I've seen and heard. I know a thing or two about freaks. Believe me when I say this—I'm not easily shocked."

"That is because you've never met someone like me."

Myra sighed. "Sissi, I see you believe yourself to be more messed up than anyone. Truth is, many people believe that. But if they could see what was going on in everyone else's head, they would know they were in good company. Everyone else isn't as 'normal' as you make them out to be. But whether you are as strange as you'd like to believe doesn't matter. What matters is that you want me to trust you, and I cannot unless I know your motivation."

Sissi nodded mutely, a serious expression on her face. "I believe you need to see something," she said and started rummaging through her pack. She took out a pile of papers and laid them out for Myra to see clearly.

And as Myra stared in shock at Sissi's paintings, she realized that the girl had told her the truth. They were not good.

They were amazing.

Chapter Thirty-Five

Obsession

As Myra examined the drawings, she could not believe that an amateur, self-taught artist created them. They looked so real, so vivid, so moving. It was clear that Sissi had been experimenting with her techniques, as the pictures varied in style and mood, but the subject matter was always the same.

All of them portrayed the same man, or probably a vampire, considering he looked like the Old World depictions of Count Dracula. He was doing something different in every drawing—fighting, riding a horse, shooting an arrow, climbing a rock, sitting on a high tree branch, looking at the moon, even *flying*, his dark cape waving like a banner behind him. Most of the time he was alone, but in some pictures he was surrounded by other figures.

Myra blinked, not sure what she was seeing. "This is—"

"This is how I imagine the Prince," Sissi finished softly and averted her gaze.

"You are drawing the Prince," Myra said. "But why?"

Sissi had turned a deep shade of red, and her next words were barely audible. "Because I think about him all the time."

"What do you mean, you think about him? You don't know him. You've never seen him. You don't even know what he looks like."

Sissi grinned sheepishly. "Am I that far off?"

"That's not the point," Myra said. "I just can't comprehend the meaning of this."

"I can try to explain, but it's complicated. You wouldn't understand."

"Look, Sissi, I am sick of you thinking you are so abnormal. Perhaps no one understands you because you've never tried to explain."

Sissi took a deep breath. "Just promise you won't judge me too harshly."

Myra smiled. "You'll find me very open-minded."

"Alright, then," Sissi said, biting her lip. "But you must promise not to breathe a word to anyone. No one knows about these." She gestured at the drawings. "Or about any of it. Telling you this is a big deal for me."

"I know," Myra assured her. "I won't say a word."

"I'm not sure where to start," Sissi admitted. "I'm not sure where it all started, to be honest. I've always been extremely obsessive about the things that I liked. I couldn't simply like something, I had to *love* it with all my heart and soul. Even as a kid, I couldn't simply pick up a book and read a passage or two whenever I had some time to kill. No, if I started a book, I had to drop everything else before I finished it. If I was forced to pause reading to eat or sleep, all I would think about was the characters and the trials they still had to face."

"So far, I can relate," Myra said encouragingly.

"Thank you," said Sissi and smiled. "I thought my passion would cool down as I grew up, but it only got worse. Reading was not enough. I kept thinking about my favorite characters, drawing pictures of them, writing additional stories with them. And worse, I was talking about them. All the time."

Sissi stood up and started pacing back and forth. Myra followed her with her eyes, but it made her dizzy.

"It took me a long while to realize these conversations were always one-sided," Sissi continued. "My companions didn't care about a word I said. To me, these conversations were fascinating, and it took me too long to see that everyone else was starting to find me boring."

"And you tried to change?" Myra guessed.

Sissi nodded. "I tried to hide. To wear a mask all the time, to smile when they smiled, to laugh when they laughed, and to pretend I was interested in their talks about who had found some new clothes, or the best way to cook rabbit, or who fancied whom."

"But you were never interested in any of that," Myra said. "You never became the mask."

Sissi stopped pacing and sat on the ground. She bowed her head, hiding her face from view. "It all seemed so empty to me, so meaningless. Doing everyday tasks—cleaning our shelter, preparing food, washing dishes—felt almost physically painful. It all seemed so small, so insignificant, knowing that somewhere out there, in my mind, my heroes were fighting for the fate of the world. That was all I wanted to talk about, but I never said a word. And so I kept pretending that I was normal, that I was like everyone else."

"You had interests no one else around you shared," Myra said. "It's not unnatural, or unhealthy by itself. You simply have the misfortune of living in a small community, so that no one around you has the same passion. If you had been lucky enough to live in a true human society with more people to interact with, I'm certain you would have found others who think like you."

"Perhaps," said Sissi. "But this experience taught me to keep my thoughts to myself, and it turned out to be useful. My companions would have burned me alive if they knew what I was thinking nowadays."

"Your companions would do that?" Myra asked in shock, and Sissi grinned.

"It was a figure of speech. We don't burn people alive. So far, at least. Anyway, after I knew all the books we had by heart, and I had drawn all the pictures I had to draw and written all the stories I had to tell, my passion was beginning to cool down. That was when I got into history. I like history from all times and all parts of the world, but for some reason I was especially fascinated by the events around the Nightfall."

Sissi paused, staring at the stream. She kicked off her slippers and dipped her feet into the water, slowly moving them back and forth to create small ripples. Sissi shuddered, but did not pull them out. The silence stretched between them, and Myra waited patiently, feeling they had at last reached the point where Sissi would reveal her secret. After a few minutes, Sissi took her feet out of the water and rubbed them, her eyes focusing on Myra once again.

"One of our people, Ikram, had written down some of his firsthand experiences," Sissi continued softly. "As I read, I became fascinated with the idea of the Prince of Darkness. I was imagining how he had gone through his conquest, and from then on, there was no way I could stop. I kept making up stories about him, putting him through different adventures, making him interact with other vampires or humans I made up. I developed him as a character, as a personality, until I knew him better than I knew myself."

"You are obsessed with a fictional character that you created," Myra said. "He may share the Prince's name, and a vague history, but that's not him. None of this is real."

Sissi's eyes blazed. "You have no idea what I feel," she said. "Do not presume to tell me what's real."

Was I ever that naive? Myra doubted that. Sissi's community lived further away from the Palace, so perhaps they were more sheltered than the Resistance. Perhaps Sissi had not witnessed her loved ones die out one by one. Yet, how could she not know what was happening in the world?

"I'm sorry. You are right, of course," Myra said. "But think about what you are saying. He is a mass murderer."

"You think I don't know that?" Sissi uttered bitterly. "I know that this is wrong. But it's stronger than me. It has taken a hold of me, and I can't get rid of it without destroying who I am."

Myra stared at her long and hard. "Sissi, why did you leave your companions? They didn't send you here to look for other survivors as you told Zack, did they?"

"I told them the same thing I told your Resistance—that I wanted to travel around and look for other survivors. I told them I would return with news. The truth is, I never planned to return. I don't want to go back there. All I wanted was to get closer to the Palace and catch a glimpse of the Prince, even if it was the last thing I did."

Myra took in a deep breath. The girl was completely insane. "It would have been the last thing you did indeed," she said. "Sissi, what exactly did you hope would happen once you met him? You don't wish to become a vampire, do you?"

Sissi's face turned bright red and she looked away.

Myra's heart stopped. *No, this can't be happening.* "You *want* to be a vampire? Sissi?"

"I don't know," Sissi said. "I've thought about it. It's not what matters the most, but perhaps it would be nice."

"Nice?" Myra wanted to punch something. "It would be *nice*? Vampires are monsters. They have killed people. They are still killing people. And you want to join them and contribute to the murders?"

"I don't want to kill anyone," Sissi said. "But I hate my life right now. I want something different."

"And becoming a bloodthirsty monster and destroying others' lives is the only option? Now you sound like Tristan."

Sissi's eyes widened. "Tristan? That's the vampire you mentioned, right? The one close to the Prince?"

"I'm not saying you are like him," Myra said. "And don't delude yourself—if you meet the Prince, you won't become close to him. You'll become his meal." She sighed. "It's your life, I suppose. Do as you wish. For now, let's focus on the problem at hand. What should we do next?"

"So you are with me on this? You don't want to see him dead?"

Myra was silent. What *did* she want? For one thing, she wanted to follow her plan. She honestly believed the Prince would meet all their demands if they held Tristan or Armida, but this could never happen if Zack killed him first.

Do you want to see him dead? Sissi had asked, and, to her surprise, Myra realized that she did not. Vladimir had killed so many. He had destroyed so much. And yet, she had held his life in her hands and had chosen to let him go.

Perhaps he deserved to die. Or perhaps he deserved to read the end of his book. Myra could not judge. But this was not about justice and judgment, was it? It was about what she wanted. And she did not want him to die.

He was no longer a faceless enemy, a monster who had killed millions. He was someone she knew. They had talked. They had discussed books, music, and history. It was strange to imagine him dead, and even stranger to wish for it.

"What are we going to do?" she repeated, avoiding Sissi's question. "We can't simply return now; there is no way to explain this."

"In any case, we can't go back to my people. They will have many questions for you and might keep us for days. And even when they let you go, they will probably send someone else with you. No, I think our best bet is to hang out around here for four or five days. Then we'll go back and say we've seen my people, reported to them, but you were in a hurry to come home, and we left quickly. I was sent to accompany you again because I know the area."

"But five days—isn't that too long?" Myra asked. "You said Zack was planning to put his schemes in motion right away."

"He can't do anything until the Prince actually goes hunting. He goes often, you said, but not every single night, so it's a matter of luck how soon he does it again. Besides, you said it yourself—Zack has been making these plans for ages. Do you truly believe he would manage to kill the Prince in five days?"

Myra was not comfortable waiting for that long, but Sissi was right. If they returned now, they had no way to explain it. Zack's suspicions of her would be confirmed, and if he distrusted her, she had no way to influence his plans. "Vlad won't be hurt in this stupid plan, I'm sure of it," she murmured. "But I fear someone else might be. And what are we going to do once we get back?"

"We have plenty of time to work on the strategy," Sissi said. "The most important thing is that you never give Zack any reason to believe Franka might be right." She paused and looked away. "I like it how you call him Vlad. It's so familiar. Don't take this the wrong way, but I am jealous of you. You've been there, seen him, talked to him, touched him. He knows who you are."

Myra glared at her. "You don't know of what you speak. This is only a fantasy to you. You have no idea what it was really like and how scared I was."

"You mean to tell me you regret these past two months? You wish you had never been captured and none of this had happened to you?"

Myra looked away, unable to meet Sissi's gaze. If she could change the past, would she give it all up? The terror, the hunger, the helplessness. The opera, the books, the writing lessons. Would she have stayed in the safety of their hideout if she had known what awaited her?

She pressed her lips together. Before her volunteering, she had been just a reader of her own life. She had let inertia carry her on and on through every single day, and had observed herself as if from far away—the life of a girl afraid to take risks and hiding from the world outside. Once she had volunteered, she had taken matters into her own hands. She had become the author of her own fate.

And if there was one single thing Myra desired most of all, it was to be an author. She looked up, meeting Sissi's eyes. She smiled, finally coming in terms with the truth. "No," Myra said. "I have no regrets."

***

Myra's heart clenched as she followed the mazelike corridors leading to the Resistance's caves. There was no reason to be worried, she told herself. There was no sign or sound of any commotion. In fact, there was no sound of *anything.*

At last, they reached the guards and she released a breath she had not realized she was holding. "What's happening?" she said instead of a greeting. "Where is everyone?"

The guard raised an eyebrow. "You're back so soon? Mostly everyone is at the barricades. Lidia can fill you in. She was there and knows better."

Myra froze. *The barricades?* What was that supposed to mean? "Where is she? Is she still there?"

The guard nodded toward the dark corridor leading deep down. "She's back. You'll find her inside."

Myra and Sissi rushed through halls that were nearly empty, apart from a few children and the elderly. Myra's heart was pounding. If it came to an open conflict, the Resistance would not last long. So far the Prince had found them more amusing than threatening, but if he perceived them as a real danger, he would not hesitate to end them once and for all.

The sound of rushing feet was the only warning they got before Thea practically landed right in front of them. "Myra, Myra, you won't believe this!" she squeaked, jumping up and down. "Zack is fighting the Prince!"

Myra's heart jumped into her throat. For a moment, drawing breath seemed like a challenge. "What do you mean, Zack is fighting the Prince?" she heard Sissi's voice as if coming from underwater. "Where is everyone?"

"They're all at the barricades," Thea replied eagerly. "I also wanted to go, but they wouldn't let me."

"What barricades?" Myra finally found her voice, even if it sounded hollow in her own ears. "What happened here?"

"A disaster, that's what happened," a voice sounded from the entrance, and she turned to look at Lidia. "Zack thought everything was under control. He thought we had them, but then all went horribly wrong. They were only three—the Prince and two more—and we had the element of surprise on our side, but it didn't help. We paid dearly for our overconfidence."

A chill ran down Myra's spine. Never before had she heard Lidia sound so downtrodden. "What do you mean, we paid dearly?" she asked, horrified to hear the answer. "No one is dead… right?"

Lidia snorted. "Oh no, no one is dead. But five of us were severely hurt and had to come back. He bit me." She pulled down her collar, revealing a bloodied bandage. "That animal bit me!"

Myra's world came tumbling down. What exactly had she expected? That when attacked, the vampires would peacefully surrender and not hurt anyone? That they could all be friends and work together for a common goal? "Was it the Prince?" she uttered. "The one who bit you—was it the Prince?"

"I think so. The description you gave fit him. Thankfully, we had many Warriors there, and they were able to stop him before he had drunk too much. One of his companions was shot—not in the heart I think—and they had to retreat. They hid inside a cave, and Zack set up barricades around the exit. Most of our Warriors are there, prepared to attack once the vamps come out."

Myra closed her eyes, her throat dry. Once the vamps came out, there would be bloodshed on both sides, and she could do nothing to prevent it.

"How long have the vampires been inside?" Sissi asked.

"Three days now," said Lidia.

"Three days?" Myra cried. "That's insane. That's enough time for the vamps to reprogram the WeatherWizard. Zack should get out of there. The woods must be full of search parties sent after the Prince failed to return."

"This is what we fear," Lidia admitted. "The woods were sunlit when we went there to investigate. Now they are cloudy the whole day. Obviously, the vamps know their Prince is out there and provide him the darkness he needs."

Myra ran her hands through her hair. "They won't just passively wait for him to come back. Vamps must be searching the woods day and night as we speak."

"I know," Lidia said. "We need to do something soon. We have to either retreat, or go inside the cave, but Zack is reluctant to attack. The vamps could have prepared an ambush inside, and they might be only three, but they fight well. And we can't just turn around and go back home—we'll never get another shot."

"I see," said Myra. "Please take us to Zack. I might be able to help."

***

Myra scanned the area around the cave. The Resistance had built makeshift barricades of stones, branches, and some furniture they had apparently dragged from the hideout. The Warriors stood behind the flimsy fence, guns and crossbows at the ready. The Resistance could take care of a few vampires in case anyone came out of the cave. That was not the problem.

The problem was the black clouds, completely concealing the sun. They were in the living woods Vlad kept sunlit during the day. The clouds could mean only one thing—the vamps had readjusted the WeatherWizard. They knew their Prince was here. She expected search parties to leave the Palace as soon as the vamps decided the weather was stable enough. That could be any moment now; she had to end this madness before anyone got hurt.

Zack spotted her, Lidia, and Sissi and waved at them. They joined him behind the barricades. "Why are you back so quickly?" he asked.

Great. Apparently Zack had indeed wanted to send her away and deal with Vlad while she was gone. "We don't have time for this," Myra said. "You need to get our people out of here. The vamps will come searching for their Prince."

He frowned. "I'm not leaving without the Prince's head."

"Then you won't leave at all," Myra snapped. "What if he never comes out? He can stay inside for hundreds of years."

Zack looked about to argue, but sighed and looked down. "Then I suppose we should go to him."

"Let me go first," Myra said. "I'll come back and tell you what's happening in there."

Zack's eyes widened. "This is what you propose? Instead of going in full force, you go alone?"

"We need intelligence," Myra said calmly. "We need to know what to expect in there. It makes sense to send a single spy before you go in, and I know the vampires better than anyone. I might even convince them not to hurt me if worse comes to worst—the Prince still needs me to finish his book."

Zack fell silent, considering her words. "Very well," he said at length. "But you will take a stake and a crossbow. And if you don't come back in ten minutes, we come in."

"Give me half an hour," Myra said as she took the weapons. Her leader nodded.

"Can I come?" Sissi asked. "I know this cave. I spent a night here while I was investigating the area. I can help."

Myra sighed. She knew very well Sissi's offer had little to do with her knowledge of the cave, and she had no time for this. "Let's risk only one life for the moment, okay?"

Sissi looked crestfallen at the rejection, but quickly composed herself. "I hope they didn't find the back tunnel," she said. "There is another exit, but it's hard to find, so they might have missed it. At the end of the cave, the tunnel splits in three. If you follow the left passage, you'll reach a large stone on the right. The passage is right behind it. I found it by accident and tried to follow, but there was a long and demanding climb up, and I didn't go all the way. But the air was fresh, so I believe it goes outside."

"Then we have another reason to act as quickly as we can," Myra said as she resolutely stepped inside.

Chapter Thirty-Six

Promises

The passage was completely dark at first, but soon Myra saw a distant light and hastened her steps. Someone had lit a torch, which meant the vampires were probably still here. She had no doubts why Sissi had told her about the tunnel—she had given her a way to let the vampires escape and prevent bloodshed. But was letting Vlad escape the best plan?

Her steps quickened as the light grew brighter. She came to a halt and drew a sharp breath. The three vampires were sitting on the ground, their backs leaning against a large rock. Armida's head rested against the Prince's chest, and she was deathly pale. Tristan was sitting next to them, his eyes closed, his arms wrapped around himself.

"Ah, look who is here," Vlad said matter-of-factly. "The prodigal daughter returns."

The other two vampires stared at her, and Myra glared back. "Oh, please, don't tell me you're angry at me for escaping. I was your prisoner, for goodness' sake. What did you expect, exactly?"

"I was expecting you to finish my book," the Prince said. "You could have informed me that was never your plan."

"Your book—of course, that's all you care about," Myra said. "You are unbelievable. You act like the beast that you are and bite one of my friends, and now you speak as if you have a shard of a reason to be mad at me."

The Prince smiled, in that way that made her want to punch him. "Ah, so this is what it is all about. I bit your friend, and now you are jealous."

Myra nearly dropped her stake. "*Jealous?* Seriously? Why the hell would I be jealous? Why would I want your stinking teeth anywhere near me?"

His grin never faded away. "You know, many would kill to get my teeth inside them. It is a high privilege."

Myra stared at Vlad unflinchingly. "You're a disgusting animal, nothing more. You bit my friend. You drank her blood. You would have drunk it all if you had the chance."

"Well, yeah," Tristan chimed in. "He is a vampire. He feeds on blood, not cookies. Or have you forgotten? And if we are to go around throwing blame, your friends ruined my shirt," he added miserably and pointed at the torn fabric below his left shoulder, underneath which Myra saw a makeshift bandage. "It was one of my favorites."

"Which is one of the many reasons why you should never wear your favorite shirt while hunting, my boy. It is a grave loss, really," Vlad said in a mock-serious tone. "This one suited you. You do look stunning in black."

"I look stunning in *anything*," the silver-haired vampire said sourly. "It doesn't mean I have to look like a dashingly handsome hobo."

"Then take it off and stop whining," Armida said. "We have more serious problems right now."

"You would like that, wouldn't you?" Tristan asked with a grin.

Myra rolled her eyes. "I'm sure you are all grieving for Tristan's destroyed shirt, but I think you should concentrate on the problem at hand—staying alive."

"You think we are in mortal danger?" Vlad challenged. "The Resistance cowards will not come in anytime soon. My people must have noticed our absence by now. I know they are searching for us as we speak. And when they find us, your friends are in for a good meal."

"Then I'm happy to tell you, you don't have the luxury to wait until 'anytime now,'" said Myra. "*The Resistance cowards* are coming. I barely convinced them to wait. And once they come, they have only one goal in mind. Killing you."

"Killing *me*?" Vlad raised his eyebrows. "Whatever have I done to them?"

"Do we really have time for this?" Myra said. "You destroyed our civilization, you murdered our friends and families, you forced us to live in exile and in constant terror, and you kept our people in a farm like animals. Because of you my friends are forced to live in hiding, surviving on rat meat."

"You say it as if this is something bad," the Prince said.

Myra snorted. "Excuse me? What is not bad exactly?"

"Rat meat was considered a delicacy in many cuisines up until the Nightfall," he said. "In parts of Cameroon and Nigeria, the meat of the local large rats was more expensive than chicken or beef. I once had the pleasure of visiting the Adi tribe in northeast India during one of their festivals, where rats are the culinary centerpiece. Many swore to me they had never tasted anything more delicious."

Myra rolled her eyes. "Vlad, honestly, I have zero patience for you to flaunt your world knowledge in my face. I might have known that too if you hadn't destroyed my culture and deprived me of a chance at getting a proper education. Besides, you are completely missing the point."

"I am not missing anything," he said. "Your point is that I am a horrible monster who has inflicted inconceivable harm upon humanity. All Resistance members hate me with a passion, and they are coming for my blood."

"Precisely," she said. "Are you in any shape to run? No one but Tristan was hurt, right?"

"His hurt is not major," the Prince said. "The real problem is we have not fed in days and our strength is diminishing by the minute."

She raised an eyebrow. "Are you saying you're desperate for blood, and you're not even trying to bite me?"

"Do not flatter yourself. As I said, we have not fed in days. We have no strength. We could not even get up. I could not bite you even if I wanted to."

She sat cross-legged next to him. "After all we've been through, is that the only reason you're not biting me?"

"No," Vlad said seriously. "After all we have been through, I will not bite you until you are ready. I will not bite you until you want me to."

Now, this was the last straw. "Why on earth would I *want* you to bite me?"

Vlad smiled, in that annoying way of his, as if he knew something she did not. "My dear girl. There is so much you still need to learn about the world."

"And I suppose you would like to teach me?" Myra said. "Now, you listen to me. Right now, I'm the only thing that stands between you and certain death, and you would do well to try to get on my good side and to stop reminding me with every word you say that you are an arrogant, insufferable monster."

"If you think I will play a role and pretend to be something I am not just to get you to help me, you do not know me at all," Vlad said calmly. "You have a stake. Go on and be done with it. Or will you chicken out like last time?"

"What last time?" Tristan asked.

Myra ignored him and glared at the Prince. "You would throw away your life to satisfy your pride?" she said. "How mature of you. Are you willing to sacrifice their lives as well?" She gestured at Tristan and Armida.

Vlad scowled at her. "That is a low blow, even for a human. The Resistance wants me. They have nothing to do with this."

"Nothing to do with this?" Myra cried. "Are you telling me none of them has ever killed a human?"

"Stop it, both of you," Tristan said, sounding bored. "Myra, you are obviously here to help us, so stop pretending you will only do it if we see the error in our ways and decide to reform. And you, my lord, could try behaving for once. The Resistance is coming, and they want your blood. We have no time to waste." He turned to Myra. "You have an idea?"

Myra was far from satisfied, but Tristan was right—they had no time to waste. "There's supposed to be an exit at the far end of the left tunnel, behind a big stone on the right. It's a narrow path and involves climbing straight up. Do you think you can manage it?"

"You are not listening," Vlad said. "We cannot stand, let alone walk or climb."

Myra paled. "Vlad, if you stay here, you will die. There must be a way."

"Can you bring us blood?" Armida suggested. "Some large animal, a cow or a pig, should suffice to get us all on our feet."

"I have nothing like that," Myra said. "And if I go out of the cave, my friends will want to know what happened here, and I won't be able to return by myself."

"Maybe you could buy us time," Vlad said. "You could tell your friends that we are prepared for their invasion."

"Buy you time for what?" Myra glared at him. "So that your people will come here and kill my friends? Forget about it. The Resistance is going to enter this cave right now and either find you and kill you, or find no trace of you. In any case, they will then leave this place and go to safety. My friends are coming here. This is not a matter up for discussion. The question is what they are going to find."

"But this is not even a question, is it?" Vlad said, his voice chillingly calm. "There is no way we can escape."

"There is a way," Tristan said softly.

"Do you have an idea, my boy?" Vlad prompted as the silver-haired vampire fell silent and looked down.

"My lord…" Tristan pressed his eyes tightly shut and took a deep breath. When he looked up again, his eyes were shining with a silent resolve. "Feed off me."

"You are out of your mind," Vlad said, before Myra could even process what Tristan had suggested.

"I have some blood left in me," Tristan argued. "If you and Armida drink, you will have enough strength to get out of here."

"We are not discussing this," the Prince said, with such authority in his voice that Myra was certain Tristan would obey.

"And why not?" the younger vampire cried. "You allowed me to feed off you when we were starving in the frozen tundra."

"That was completely different," Vlad said. "I had enough strength to spare, and we were in no immediate danger. If I feed off you now, you will be completely spent. If this way out is anything like what Myra describes, I cannot carry you. I would have to leave you here to die."

"And if you don't do this, we all die," Tristan said.

"Then we all die," the Prince replied.

"My lord, you are being ridiculous. If we listen to you, we all die. If you and Armida drink my blood, then you two have a chance to escape."

Vlad lifted himself on one elbow, fully facing the younger vampire. "Tristan, my child, you know that if someone stays behind, it will be me."

"My love, this is madness," Armida protested immediately. "So many depend on you. What will happen to our world if you perish?"

"I think I know—" Myra started, but Tristan interrupted her before she could continue.

"And why is that exactly?" he challenged. "Give me one good reason why it should be you who stays behind."

"For one, it would make more sense. I sired both you and Armida. My blood will give each of you more strength than yours could give me. Besides, officially I am your Prince, and you are my subjects. I am sworn to protect you."

"You know what? I am tired of you trying to protect me," Tristan growled. "I am not a child. I am centuries old, and I am strong. I am more than capable of taking care of myself, and of others. But no, it is always you who has to make the sacrifice, always you who has to help and protect everyone, and at the same time you refuse any help offered to you."

"I am far from thinking you weak or helpless," Vlad said seriously. "But you have suffered more than enough already because of my ill judgment. I will be damned before I let you take any further hurt."

"Well, guess what? It is not for you to *let* me suffer anything. What I am going through is my own doing, and my own choice. Or are you saying you should have taken that choice away from me?"

Vlad's gaze darkened. "Perhaps I should have."

With speed that belied his current weakness, Tristan grabbed the other vampire by the collar and pulled him forward. "Say that again," he snarled, "and I will drain your blood here and now."

"Go on," Vladimir said calmly.

"Yes, Tristan, please go on," Armida said, rolling her eyes. "It is not like this was what the Prince wanted all along."

The vampires continued glaring at each other, and Myra could take it no longer. "There might be—"

"Stay out of this, girl," Vlad snarled.

"Vladimir, listen to me," she cried. "If you two are quite done with your sappy melodrama, you would do well to be quiet and listen. I actually have something to say."

"Sappy melodrama?" Tristan echoed in disbelief, while Vlad simply stared at her and Armida chuckled.

"I am sorry," she said. "But I needed to get your attention. I think I know how you can all walk out of here alive."

"Very well," the Prince said. "You have our attention. Speak."

Myra hesitated. "For starters, we begin with Tristan's suggestion. You and Armida drink his blood and are strong enough to leave."

"If this is what you have to say—" Vlad interrupted, but she glared at him.

"Will you just listen for once? The Resistance will arrive soon and take Tristan prisoner. They will not kill him."

"Right," said Vlad. "They will invite him for a hot brownie with vanilla ice cream and a pint of warm blood, as they do to all other vampires they capture."

"The Resistance has so far killed anyone we have captured," Myra said calmly. "But Tristan is different. I can make them keep him alive, and when the time is right, I can help him escape."

Vlad pushed himself on his elbow to turn towards Myra, this time with real curiosity in his eyes. "How is Tristan different?"

"Hey, are you saying I am *not* different from all those blunderheads that got themselves captured?" Tristan cried.

"What a nice way to talk about your deceased companions," Myra said.

The silver-haired vampire shrugged. "I have on numerous occasions expressed my extreme dislike towards other vampires. I fail to see why you are so shocked."

"How is he different?" Vlad repeated, his eyes never leaving Myra's.

She hesitated. "You know that our ultimate goal is to destroy the WeatherWizard. Our commander wanted us to kill you to create chaos, but I suggested that your death wouldn't help us. I told him, and the rest of my people, that our only chance to have the Wizard destroyed would be to make you do it yourself. I told them you would do anything for Armida and Tristan and suggested we try to take one of them prisoner and demand the destruction of the WeatherWizard in return for their life."

"You did *what*?" There was no anger in his voice, just bone-chilling cold.

"Oh, please, don't tell me you are shocked," Myra said. "We are enemies, Vlad. Enemies. We have never been anything else. I want to destroy the Wizard and bring the sun back to us. You think that a few deep conversations and hunts and dances will change that?"

"So this has been your agenda all along?" the vampire said. "And now you ask me to leave Tristan behind, so you can later force me to destroy the WeatherWizard?"

"You're not listening," Myra said. "Yes, I do want to destroy the WeatherWizard. But not like this. One day I will destroy it and give this world back to humanity. But not today. Today you will escape, and you will leave Tristan or Armida behind. I will help whoever stays behind escape, and I will ask for nothing in return."

"You would do that?" Vlad looked at her quizzically. "Alright, let us for a moment assume that you would one day achieve what you fight for and give this world back to humankind. Let us say it is in five years, or a year, or even a week. You know that every human that dies under my rule after today will be on your conscience."

"You think I don't know that?" Myra said, blinking against her tears. "I'm simply trying to do the right thing. There is no need to make this harder than it already is. I have told you my plan. If Tristan or Armida stays behind, I can guarantee their safety."

"What if I stay?"

She shook her head. "I'm sure my friends will stake you here and now. No, Vlad, it has to be Tristan or Armida."

"They have no idea what I look like," the vampire argued. "I can stay behind, and you will tell them I am Tristan."

"They know enough," she said firmly. "You have to trust me on this."

"In that case," Armida said, "I suppose we should decide which one of us is more suitable for the task."

"Maybe my lord should decide?" Tristan suggested.

Vlad looked positively miserable. "Thank you so much, my boy. This is exactly what I need right now."

The younger vampire grinned sheepishly. "I suppose it must be hard for you. For the first time you are forced to let someone else take the fall."

"I am glad you are enjoying yourself," Vlad grumbled.

Tristan smiled. "I admit, I do find your predicament rather amusing, but causing you pain is the last thing I want. This is the only way. You must let us do this."

"Oh, I must?" Vlad raised an eyebrow. "Last time I checked, I was your prince. And as such I order you both to feed on my blood and leave this place."

"Then you must stake me for treason," Tristan said, "for I will disobey."

The two vampires continued glaring at each other, and Myra and Armida exchanged an exasperated glance. "Will you stop this?" Myra said. "The Resistance could arrive at any time, and you're growing weaker. We have to act, and now. And no, Vlad, it has to be either Armida or Tristan who stays behind if you want all three of you to live through this."

"Tristan, muffin, I think it is obvious which one of us is better suited for captivity," Armida said. "With your disability, and—"

"*Disability?*" Tristan cried. "I. Do. Not. Have. A. Disability," he enunciated, his voice low and dangerous.

"Indeed?" Armida challenged. "It interferes with your daily affairs, and it makes your life harder. I think this fits the definition closely enough."

"I am strong," Tristan snapped. "I am as strong as any vampire. And I do not let this interfere with my life and actions. I can face captivity as well as you, if not better."

"And what if the pain becomes too strong?" Armida asked. "And instead of feather beds and servants and chocolate and your sire's blood to distract you, you are deprived of all comforts, mistreated, and locked in a dank prison?"

"I can deal with it," the silver-haired vampire said firmly. "My life has not always been feather beds."

"What if they take away your hairbrush?" Armida asked mischievously, and Tristan bristled.

"That is enough. I came up with the idea in the first place. I can do this, and I am doing it."

"Tristan, it is wrong of me to order you anything," Vlad started softly. "But I beg you. There must be another way."

"There is no other way," Myra said. "And there is no time either. You have to do this now."

"Please, my lord," Tristan said. "I want to see you again, out of here. I want to do this. I want to let the Resistance capture me, and when I escape, I want you to be there, waiting for me. Can you do this for me?"

Vlad was silent, and Tristan tried again. "Centuries from now, none of this will matter. We will not even remember that we were here, in this cave, fearing for our lives. The world will belong to us, just as it once did, and we will not have a single care. But in order for this day to come, we must endure this trial today. We have countless years ahead of us. Do not throw them away only because you want to spare me a bit of pain."

"I would have kept you away from any pain," Vlad whispered.

The silver-haired vampire smiled. "I know. But we must do this now. I can get through this. Can you?"

The Prince nodded, and Myra breathed a sigh of relief. "I'm sorry to push you," she said. "But we really must hurry."

Vladimir turned around, facing the younger vampire, and smiled sadly. "I am sorry, my boy."

Tristan shook his head. "It is the only way. And I told you, I am strong enough to take this."

"No, not about the blood," the Prince said. "Though I am sorry about that too." He paused. "I was talking about what you said earlier. I am sorry I made you feel like an overprotected child. I wanted to keep you safe, and I wanted you to be well, to be happy. I see now that putting you in a golden cage was not the right way to achieve that."

Tristan reached out, grabbing the other vampire's forearm and squeezing tightly. "But you never put me in a cage, my lord. On the contrary, you set me free. You broke my chains, and you gave me wings to fly."

"Tristan, you are not using your forfeited poetic skills to try to say goodbye, are you?" Armida said shakily. "You are not saying goodbye, dearie, and we will not hear it. You are coming back to us; that is the agreement."

"Of course," Tristan said firmly. "Let us waste no more time. If you have something else to say to me, we can talk when I come back home."

Vlad locked eyes with Armida. "You start. Drink as much as you need. Not a drop more. And be slow and gentle—he is not a meal."

"As always," Armida said, and to Myra's complete shock, she leaned forward to give Tristan a slow, sensual kiss. In what way this was necessary for the blood exchange, she could not imagine. Even stranger, Vlad did not seem to mind, or even be surprised by what he was seeing.

"My handsome, brave, sweet darling," Armida whispered as her kisses moved down the silver-haired vampire's neck. "We will not leave you here. We will get you back, and then we will all be together forever." She started undoing the strings of his shirt, giving herself better access. "Oh, dearie, I can smell your blood flowing underneath this flawless skin of yours. So sweet, it intoxicates me. You know how much I love the taste of your blood, darling. I am not certain I can ever stop."

Her teeth sank deep into Tristan's chest, and she hungrily drank the lifesaving fluid. Tristan's body stiffened, apparently sensing that losing so much blood in his current condition could not be good.

"It will be over soon," Vlad whispered soothingly as he steadied the other vampire's head. "The pain will go away." He went on speaking in a language Myra could not understand, and she felt tears prick at her eyes.

After a while Armida raised her head, her lips red with fresh blood. "My love, what are you doing? You need to drink too."

The Prince's brow furrowed, and he shook his head, but Tristan turned around to look up at him. "My lord, please. I want this."

Vlad briefly closed his eyes, and when he opened them, he leaned forward, sinking his teeth into Tristan's neck. Armida bent down and continued feeding. All three vampires grew pale and translucent, and Myra could see the veins pulsing underneath their skin.

Myra watched transfixed as the three vampires shared blood, shared life. By all rights, the scene was disgusting and terrifying, and yet there was something strangely fascinating about it. The three vampires were so close at that moment; they were as one single being. They were connected in a way no humans ever could be. And they seemed a part of something bigger, something ancient. A part of tales and legends and songs of forgotten times, when mythical creatures walked the earth. A part of the very fabric of the world. And for a brief, treacherous instant, she wanted to be a part of it too.

Tristan's eyes fluttered, and with a sigh, he let go of consciousness. The other two vampires barely seemed to notice and continued drinking thirstily, as if all that mattered was the life-giving blood that now flowed into their veins. But then Vlad looked up and pressed a piece of cloth against the wound at Tristan's neck to staunch the bleeding.

"This is enough," he said.

Armida frowned. "You have barely eaten."

"I've had enough. I am able to walk, and so are you."

Vlad stood up and took a step towards Myra, and before she could comprehend what he was doing, he grabbed her and turned her around, his strong hands holding her arms to the sides in a viselike grip. His teeth scraped against her neck, and Myra's heart hammered as a lump formed in her throat.

"My dearest girl," Vlad whispered in her ear. "Did you not know that after feeding, I would be strong once again? I may not be at my full strength, but I am still stronger than you. Did you not think that I could drink you, feed what was left of you to Tristan, and take him to safety? Did you truly think I would leave my friend in captivity and danger?"

Myra wanted to slap herself. Honestly, it had never occurred to her that Vlad would be strong enough to overpower her. She tried not to panic and took a deep breath, until her heartbeat slowed down. "Of course I knew that," she said, her voice strong and confident. "I was well aware that drinking Tristan's blood would make you strong enough to bite me."

"And yet, you never ran and never tried to stake me before I drank," he said.

"You claimed you wouldn't bite me until I was ready," Myra said calmly, even though she had no idea if she could trust a word he had said. "You told me you were no liar. I trust you."

He released her and smiled at her, as she turned around to face him. "I am glad to hear it, because I trust you too."

Myra forced herself to smile back and released her breath. If this had been a test, she had apparently passed it.

He broke their eye contact. "Do you have any idea what Tristan means to me?"

Myra nodded. "I do."

He shook his head. "No, you don't. You could never begin to understand. And now I choose to let him suffer and to leave him in mortal danger instead of hurting you. I hope you appreciate this and will pay me back in kind."

"Tristan told me how you met," Myra said. "Why did you choose him as your protégé out of all other humans? Why was he so special?"

"That is a long story," the Prince said. "We can talk more the next time we see each other."

Myra's breath caught in her throat. She had believed this was to be their last meeting. "You plan to meet again?"

"Of course. You still have a book to finish. I will not let you go until you have given me the complete manuscript. Besides, I already told you that you have a major part in one of my larger plans. The recent events did not cancel my plan; in fact, they might have sped it up."

Vlad knelt down, took off his coat and wrapped it around Tristan's body, fastening it at the neck with his golden pin. "Make sure he knows he is not abandoned."

"I will," Myra said solemnly. "And I'll help him escape as soon as possible. I swear it."

To her surprise, Vlad stood up, held her hand gently and kissed it, his eyes never leaving hers. "Thank you, my lady. What you are doing is beyond honorable. It will not be forgotten."

She signed. She preferred him when he was cocky and annoying; it was a lot easier to deal with him then.

"There is one more thing," the Prince said. "You must find a way to feed him as soon as you can. He has lost too much blood. He can survive in this condition forever, but it is not a pleasant state for a vampire. He will be haunted by painful nightmares until he regains consciousness; you must not let this go on for any longer than necessary."

"Of course," Myra said. "Go. I'll take care of him."

With a last look back, Vlad and Armida disappeared around the corner. Myra followed shortly to ensure that the vampires had found the way and moved a few stones around to conceal the passage. After she decided Vlad had enough of a head start in the unlikely case that Zack decided to look for the hidden way out and follow, she hurried to the exit.

Chapter Thirty-Seven

The Right Thing

"What happened in there?" Zack cried as soon as he saw her. "I was about to send reinforcements."

"He is gone," Myra said. "The Prince isn't there." She wished she could just say there was no one in there. It would save a lot of trouble, but she knew Zack would go in himself and check anyway.

"What?" the General cried. "How did he escape?"

"I'm not sure," Myra said. "I guess they found the passage Sissi mentioned. I myself couldn't see it. But Zack, luck is on our side today. One of the vampires, Tristan, is left behind. Apparently he was too injured to go on."

"Great," her leader said. "One more vampire we get rid of, and the Prince remains untouched. Our progress is too slow."

"You don't understand," Myra said, trying to sound excited. "This is the vampire I told you about. The one close to the Prince. We can keep him a prisoner and demand whatever we want." Even as she spoke, she felt strangely dirty. Zack was her leader and her longtime friend. She was deceiving him now, and for what?

Yet, even as the doubts assaulted her, she realized that there was no other way. She could never bring herself to kill Vlad. Before she had left on her mission, the Prince had been the Enemy, a faceless name that had to be eliminated. Now he had a face, and a story, and thoughts and feelings. Yes, he was a monster, but she knew him. She had talked to him. They had discussed her stories and his.

And, most of all, he could have easily bitten her, drunk her or fed her to Tristan. He had held her in his arms like a ready meal, and she had been completely helpless and unable to put up any fight. Yet, he had kept his word, and she would keep hers. If she betrayed Vlad now, she would be worse than him, worse than a vampire. She would find a way to destroy the WeatherWizard, but not like this.

Zack frowned. "The Prince left his companion behind to be killed, and now you claim he would destroy the Wizard in exchange for his life? This makes no sense to me."

"We don't know what happened," said Myra. "Perhaps the Prince went to look for help and is planning to return with reinforcements. We should act before that happens."

"Fine," Zack said. "Let's see this very special vampire of yours."

The two entered the cave, followed by Sissi and the Resistance Warriors. Zack lit a torch to light the way. "Is he dangerous?" he asked.

"He's badly hurt and unconscious," Myra assured him. "There is nothing to fear."

They reached the place where the three vampires had stayed, and the humans formed a circle around Tristan. Zack stepped forward, examining the unconscious form.

"These are the Prince's coat and pin," Myra said. "He wouldn't leave them with a vampire who meant nothing to him."

Zack undid the pin and shoved it in his pocket. Then he removed the coat and folded it carefully.

"What are you doing?" Myra said sharply.

"Are you worried about the prisoner's comfort? We will send these to the Prince as a token, to show him we have his friend." His eyes narrowed, and he stared at Tristan's chest.

"Zack, what is it?"

"We wounded him once," the General said. "He is freshly bandaged in three places." He used his dagger to tear off Tristan's shirt and undo the bandage around his chest. A few gasps sounded as two puncture wounds were revealed, still bleeding sluggishly.

"They fed off him," Thomas spat. "His own friends fed off him!"

"They make me sick," Zack said and stood up. "Myra, after this there is no way I'll believe the Prince would give up his kingdom for this one. He drank his blood!"

Myra shuddered. If she could not convince Zack to follow her plan, they would stake Tristan. "You know, among vampires, drinking someone's blood is considered a sign of affection."

Zack used the tip of his boot to turn Tristan's head around to get a better look at his face, which made Myra very grateful Vlad was not around to see this. "Are you sure you don't want to keep him alive just because he is such a pretty boy?" he asked.

"Zack, we don't have time for this," she said. "The Prince cares about him. We should at least give it a try."

"Myra is right," Sissi chimed in. "And my people agree with her."

Zack turned to her. "The Survivors know of this plan?"

"My people have always been looking into ways to control the Prince. We were never thinking as big as you, never even considering we could make him destroy the Wizard. We were thinking more along the lines of safety and protection."

"And you discovered something?" Thomas asked.

"We hadn't, not before I left. But when Myra and I were home, my friends told me they had interrogated another vampire, and they've reached the same conclusion. The best way to make the Prince cooperate would be to capture this vampire."

"This one in particular?" asked Zack.

"They said his name was Tristan and that he was silver-haired. He is dear to the Prince, from what they learned."

Zack looked at Myra. "You never told me the Survivors agreed with your plan."

"Was it necessary?" said Myra. "Does the word of strangers you have never met mean more to you than mine? When did this happen, Zack? When did you stop trusting me? You think my time with the vampires made me like them? If anything, it made me hate them even more." Her voice was laden with bitterness, but not for the reasons Zack probably believed. Her friend had every right not to trust her.

The General averted his gaze. "You are right. Forgive me. Alright—we take this one prisoner and keep him alive. We will send word to the Prince soon."

"We have to feed him," said Myra.

Zack's eyes widened. "Beg your pardon?"

"We have to give him some kind of blood. Any blood of mammals or birds would suffice."

"And why should we do that, exactly?"

"Because otherwise he will remain unconscious," Myra said, realizing as she spoke that this did not sound convincing at all.

"Which is bad, because…?"

"We might want to question him," she tried.

"We already know everything," said Zack impatiently. "We keep him alive, we demand the Prince switches off the Wizard, he refuses, we start sending fingers. If the captive is unconscious, he'll be more manageable."

"This is a bad idea," Sissi said. "If a vampire stays without blood for a long time, he suffers severe brain damage. What if the Prince wants to inspect the goods before the exchange? He won't meet our demands if his friend is brain-dead."

"Are you sure about this?" Zack asked. "This is the first time I've heard anything of the sort. Perhaps one of your prisoners lied to you to make you feed him."

"Oh, I'm certain," Sissi said confidently. "I've seen it firsthand. We did experiments."

"Fine," Zack said. "We can spare a few rats from the farm."

"We should also rebandage his wound and find him intact clothes," Myra suggested.

Zack rolled his eyes. "Now you are pushing it. He is getting better treatment than any of us. Tommy, get him up and let's go home."

A shudder ran down Myra's spine as she watched Tristan's silver head loll listlessly as Thomas picked him up. She had a bad feeling that she had made a promise she could not keep.

***

Myra suppressed her impatience as Thomas secured Tristan to the prison wall with titanium chains. The vampire was completely drained; he could never try to escape on his own or pose any threat to them. "When are we feeding him?" she asked.

"Tomorrow," said Zack. "I'm certain he won't get brain damage in a night. Our prisoners have gone without food for longer."

Myra sighed. The arrangement was far from ideal. She had promised Vlad to take care of Tristan. The Prince had spared her life, when he could have easily drunk her and saved his friend. He trusted her, and so far she had done nothing to deserve this trust.

She wished Zack a good night and returned to her room. As she closed the door behind her, she leaned her back against it and slid down to the floor. What was she doing? This had been her plan all along. Myra had wanted Tristan captured not to save Vlad's life, but because she believed it was the only way to destroy the WeatherWizard. And now that Tristan was in their hands, she was going to let him go?

This would be the end of her plan. She was certain that if they let Tristan go now, they would never be able to recapture him. She was going to forfeit the fate of humanity, and for what? For a promise she had made to a bloodsucking fiend?

Tears slid down her cheeks, and she quickly brushed them away. What had she been thinking when she had made that promise? She could not go back on it now—it would not be honorable.

Honorable? And what did vampires know about honor? Vlad had promised her to let that boy go if she finished her story, and yet he had killed him. He had sucked the child's blood right in front of her, not because he was hungry, but because he wanted to teach her obedience.

I never said I would let the boy go, Vlad's voice sounded in her head, in that mocking way of his. *All I said was that I would kill him if you did not finish your story. I never said I would let him go if you did.*

Whatever. Did it make any difference? The Prince was a master of words, and he had used that skill to deceive her. He claimed he had never lied to her, but he had misled her with twisted words. No, he had no honor. Yet if she broke the promise now, she was no better than him. She was a human. She had to do the right thing. If she won the war but lost her humanity in the process, it meant the vamps had truly won.

For the first time, Myra admitted to herself that while she had been in that cave, watching the three vampires trying to save each other's lives, she had been more concerned with getting Vlad out of there than with accomplishing her plan. She just could not understand why.

She wanted him to hear the end of his book, she told herself. She did not want Vlad to die before he had heard the ending and told her it was good.

Yes, and that was a very good reason to doom hundreds of lives.

She could not simply destroy the vampires. There were so many questions burning in her mind. Why was Tristan in constant pain? Why had Vlad turned him after his initial refusal? Why had Vlad picked him in the first place? How had Vlad met Callisto and what had happened to his mortal family? Why had they separated? And, more important than anything else, what was this plan that Vlad kept talking about and what was her part in it? She had to know or she would go mad with curiosity.

Myra buried her face in her hands, her thoughts spinning wildly. The Prince had destroyed so much, and yet he had created something beautiful. The Palace was a masterpiece, with its libraries, and galleries, and theaters. He had created a beautiful world, and she was loath to see it gone. And, as much as she hated to admit it, this world would be a much duller place without the Prince in it.

And much safer too, she told herself bitterly. *A much better place to live and love and create, to raise kids and watch them grow without a constant threat hanging over their heads.*

She raised her head. It was not just about the book, or doing the right thing. After all she had been through, she had no desire to fight Vlad anymore. She vividly remembered the disappointment she had felt when she had seen Lidia's bite. Had Myra honestly expected the vamps would not fight back when attacked? She winced, suddenly realizing that was exactly what she had hoped for all along. She had thought that perhaps they could somehow reach peace. That they could somehow coexist.

Am I crazy? How could humans and vampires possibly coexist? Yet, vamps had lived in the human world for millennia before the Nightfall, keeping such a low profile that they had faded into legend.

But vampires had not truly lived at the time. They had been forced into hiding, deprived of many freedoms and pleasures human civilization could provide. Humans had ruled the world, and vamps had been parasites, living on the periphery. Now they had taken over, and humans were reduced to livestock.

No. Humans and vampires could not rule together in peace. The world would always belong to one, while the other was oppressed. The war could never end.

None of this mattered now. She had made a promise, and she had made her choice. One day, she would make her move to destroy the Wizard, but today was not that day. Now the only question was how to help Tristan escape, and once she found a way, the fight between the Resistance and Prince Vladimir would resume from square one.

Myra stood up and reached out to extinguish the single candle. But before her fingers had closed around the flame, killing it, she let her hand drop and decided to let it burn.

Acknowledgments

This book would have been very different without my talented beta readers and editors. Special thanks go to Eliza, Cady, Kellie, Anaiya, and Cate. One thing I learned on this project is that it takes a village to write a book. I owe a debt of gratitude to Nadica for creating the memorable cover and character art.

64929676R00324

Made in the USA
Charleston, SC
15 December 2016